Book 2 in the Seekers Series

THE EMPEROR THE RING

JEFF GAURA

ISBN: 978-1-961879-54-6 (Paperback)
ISBN: 978-1-961879-55-3 (Ebook)

Printed in the United States of America

Foreword to the Second Edition

This second edition contains additional content to ensure that future books are coherent and consistent in their storylines. Between the first publication and the second, I spent hours reviewing the story to ensure that it worked.

Foreword to the First Edition

An overwhelmingly dishonest theme coming from our current instructors is that things are bad and are getting worse. Social unrest movements start with the mass distribution of the "things are bad" message using images on social and traditional media. Then, they report to us with a matter-of-fact approach that the future is on a collision course to be worse than today. And with that claim, they proceed to say that it is OK to sin, and we need to sin to make things right or get our fair share. We burn other people's property and throw things at them. We attack them with words and weapons, thinking it will help our cause to make a place for ourselves. It is sick, and there is nothing new about it. In fact, it was alive and well during the Roman Empire and worse than it is today.

As a part of writing this series, I felt compelled to academically explore a day in the life of someone living in first-century Palestine. Before I finished reading the work of two different authors, I realized that there is no doubt that modern Christianity and the people who claim it as their faith have it easy! Where do I start to compare the present to the first century? To begin, 25% of us are not slaves. Neither Jews (historically called "Ebreet") nor Christians today are beheaded in public, with 50,000 people watching and laughing. I know of no places on earth where mass crucifixions occur, organized by highly trained government engineers to address the time requirements to kill several hundred people a day on limited soil and the disposal of the bodies to minimize flies and pestilence. We have relatively no clue what it means to be repressed.

Ancient Israel, in the time of the Roman Empire, had all those things. To say that the Ebreet and Christians from Israel were oppressed is like calling Mount Everest "another big hill." Freedom under Roman rule was an all-or-nothing proposal. You either had all available freedom or you had nearly none. Today, there are many shades of freedom, and the global middle class includes more than a billion individuals (and growing) who are Christ-followers. Our life spans are longer, our access to health care is advanced, our housing is safe, our transportation is cheap, we assume electrical power is readily available, and we have universal education. Global poverty is at an all-time low since this has been a measurable event.

Each time I hear a preacher talking about how things are going in the wrong direction and have been for quite some time, I wish I could pick him up and dump him in ancient Israel for a month and then put him back in the pulpit, filming the entire event. He would slap himself silly as he admits his false conclusions. And there is no better time to see a man's character than when he discovers he is wrong.

We are in the golden age of freedom as Christ-followers. We are in the golden age of freedom as humans; do not let the uneducated fools of social unrest dupe you that we need to somehow repent from our past and change. The evidence is bulletproof. We have changed and we are better. History proves this from all perspectives greater than a century or two at a time.

Yet, one point of greatest interest is consistent between those two times. Jesus works on one person at a time and one relationship at a time; relationships of eternal significance cannot be mass-produced. All of us get to know the One Person of God through something one of His current followers shared with us. It is always unique, always circumstantial, and always changes eternity as it happens. In that sense, the first century was just like today.

My first date with Jesus happened while wearing a guitar on a stage in a US church. The pastor had asked for people to apply to become the new lead guitarist at a synagogue I had attended exactly one time. They gave me the job, failing to ask me if I believed in what they taught. I had just come back from a multi-year stint in the Peace Corps and I was looking for a place to fit in. In my mind, I was being culturally sensitive. I knew that in rural South Carolina culture, a normal life included going to synagogue on Sunday. After a couple of weeks of "performing" at the worship service, I had a personal experience with a Living God that I did not previously know. I cried on stage moments before I was to "perform" for several hundred people. Another member of what I called the "band," but what they called the "worship team," told me that the Holy Spirit was upon me.

In the way that God wants us all to have faith like a child, I complied, asking a question openly and with ignorance, "Who is the Holy Spirit?"

Dennis, the keyboard player, watched and listened, and moments before we began a worship set of Maranatha music, I gave my life to Christ. Dennis thought the event was hysterical and his laughter helped me stop crying long enough to play an opening riff for the first song. That day, I cannot tell you if my Fender Stratocaster was in tune or if it was turned on. I just played, closed my eyes, and said, "Wow!" as I heard the singer's words and connected with the content for the first time in my life. I had been playing these types of songs for a month, and I was more concerned with the patterns I would play as we transitioned from D to A minor than the Creator of the universe for whom I was playing.

I remember the colors of that moment. I remember the slope of that rental facility floor that I had to walk down and walk up as I transitioned from church member to lead guitarist and back. Certainly, that pastor got an "F" grade for not screening me before permitting me to lead his people in worship. Yet, is it not true that God can use all things for His glory, including the mistakes in church and the mistakes by the church? I claim to be the evidence that this is true. My characters in all three books in the Seeker's Trilogy reflect that heart of God.

This is a work of historical fiction that borders on the edge of nonfiction. The main characters are a couple of adolescents who encounter life's tragedies and are forced to address the world on the world's terms, using their passion for adventure and the power of togetherness. They navigate racism and repression. They fear false accusations of crimes. They get traumatized repeatedly, yet they persevere. They know they are damaged, too.

My creative mind saw a place in the history of the world to allow some unique events to be possible. I found real places on the map and included them. I found places on the map where there was nothing, and I made something up and put it there. I built upon what I had already done in the first book. It was an easy story to develop, and I imagine the characters in this book from a third-person view, for which I am invisible. During those moments the primary characters of this book are alone, I imagine myself talking to them and guiding their choices as best as I can. That is what Christ does. That is what my parents did while they were alive.

My closest circle of friends is in the latter years of their lives and I often talk to them about what goes on in the head of Jeff, the writer. I think about the legacies that they will be leaving as their bodies fail and they depart this world to enter eternity. Part of their tales has inspired me to write, for I perceive that I will outlive all of them; at least, that is what the actuaries tell me. My prayer is that my passion for writing does not waiver as I lose them from my circle. They are irreplaceable to me.

I hope you like this second edition of the book. Several people say it could be made into a movie. For now, just let the story unfold.

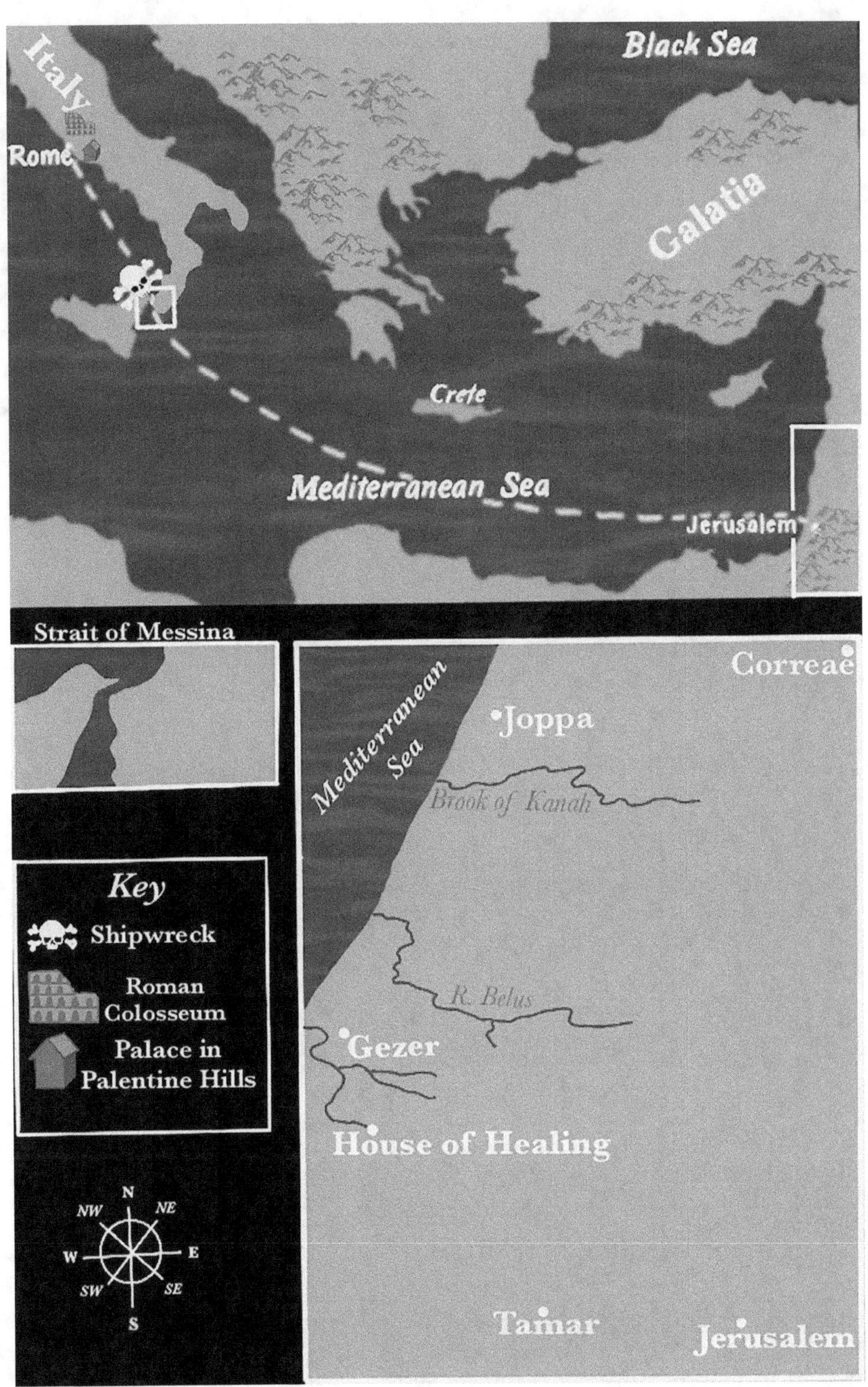

Black Sea
Italy
Rome
Galatia
Crete
Mediterranean Sea
Jerusalem
Strait of Messina
Correaë
Joppa
Mediterranean Sea
Brook of Kanah
R. Belus
Gezer
House of Healing
Tamar
Jerusalem
Key
Shipwreck
Roman Colosseum
Palace in Palentine Hills
N
NW
NE
W
E
SW
SE
S

Prologue

Recorded History and context

The year is AD 83. Less than fifty years have passed since Yeshua has died. Tales of his teaching and resurrection have partly spread, but most have no idea who he is. Since the destruction of the Temple almost seventeen years earlier, the members of The Way have changed names and now called themselves "Yeshuians." Their numbers are growing all around the world. However, Roman authority continued to grow and expand, and much of the wealth stored in the Second Temple of Solomon was lost or taken back to Rome for use in Roman public work projects under Vespasian's son, Titus. Local Pharisees and Sadducees took a small lot for preservation.

Israel was now a separate unit of administration in Rome's eyes, and it was called *Provincia Judaea*. The Ebreet spoke the name "Israel" amongst themselves; but in the common tongue of Greek, the land in which they lived was now called Judah by all. It was a crime to call it by its older name.

Taxes were collected and sent to Rome; but under Titus, Judah's tax burden was reduced. Titus replaced his father, Vespasian, in AD 79 after sacking Jerusalem and destroying the Temple. Although many feared that Titus would be ruthless, he was found to be a great leader and open to new ideas. His reign was a few years and he died of what were believed to be natural causes. He was succeeded by his younger brother, Domitian.

Synopsis of Book 1: Correae Chronicles

Yeshua came and left, and the Roman Empire continued its control of Judah and its people, the Ebreet. Emperors changed many times after the death of Yeshua, but the Roman power and authority did not. Some people followed the message of a risen Messiah, but most dismissed the stories of His time on earth, as not all the promises of the prophets had been fulfilled by His deeds while He was living.

A teenage girl from an Ebreet village of Correae in the northern territories of Napthali succumbs to the sin of fornication. She decides on the night of her older sister's wedding to travel to Jerusalem to sacrifice at the Temple to atone for her sins. Her father gives her the money he had intended to give to his future son-in-law as a dowry and blesses his daughter and her courage. She takes minimal supplies and sets out on foot in the middle of the night to reach Jerusalem and make her sacrifice. According to what she had learned, she could receive a bead of penance and it would rid her of the guilt and shame caused by her fornication. Then she would be able to start life anew and perhaps one day get married to a nice Ebreet man like her sister did.

Her journey was filled with extreme experiences. She watched a random beheading and saw the brutality of the Roman Army and their lack of concern as they called unruly Judeans. She met Barnabas and some of his contingent on her six-day journey to the Holy City. Barnabus tells her she does not need to travel to the Temple to atone. She needs merely to accept that a Messiah has come and that faith in him cleanses us of sin. She cannot believe that forgiveness is that easy and so, she continues her journey. She arrives outside the walls of the famed city to find the city surrounded and closed off by several Roman legions set on destroying the city as a penalty for defiance against the emperor's claims of authority. The Roman military barred the city gates for four months, allowing no one in or out, as they starved the city into submission. Yael overcomes her dismay at seeing that there is no way inside of the city, but she does not give up. She sets out in the middle of the night to find a back door entrance. She stumbles upon one of the many hidden tunnels from the days of King David that lead into the city and travels under the city; she finds herself face to face with Mishi, a young rabbi and headmaster of the Temple School, who was building a bunker under the temple to keep the Romans from finding him and his students. She asks to participate in the ritual of atonement to free her of guilt and give her the ability to start life anew, but there are no animals left to sacrifice. The young rabbi cannot help her with her grief but listens to her confession. He also confesses his sins to her and the two of them connect. She quietly leaves Mishi's apartment in the middle of the night and backs out through the secret tunnel hoping to buy an animal, bring it back into the city, and receive the all-important bead of atonement.

After she leaves the city, she is discovered by one of the Roman troops and in her fear, she offers her body to a Roman soldier as a way to escape danger. The soldier proceeds to rape her and she unknowingly becomes pregnant. The same day she is raped, the Romans begin their siege on Jerusalem, and she watches the city and the Temple destroyed as she experiences the trauma of feeling filthy and unworthy of love. She meets an old woman who shares with her a story of the risen Messiah that matches what she heard from Barnabas, and she begins to find peace in the midst of her darkest moment. This old woman speaks prophecy about her great faith and her future children and grandchildren, but she doesn't understand the message.

Back inside the city, Mishi is taken prisoner after the Romans enter the Temple grounds, and he becomes a slave of Rufus, the Legate over the 4th Legion. Rufus is the son of the centurion Cornelius from Caesarea and the second in command of the siege. Rufus was one of the architects who destroyed the temple. Rufus, too, had heard tales of this risen Messiah from his father, and he tasked Mishi to interview as many different sects as possible of people about their stories that there was a savior on Earth named Yeshua. The evidence is strong and they begin to believe that the stories deserve full consideration.

Meanwhile, the old woman who comforted Yael introduces her to an underground synagogue of the followers of The Way and she reconnects with Mishi. The two of them are commissioned by Luke, a wounded traveling doctor and rabbi who had firsthand experience of Yeshua and His follower Paul. The doctor commissions the two of them to transcribe his message and they make multiple copies to send to the small and floundering synagogues within the empire. These writings become the Book of Luke and the Acts of the Apostles.

As Mishi and Yael work together in the days after the fall of Jerusalem, Mishi falls in love with Yael despite being pregnant with another man's child. Although it is unthinkable for a rabbi to marry a woman who is pregnant, he recounts the story of how Yeshua's birth came to pass. He enters into *Erusin*, or engagement, with Yael in a most public manner. Rufus is offered a chance to retire from the Roman military and stay behind, and he takes this opportunity. He also becomes engaged to Gesher, an Ebreet from the tribe of Dan, who also has a child with another man. Rufus escorts Mishi and Yael back to their home village, where Mishi can formally petition Yael's father for her hand in marriage. Rufus spends six months traveling the Roman empire, distributing copies of the transcriptions that Yael and Mishi completed. Yael's *Erusin* with Mishi is now complete. Mishi tells the village the story of Yeshua and many are saved. Yael tells her sister that she is pregnant, and her sister tells her that she is also pregnant.

Book two, *The Emperor and The Ring*, continues more than seventeen years after Titus becomes emperor.

Chapter 1:
The Complications of Being
a Celebrity Rabbi's Son

Yael stepped outside and looked in amazement at the completed school next to their small but quaint house. It started as her husband's dream, but now that it was real, it occupied nearly all of their time and energy.

It was magnificent, with dormitories for 600 and classrooms for up to 14 simultaneous teachers. Sixteen years earlier, this land was a field outside of town where her in-laws grew grains and vegetables. She was a new mother and baby Caleb was at her breast. She had a pause in her housework and she put her hands on her hips to admire all the activity at the school, knowing that parents from all of the twelve tribes sent their children here to learn. The Tamar Boarding School, as they called it, was the lone school in the Holy Land that focused on teaching the new Torah of a Messiah named Yeshua, who came to save us from our sins.

Despite her responsibility to oversee the instruction of 100 young women about literally everything, she had a young man to parent, and there was no one in the world she loved more than her son, Caleb. However, he now stood more than a head taller than her and had been training to be a warrior under his Uncle Rufus' tutelage.

"Little One, come in to help with dinner, please!" yelled Yael from the door to their home. The house was plenty big for the three people in their family, but it seemed small to Caleb. It seemed like every other night, they had house guests. He could tell by his mother's tone that they were having guests again, and he could all but anticipate what she was about to ask.

Caleb had been practicing archery, as he did most afternoons. His uncle convinced him that 200 shots a day would make him an expert. He took 250. His uncle told him he would default to his training in times of difficulty. Caleb wanted that skill and did not miss a day of practicing swordsmanship or archery.

"Caleb, come on!" his mother repeated. He looked up and saw that his mother was wearing her thick cloak and a scarf, standing under the front porch. The day was overcast and it did not warm up enough for her to go outside without layers. The winter season should have been over in this part of ancient Judah, but it hadn't left yet. Living near the edge of a desert meant sparse vegetation and limited water, but it also made the cold season short-lived. Either way, she needed her son's help to finish the preparations, and he needed to stop shooting before he got his 250 shots. He was already at 210 and he knew his mother couldn't do everything. Caleb's cousins all had slaves, but his parents insisted that they do food preparation for guests without them. She told everyone that she was a slave to Yeshua for his blessings of a healthy baby. She was proud that he had become such a fine young man and loved how she had raised him alongside her sister's daughter, Eliza. The two were nearly the same age and they had spent more time together than apart.

As Caleb approached the home at a slight jog, Yael smiled and reached out her free arm to wrap it around her son. As he entered the doorway, her other hand lifted a small basket of vegetables that she intended to cook that evening. She called him "Little One" as a term of endearment, but he was anything but little. He weighed twice as much as she did, but that did not deter her from trying to wrap her cloak around him and kissing him on the cheek. He did not share with anyone, but he cherished his mother's kisses. He smiled, rhetorically asking her what she needed.

"Your father has been sitting at the feet of the leaders from Pergamon all day, and he sent a message that we will have three more guests with us for dinner and bed. They will be sleeping in the guest room, and I need you to make sure it is swept clean and that the mats are aired out, along with the blankets and pillows. Put an extra blanket in there, too. Those Peragomians are scared of the cold." Mishi knew his mother did not know these men and didn't care that she had a tendency to be prejudiced. It seemed like other people from her hometown of Correae were that way, except for Eliza. She would get to know them first.

Caleb acknowledged his mother's request as she began to walk away to do some other chores.

"With all these people coming and going into our home these days, I do not know what I would do without you, son. I need to carry those things down to the river to clean one of these days," she said, turning around and leaving him before she finished the last sentence. He hated how she would walk away from him while talking and mumbling. He seldom understood the end of her sentences. Regardless, he needed to do what she said. Being the son of the first-ever husband and wife rabbi team meant everyone looked at him. His father had been teaching him that since as far back as he can remember.

Caleb bowed his head respectfully and took off his sandals, leaving them outside the door to the room, as all Ebreet boys are taught to do. He felt the warmer air of their central fireplace as he stepped into their home with walls made of dried straw and mud. Although his mother's request was purposeful, his mother also often gave him stupid chores meant to make him stay near home. He figured out she just wanted him to be there. He liked home, but he liked to explore the deserts and the forest, track and hunt, fish, shoot his bow, and get lost discovering God's creation. Yet he knew his mother made sacrifices for everyone, and this was the least that he could do for her.

Deep down, Caleb thought his mother gave him these chores because of her disdain for his desire to hunt and kill wild game. He would bring home his wonder for God's creation and would try to talk about the joy he experienced as he hunted; she would find ways to get him to stop. Sometimes, she would interrupt him. Sometimes, she would ask him to do chores. Regardless, she hated hearing about how an animal would be tracked and killed, and create feelings of thrill inside of her child. It made her feel like she had failed as a mother.

Her feelings could not change his heart. Everyone knew deer hunting was Caleb's favorite pastime. He didn't see it as murder, as was mentioned in the Ten Commandments of the Torah. His mother didn't see it that way. Fortunately, his uncle understood him. Uncle Rufus would listen without judgment as Caleb would complain about his mother's reaction. Rufus consoled him as best as he could, telling the young man that his mother was very much like other mothers, trying to protect their children from getting numb to the atrocities of the world. Rufus, after all, was the one who taught him to hunt.

Rufus loved Caleb like a son. Rufus' wife, Gesher, and their son, Nathan, were killed in a freak accident when Caleb was little, and Caleb didn't remember either of them. Rufus seldom spoke about them, but his mother and father had told Caleb that Rufus was not an uncle but more of a second father. Things that Rufus should have done with his son; he did with Caleb instead. Considering how great of a warrior Rufus was, the community expected that Caleb would be no different.

Men from all over the twelve tribes who knew Rufus' father, or knew Rufus, reminded Caleb that he was being trained by an elite warrior who knew many emperors on a first-name basis. The claims made Caleb proud to call him uncle, and Caleb was hungry to learn. On his 14th birthday, Caleb entered an archery competition and he won it ahead of more than 200 other competitors. Rufus affirmed Caleb's skills, telling him that he would have put him in his legion as a lead archer if he were still a Legate in the Roman Army. Caleb knew that was a compliment, as a Legate or Legionnaire had 5,000 men under his command. Caleb needed no one to remind him to practice. His desire to remain excellent created a discipline seldom seen in a young person.

Caleb was a teenage boy but didn't look like one. Anyone looking at Caleb would underestimate his age. Despite his young age of sixteen years, Caleb was already taller than most men and he was more muscular than a highly trained Roman soldier. He was school-aged, and he and Eliza had one school cycle remaining before they would enroll. Most boys get taller first and thicker later. Caleb grew up and out concurrently. In fact, his physical presence scared people who didn't first know him as "Rabbi Yael's son".

What caught the attention of nearly all who came to the synagogue to learn from his parents wasn't Caleb's size but his non-traditional grooming habits. Caleb kept his hair short like the Egyptians did, but he also sported a thick and shortly trimmed beard and mustache. Ebreet barbers were of no help; he would visit an Egyptian barber near Joppa on the coast to get his hair cut and hear stories of Egypt and its rich history. Caleb loved the experience and he loved how his hair felt after the barber was done. While sitting in the man's chair, Caleb would speak the language of Egypt, and he developed good fluency over the years. During one break from Midrash, he traveled overland to Egypt, as his father had an assignment at a synagogue in Alexandria. Caleb could not stop talking about how much he loved the journey to Alexandria, the people he met along the way, and how good the food tasted at the different stops. Fondness for other cultures was a part of Caleb's identity, and his parents were proud to foster that.

His father helped him make that cultural bridge as they traveled, as Mishi was a chameleon of people and places. He would go with Caleb on his trips to the Egyptian barber, wearing his pastoral clothing for no other reason than to start a conversation about why his son was getting a traditional Egyptian haircut. His presence as a rabbi in a new faith led to a conversation about the Messiah. Caleb watched in awe as his father would maneuver his words to get people to listen to his stories, as his command of Egyptian was poetic and rich in meaning. More than one Egyptian called him their "Palestinian brother" when they would introduce him. Caleb was said to walk in his father's footsteps. Little did he know that being called a Palestina was an insult in the eyes of the Romans but spoken in a spirit of playfulness with the Egyptians.

Caleb's beard represented a wonderful story that Mishi could use as he explained the big shift in the faith within the twelve tribes. In addition to the Torah, the message of the risen Messiah and a new Torah were included in many of the synagogues in Judah and Egypt.

Caleb's father did not thrust those sorts of dress and grooming expectations on his son, nor did he do it in his synagogue in Tamar. He taught that Yeshua would not have cared what his son looked like; it was, after all, the state of his heart that he came for.

Caleb received no special treatment during the school year, though his cousin Eliza did. Mishi taught his son the same thing he did to all the students at his new and quickly growing school. The Messiah came for all, including those with different hairstyles, and we are saved by grace and through grace. For Mishi, that meant his son could have any hair type he wanted, which included short hair and a trimmed beard. And his wife, Yael, taught the girls the same message about how they appear in front of the community. She told them to dress and behave appropriately, but not necessarily as everyone else does. They were responsible for ensuring that their dress did not cause any of the boys to stumble. That was Yael's first message as the mentor for all the young women who traveled to Tamar to sit at her feet and learn. It was no secret that Yael's students all loved her and performed at or above the level of the boys. The freedom that Yael shared with them, which came from a belief in a risen Messiah, inspired them to think that they, too, were free. Although none of them ever became rabbis, they all were leaders in their future homes and villages. Soon, Yael knew she would be teaching a second generation of young girls whose mothers grew up loving the Messiah. She couldn't wait.

However, her niece Eliza received special treatment. Her sister had one child, and Yael loved Eliza as if she were her own. She was present the day Eliza was born, and one time, while her sister Katie was sick, Yael breastfed both Caleb and Eliza as Katie recovered. Eliza was the daughter that Yael did not birth herself.

During the school cycle, Eliza didn't live in the boarding school with the other girls. She answered, "I live with Aunt Yael," and she was proud to announce it as others asked where they could find her after school. She kept clothing at her aunt's house and she had her bed, mattress, quilts, and a pillow on the other side of Caleb's bedroom. She called it "her family's home in Tamar".

Yael assigned Eliza chores as she did Caleb and gave Eliza extra tutoring in language and mathematics. Eliza and Caleb grew up as playmates, and neither of them was shy about interacting with the opposite sex because of the time they spent together.

Eliza helped Yael in the kitchen or the school offices; during times Caleb hunted, Eliza listened to her aunt tell stories about her many trips to work with The Way back in Jerusalem, and she looked forward to the weeklong trips they would make to teach and uplift the poor who believed. In Jerusalem, they would stay in the home of an old woman whom Yael respected more than nearly anyone Eliza had ever met, and the old woman would cook, sing, and kiss them every time they visited. Eliza spent many evenings listening to the two of them tell stories and loved to hear two women talk about how much they loved travel and adventure. Her mother did not speak like that.

Eliza grew up watching the Tamar Boarding School expand. It started as a dream that Mishi's family had; but after the fall of the city of Jerusalem, their dreams came to life and expanded beyond anything they could imagine. Many who were inside Jerusalem during the seizure and destruction of the Temple were either enslaved or fled for their lives. Mishi and Yael avoided this, and they stayed around and helped Luke transcribe the scrolls of the early Yeshuian faith, called the Gospel of Luke and Acts of the Apostles. In addition to having the original Torah used by the High Priest and these two new writings, they also had the original scrolls written by Yeshua's half-brother, James. With the combination of these ancient and new teachings, they established a new kind of school. They taught everything that a student might learn in Ebreet School in Bad Safir and Bad Midrash. They added education in the message of Yeshua and the forgiveness of sins revealed to Ebreet and Gentile. And, as tales of their passion for teaching and Yael's investment in intelligent young women spread, people from all over the Holy Land sent their children to learn under this husband-and-wife combination. Eliza grew up with friends from Dan, Manasseh, Issachar, Simeon, and Reuben. Some Edomite girls attended and none of them seemed prejudiced against the other.

Yeshuian synagogues were now found nearly everywhere in the Roman Empire, and the number of followers was growing continuously now that the message was available for Yahweh's chosen people and the Gentiles. Yael and Mishi were happy together, and Caleb watched his celebrity parents impact the world. In the last two years, other larger cities sent contingents to Tamar to learn from Mishi and Yael how to make schools like theirs. Eliza and Caleb had the best seats in the world as these great leaders would sit on the floor of their home, seeking guidance from a husband-and-wife team. Eliza could see that her aunt and uncle were changing the world, and it inspired her.

The two children didn't share the same home village, and yet both of them grew up with the heart of explorers. Caleb liked hearing tales of those who came from faraway places; but for the most part, those tales were brief, as men came to the village of Tamar to listen to his father and mother and not talk to them. For every new story, he had to listen to ten old ones. Caleb yearned not just to visit these faraway places but to explore them. He wanted to walk their mountains, fish in their rivers and lakes, and track new and interesting game. For the most part, he didn't care about their food or customs. He had fond memories from his trip to Egypt and just wanted to meet people from other places with unique histories, as those discoveries made him feel alive.

His mother did not understand his desire to connect with Creation, but his father did. He knew that the connection between Creator and creation for his son was tightly knit.

"Abba, you have told me many times that you want me to know the Creator," Caleb would say. Mishi taught his son to use Aramaic, as he would call him "father". He liked the informality of it, and he wanted his son to know God the Father as a friend.

"I love creation, even though you tell me it has fallen from its original grandeur. I feel like I can see the Creator in creation better than I can in school. I want to visit and explore like the time you and I went to Egypt. I want to see the pyramids and the great volcanos. I want to see these synagogues and islands around the empire. I want to visit Gaul and Britannia, too. That would be my dream. To do that, I need to join the military like Uncle Rufus," Caleb added. His father had known for years that his son would one day ask his blessings to do this.

"You have my permission and my blessing to join the army, but I want you to finish school first," Mishi said. Caleb agreed, and he used that to motivate himself to do well. He looked forward to becoming a soldier; this agreement gave them peace about their compromise.

Mishi knew his son's choice to join the military made sense. Caleb's combination of physical strength, discipline with weapons, and academic knowledge of history and culture would make for a bright future. Rufus guessed he would quickly reach the rank of Centurion and make a name for himself. All the soldiers that regularly patrolled the roads in and out of Tamar knew it to be the home of Rufus and his nephew, and a great leader was being formed in their midst. No Roman soldier, not even his uncle Rufus, could catch Caleb in a footrace of any distance. The weight of Roman armor and Caleb's familiarity with the surroundings around Tamar made him slippery. He was more than adept with a bow and gladius, and his expertise demanded respect. He could kill from a distance and outrun any pursuit. As a sign of respect, both for his skills and his Uncle Rufus, Caleb was allowed to travel openly displaying weapons, camp anywhere, and not pay a hunting tax after he harvested fresh game. Rufus remained exempt from Roman law; therefore, the army informally extended that privilege to Caleb.

Caleb's hunting passion started at an early age. Uncle Rufus asked him to go with him one morning before school, and their routine of hunting twice each week continued through puberty. Caleb looked forward to hunting treks with his uncle, and he would often knock on his uncle's door when it was time to leave if his uncle accidentally slept too much. Once they reached the hunting rounds, neither of them spoke while they waited for the game to arrive, but the trip to the hunting grounds and the return were Caleb's moments to take in stories that he could share around the nighttime campfire. Caleb could listen to Uncle Rufus all day as he described the campaigns he participated in. Caleb loved to hear about distant places like Britannia and Gaul. Pale-skinned people and the overtly green backdrops seemed so different than life in the deserts of Judah. The tales of rain coming from the sky every day on the island of Britannia were perhaps the most unbelievable of all Rufus' tales to a boy growing up a day's ride by horse from Jerusalem.

For Rufus, the best part of mentoring Caleb wasn't that he was a great student. Rufus loved mentoring the young man as he had tremendous courage during stressful situations. A wounded bear did not scare Caleb any more than a desert cyclone. He always displayed self-control when challenged, and he seldom gave into his natural desire to have outbursts when things didn't go his way. The best part for Caleb was that his uncle's life was not separated into two parts like his father and mother's were. Rufus's before-Yeshua and after-Yeshua life habits remained the same. Caleb idolized his uncle's success and composure, and he wanted it for himself and his family one day.

"My boy, it is said that when the student is ready, the teacher appears. This is inverted for you and me. The teacher was ready first, but the teacher did not know it!" Rufus would say, laughing and hugging Caleb as if he were his son.

The hunting gave Caleb something else to think about other than the topics the rabbis taught him in school. Seldom did the rabbis teach them with authority that came from practical experience. Most of his teachers were rabbis in training; his mother didn't like the word disciple, but certainly, they didn't know as much as she and his father did. He knew that his parents were using their local school to train the next generation of teachers, and he respected that. But they didn't know nearly as much as his parents. When Eliza was in town, he knew his mother would provide extra teaching and insight each night to make sure they understood. Eliza was a better student than he was, and Caleb felt no intimidation during the times Eliza led conversations about either the old or the new Torah. He respected Eliza's intelligence and she respected his physical presence. Rufus reminded him to respect his parents for no other reason than he did.

"Your mom and dad have a great way with words, young man. I can sit at their feet and listen to them for hours at a time," Uncle Rufus would tell him. "The world needs to hear their stories, and you and I are here to help them. It's our job to keep them protected and safe, and the tools you and I use work alongside your parent's tools. They study the Torah. That is why you and I practice with bow and blade on most days." Caleb needed no convincing. He accepted this role with pride and knew it was honorable.

"I think Eliza is like my parents. She knows Torah better than anyone else at school, and she talks about it and does not struggle to remember details. She is also fragile, like my mother. And she is a great teacher," Caleb told Rufus.

"It will be your job to protect her, just as it has been my job to protect your mother and father," Rufus said. That made sense to Caleb.

Chapter 2:
Prevent the Past from Recurring

That evening, Rufus ate dinner at Caleb's house, as he had done many times before. Caleb was thinking about his cousin Eliza and the comparisons made earlier.

"Uncle Rufus, how did it come to pass that you would be my parents' protector?" He wanted to know how they met and how Rufus traveled with them during their times away from Tamar, fully armed with bow and blade.

"During those weeks your mother was writing down what Rabbi Luke told her, all three of us decided that spreading the message of Yeshua did not require the path of suffering that the Apostle Paul took. Your parents did not need to get stoned, thrown in prison, and physically attacked while they proclaimed Yeshua to be the Messiah. Instead, my men and I created a system to escort them during their foreign travels to make sure they get a chance to tell the Greatest Story and not be attacked or imprisoned." Caleb thought that he would love to be a part of Rufus's team of protectors one day.

"You may do this same thing for someone dear to you one day. Maybe your cousin, Eliza?" His mother rhetorically said. Caleb looked at Rufus, and the two of them smiled. It seemed more than coincidental that his mother brought up Eliza a few hours after Rufus did. It was easy for Caleb to envision himself defending her.

Caleb was one of the few people who knew Rufus' best friend was Titus, who now served as the Roman emperor. Caleb would often press him on the subject of that relationship, and Rufus indulged him with stories of his and Titus's antics during their years serving together. Caleb had not heard Rufus retell those stories to his mother and father. He wondered if they already knew them or did not want to know them. It was time to bring that subject into their conversation.

"Uncle Rufus, you knew Titus. Tell me more about him," Caleb asked.

"Titus is a great warrior and an excellent judge of character. But, he is shrewd and addicted to sex. He gets things done and he listens as others share their passions. He is an encourager, and that is what I admire about him. However, I did not like that he loved laying with different women at night." Caleb could tell that his uncle was covering up a wound.

"I don't want anything to happen to your mother and father, so I protect them from men like Titus who share a lust of the flesh. If I can prevent one rape or an attempt at murder, all of my trips with your parents will be worth it," Rufus said.

"Has anything happened like that in our family?" Caleb asked. Rufus quickly looked up at Yael, and she shook her head no. Rufus knew what she was saying, but Caleb didn't.

"That is not my story to tell," said Rufus. With that, he got up and left to go back to his house. It was time for a family discussion that did not include Rufus.

Chapter 3:
On Correae's Secret

Katya and Matthew had made a wonderful life, and they lived in one of the wilderness regions of Naphtali near the Golan Heights. Their small village of Correae had doubled in size since they had married, and it now supported nearly a hundred families. In the seventeen years since she had given birth, Katie's daughter had grown into a mature and beautiful young woman. Eliza had a brilliant memory and she demonstrated courage and leadership skills that impressed all the village elders. Matthew would joke that his daughter could have any man in Judah that she wanted, but few would be able intellectually to stay with her. And her skill at negotiating and bargaining in the marketplace had no equal.

Matthew was one of Correae's leaders and his role in security was unequaled in its importance. With the additional population, the village decided to use more of their gold stockpiles to hire additional rabbis to teach the children. Correae's residents received more education than nearly all Roman citizens and most Ebreet from the other eleven tribes. After all, this hamlet was wealthy, as they mined a secret vein of gold outside the village. It required an educated and organized workforce to mine, smelt, mold, and distribute the precious metal without drawing the attention of the Roman Empire.

Despite this growth, the center of the village where the children played, festivals were celebrated, and the elders decided on communal affairs, had not changed in size. It seemed like kids were outside screaming and chasing each other during all waking hours.

All this growth was not organic, nor did events of a predictable nature cause it. In the days and weeks after the Roman armies destroyed the Second Temple, the economy it supported collapsed along with it. No longer were street merchants selling to pilgrims coming to the Temple to atone for their sins. The quaint inns and food services within walking distance of the Temple grounds disappeared in a flash. Those who worked in that industry had to leave to find work, and some of them ended their journey in Correae, a six-day walk from the City of David. These migrant workers traveled north to the end of the road to restart their lives. However, since it was near the northernmost edge of Naphtali, less than a small handful of those escaping Jerusalem traveled this far. Correae was isolated because there was a single path into the village that supported carts, wagons, and caravans. Most who arrived did not spend the night, as there was no inn for transients. But a few of them arrived with essential provisions, and they came for work and to start a new life. They engaged the community leaders in a humble enough manner to receive a plot of land on loan so they could camp, farm, and eventually build a home. Most slept under the stars and lived on whatever reserves they brought with them.

Many migrants arrived and immediately left, but some stayed and worked for a few days for food and a few shekels at harvest time. The lack of permanent work discouraged most of them, seeing life in Correae as a dead-end. A few arrived with a spark in their eyes, willing to work hard. They were grateful for a chance to start their lives again in a place where the idea of a risen Messiah was respected. Once they accumulated enough wealth to pay back the loan used to buy their land and build their home, they were well-received by the village leaders, and they quickly melded into the community. It was common for the community to celebrate once a family climbed out of their debt, and they would be celebrated with gifts and a huge community meal.

Those who camped built homes and decided to settle into a long-term life in Correae needed to prove their loyalty before they learned of the presence of gold and how the village managed that wealth. It was Matthew's job to screen those who stayed, learn their personal stories, and share his findings with the elders. If the elders selected a traveler to become a citizen, it was Matthew's job to teach them what responsibilities came with that citizenship. He would also lead them on their first tour of the gold mining operation, studying their facial features and non-verbal responses to see how much they could be trusted. The elders trusted Matthew's judgment in this area. He was able to read people and their motives.

The mine required a small number of skilled people to extract what the community needed, as the value of gold had increased under Roman occupation. However, the most trusted and time-tested of Jerusalem migrants, those whom Matthew had properly screened, worked in the gold mines. The rest farmed and raised livestock. After all, a single greedy man or woman could ruin this experience for all the residents of the village.

Chapter 4:
The Love of a Husband

The elders reminded Matthew each season that the village's survival was contingent on his successful screening of refugees and migrants. If Matthew missed one detail about their habits or how they responded to stress, a simple slip of the tongue could doom the entire village.

The truth was that Matthew did not consider his job to be the most important part of his life in Correae. He saved the title of "most important job" for his role as husband to his childhood sweetheart, Katie. He spent much of his time patrolling the village perimeter and was keenly aware that if there were an attack by Romans against their village, he would be one of the first ones engaged in battle with the enemy. And he would be one of the first to die. He was not a well-trained soldier either.

He and Katie lived in a well-kept but small home next to Katie's parents, very close to the commons. He and his father-in-law were required by Ebreet tradition to complete the construction of that home before he was allowed to marry. As such, his efforts to make that structure into their home were his highest priority. It was in his efforts to build that home that he showed Katie his love for her. Since that event, he considered all of his labor a gift to his bride. Their daughter Eliza grew up hearing her father tell her mother of his love for her before he left for work. Those were also special moments for Matthew's girls. Matthew barely spoke one word for every ten that Katya spoke, Eliza's mother would say, but his words filled her soul, and she treasured them. Her favorite moments occurred as he left and came home, as those were the moments he most filled her soul.

"Katie, my dear, I am leaving for work. While I am gone, I will think about you and remember you. Love is not a strong enough word for what I feel for you. While I am away, coming home will be the most important act I perform each day. I promise not to take you for granted, and I want to be next to you as much as I can once I return."

As he stood in front of her before turning to walk away, she opened her soul in an attempt to reciprocate his warmth. Yet his words were of a depth that she could not equal.

As he left her, she would say, "You are a good man, Matthew." He knew this, but her simple affirmation meant as much to him as his words to her. From her conversations with her friends, she knew that not every woman had a husband who adored her. She was not about to lose that connection.

Eliza grew up watching her parents, and she knew what love looked like.

Eliza got her looks from her mother. Katie was beautiful and strong by any standards. She had perfect olive skin and deep green eyes with a beautiful smile that endeared her to everyone she met. She kept her hair short, and she loved to laugh and make others laugh. She offered the best wine her coins could buy to anyone who came by for a visit, and she was full of affection for anyone who stepped onto her property, whether they wanted her hugs or not. People found themselves amazed at how quickly they felt comfortable enough to share with her from their hearts, and she felt comfortable counseling people. She had light brown hair, just like her sister, and perfectly straight white teeth, a feature that was most uncommon in Naphtali. Being a native-born citizen of Correae also meant that she grew up eating a lavish variety of foods; her immune system was strong, and her bones and muscles were large by Roman standards. As Matthew would tell his closest friends, Katie was an eleven on a scale of one to ten. Every bone in Katie's being knew that Matthew was sincere with his words.

Her strength was of the kind common to women who had been born and raised in Correae but uncommon in most places where the community was wealthy. As her contribution to the village, she had spent many days lifting and carrying gold ore baskets from the edge of the river to the smelting furnaces. The path from the mine to the smelting operations was through the river, walking upstream. She developed a good sense of balance as she carried heavy baskets of rocks in the seasonal currents of the Jabbok River. As such, neither cold water nor heavy loads concerned her. Her ankles were resilient, and he legs were strong. Her midsection was highly muscular, and any flowing gown or ceremonial robe she wore made her feminine curves stand out and excite Matthew. After Katie had donned beautiful robes, put on jewelry, and bathed, she would present herself to Matthew. His excitement was obvious to everyone. He would tell her that she excited him as much as she did on their wedding night. The two of them would publicly embrace and they would kiss passionately, with no regard for who was in their village and watching. Eliza grew up with her parents as the model of what it means to be a husband and wife.

Yet, that toughness and her willingness to drink and share wine did not prepare her for the adversity that is a part of parenting. It was now time to have a conversation about sending Eliza off to her sister and brother-in-law again. For the last three years, Eliza spent fifteen six-week intervals living with her relatives. During the day, she studied at the Tamar Boarding School; after school and on their day off, she helped her sister and brother-in-law with household chores. After these six weeks ended, she would come home for one to two weeks, and the cycle would start over. Eliza learned many skills that her mother did not have, like speaking common Greek, Latin, and Aramaic and using the vernacular and the accent of a Roman army officer. However, during all these travels and spending nights in villages along the way, Eliza also acquired a love of adventure. And the last time she came home, she did so before her escort was ready, and she traveled across Benjamin, Ephriam, Manasseh, Issachar, and Naphtali alone. Eliza's apparent disregard for safety angered everyone in Tamar and Correae. She traveled through wilderness and wild animal ranges as well as mountainous routes that required route finding and careful planning to manage her water reserves.

However, she made it home without any negative consequences, and she was alive with stories of the people she met and the events she experienced on the way home. Her family did not know until the next day that she traveled alone, as she arrived at dinner time and she spent nearly all of dinner telling tales of her time away. No one asked her where the escort was. For that, her mother and father felt guilty for not reprimanding her and angry for her apathetic approach towards safety.

The next morning, after Katya learned that her daughter traveled six days alone on foot, she was furious. However, in her rage, she saw how well-adjusted her daughter behaved and she realized she did not know how she felt about Eliza's decision to deceive her. It brought back memories of her younger sister. Yael left in the middle of the night to go to Jerusalem and told no one other than their drunk father. Katie decided that her daughter was old enough to hear their family's secret story. Her reaction would determine how much freedom she could give Eliza; she was becoming a woman and needed to know that her mother trusted her.

After the morning meal, Katya left the job of cleaning to their slaves. She turned to Eliza and said, "Let's take a walk." The two of them left and began traveling up the hills behind the village, away from where everyone else was coming and going. Neither the agricultural fields nor the mining operations were in this direction, and the trail was rocky and seldom traveled. Once they had walked far enough away so that no one could hear them, Katya sat her daughter down on a large boulder that had some snow on it and told her daughter a story.

"Little One, your aunt knows this path better than I do, as I do not go much higher than this." Eliza knew her mother did not have her aunt's sense of adventure.

"Mother, why are we up here?" Eliza asked, showing some concern. Katya took a deep breath and took her daughter's hand.

"I promised you a story, so here it is. Your aunt walked up here and far beyond, and it required a strong dose of courage that I didn't have. She wanted me to go with her, but I was too scared to go. She used to tell me she wanted to go high enough to see the great river

Jordan. I thought she was being stupid, but she was serious. One time, she talked our teacher's nephew into taking the hike with her. Once they reached the top of the hill, she was sexually intimate with him. He left the village the next day and she was devastated." Katya waited to see what her daughter's reaction would be, but she couldn't read her. She counted to five before she added, "So, young lady, that was the first time Yael went traveling without a village escort."

"But Mom, I would never think about doing that."

Katya had recently had a conversation with her daughter as to how procreation works, and she considered telling her daughter this story at that time, but she withheld it.

"Perhaps you wouldn't, but sins like that tend to keep themselves secret. Your aunt told no one for a year. Then, during the night your father and I got married, your aunt asked our father for coins so she could travel to the Temple in Jerusalem to offer a sacrifice as is commanded in the Torah. She sought to restore herself before the eyes of Yahweh before she could restore herself to me and our family. She embarked to Jerusalem alone, in the night, while the rest of the village celebrated my wedding."

Eliza was taken aback, and Katya gave her time to process the story before continuing. Katya kept her grip on her daughter's hand. Katya allowed Eliza a moment to cry before she continued her education.

"When your aunt was on the way to that city, she had to watch the beheading of an innocent Ebreet woman by the Romans, and a Roman soldier raped her. However, it was during that time that she met your uncle Mishi, and I know she has told you that story, hasn't she?"

"She did tell me that story, yes!" Eliza said, relieved to have something positive to talk about.

"You know what makes your aunt so amazing is the part of the story that you do not know, but it is time for you to know. She became pregnant by that Roman soldier, yet your uncle Mishi decided to marry her and take her as his wife. He could have had her stoned for her insidious act of becoming pregnant out of *Erusin*. Instead, you know what he did? He forgave her, showing all of us how deeply the Messiah forgave us for our sins. I tell you right now that your uncle's act…"

She paused to wipe a tear from her eye.

"Your uncle Mishi's choice to take my sister as his bride and treat her like royalty, just as your father treats me, is worthy of…"

With that, her mother stopped, turned towards her daughter, and embraced her in a hug. She was sobbing, as was Eliza. Once she composed herself enough to continue, she held Eliza's face with her hands and looked her directly in the eyes.

"My sister and I have been blessed to marry honorable men. Your father and I want the same thing for you! When you travel without an escort, we become scared of what might happen to you," she said. Katie knew the hardest part of this story was in front of her. She took a deep breath and continued with what she needed to say.

"What I love about your aunt and uncle is how they reflect the faith that they taught us about. It is their commitment to the revelation that the Messiah has come that convinced your father and me that they were telling the truth." Eliza knew that, but this was the first time her mother spoke those words. Katya stood up and stretched. The fatigue of her conversation demanded it of her stiff body that came from carrying gold ore all day. The next part of her story would strike her daughter with force, and she wanted to be able to hold her daughter when it happened.

"Eliza, the truth is your aunt delivered the child that the Roman Soldier created. He is your cousin Caleb."

"Mom! Caleb is a bastard? He isn't my cousin?" was all Eliza could say. Katie pulled Eliza into her and held her, giving her a moment to process what she had heard. Then, she answered her daughter.

"Caleb is your cousin as much as Yael and Mishi are your aunt and uncle. Caleb has been raised as the son of a rabbi. Your aunt and uncle have happily shown the world what it means to be a Yeshua follower, and the two of them have literally changed all of the people who live in Benjamin. Ask anyone, and they will see he is their son. That means he is your family, Little One. Don't you think differently."

"Mom, I had no idea."

She motioned for them to start walking back home. She held Eliza's hand as they descended out of the Northerns.

"My heart fluttered when I heard you traveled alone. I think of all the bad and all the good that happened to your aunt as a result of going into the wilderness by yourself. I do not want anything other than good for you. You know that, right?" Eliza nodded that she understood.

"For your aunt, the good was greater than the bad. I do not want the bad to be bigger than the good for you."

"Mom, but Caleb…" Eliza started, but her mother stopped her.

"Now that you know the truth about those events, you must promise me something."

"What?" said Eliza.

"Eliza, you cannot treat Caleb any differently than you do today. Do you hear me? The two of you have grown up together, and your aunt and I visited each other many times every year so you two could play together and be raised together. He is your family as much as I am," she said as she waited for her daughter to respond. Eliza finally nodded in agreement as she felt the sincerity of her mother's request. Kayta was far from done teaching her daughter the points she wanted her to remember.

"Caleb is fully a man, and God chose him to carry on our people's traditions, no matter what his blood is. Do you understand me?" Katya pointed her finger at her daughter and spoke with a seldom-used authoritarian tone. She felt guilty that her little sister was raped and she had been unable to help. A part of that anger and self-loathing and not being there for her little sister was becoming visible now.

"I'm sorry, mother," she said. Katya smiled at Eliza, and they quietly walked down the hill until they reached the bottom. They didn't speak, as Katie wanted her words to have time to meditate inside of Eliza.

Despite all of the female traits that puberty had bestowed upon Eliza, Katya knew that Eliza's love of a great adventure was a mirror image of her aunt's. As a woman living in an isolated Ebreet village, Katya had not yet decided if this was a curse or a blessing. As a woman who had not experienced much of the world, she admitted to her husband that she was jealous of her daughter's courage to tackle the unknown and walk through lands owned by five different tribes without an escort. Either way, she was proud of the woman she was becoming.

Eliza was in a bit of shock as they came down the hill, as Katie wanted her to be. She knew the adventure side of the story but not the raping part. She knew her aunt was the same age as her the night she departed for Jerusalem.

"Mother, I will be more thoughtful in the future," Eliza promised. Katie believed she was sincere. After they got home, they had a quiet evening together, but Eliza could hear her mother telling her father about the conversation in the next room.

"Do you trust her?" she heard her father ask. Her mother mumbled that she did. With that, Eliza closed her eyes and fell asleep.

The next morning, the conversation about walking back to school resurfaced during breakfast.

"Mother, I want to honor our family. I won't do anything to endanger us. Please trust me," she said as her tears came to an end.

"I know you do not want to do something stupid," Katya told her. "But, you have no experience with the evils of this world. Your father must decide if you are ready to face the world without us by your side."

"But, mom! I heard you and dad talking, and you said I could go!" Eliza said.

"No, I said that I trust you. He must decide if you can go. This is his decision as the head of the household."

Chapter 5:
Eliza Sees Her First Rainbow

Eliza knew better than to raise her voice toward her parents, but she was on the precipice of saying something she would regret. She spoke with authority but not with anger. She used a tone like she had heard her mother use yesterday in the mountains. It was the same tone her aunt used as she taught in a room full of young men who challenged her authority as a female teacher of the law. Even though Aunt Yael was the scribe for Rabbi Luke's gospel and the Acts of the Apostles, leaders throughout the twelve tribes considered Yael's place as an instructional rabbi to be in an "improper position within the community of teachers". However, once they came to hear her teach, they changed their minds.

Eliza idolized her aunt's use of knowledge and experience as an act of defiance. In fact, all of Eliza's thoughts and beliefs about her aunt came out in this family conversation.

"I have made the trip between here and Tamar fifteen times!" Eliza exclaimed. "I know every step and all the back roads. I know signs to look out for, where to stay, where to stop to eat and drink, and how long it takes between villages. Uncle Mishi and Aunt Yael have taught me how to talk to Romans outside of our village. I speak better Greek than either of you two. I can use their accent, father!" Her parents looked at Eliza's body language and listened to the emotion in her words. Eliza looked at each of them one more time before she continued.

"I have made this trip since I was ten weeks old. I do not need an escort anymore." She had her hands on her hips, and she expressed her exasperation most compellingly.

Her father was level-headed, and Eliza knew she might lose her case to travel back to school by herself if she raised her voice. She wanted to ride her horse to Tamar without asking her father to leave work for a week to make the trip. Yet, she had something new to consider. She knew the truth of her aunt's journey, and she knew it was a matter of time before her father mentioned that he did not want to see what happened to Aunt Yael happen to her.

"Matthew," Katya said. "She is your daughter, and she is our daughter. I treasure her in ways that no one but you can understand." Matthew looked at his wife and smiled. He loved Katie more than anyone in the world. His kiss on her forehead was more of an acknowledgment that he heard her and valued her input. He looked his wife in the eyes and spoke to her.

"Katie, I do not want to lose her, either," Matthew answered. "However, she makes a reasonable argument. She has made this trip alone and she knows the way, but I do not like the idea. How will we know if she made it there safely or if we need to go looking for her?" Then, Katya said something Eliza was not expecting her to.

"Matthew, she knows what happened to my sister. I told her everything, now that she is becoming a woman. At this time of the year, there is a need to have you here, and you can go and bring her home the next time you and Effron head to the coast to trade." Matthew and Katya had already talked in private, but Katya needed to say that while her daughter listened.

Matthew positioned himself in front of his daughter. He put his hands on her shoulders and looked her in the eye. "No Ebreet father should entertain such a foolish conversation as this with his only daughter. Your purity and your well-being are my responsibility. Your safety lies upon me, above anyone else, to keep and maintain. You are no exception to Ebreet tradition nor the laws under which we all must live. You have not yet had your Bat Mitzvah and cannot make decisions for yourself yet."

Despite all those words of caution, Eliza could sense that a yes was coming, but she needed to maintain her composure until she received it.

He pulled his hands off of her face and held her hands. He took a deep breath and kissed her on the forehead in the same way that he kissed his wife. "However, the world is different, and I agree that you would not be any safer traveling with me. Our horses can outrun the Roman ones, and you know the way. Come, Eliza, receive your father's blessing. You can go alone."

There was no defense against a father's love and words spoken in love. Eliza melted. Her mom was right, Matthew was a good man.

"Thank you, father," she said, allowing herself to cry a few tears of happiness. He reached up to wipe away the tears that fell from her eye, but she turned her head away from him, feeling shame for shedding tears for him to see. He was, after all, the greatest man in her life. She desired to appear brave and strong before him, and her tears did not help her achieve that outcome.

"It is time to trust you, Little One," he said, motioning her to kneel in front of him. As was the Ebreet tradition, she placed her hands underneath his upper leg as he sat cross-legged. She closed her eyes and leaned back. Her father closed his eyes and raised his hands to heaven. He spoke a prayer from his heart.

"Yeshua, our Messiah, please send Your spirit of protection and take care of our daughter as she crosses the lands of the twelve tribes to reach her school. May the roads be free of crime, and may her eyes, ears, and mind be fast to discern any dangers that come upon her. I beg for her protection in the name of Yeshua's shed blood. Amen."

They all stood up, and Matthew would not let Eliza leave without one more message. "I know that you feel more alive as you travel and experience new things. Remember, my daughter, you are not alone. Keep your family's teachings as close to your heart as you can. During those moments when all light fails, God will be there. He will provide for you the courage you did not think you had."

"Yes, father," was all Eliza could say before her voice cracked.

"You can leave tomorrow right after breakfast. Make sure that you get all your provisions packed and your horse fed and groomed. Get Ishmael to look over the horse's shoes, bridle, and saddle before you leave. I want you to make sure that all things are in the best of order. And take ten extra gold and twenty copper coins in case something happens. You know where I keep our money." Eliza thanked her father again as he left to visit some of the village leadership to discuss what he had decided. He promised to be home before they went to bed.

Eliza was overjoyed, and she hugged her mother as soon as her father had left. She could not wait to tell Aunt Yael about all of her exploits traveling by herself. For an Ebreet girl in the time of Emperor Titus, this moment was as magical as seeing your first rainbow.

Chapter 6:
More Forgettable Stories

Caleb's outward physical maturity disguised his age. Everyone assumed he had completed his Bar Mitzvah and was making decisions on his own. However, he had not, and he had an obligation to route all his decisions through his parents. When guests came to visit, he would sit quietly, answering questions when asked. Tonight's Peragomians told stories of miraculous events that they witnessed. There were tales of a dead man who was brought back to life and another of a pond used for irrigation that was completely refilled in the middle of the dry season. Caleb had seen some of these events with his own eyes, so he knew that they were real. They were proof that God existed. It felt like a grand story was an admission ticket to his family's house for dinner. Yet, he had no stories of his own to tell - at least, not yet.

Caleb found that there were a few guests over the years who loved hunting and fishing as he did, and they would tell him of great places to stalk game, sometimes with the same passion that they had for the tales of how Yeshua moved mountains. They were his favorite kinds of guests. Fortunately, his father took all the maps from the Temple with him, and they were now kept in their synagogue. These guests would tell him of the best places to hunt; he would often get them to walk back to the synagogue with him the next morning and show him on the maps where game from their locality would travel during different seasons. He wrote codes on the Temple maps so he could refer to them in the future if he reached their part of the empire. Initially, his father got upset at him for defiling the writings of the ancient temple. Later, he agreed that the borders of Rome were changing so quickly that the maps were out of date. In fact, Caleb now called Solomon's maps of the twelve tribes his hunting maps. Rufus had watched Mishi's change of heart and quietly loved it. He was allowing his son to make decisions without the Bar Mitzvah.

"Young Caleb, there is much you must know to understand our faith," said the leader of the guests on this particular night. "We want to invite you to visit us and our synagogue one day in Antioch. Perhaps we can go hunting for eagles while you are there." Shooting an eagle with a bow was an exceptionally difficult challenge, but Caleb was excited for the opportunity.

"Challenge accepted," Caleb said.

Caleb had received invitations to visit these newer Yeshua-based synagogues many times. However, since this man mentioned hunting, Caleb committed to one day going to Antioch and perhaps visiting the synagogue as well.

"To begin with, we heard you refer to us as members of The Way. We are now called 'Yeshuians' or 'Yeshua Followers,'" this man said.

"Yes, sir," Caleb replied. Caleb readily allowed himself to be corrected by those whom he respected. In his mind, anyone who proclaimed that they were an eagle hunter was a respectable man.

For a seemingly unending period, these men told stories of the events from Antioch that engaged Caleb. There were tales of a woman being raised from the dead. There was a story of three young boys who turned rocks into bread while they were lost in a cave; when the boys were rescued a week later, there were three loaves in the cave with them, still warm. There was a story of a time when everyone in Antioch had the same dream of three men riding into their village on horses. The same evening, three men rode into the village on horses, all weeping. The leaders of Antioch approached the men, telling them they had been expecting their arrival. The men dismounted their horses and were led to the center of Antioch, and different members of the village began telling them of their dreams the night before.

People from all corners of Rome would come to read the writings that Caleb's parents stored in the vaults, including the original scrolls from the Second Temple that Mishi saved. Last month, scribes from Thessalonica and Cyprus had come to make copies of those scrolls to take back to their synagogues and schools. There were now two scrolls from the teacher, Paul. His stories were important, as they came from Rome and were the most talked about of all the writings in their vault. To most visitors, the inside of their synagogue was more a library than a synagogue.

As the men got up to retire for the evening, Mishi turned to his son and said something that he knew would be more interesting to him. "It is near time to begin another semester of school. Although I haven't received any word yet, I would expect your family from Correae to be arriving soon. That means you can take your cousin hunting with you again."

"That's great! You know, father, Eliza hates hunting. Uncle Matthew, though, he likes it!"

Neither of them had any idea Eliza would be coming alone.

Chapter 7:
Eliza Travels to Tamar

Eliza woke up early, full of excitement. She had the servants prepare her breakfast quickly. She skipped drinking tea with her mother to get her chores done as fast as possible. Katya saw that her interest was elsewhere, so she let her out of some of them. Katie needed to get herself ready to travel, and it would only help if Eliza left a bit early.

"Eliza, please double-check everything. Take anything from the house that you think you might need to be safe," Katie said. Eliza politely acknowledged her mother, but Katie could tell that Eliza was prepared and didn't need her help.

Eliza did not need much time to get ready, as she had made all the necessary arrangements the afternoon before once she had received her father's blessings. She needed to make a short trip to the river to fill her two waterskins, and then she would be ready to leave.

She told her parents that she would reach Tamar late on the third day. Her horse allowed her to cut her travel time in half as long as the paths were open. She would stay at safe houses where former students of her aunt and uncle now lived, and she would use the main roads for the first two days. She would leave Roman roads on the last day and instead cross through two different forested sections to reach some remote roads north of Jerusalem that avoided Roman encampments between Jerusalem and the sea. Those encampments were places where bad things happened to the Ebreet with no accountability for the perpetrator.

Her father had a great sense of direction. He made her recall the route she would take to the Tamar, making sure she would avoid Roman training camps. He also asked her where she would stop and let her horse drink while she rested. Once she answered the last question, he playfully did what he always did.

"Ok, get out of here before I change my mind!" She knew he was being playful, and she stepped up to him, kissed him on the cheek, and said, "Goodbye, Abba." Then, she walked towards her horse to leave on her journey.

But she was stopped immediately as some of the village elders approached her. "Please, we must talk to you before you leave."

Eliza knew to listen; her father showed great respect for these men, and she would be reprimanded if she didn't do the same. She assumed she would be warned of dangers again, no different from what her parents had already told her. They stood around her in a circle, and her parents joined. From their body language, it was obvious that her parents knew the words about to be shared. The mayor was there, and he spoke first.

"Eliza, this job is one that your father must do as the assimilator of new residents. However, the village has decided that I shall do it with you. This message is too important to leave to chance or misunderstanding."

Eliza was concerned, and she looked at her father for validation.

"It is okay, Little One," he assured her.

She returned her gaze to the mayor as he began. "Our village's success is built around our secret gold mine. In the event that you are taken by the Romans or other angry factions of Ebreet, you must let that secret die with you. You do not have permission to share the secret of our wealth, even if it means you give your life. Our village is more important than anyone's life. You must understand and embrace Paul's writing as he says that you are to offer your body as a living sacrifice, holy and pleasing to God." The mayor waited for her to acknowledge what he had said.

"I understand," she said, which was all she could muster. "So, are you expecting me to kill myself if I am caught?"

"Of course not!" said the elders, almost in unison. "The opposite is true. You must fight and try to escape at every chance. Defend yourself! Don't be paralyzed and let them kill you. Fight back! There are many stories in our history of Ebreet killing their oppressors."

Eliza let out a sigh of relief and thanked him for his clarity.

"Since you are carrying a great deal of gold," the mayor continued, "you will need an alibi to explain where it came from." With that, one of the elders gave her a bill of sale and a large pot of frankincense to show where her current wealth came from. He instructed her to tell anyone that she intended to barter gold for another's harvest. He instructed her to carry the gold on her in several different places. She wanted to tell them that she already knew this strategy and was going to show them her three leather pouches where she carried her coins, but she wanted to leave. She nodded in agreement and bit her tongue instead.

As the mayor finished sharing, her mother put a hand on her shoulder.

"Your aunt and uncle taught us how to use the gift of the Holy Spirit. This is one of those moments where we will call upon His power."

Each person placed one hand on the young woman, and her father began to pray. Matthew had the responsibility of being the spiritual leader, and he spoke first.

"Father, You told the Levites to lay hands. You told Moses to lay hands. You told your apostle Paul to kindle afresh the gift of laying of hands. As Your prophet Luke shared with my sister and brother-in-law, You desire us to come to You and ask You for Your touch. We pray for the Holy Spirit to send His anointing on my daughter as she begins a journey away from our protection. We live in trying times, as our ancestors did before. We thank You, in advance, for the power of Yeshua protecting our daughter as she crosses the remnants of the Promised Land."

He leaned forward and kissed his daughter on the forehead, and the elders started humming, chanting something that Eliza could not understand. She began to sob, even though she did not know why.

Her mother spoke. "God, bless our daughter. Cover her in Your protection as she travels into what used to be the lands of your people but is now the lands of the enemy. Keep her safe. Keep her eyes sharp and her mind alert. Let her see the path before with clarity that the world cannot understand. Treat her as Your precious daughter, just as her father and I do."

"Thank you, mother," she said, giving her mother a big hug. Prior to Yael becoming a rabbi, it was unheard of for a woman to lead a prayer that included village elders present. In Correae, it was now common. Katya occasionally led public prayer as her sister had paved the way for this to be spiritually acceptable.

The elders stopped chanting and everyone took turns embracing Eliza. The mayor reached into his tunic and took out a large bag made of leather, tied with a string. "Normally, the eldest person from the village pays for rabbinical services for the education of its youth. This transaction is hidden from the students. Since you have excellent intuition with all financial dealings, we permanently extend this task to you. Take this bag and give it to your uncle after you are settled into their home. It contains a tenth of a talent for your education for the next cycle for you and your cousins and an additional tenth of a talent as a donation to their charity work. Until you arrive, do not take it out. In fact, keep these gold coins out of sight from anyone you meet. We stamped them as they came from our kiln with a Roman inscription like others we have found so that no one can trace them back to our village. However, this is enough gold to justify killing you and leaving you on the side of the road." She acknowledged what they said with a nod. She was not scared of what she might have to do to survive. If nothing else, her aunt told her that she must be brave, no matter what that meant.

Then, the head elder handed her the bag. She took it and was amazed at how heavy it was. These were real golden coins without any impurities, most likely smelted yesterday. She placed them in her saddlebags and secured the drawstring. Once she was done, she was ready to mount her horse and depart, but the head elder put his hand on her shoulder as she prepared to jump on her horse, making her stop.

"And this is also for you." He handed her another allotment of coins, including copper, bronze, gold, and several made from silver, the most precious and expensive ore.

"Spend this on yourself. You have our permission to purchase something nice for yourself or your classmates. You are of age to Bat Mitzvah soon, and perhaps even marry. You need not account for how you spend it, but I am sure that you will." Although this purse was smaller, it reinforced the importance that the village placed on those whom they educate and tithing to those who serve the Lord. And with that, Eliza mounted her horse and began a trot out of town on the road out of Correae.

"See you soon!" her mother yelled as she departed.

Little did Eliza know that her parents would be half a day behind her.

Chapter 8:
A Difficult Family Reunion

Three days passed, and Eliza reached Tamar without incident. Each of the synagogue communities she stayed with on the previous two nights had been welcoming. As instructed, she arrived at the very end of each day, a few moments before sunset, as she did not want to draw any attention to her arrival or departure. Each place she visited provided for her needs, and she did not need to use any of her food for dinner or breakfast. Her horse received grooming services and all the fodder it could eat. She had perfect weather. She did not need to use her heavy cloak for warmth against the wind nor her deer hide for rain protection.

In her mind, the best part of her solo adventure was that she did not spend a coin. Eliza loved managing finances and found pride in keeping her spending reigned in. She felt pride as she rode her horse in the wilderness between villages, knowing that her village leaders had entrusted her with managing some of the finances. She dreamed that perhaps, one day, she would become a businesswoman or village treasurer. Perhaps she would be both.

On her trip through the forested region, she decided to give the two different sections names. She called one section "the North Forest". The second forest was "the South Forest"; although it was smaller, it had more wildlife. This trip was no exception, as a fox was carrying a recently killed rabbit in its mouth, not a stone's throw in front of her as she entered the forest.

No one would understand that the lack of incident was the worst part of the trip. She had to admit to herself as she neared Tamar that she had hoped for more adventure stories, but there was nothing of significance to talk about. Long before sunset on the third day, she found herself in sight of the arched entrance into Tamar. She could see smoke coming from the chimneys of the homes, and there were distant voices on the horizon, as the sound carried a long way this time of day. Her heart raced in excitement, and she prompted her horse to go faster.

After passing through the arches into the hamlet, she went directly to the school, bypassing her parent's orders to go to her aunt and uncle's house. She found the school full of activity, as school was scheduled to start two days after the upcoming Shabbat. She saw many of her friends doing the same thing she was, checking in at the dormitory and confirming which rabbi they would be sitting with during this school cycle. Village volunteers were readying the school grounds, making it look beautiful. Firewood was being delivered and stacked outside the boys' and the girls' dorms; and a wagon full of grains, oils, potatoes, olives, oranges, and lentils had already been delivered. Enrollment at the school was now nearly as great as the village's entire population, and some builders and Roman administrators from the coast had come to survey where the next buildings would be placed. Last year's farming expectations were met, and slaves and citizens were moving the last of the extra wheat straw into a large mud house for storage for the wet and cold winter months ahead. Some flowers had been planted outside the window in the office where the rabbis worked. There was also new thatched reed grass on the roof to keep the facility waterproof during the rainy season and cool during the hot season. The school looked nearly ready.

Before she took ten steps onto the school's grounds, she was knocked to the ground. She looked up to see her cousin, Caleb. He laughed and apologized in complete insincerity.

"You donkey! That wasn't an accident! Why did you do that?"

Her words made him laugh harder. "Eliza, how've you been? And where is everybody? Where are your mom and dad? I want to go hunting with Uncle Matthew."

She raised her hands over her head and pointed at herself from above. "You are looking at my entire entourage!" Her smile was rich in symbolism, as she knew that Caleb did not yet have permission to travel alone outside of Benjamin or Dan.

"Wow," he said. He paused and was obviously jealous. He forced himself to smile, but he didn't say anything. Eliza smiled back, feeling for the first time since she left that she had accomplished something worthy of Caleb's praise.

"You are not jealous, are you?" she said, reaching out and holding his massive forearm. He frequently practiced with a gladius, and he had larger forearms than anyone from her hometown of Correae.

"Your parents let you come here alone?" he responded. His inability to answer her made her day. She smiled.

"All by myself!" she said.

She knew his story, as the two of them had talked about it before she left to go home by herself. He knew the hills and caves of the area better than anyone, but he had not tried to seek permission to travel overnight by himself. He was the son of two Ebreet rabbis, a most unique status in the history of all of Judah, and the thought he would get his parents' approval to do such a thing seemed impossible.

Eliza smiled and put her hand on her hips. She loved the satisfaction of doing something her cousin could not do. He was bigger, faster, and stronger than she was, even though the two of them were born ten days apart. It made her effort to convince her parents to let her travel alone worthwhile. They joked a lot, as teenagers do, and the two of them sat down as Eliza shared every boring detail that she could remember from the journey. Caleb showed interest as she talked about the fox and rabbit she saw on the way, asking her lots of questions about the size of the fox and whether or not the rabbit was moving. Eliza did not care about that and got bored quickly.

She heard her aunt's voice coming from their home, and she stood up and ran towards her, abruptly breaking off the conversation with Caleb. She and her aunt embraced as two Ebreet women could, with kisses on her cheeks and lips, and lots of blessings poured onto each of them. Neither of them hesitated to tell the other that they missed them and loved them. Caleb watched them, and he smiled. Eliza visited consistently, and he felt that life was normal during the school year if he could hear her talking to his mother. He was glad that she had arrived safely, and he loved her from the bottom of his heart. He had no siblings, as his mother had difficulty during childbirth, and Eliza was the closest thing to a sister he had. Yael spoke to Eliza first.

"Oh my, you have grown up, my dear. You are most certainly looking like a woman in all the right places. And, of course, you have all the curves of a woman and look more and more like your mother…and me!" Yael's sense of humor could make Eliza laugh, no matter how moody the teenage girl got.

"Eliza, would you like to help me make dinner?" She put her arm over Eliza's shoulder and walked her into the kitchen. Caleb went to get Eliza's bags from the horse, and he quickly returned, placing them in the bedroom where the two of them slept.

"Auntie, I brought some of Correae's olive oil with me. I want to use that. Is that okay?"

"Yes! Yes! Let's use that. Home always tastes better." Without hesitating, Caleb retrieved the oil from Eliza's bag and brought it to them in the kitchen.

They began their continuous chatter and dinner preparations. Yael and Eliza had a lot to catch up on. Caleb ran off to play with his friends.

"Auntie, can I ask you some questions?" Eliza said as they settled into their normal routine in the kitchen, with her two slaves assisting her in preparing all the materials.

"Of course." Yael could sense Eliza's hesitancy.

"Mom told me about how you left Correae to travel to Jerusalem for redemption. Part of that story I had heard before, but I did not know about why you left until a few days ago."

Yael smiled. She knew this day would come, and she knew to let her older sister initiate the conversation after Eliza had started her monthly bleeding.

"In our culture, we teach young men and women the importance of purity before marriage. I tested those boundaries with a young man whom I did not know, thinking he would be special to me one day. He did not share my intentions. He wanted to have a good time and discard me like an old rag. I made two mistakes that day. I decided to ignore the teachings of God, and I decided to trust that boy. The first one was my mistake. The second one is a natural error that anyone can make. God forgave me for the first one, and I forgave myself for the second one." Yael continued to work as she told the story, knowing that Eliza idolized her and would be watching and listening to her every word.

Eliza did just what Yael expected. Now that she was a woman, she no longer looked at boys as stupid rats, as she used to. She knew that one of them would be her husband one day, and she felt a burning desire to share what she had been thinking.

"Auntie, I don't think I am going to marry the first boy my mother and father select for me. Your story scares me. I am sure that I am going to wait till I am older and have seen the world," she said.

"My sister and I have talked about you and talked about that. You can take all the time you need to get married. Our family is full of very fertile women, and you can have children later in life if you want. Yahweh Himself knows you are beautiful and smart enough to have any man in Benjamin like I did." They laughed, and Eliza got another hug from her aunt.

Now that Eliza was of childbearing age, thoughts of what her husband would be like appeared in her mind on occasion, and Yael would ask Eliza to describe her husband. Eliza liked talking about these kinds of questions, and she knew she could speak without filter with her aunt. Yael told her how God provided her with Mishi, a man smarter and more tolerant of different kinds of people than she was, and she knew she could follow and trust him. For Yael, a man she could follow was most important.

"We learned from our dear friend Paul during our time in Rome before you were born that God uses all things to bring Himself glory. I told Paul my story, the same one your aunt told you. He laughed! Do you know what he said? He said he used to kill Ebreet, and now God had used him to teach others how to save themselves for eternity. I gave up my body and got to see God transpose my sin into the Gospel of Luke and the Acts of the Apostles. It seems like God has a sense of humor."

Eliza started laughing as she had heard tales of Paul repeatedly.

"Oh, I was not expecting him to laugh. But, it helped me see things as more than tragedy. Good came from that event," Yael said. She paused and was anxious to share what came next. Yael knew what was coming by Eliza's body language.

"Mom also told me that a Roman soldier raped you and that Caleb came from that rape."

Yael put down her wooden spoon and looked Elize directly in the eye.

"Yes, this is true."

Eliza began to cry. She hated crying in front of her aunt, as she wanted to prove herself to be a strong woman. Tears seemed to make her feel like a failure. Yael held her until her crying stopped.

"I am so sad for you. Mom said that I must not treat Caleb any differently than before I knew this. She said Caleb is an heir to God's kingdom like any Ebreet or Gentile who accepts his gift." That comment made Yael smile.

"Your mother understands the message of the Messiah. Yeshua did not come for the Ebreet. He came for everyone who sins - which is everybody!" Yael paused to wipe the tears from Eliza's eyes as they laughed hysterically.

"I hate this crying! I did it before I left to come here, too!" said Eliza. Yael drew her into her chest and held her head while rubbing it.

"The best part of that story has been your uncle's demonstration of his love towards me and Caleb. Your uncle has given every moment and every extra coin he has to raise and love Caleb as if he were his own blood and flesh. Caleb feels this love, and the two of them love each other. But sometimes, it is obvious that they aren't of the same blood. Caleb is very strong and fast, and my Mishi is not!" That got a big laugh from everyone, including the two slaves helping them in the kitchen with food preparation.

Eliza had seen and heard many stories of Caleb's physical prowess. She loved how he could run fast one minute and carry such heavy loads the next. Caleb had been a hunter of great skill for many years, but lately, he seemed better and more compassionate than before. He would give the meat away from his kills to travelers who looked to be in need. Sometimes, he would take a deer he had harvested to a family in the next town whom he knew had no land of their own and give it to them, along with his allowance for the month. Eliza would tell him that one day, he would be a great husband and father, and she looked forward to meeting the woman he would pick as his wife.

"I think he learned the skill of protecting and sharing with those who are less fortunate from Uncle Rufus. Both of them have big hearts like that," she added. "Now that he has transitioned into becoming a man, I am glad that he hunts game instead of women."

They began laughing again.

"Auntie, as I was traveling here alone on my horse these last three days, I thought about what it must have been like for you the first time you left Correae to travel alone to Jerusalem," Eliza said.

"I had to find water and get out of the way when caravans would pass me on the Jerusalem highway. I met some wonderful people and half of the time; I walked at night. I learned a lot during that week of walking. At the end of the walk, I met your Uncle Mishi. Now we are done talking about the men in our lives today, okay? It is time to feed them! Go get your cousin," Yael said.

Eliza went outside and called for Caleb. He was hungry and arrived quickly, sneaking a piece of bread from the oven before his father entered and blessed the meal. They all sat and ate together. As dinner was winding down, Mishi spoke up for the first time that evening since blessing the meal. Caleb was already on his third portion of bread and mutton while the women talked incessantly, barely eating their food. "Yael, let the slaves take care of all the cleaning. It is time to talk to our son about his past. Since Eliza arrived here by herself, I believe she is old enough to hear this story. Caleb will need her support. She is his family."

Mishi turned to Caleb and could see the boy looked shocked. "Young man, come sit next to me."

Caleb did not hesitate. That left Eliza sitting next to her aunt. With that shifting of seats complete, Mishi began.

"My son, you have heard how I met your mother in an abandoned tunnel left behind from the days of King David underneath the city of Jerusalem. Neither of us was much older than the two of you are now. You have also heard how we were moved by the Holy Spirit and helped Luke record the words spoken to him by Yahweh Himself. It is the content of those stories that brings people from synagogues all over the Roman Empire to us. What I did not tell you is an important piece of information regarding how you came to be my son."

Caleb looked perplexed. "What? What do you mean, father?"

His father had taken him into the wilderness just this year and explained to him God's plan for procreation and how that plan works. One man and one woman come together, and through this union, children are created. It is an act of love that occurs once a man leaves his parents' home and builds a home for himself and his bride. Then, they have sex and create offspring.

"You know that I met your mother in Jerusalem. What you do not know is that she came to Jerusalem to atone for a sin she had done a year earlier that she hid from everyone."

Caleb looked at his mother. "Mother, what sin?"

Yael began to look pale, and she reached out and put her arm around Eliza. "Keep listening to your father."

Eliza noticed her aunt's tears as she spoke, and her view of her aunt forever changed at that moment. Her aunt did not look the part of a great teacher and the leader of a movement of strong women. She was no longer a teacher of the old and new Torah, revered for her insight into how to read and write many languages. She was now a woman who remained a teenage girl at heart, who had yet healed from a hurt from half a lifetime ago. Instead, this great woman now looked frail, ready to begin sobbing.

"Your mother had sexual relations with a boy who was temporarily staying in Correae, and the guilt made her suffer. She left to come to Jerusalem to sacrifice at the altar in the Temple to atone for her sin, as was our custom."

Caleb looked at his mother with his mouth wide open.

"Mother? Is that true?" he rhetorically asked.

"Yes, my son. That is what happened. That is what I did," she said, making sure to point out and separate her choice from its impact. Once Caleb returned his gaze to his father, Mishi continued.

"After your mother and I met, she secretly left the city to find a suitable sacrifice so I could lead her through our ritual of atonement. After she slipped through the tunnels under the city, she found herself in the fields in front of the city. A Roman soldier raped her, and your mother became pregnant. Son, you are biologically someone else's son."

Before Caleb could speak and attempt to unwind the mystery just revealed, Yael began to talk to her son with a cracking in her voice that neither Eliza nor Caleb had heard. "During the days I was falling in love with your father, I worked with him nearly every day. I did not know I was with a child! We were consumed by the task in front of us of recording the Word of God, and we spent nearly every moment together, taking turns writing what Luke spoke to us. I did not notice that I missed my menses. Your father was far from his family, and I had left Correae in the night. No one other than my father was aware of my choice to travel to Jerusalem alone. Your father and I bonded during our time in Jerusalem. They were the best days of our courtship."

The teenagers were speechless. Eliza had been given the high points of the story, but she did not know these details. It was unheard of for women to speak about their monthly cycle in the presence of men. Mishi again spoke.

"I was falling in love with your mother before I learned that she was carrying another man's child," he said. "At the same time, I was learning from Luke that our Messiah was conceived by someone who was also not His earthly father."

Mishi gestured for his cup to be filled with some red wine. The children saw him do this less than once per year and on special occasions. Once it was filled, he motioned for the servants to pour themselves a cup and join them. Caleb admired his father for his willingness to include slaves in all their affairs. He was now beginning to see that despite being a bastard, he was loved by this man like a son, just as these slaves were loved and considered part of his family.

"As we are taught in Luke's story, Mary's soon-to-be husband had the choice to leave her, without disgrace, once he learned that she was carrying someone else's child. He could also have chosen to have her stoned to death. Rabbi Luke told me that Yeshua forgave all of us for our sins from the past. In exchange, the Messiah asked us to follow Him."

"So, you married Aunt Yael, knowing that she was with child from another man?" asked Eliza.

"Yes, Little One, I did. Memorize the next words I am about to share with you. Are you listening?" he said. She nodded yes.

"It was the best decision I have made since my birth." He lifted his cup and toasted with the two slaves. Caleb and Eliza looked at each other in complete awe at Mishi's humble character.

Yael had been holding her niece closely, resting her head on the sixteen-year-old's shoulder and caressing her dark brown hair. Now, she was lightly weeping.

"I love you," Mishi said to Yael, lifting his cup to toast her again.

Mishi smiled at his wife before returning his gaze to his son. "Caleb, this event does not change the legitimacy of the love your mother and I have for you. You are our son, and we have raised you to be an Ebreet and a God-Fearing Yeshuian. Your Uncle Rufus has raised you to be a warrior. You are a unique and powerful young man. Although no one here will know your biological father's name, I am your father on earth, as Yahweh is your Father in heaven. Your mother and I believe that you need nothing else. You need no one else, perhaps other than a wife of your own, one day. And don't be confused about your cousin. Eliza loves you just as much now as she did before."

"More than before," Eliza said, reaching out and interlocking her fingers into Caleb's massive hands.

Caleb was thoughtfully silent, but Eliza was bursting with questions. "Aunt Yael, how did all that happen? With the Roman, I mean."

Yael told the story as best as she could of seeing her first behemoth outside the city walls and being sexually assaulted by the man overseeing the beasts. She talked of shame, the old woman outside the city, and the house where Luke lived, where everyone knew what happened to her yet included her in all their affairs. But she also talked of what she learned.

"Romans made slaves of Ebreet peoples, and they made slaves of themselves. They follow the emperor, and they fear him more than we do. They fear that they will be humiliated, that their family will be banished and perhaps killed. As Yeshuians, we are commanded not to have that same fear. No matter what happens to our bodies on earth, we will see our Savior in heaven one day. Our brother John received a vision from the Messiah, telling us that we once again will have a New Jerusalem, far bigger and grander than the one that your father and I knew. This is the hope that allows me to continue. I carry this hope with me. Above all other children in that school, I love the two of you the most."

Yael paused as she once again displayed the aura of a polished and courageous speaker, capable of commanding an audience with the authority of her voice and the authenticity of her tales.

"There can be no doubt as I replay these events of my life that God's word is true. He uses all things for His glory, including my rape and Caleb's birth. The very day that I was raped, the Romans sieged the city, and eventually, they destroyed it. Words cannot describe the despair I felt that day. God provided and answered my prayers before I spoke them. I met the old woman you now know, Eliza. She guided me in my despair. Had I found a sacrificial animal and proceeded to get your father to perform the ritual of atonement, I would most likely have secretly left Jerusalem and returned to Correae, never meeting Luke, your uncle Rufus, or any of the brothers and sisters. I would not have become a rabbi. I would not have found a man who I could marry and be completely honest with, and perhaps I would live a life of shame at my father and mother's home in Correae, as no Ebreet could marry a soiled woman. God has protected me from this outcome. And now, I get to teach all these beautiful young women the greatest story ever told."

She paused before continuing, making eye contact with all three of her family.

"Look at us now. We have been given the gift to teach others for the remainder of our days and raise our son to be a man. I could not possibly have had a better outcome, I tell you the truth."

"Son," Mishi said, "As your mother and I discussed telling you this tale, she did not want you to think of her as a victim or me as a heroic rescuer. Others have tried to portray us in these roles, and these depictions are not right. You filled our lives with joy and restored hope, but your presence in our lives has also healed us. In the same way, your mother was a sinner and needed atonement. I, too, was a sinner. I have not told you this story, but I was hiding rations and supplies under the old Temple so that I could survive after the Romans sacked the city. All the while, I watched men, women, and some young children starve to death. I had lots of food to share with them, but I did not. Had your mother not left hastily, I would have survived under the city for half a year, long enough to avoid Roman scrutiny, and I would not have met Luke, Rufus, or any of the people you now see coming to our house. And I would not have been able to build this school." Caleb had shock on his face, and he processed what his parents were telling him.

"Why are you now telling us this?" asked Caleb.

Mishi looked at his wife, and she answered him. "Some people have been told a milder version in the synagogues and towns around us. We did not want you to hear this story from someone else, as this is a story about you and your past. You needed to hear it from us. Now, you know why you are much taller and stronger than your father!"

This comment broke the tension in the room, and everyone began to laugh. His parents got up and approached their son, embracing him and telling him that they loved him. He loved the affection and smiled broadly. He leaned over and kissed Eliza, and she reached up and held his cheek, smiling and happy for him. Once they stopped, Mishi took his wife's hand and stepped a few steps away.

"And since Eliza is now traveling through the land of the twelve tribes, we have decided that you can do the same."

Caleb's eyes widened. "Are you serious?"

"If you can track and hunt wild animals, you can travel the roads and cities and explore. We place no limits on you. You talk about Egypt like it was your second home. I am not worried about you. God has already done great things with you, and I am assured that you will yet do great things for Him!"

Caleb looked at Eliza like a little boy who just had his first bite of watermelon for the season.

"Thank you, Abba," he said, embracing the man with a big hug.

Once they stood up, Eliza wrapped her arms around Caleb and cried for what she hoped was the last time today. "Cousin, my love for you has grown today. Consider me part of your family for all times." He leaned over and kissed her, lifted her, spun her around, holding her next to his chest. They both laughed as he took her in his arms, and they appeared to be like lovers. Normally, lifting a woman, kissing her, and spinning her was reserved behavior during Erusin. Erusin was a public announcement of a lifelong commitment. Caleb had been embracing Eliza since he learned about how his father did it with his mother. And he knew Eliza loved knowing how special she was to him and hearing him say I love you out loud and in public. And she loved how his beard would tickle her face when he kissed her.

He dropped both arms on her hips, and she interlocked her fingers in his hands. Although this made them seem like lovers, they were not. They were family, and now they knew the entire truth about who they were. There were no secrets left. Mishi took that moment to embrace his wife and kiss her as well.

"When can I start traveling alone?" Caleb asked with timidity.

Both parents chuckled. They anticipated that question.

"Your mother and I would prefer it if you two could do it together this first time. The school opening is delayed for a few days as the Romans need to inspect the grounds. You can go tomorrow if you like." Caleb and Eliza looked at each other as if they were about to celebrate a holiday again.

"Tomorrow morning it is!"

Chapter 9:
Not a Typical First Adventure

The next morning, before breakfast was served, Caleb asked Eliza to help him make his provisions for winter travel. She took her uncle's backpack and put a bedroll on the bottom of it, wrapped in a deer-skin to keep dry. She put a tinder kit along with some flint in a small satchel and attached it with some leather straps next to the wooden pack frame. She took two of her aunt's old water skins and filled them, attaching them to the top of the pack. She pointed at Caleb and gave him a task.

"Put this on so you can feel how much this weighs. You need to get used to it." Caleb held no disdain for hard work the way the boys in Correae did. They complained, and Eliza found their unwill-ingness to be despicable. Caleb gladly accepted it; Uncle Rufus had taught him that the effort of carrying a heavy object made for a good man more than a good soldier, and Caleb wanted to be that kind of man. Eliza admired him for it. He and Eliza had been taught that one day, a man and a woman shall become one flesh, and the man will rule over her. Caleb wanted to be an honorable ruler, and he knew that practice would help. Eliza wanted a man who willingly worked hard, and Caleb was her silver standard.

Caleb put the pack on and adjusted the straps on each side to get the most comfortable fit he could. He quickly took the pack off and opened the top up. "I need to add the good stuff, now," he said, and he came back with his sling, a quiver of arrows, his shooting stones, two knives, and two metal cups and bowls. "Now, that will give me what we need to eat," he said with a lot of pride. He put his bow over his shoulder, hit his chest, and signaled he was ready to go.

Eliza rolled her eyes at his display of bravado and put her hands on her hips. Then she spoke, sounding a lot like her mother. "You know, there are cutlery and plates at the inns. We probably don't need those."

"But what if we do? What if I kill a lion and we camp and eat in the wilderness?" She looked him in the eye, not sure if he was being a braggart or serious. She decided he might actually do that and needed to respond accordingly.

"Cousin, you just might kill something big. Let me go get something, just in case." She left and came back with salt, spices, and a filet knife meant for larger game. She also brought dried meat and fresh bread.

Caleb pointed to the dry meat. "We will not need that junk. We will eat fresh meat. God will provide." His tone conveyed his level of confidence. Eliza had seen him kill many times and had bragged about him to the people of Correae for years. He didn't need to justify himself. However, she had also been with him during times he was unsuccessful.

"But you might not provide. That is why we have your mom's food." She smiled at him and held up two loaves of hot bread that her mother had just taken from the oven.

Caleb stuck his tongue out at her, and they laughed. He knew she was right to plan for the unexpected. He lifted her upon the horse and soon, they were underway.

The two of them selected Kedron, on the river Gath in ancient Philistia, to be the first foreign land they would visit together. The Philistines were as much overrun with Rome's heavy-handed rule as the twelve tribes. Caleb's parents repeatedly warned them about approaching groups of Philistine men or groups of Roman soldiers who looked bored, as if they were identical with their intent to harm. Mishi told the two of them what to look for and how to speak to Roman militia if they had an encounter. He helped them practice speaking Greek slang that all Roman soldiers would understand. He also taught him hand gestures and told them to use them if the situation required it.

Before leaving, Eliza gave her uncle the tithe from her village, but she left the education coins inside her bedroom with her blankets. Those would go to the school treasurer once classes commenced. Uncle Mishi accepted the tithe and put them on the top of the small wall in the kitchen. He reached inside and gave four coins to each of the slaves, instructing them to give them to the rabbi in charge at the school to pay for their children's education this session. All were speechless except Yael.

"Husband, you are a man after God's heart. Education is a beautiful investment and a great way to show you care," she said, kissing him on the lips without embarrassment. Neither Caleb nor Eliza responded to this display of affection, as it was allowed inside of one's home. However, the slaves were overcome with gratitude, and they placed their hands in a prayerlike position and thanked Mishi for the gift.

The trip to Kedron was fast and easy. Eliza rode on a horse, going slower than she otherwise would since her cousin was walking and running next to her. As they reached the outskirts of Kedron near the river, he spotted three deer.

He grabbed the horse's reins and gestured to Eliza to cease any conversation. She nodded, already feeling the excitement of the hunt that was about to happen. She slowly stepped off the horse, and Caleb reached his bow and took out the quiver of arrows. He stayed low to the ground, notched a single arrow, and began to stalk the deer.

From experience, Eliza knew that this could take considerable time, and there was a real chance he would come back with nothing but a bad attitude. Or, it could be fast, as she wouldn't have time to go to the bathroom before he called for her to come and look. She reached for a water bottle and took a deep drink while her cousin left her field of vision. She decided to sit and wait for her cousin while she prayed for his success.

Before she could finish a quarter of water, she heard Caleb calling her. She mounted her horse and quickly crossed the hill that separated them. Caleb was on one knee, already bleeding the deer.

"She had no idea I was coming. She should have. The shadow of the afternoon sun should have given me away. Stupid animal forgot to use her eyes." He made another cut in her abdomen, pulling out the entrails.

"Do you have to do that now?" Eliza commented with disgust as all the innards fell out and hit the ground.

Caleb did not have any interest in responding.

"It sure did not hurt that I was a good shot! This deer will provide you and me with some fresh meat, just like I told you. And, it gives us a reason to go to the market to sell the rest." He lifted his arrow and showed it to her. "This arrow has already killed three deer this season. It's my favorite."

Caleb knew that the idea of entering a marketplace with something to sell was Eliza's love language. That promise helped her set aside any repulsion she was experiencing. Many of the boys in her village would go out hunting, but few succeeded as quickly as Caleb did. That deserved some acknowledgment, but she did not want it to go to his head, so she said nothing. Deep down, though, she was impressed.

"Let's take this to Kedron right now!" He pointed to the city ramparts, less than a league away. "We can sell most of this meat, as the markets will be open, and this time of day, fresh game sells at a premium." He hoisted the deer onto his shoulders, and after all the bleeding was complete, he began walking.

"What about your stuff?" Eliza asked.

"Oh, would you mind carrying it for me? This animal is heavy." She shook her head as he slung the dead animal over his shoulders and began walking to the city walls. She knew that animal weighed nearly as much as he did, so she picked up the pack, attached it to their horse, and began following him towards the city walls without any sense of resentment. She knew he was going to the market for her well-being, anyway.

As he predicted, Eliza all but ignored him once they entered the market. Caleb was merely the meat-carrying guy. She negotiated a great price for fresh deer, as it could be stored outside for much of the remainder of winter. They left the market after selling the deer to two different butchers who treasured different cuts of the animal. They left with several coins of various types, all legal tender in Roman-occupied lands. Caleb and Eliza were happy with their efforts, but it was also time to arrange their evening accommodations. Neither of them had been to this city before, so the act of selecting an inn and ordering dinner would be new to them. Caleb needed to bathe and change his shirt; he smelled after cleaning and carrying the deer.

They negotiated a room at the inn near the local synagogue and found that the manager of the inn was a Yeshuian. Thinking it was safe to speak freely, as there were no Romans present, Caleb engaged the innkeeper in a brief conversation about killing the deer and bringing it to be sold while the meat was fresh. Eliza looked around at the other people in the inn's lobby, and she also felt a bit safer than she had expected. It was very much like her experience traveling to Tamar from Correae a few days earlier.

Caleb introduced her to the innkeeper. "This is my cousin, Eliza, from the village of Correae, up in Naphtali. She attends school with me. We are traveling in the area, and we need a room for one night. Two beds, please."

Eliza smiled. She did not know if truthfully disclosing their actual names was the right decision, but it was too late to undo it now. Caleb had a habit of being quicker to speak than to think. They ate dinner and talked to a few people. Then, they went upstairs to sleep.

Their night in the inn was uneventful and the sounds of the city first thing in the morning reminded them that they were no longer in a village. Men and women were outside making lots of noise and selling their goods; and the natural order of pre-dawn and sunrise in an Ebreet village was not present. There were no sounds of roosters, nor were there any smells from cooking fires and fresh bread.

After they mustered the courage to get out of the warm blankets and step into the cold room, they got dressed. Eliza led the way out of the room and towards the banqueting partition of the inn. They ate a breakfast of yesterday's bread, hummus, and dried apples. They each drank two cups of hot tea mixed with camel milk and honey to warm them. Eliza paid for the room and the food and noted that this inn was nice enough to return to one day.

Caleb followed his cousin's lead that it was time to go. After washing their hands, feet, and faces, they retrieved Eliza's horse from the manger, giving the attendant a copper coin for his efforts. Eliza mounted the horse and Caleb walked next to her as they left the city.

Tamar was a few hours away from Kedron, and the trip went quickly. They sang school songs along the way, and they each offered up a prayer for the safety of the children and the school, saying that they had a powerful educational experience during this cycle. After they crested the last hill before the plains surrounding Tamar, they stopped suddenly. Eliza had horror in her eyes, and her heart began to race. Caleb quickened his breathing, reaching for his bow and quiver, and made sure that both of his hunting knives were securely fastened to his lower legs. He put on his leather bracers and gauntlets that Eliza didn't know he carried, and he stood up to take in every detail. He kept one arm on Eliza's shoulder to calm her.

Although his family's village was far away, the two teenagers could see that some of the buildings near the center of the town were on fire, burning as if struck by lightning.

"What did they do?" Caleb asked rhetorically. Eliza stood, paralyzed, while Caleb's focus was now on all the activity happening. He began quietly murmuring as he sized up what his uncle taught him were called "the actions of the enemy". He counted out loud and nodded his head as he methodologically went from left to right.

For her part, Eliza was unable either to move or to speak, but her heart was already beginning to break. Sounds carried well from the school to the top of this hill. They heard women shouting and saw some horses and camels running outside of the village that should not have been there. Fear entered both of them as they listened and heard mostly Greek. That meant Roman soldiers or foreign marauders were down there.

"Yes, Eliza. Something is wrong," said Caleb in a quiet and calm voice as he finished counting. Eliza had finally gotten off of her horse and was about to yell down to them, but Caleb put his hand over her mouth and whispered. "Quiet! We must remain in control of our emotions. They do not know we are here or who we are, and we need to keep it that way. Tie the horse off and walk down there with me." *Giving her a specific task might calm her and engage her,* he thought.

Eliza nodded and regained control of her breathing. He took a long drink of water before offering it to Eliza. She took a deep drink and set the water skin on the horse. "Just breathe and follow my lead. We have got to stay calm." Caleb took her hand, and they quickly went down the side of the hill.

They followed an animal trail to the village edge, staying off the main road. The animal trail provided tree cover and places to stop and reassess the situation. Caleb remained levelheaded, but Eliza found herself breathing rapidly and occasionally, she felt panic. Each time this happened, Caleb would stop and hold her head and stare into her eyes, telling her to keep a cool head and not do anything to draw attention towards them. He spoke with authority but quietly.

"I trust in two things right now. I trust in my skills, and I trust the stories I have heard in my life of how the Messiah hears our prayers. I will do my job, and I need you to pray." He maintained eye contact until she acknowledged him. His uncle told him to do that in order to keep the new troops from going into shock. Eliza was about as useless as a new troop.

"Caleb, I trust you," she said.

"Good. Let's keep moving. I have to try to stop this," he whispered.

They reached the edge of town and ducked behind a tree that provided them cover. He also needed to keep them out of sight of the town's residents, as they might also give away their cover.

"There," Caleb whispered, pointing at a horror on the edge of the town square. On the ground lay several dying residents, most of them bleeding out, and eight Roman soldiers were bringing more villagers to the center of town where what appeared to be a centurion stood, holding a gladius of high-quality Damascus steel in his right hand.

The centurion spoke loudly as four villagers were presented to him.

"Tell me. Is it true that the school teaches that there is another God besides the emperor?" All of his men remained quiet as they awaited a reply from the villagers.

The villagers did not answer his question. They knew the penalty for publicly worshipping another God besides Caesar was death, and they were scared. Two of them were women and they began crying hysterically. One older man was composed enough to answer the soldiers, hoping to protect the women.

"We are no threat to you or the emperor. We are a small Ebreet village thousands of leagues from Rome. We pay our taxes and keep the peace. Please do not kill us."

Without a second warning or any advanced notice, the centurion thrust his sword through the guts of the man, ignoring his pleas. Caleb looked at the face of the sword holder and studied it. He could tell that the centurion was trying to set an example with this one. He found himself thinking back on all the different lessons his uncle had taught him about how the Roman military dealt with insurrection. He nodded as he processed what he saw, reflecting on his uncle's teachings. He knew he needed to be slow to judge if he was to keep himself and his cousin alive. He compartmentalized the reality that he knew this man; he needed to focus on saving the rest of the town and not get angered by the loss of one man.

Eliza had the complete opposite reaction. She vomited, and she gestured as if she was about to cry out, but Caleb grabbed her, whispering, "Cousin, if you make a sound, we die!" She spat out the vomit that remained in her throat and cleaned her face with her robe. She also knew the man, and he would bring oranges to all the little girls when she first enrolled at the school. He did it with all the first-year students every week, and he would play games with them at lunchtime. He was jovial and didn't deserve what happened to him.

The centurion turned towards the other man in the lot. "Perhaps you shall answer my question!" he yelled. The two remaining women fell to their knees and began pleading for mercy in their native Ebreet language.

Caleb looked away from the gruesome scene to see what else might be happening and his eyes found something more frightening.

Near the village well, he saw his aunt and uncle being placed on a large cart. Aunt Katya was crying and Uncle Matthew was battered, lying down. Matthew appeared to be attempting to sit up.

"Look, Eliza! It's your parents. They must have arrived this morning to surprise you!" He stopped whispering for a moment and looked at the situation one more time. He had information to know what to do next.

"Stay here and take this knife to defend yourself. I'm going to free some of these people." He did one last survey before returning his gaze to Eliza.

"Keep the knife hidden and close to you until you can strike someone without having to extend your arm all the way. Let them get close before you strike. The blade is sharp and will penetrate armor and flesh with little effort. You do not have to drive it into them with all your strength. Just push and do not stop until it is all the way in. Once it's in all the way to the hilt, leave it. Then, run to the horse and go home. Tell everyone what you saw."

Eliza nodded in agreement and pulled herself together. She knew she needed her wits about her now. She wiped the tears from her face and took a deep breath. She was traumatized, but she had something she needed Caleb to do.

"Caleb, we must pray first together! Remember what we were taught? 'Where two or more are gathered in my name, so there I will also be.'" Caleb let his guard down as he took a deep breath and agreed with Eliza.

They took each other's hands and spoke the prayer. Caleb led it. "Yahweh, Lord Yeshua, thank You that You are in heaven. Your name is great. May Your heaven come to earth as it is with You now. Give us our daily bread and forgive us our debts as we forgive our debtors. Especially today, deliver us from this evil. Amen."

At that moment, Eliza looked at Caleb like a dog might look at its master. Caleb looked like a soldier and a warrior, ready to defend her with his life. She spoke to him, using the tone that her mother would use as her father would leave in the mornings.

"Caleb, you are a good man. Go, Cousin. Do what you need to save our people." She pulled him towards her and kissed him.

"Thank you," he said. He crouched down so as not to be seen and went to the side of the village where the soldiers were not looking. It was time to apply all that his uncle had taught him to defend the people in his village.

Chapter 10:
Mission Field at Home

Caleb quietly and thoughtfully circumnavigated the houses on the edge of the village to the place he wanted to stage his surprise attack. He counted eight Roman soldiers in the village that needed to be neutralized. The centurion with the steel gladius was obviously the leader, as he was giving orders to the other seven. It was not yet midday and Caleb concluded that they were not drunk on wine. He couldn't tell if the centurion in charge was just angry or trying to command respect, but he yelled at everyone and was emotionally charged. Caleb continually looked at his aunt and uncle, hoping that he could make eye contact with Uncle Matthew. Other villagers saw him as he gestured to them to remain quiet as he readied his attack plan.

After he rounded the outside edge of the house closest to the center of the village, Caleb finally made eye contact with Matthew. He saw his uncle's eyes bulging as he recognized his nephew. Matthew shook his head, trying to prevent his nephew from taking an unnecessary risk, but Caleb already had a plan. Caleb raised a finger to his lips to tell his uncle to be silent. Matthew made no gesture acknowledging him but stopped looking at him and returned to holding his scared wife.

Rage boiled in Caleb's veins as he saw the damage on Matthew's face. Aunt Katya at least looked unharmed. He had heard stories of Romans destroying villages and enslaving the residents, but he had not considered that it might happen to his own family. The evidence around him was dispelling his fantasy that his family was immune. Enslavement was, in fact, in process.

He felt a desire for revenge, and he knew he could kill or wound several of the soldiers before they knew what had happened. And that was a better idea than becoming a martyr. The leather armor on the seven looked too thin to stop his arrows, as he kept all of the ones in his quiver sharp enough to penetrate a deer's hide. He decided that he was going to take out the leader and eliminate a few of the perimeter soldiers. Then he would kill the remaining soldiers as they fled on horseback to get help. He knew that if just one of them lived, an entire squad might descend on the village as retribution. He had to get them all, or he would become a fugitive.

Next to the last house was a village stable where livestock was kept during the night. Caleb moved behind the horse stalls and he readied his first arrow. He knew there would be two soldiers in front of him once he stepped out, and he would be at their backs. With the focus his uncle taught him, he turned the corner and used the element of surprise. He launched his first arrow at a soldier into his upper back, directly into his heart. Without thinking, he reached into his quiver for the second arrow, knowing the other soldier would quickly turn to face the attack. Before the second man could identify what was happening, Caleb's second arrow found his neck, making the man stand upright but unable to speak for a few moments. Caleb stared the man in the eyes. Finally, the man fell to the ground without speaking. He could not take the risk that they might speak, so he quietly removed his hunting knife, slitting each man's throat. He wiped his knife clean using their pant legs and he put it back in its sheath on his lower leg.

He remained on one knee, surveying the situation.

The reaction that Eliza had moments earlier was now upon him. He turned his head to the side and vomited. Among the pile of corpses that the two soldiers had made lay his mother with no life left in her body. His father lay next to her, bleeding out from the gut but alive. He saw Caleb and spoke to him with as much effort as he could muster. He needed to stop and start as a spear had pierced his diaphragm, and his ability to breathe was permanently compromised.

"My son! These are fools." He held the spear with his remaining strength and attempted to breathe. His diaphragm was destroyed, and he could not sustain enough air to speak in sentences.

"Do not let them, Caleb." That sentence taxed his father, and he shook uncontrollably as he fought for air like a man drowning in open water.

Caleb was overwhelmed as he saw the trauma of his father dying in front of him. His hands began to tingle. Caleb's breathing became shallow and he felt paralyzed to move. He had no memory of practicing for a moment like this. His self-control and mental focus were now beyond his emotional reach. Yet Caleb defaulted to his training, just like his uncle said it would. He looked around to see what else was nearby.

In front of his parents lay three more dead people. Two looked just like the others in town, but Caleb recognized the third. It was his uncle Rufus. Rufus held a wooden rake in his hands and was wearing no armor, but his stomach had been cut open. Caleb moved towards his hero and he felt like he might vomit again. Then, his dying father spoke to him from behind.

"Go tell the world," Mishi said. He stopped short of finishing his sentence.

Caleb yelled out, "No!"

The centurion heard him, and his element of surprise disappeared. He ordered two soldiers to turn their attention away from the two hysterical women, pursue Caleb, and kill him. The two soldiers saw that their comrades had just fallen, and they began moving Caleb's way with their gladius in their hands.

Caleb hastily executed his plan. His uncle's body was closest, so he reached down, taking up his uncle's gladius. His uncle had taught him how to use this weapon in his early years and the strategy on how to use it was ingrained into Caleb's fighting tactics. Rufus looked him in the eye and grunted something. Caleb couldn't make out the words as Rufus's diaphragm was destroyed, but he knew what his uncle meant. Caleb removed the ring from Rufus' left hand. Then, he took the gladius and pressed the sharp tip into his uncle's chest, giving Rufus the end that he sought. Caleb felt tears pouring from his eyes and the blade came out the other side of Rufus' chest and bent over to kiss Rufus one final time.

As Caleb turned and refocused, he saw that the two Roman soldiers were closing in on him, but the weight of their armor made them slow. Caleb stepped back over the pile of bodies, quickly notched an arrow, and fired it at the soldier closest to him. Neither soldier was expecting a fast response, as the Ebreet were not militarily aggressive. Once the first arrow hit its target, the other soldier stopped, and that was all the time Caleb needed.

Caleb notched a second arrow and shot the second soldier in the heart. He fell over dead, buying Caleb more time. He heard his father coughing and Caleb ran to his father's side. He had at least one more moment left with his father before he would have to face the centurion.

Mishi spoke in Greek, as it was easier, and his breathing was now very difficult. "Run!" he said. His voice was weak, and the coughing lifted his chest off the ground.

Caleb leaned over his dying father. "I will kill them like the deer I killed yesterday!" he vowed.

"Save Eliza."

"I will, father," he said as tears of rage rolled down his cheek. Caleb's hand ached as he gripped his weapon with all of his strength as he coped with his rage.

With that, Mishi breathed his last. As Caleb saw his chest stop moving, he changed his focus. There were three remaining guards wielding swords, and two were nearly on top of him. He jumped and launched another arrow into the gut of the one closest and it pierced through his leather armor, embedding itself in his diaphragm. Caleb turned and ran around the opposite side of the stables to give himself some more time. One of the remaining warriors stopped to help the injured soldier, and Caleb shouldered his bow to switch to his uncle's gladius.

The centurion was not as naïve as his men and could tell that Caleb was trained in the ways of combat. Caleb rounded the corner of the stable that he had hoped would give him an unobstructed view of the leader, but the centurion knew that Caleb would take this route, and he beat Caleb to the corner of the building. The centurion's sword was already moving to attempt to decapitate him as he stepped around it.

Caleb raised the arm holding the gladius, but he could not get it up high enough. The force of the strike hit Caleb's blade and knocked it from his hands. All the years of fighting with dogs had taught him that once a dog has your arm in its bite, the best strategy is to let it go limp and maneuver your body to attack back better. As the blade struck him, he let his arm go limp, and he fell to the ground, rolling towards the centurion. Caleb was now on the ground and the centurion was preparing to strike him from above as Caleb reached down and withdrew his hunting knife from its sheath on his calf. With his left arm stinging from the force of the impact, Caleb used his right arm to drive the knife into the exposed calf of the Centurion, deep enough to get to the bone. As the Centurion screamed, Caleb had another move to make. He steadily pulled the knife down the full length of the man's calf as if he were skinning a fish. He pulled it out once it struck the top of his boot. He rolled over two times to create distance between himself and the centurion, as he knew the centurion could now no longer walk. He had shredded his calf muscle and the tendon that supported it. If the centurion survived, he would not walk normally for the rest of his life. The centurion was focused on his pain and forgot Caleb was there for a moment.

Caleb stood up and yelled at the centurion, "Why did you attack and kill these people? What did they do to you?" He made sure he used the slang Greek his parents had taught him. He knew that if he called the villagers "my people", it would be days before the Romans determined who he was and began a manhunt throughout the Holy Land looking for him. That is not what his father wanted. He knew that his best hope of protecting his cousin was to remain anonymous.

The centurion was enraged and attempted to step forward to get close enough to swing at Caleb. But Caleb knew his reaction would be his doom. Caleb allowed him to swing with what he hoped would be his maximum effort. The man met his expectations and the blade zoomed past Caleb at a very high speed.

As soon as the blade passed him, Caleb lunged and struck the centurion in the underarm of his exposed shoulder, knowing that this stab would cause the centurion to place all of his weight on his destroyed calf. The centurion cried out as he forgot that his leg could no longer bear any weight, and he focused all of his attention on removing the weight from his wounded leg.

For Caleb, this moment felt like the world was moving at half speed. Despite his rage, his combat movements were without emotion. As the centurion adjusted his body weight, Caleb calmly stepped forward and ran his hunting knife across the man's throat, opening it up.

The centurion was in shock, but he was not yet dead. He moved his right arm rapidly, and the plate armor on his elbow struck Caleb in the head, causing his eyes to see what he thought was lightning. Stunned, Caleb stood motionless, attempting to keep his balance. He knew that he need not maintain any defensive skills, as the centurion's efforts to strike him would further open the wound in his neck, and the blood would already be uncontrollably flowing out. He would be dead within three breaths. However, blood was now pouring from Caleb's head and his vision was obstructed. He wasn't sure what he was seeing now. Caleb's injury would soon have him in a state of shock, and he would be an easy target for the remaining soldier.

Caleb stood nearly motionless, holding the wound on his head as he recovered from the blow. His hearing worked and he heard his aunt and uncle yelling at him to beware of the other soldier who was now approaching him. Without a clear vision, he could not use his bow. With shooting pains in his forehead, Caleb was not ready to fight again. Yet, as he prepared to run away, he remembered his father's last words. "Save Eliza."

He turned and ran. The remaining soldier in full combat gear could not sprint as fast nor run as far as Caleb could. He made his way through the village center towards the tree on the outskirts of town, where he hoped Eliza remained. As he approached her, the one working eye could see that she was right where he left her. Once he reached it, he stopped and tried to look her in the eyes. Blood covered his shirt and pants, and the centurion's blood was all over his legs and sandals.

Hidden from the remaining soldier by the protection of the tree, she looked at him and said in a low tone, "Caleb, your face! You need healing!"

Caleb nodded his head in agreement. He knew that. His head hurt. Eliza tore a piece of her thin, inner cloak and put it on his forehead. He reached up and held it in place. Eliza peered around the corner. The remaining soldier was angrily yelling out, calling for others who must have been in the area that Caleb did not see.

"Caleb, I talked to my parents. I promised them that we would come back for them." He nodded an acknowledgment.

"We cannot stay here. These men will tell others and hunt us down. We need to get out of here right now." Caleb was not negotiating with Eliza and she understood what to do. It was time to leave and regroup.

She grabbed his hand and the two of them ran back towards the top of the hill, where they left their horse. Caleb was now a murderer of a Roman centurion and the price on his head would be great. With limited vision and substantial blood loss, he was losing control of his senses. He was finally scared.

Chapter 11:
House of Healing, Part 1

"Good morning, Caleb, son of Rabbi Mishi and Rabbi Yael."

Caleb opened his eyes and saw two men standing in the room, silhouetted by light from the window. They wore Rabbinical robes just like his parents. They were smiling at him and each other, obviously glad that he was OK.

"You look like my father during the Passover," Caleb said, making both of them laugh. He heard Eliza laugh and noticed that she sat on the bed with him, holding his hands and thanking God that he was awake. The two of them made eye contact and Caleb smiled at her beautiful face.

He looked away and saw that his bed was luxurious, covered in linens made from Egyptian cotton. The pillow was soft, obviously made from bird feathers. He looked out the open window on the opposite side of the room and could tell he was at least on the second floor. The cold winter air was coming in through the open window, but it felt good against his face.

He looked back at Eliza, who remained smiling. The Rabbis put their hands upon him and gently moved his skin, showing their joy that he was alive. Caleb could tell she must have been his prayer warrior since he had arrived, and they were merely acknowledging that Yeshua had heard and answered her prayers. However, Eliza was experiencing her own trauma and she erupted on him as if he had thrown cold water on her.

"What happened?" he asked.

"Caleb, you attacked and killed seven Roman soldiers, one of whom was a centurion. That carries the penalty of death by crucifixion! What were you thinking?" Before he could answer her, the rabbis added to the conversation.

"Young man, you were equally brave and foolish to deny Romans their authority," said one of the rabbis.

Caleb replied without thinking. After all, speaking first and thinking later was part of his childhood identity.

"What are you talking about? They had just killed my parents and were capturing people from my village! What did you think I would do? Let them kill us, too? My father told me to save Eliza. That was the last thing he said before he died." Caleb held back nothing with his tone and body language. He could not understand how they could be upset with him for doing the right thing. After a moment of silence, he slowly used his arms to push himself off the bed. The motion was much easier than he thought it might be.

"Oh, that didn't hurt to sit up. Your words, though, they hurt!" Caleb said with a full serving of sarcasm. Eliza felt shame and knew that she needed to apologize.

"Caleb, I am sorry. I didn't mean that. Thank you for protecting me," Eliza said. Caleb, too, needed to own his unnecessary rage.

"Rabbis, I am sorry for that outburst. My mother and father taught me to be better than that," Caleb said.

The rabbis said nothing but smiled and offered him some water to drink and wash with. They also gave him a towel to dry off with.

"Caleb, I am glad you are awake and talking." Caleb gestured for Eliza to come to him, and he hugged her. Eliza repeated her apology, and he put his arm around her. Caleb looked at the men and told them what happened. They didn't have many questions, as his story corroborated nearly everything Eliza had already told them.

"I do not think they will figure out who I am or where I am from since I described the villagers as 'these people' and not 'my people'."

The men looked at each other and nodded in agreement. "You are probably right. We see that you are quick with your tongue and your weapons, especially considering what was around you. Your use of non-Ebreet Greek was brilliant. Yahweh's angels were looking out for you. However, the loss of a centurion will demand retribution.

We are glad that your instincts took you to this place." Caleb had no idea what that last phrase meant.

Caleb looked at Eliza and asked, "This place? Where are we?"

"I went back to Kedron and the people in the synagogue sent us here," she said. Caleb nodded. That sounded smart. Then one of the rabbis answered with the details Caleb was looking for.

"You are in the House of Healing on the hill behind the city of Kedron. Your parents have visited us many times in the past." They paused to look at each other and then back at the two children.

"We are sad to learn of their passing. We ask that you stay with us for some days, as you have experienced trauma and loss, and you must heal. For today, we ask nothing of you but to answer some questions and let us care for you. Can you do that?" Caleb knew that they were trying to help as graciously as they could. But they also knew he was a warrior with a potential price on his head, and he wouldn't behave normally until he felt safe again.

"I am too confused to do anything else," Caleb answered. "I submit to your care." The two rabbis exhaled their anxiety and helped him take a few steps to test his balance after his head trauma. His steps appeared fine, but he was slow.

"How did you acquire such shrewd hunting skills, considering that your parents are some of the most unlikely people to shoot a bow or swing a blade in all of Judah?"

"My uncle did."

"Ah, Rufus. So, you were his disciple?" they asked. Interesting question.

"I guess I was. I was not fond of all the ceremonies that my parents made me participate in. I loved hunting in the wild. I merely wanted to be a normal boy from Benjamin, not the son of royalty. Rufus taught me all of those hunting skills." The men looked at each other and smiled.

"Your parents all but walked on water. Their teachings about the Messiah taught us a way to live without the rules and rituals of old. They taught us about freedom that we could not dream of. We are committed to allowing you to stay here as long as is necessary. However, you have defied the rules of Caesar and his lineage, and that carries the penalty of death for all who help you. We have agreed to lie to any authorities about your presence with us. This is a courtesy we are extending to your family."

Eliza spoke up since Caleb had yet to respond.

"His uncle taught him the joys of hunting. And my dad. His uncle, I mean our uncle, was a Roman legate before he retired and joined us," she said.

Caleb nodded, agreeing with Eliza. The rabbis spoke to Eliza but pointed at Caleb.

"He probably saved your parent's life today and that of a few others," they said. "For now, let's let him rest." With that, the two rabbis left, motioning for Eliza to join them.

"That is ok. I will stay here," she said. Caleb motioned for her to lie back down with him, and he held her, looking into her eyes.

"Thank you," Caleb said, trying to close the gap between him and Eliza.

"You are welcome." Eliza paused for a moment before speaking.

"You were delirious after the wound on your head got worse, and I put you on the horse with me. I rode directly here and these men tended to your wounds. While you were asleep, you kept dreaming out loud, saying, 'We have to get to Titus! We have to see Titus!' What are you talking about?"

"I was dreaming out loud?" he questioned, using a tone of astonishment. He looked up at the ceiling and began to speculate now that he was conscious.

"Eliza, your parents are probably now slaves. I am a fugitive, but you promised that we would get your parents back. The best way to do that is to get assistance from Rome. I grabbed Uncle Rufus' ring. I think if we can get an audience with the emperor, I can show him the ring of his best friend and we can convince him to write us a royal decree that will free your parents."

"How well did that work for Moses as he repeatedly approached Pharaoh, asking him to let our ancestors go?"

"I thought about that. We have a relationship with Pharaoh. We know his best friend as our uncle!"

She did not say anything back but stared at him with an open mouth. His mother told her again and again to be quick to listen and slow to speak. She did that and finally opened her mouth.

"Caleb, I like it. That is a pretty good idea," she said. But what she didn't say was that his idea was full of adventure as well. But she wouldn't give him the words of affirmation he was looking for. She couldn't wait to go to Rome. She had no idea that she was daydreaming while staring at Caleb, and he felt confused.

"That is all I have, Eliza. Why are you looking at me like that?" he said.

"Well, your plan sounds good. I was thinking of going home and getting the elders to give us enough gold to buy my parents freedom. We have enough of it, I am sure, but I do not know how much a slave costs, nor do I have a clue where they are now. And if we do find them, what is to say Romans won't just take the gold and make all of us slaves?"

She did not wait for him to answer her.

"I do not think the village elders would get deeply involved in their rescue, though. They always place the village ahead of the individual. They would tell me that this is the way things are. But I do not want to give up on them. I want my parents back! Why did they follow me to Tamar?"

She put her head back on Caleb's chest. He kissed her head and rubbed her hair, reminding her that she was his family now. Her affectionate response meant the world to the young man, and he loved holding her.

"Cousin, I do not know what to say. My parents are dead. I saw my dad breathe his last," he said, rubbing her head gingerly. He took a long pause before speaking again, and he quietly cried as her head rested against his chest. She could feel his diaphragm move as he would cry, and she began to cry with him. His mother was her hero and she also needed to mourn.

"Father told me more than once that the Messiah said it is a great joy to die for your faith in Him. He asked me to promise not to mourn his death if that happened, and I agreed. I do not know how to do that, though," said Caleb, wrapping his huge arms around

Eliza. She closed her eyes and let him care for her. She, too, was hurting. After some more silence, he spoke again.

"Mother agreed with father when he said that not even death could separate her from Yeshua, and all I can think about now is that she is with Him. Did your parents tell you about the teachings of John and the stories he had of what the new kingdom of God is like?"

"I learned about that from your mom, not mine. My mom did not talk about Yeshua very often. She told me, 'Ask your auntie!'" With that, they erupted in laughter, Eliza imitated her mother perfectly. Once they stopped laughing, she continued.

"We have got to do something, cousin. Something is better than nothing. I do not know if I like your plan or if it works, but I'm in. Let's go to Rome and get an audience with the Emperor, and use that Ring that you carry now. Uncle Rufus talked about Titus a lot. I feel like I know him."

"We are barely old enough for a bar or bat mitzvah, and we are going to try to get an audience with the ruler of the world! That would make our parents proud!"

"Agreed! It's on the other side of the sea, and the last time I checked, we do not have a boat and neither of us has any experience in this sort of thing." Caleb's sarcasm was a cover for his confidence. Eliza could look at him and see that he would figure out how to cross the sea and meet with the emperor, even though he didn't know where to start.

"Well, thank you for supporting my ideas. That is what my mom did every time my dad came up with something that he had not done before. It worked for them." Caleb said.

Eliza rolled her eyes. "I am your cousin, not your wife. Frankly, this idea stinks like camel hair after a summer rain. That might be why I love it so much. And, Caleb, I love you. You know that, right?"

Caleb hesitated for a moment, but he needed to unwind her affirmation. He jumped on Eliza and held her down, starting to tickle her under her arm. "Well, daughter of Katya and Matthew. What wisdom can you share?"

Eliza tried to get up, but she was laughing too hard. She tried to tell Caleb to stop, but he refused and continued to tickle her. He did not give her a chance to finish her words and she screamed each time he found a new place to tickle her.

His parents were right. She was his family now. It would be troublesome if she weren't.

For now, though, the rabbis had promised to care for them. They needed time to heal and plan.

"I am hungry!" said Caleb.

"Me, too," Eliza added. "I have been here since lunchtime yesterday. The day is already halfway over. Let's find something to eat."

They both got up and went to find the kitchen.

Chapter 12:
House of Healing, Part 2

Caleb and Eliza lived a sedentary life for another three days in the "House of Healing". Two other boys from Tamar also appeared at the house a day later, and the rabbis anticipated more children coming. Too many families were lost or carted away into slavery, and the children were the most susceptible to trauma in the aftermath. Caleb and Eliza were able to connect with them, as all of them lost their parents during the attack. Dor and Benji were the two rabbis in charge of trauma care. The two young men were up early and went to bed late as they cared for everyone who was experiencing loss from the Roman attack. Eliza was mesmerized as she listened to them and watched them perform what she thought were miracles. They would ask questions and let the boys start to come to terms with their loss. Both men would cry as the boys would tell their stories, and Eliza would watch and cry with them. People cried all the time, but these two young men knew how to help all of them start on the road to healing.

Dor, the eldest rabbi, saw Eliza and Caleb leave the kitchen and walk outside the city walls. He followed them. Once he found them, he began his craft of helping them come to terms with their new life.

"Shalom. I wish to talk to you about your experience in Tamar a few days ago. Are you open to talking about what happened?"

"Sure, I guess," Caleb said, as he was required to speak as the oldest male in the group.

"You are the son of two murdered parents. Can you tell me what this makes you feel?" he asked.

Caleb paused. Eliza looked at Caleb with interest - she was not used to seeing him think before speaking.

"Rabbi, I do not know." Caleb began fidgeting with his thumbs, and Dor could see that he was grinding his teeth.

"Are you sure?" Dor rhetorically asked.

"No, I do know! I feel glad that I was able to kill some of those Roman bastards. Those seven can no longer do that to anyone else!" His anger and indignance were obvious. Eliza saw their situation more clearly than Dor did, and she looked at him with concern on her face. She was scared. She and Caleb had talked on the ride to this city a few days ago, and she knew he was trying to make peace with the discovery that he was a bastard and knew that in his rage, he was expressing a bit of his own self-loathing. She didn't want this to be Caleb's new identity. She looked at Dor with her eyes wide open, hoping he could see her concern. Dor was one step ahead of her.

"Tell me about your body language right now. Is your teeth grinding of someone glad?" the rabbi asked in a flat tone. This time, Caleb didn't need to think.

"No," Caleb admitted. "It isn't. I am not glad. I am mad that they're gone. My parents served people! Why does the world kill people who are doing good?" Caleb's fist was clenched tightly as he raised it to the sky. Eliza looked at him and quietly stewed. She didn't like this angry version of Caleb. Dor continued with his counsel as if Eliza wasn't there.

"Caleb, you are learning the great lesson that seeking revenge does not remove the pain or the truth of the tragedy. Vengeance is the Lord's possession, not ours. I am sure you have heard your parents teach this. After all, I learned it from them!" Dor smiled and looked at Caleb as if he were a two-year-old having a temper tantrum. Caleb smiled. He needed a good memory of his parents and Dor gave him one that he didn't know about. Dor looked at each of them and shared an extended smile and a touch on each one's shoulder.

"Little ones, both of you have much sorrow and grief to process, and I share it with you. You have done nothing wrong but neither have you been abandoned by God." He paused to let those words begin to sink in. He knew that the more they understood how inseparable those two claims were, the more likely they would be able to find peace.

"We have prepared a gathering for you this evening, and the community wants to be with you." He gave each of them a hug and a kiss, and he led them back through the city and up the hill.

That evening, nearly 40 children, all of whom Eliza and Caleb knew, had been sent to the House of Healing. All of them experienced great loss during the attack. Their grief and anger would have been too much had the rabbis in the House of Healing not been there to help them. These men had guided many who had lost loved ones at the hands of the Romans, and they knew how to begin the healing process after deaths caused by the atrocities of war and enemy occupation. Indeed, that is why the House of Healing existed.

Caleb was beginning to make peace with some parts of the truth. He had seen his father and mother for the last time. Eliza had lost her favorite aunt and uncle, and her parents had been captured and put in chains by Roman soldiers. Eliza's plight was exacerbated in that she was uncertain about her parents' whereabouts. She thought they probably were being transported to a Roman slave market, perhaps to be sold, but she did not know. She also knew they might already be dead. The rabbis did not make light of the reality that her parents had lost their battle for freedom and that nothing short of a royal decree or a lot of Roman coins could undo that.

That evening, all the children walked to the local synagogue with Dor and Benji. Word had gotten out that there were the children of two great teachers who had been martyred the day before. The community served a great feast for the youth. Nearly everyone spoke to Caleb, reminding him that their parents had made a great difference in their lives, and he should be proud of them. One younger woman told Caleb the story of how his parents had performed a joint wedding ceremony for her and her sister a few years earlier. Caleb was finally able to smile as he learned that their first-born son was named "Mishi", after his father. They introduced the boy to Caleb and the rage in Caleb's heart all but disappeared like fog does mid-morning.

Caleb bent over and extended a single finger to the boy. He took it. "You have a beautiful name, Master Mishi. Did you know that was my father's name?" Caleb was not experienced with teaching young children, but he had seen his mother do so and he used words and tones that he thought his mother might use. The little boy nodded, a bit afraid and perhaps in awe of the man in front of him who towered over everyone else in the synagogue.

For the most part, though, Caleb seldom spoke other than to thank the visitors. He kept looking around to make sure he could see the little boy. "A piece of my father lives in him now," he said to Eliza. She looked up at Caleb as he spoke and she didn't have words to tell him how much she loved him. All she could do was allow herself to fall into his chest and rest her ear on him. He bent over, kissed her, and began to rub her hair. She could see that this little boy was a big part of Caleb's healing.

But this night was dedicated to honoring their loss. Many of the other students had the same experience that Eliza did. Their parents were taken away and no one knew where they were. Some would find their parents. However, there was no certainty. Yael and Mishi were dead. Caleb received tears and hugs of shared grief; Eliza got words of encouragement and a promise that others would pray that she would find them in the days ahead.

After the meal, a few people volunteered to clean everything. The elders sat them down next to the altar, and everyone began to pray and speak in tongues. A man from Thessalonica translated for them, and many people claimed to see Caleb and Eliza being used by God in the days ahead to do great things. The prayers continued for a short time before the lead rabbi stood at the altar and called forward a group of young girls. They were dressed in white clothing with perfectly groomed hair that had been let down, attire normally reserved for special ceremonies or alone time with their husbands. All the girls were virgins, as was required of members of the worship dance team.

One of them stepped forward and spoke to Eliza and Caleb. "Your mother, young Caleb, and your aunt, young Eliza, was our favorite teacher. She convinced us that, as women, we can control the outcomes of our families more than anyone else. She was more than just our hero." The girl had to pause to wipe the tears from her eyes before she could continue.

"Rabbi Yael was our friend." She needed another to express her grief before she could continue. Dor introduced the group and their intention.

"The girls have created this worship dance, and they wish to perform it for the two of you." The lead girl spoke up again.

"Please be patient with us, as we have never performed it. In honor of Rabbi Yael, we commit to keeping this performance private until we are with the Messiah. This is the only time anyone will ever see this dance," she finished telling them of her commitment before she covered her face and wept. Caleb reached over and interlocked his fingers in Eliza. The power of the moment was great. Dor could see that they were crying and he knew that sharing grief like this was a requirement if they wanted to see the world in a better light.

Those in the gathering who had not yet mourned now did so, knowing that they were witnessing a unique event. A young boy carrying a drum made from goat hide and another boy with a flute came from the other side of the altar and played a lament. The girls separated and began the dance. Their motions were graceful and they alternated between approaching the altar and gliding away from it. This went on for some time before the girls stepped to surround the altar and locked their hands together. With that, each of the girls sang a short prayer for the martyred teachers and asked for God's peace to pour itself on all those who felt the loss. As each girl finished their prayer, they knelt before the altar with their hands held high.

Once each girl had finished and all of them were kneeling, the room was silent, and many in attendance returned to their weeping. After a time, Rabbi Benji came up and thanked everyone for attending and dismissed them. One congregational member asked if they were taking up a collection for the children, but Eliza quickly dismissed the idea, asking for the money to be sent to help rebuild the damage done in Tamar. Each of the girls from the worship group came forward and embraced Eliza, as was an Ebreet custom, stepping to the side to allow the next girl to come forward. As the last dancer finished her embrace, they all placed a single hand on Eliza and lifted their remaining hands to the sky. The first girl spoke a prayer for Eliza, inviting her to visit them again. Eventually, the rabbis dismissed the crowd and everyone raised their voices, saying, "So be it." They began leaving the synagogue and walking home with their lamps guiding them.

The outside weather was in juxtaposition to the spirit inside of Caleb and Eliza. It was cold and snowing outside the synagogue, as the elements of winter had reached the heart of Judah. Eliza and Caleb walked to their room, but they felt disoriented from the impact of this evening's event. The exhaustion of the evening's corporate sharing had spent all of their emotional energy and they were ready for bed. The other children left to go to their new homes. Eliza and Caleb slept all night long and shared their dreams as they woke up.

And they knew it was now time to go to Rome to seek an audience with the Emperor by way of Rufus' Ring.

Chapter 13:
Departure from the City

By the fourth morning, all the swelling on Caleb's forehead where the centurion's armor had hit was gone, as was the stinging in his wrist, thanks to the skills of the herbalist in the house. Caleb already knew how to clean a puncture wound caused by an animal, but he knew nothing of what types of plants and leaves to put on this sort of wound to speed up healing. The herbalist talked through how she prepared the plants that she used and showed Caleb how she stored them. She shared all the best places to find them and encouraged Caleb to begin collecting them, as these plants had a use. Caleb felt as if he were in school again and it felt good to be learning something new that he could apply to his life. He wondered if this healer was also one of his parent's students, but he did not ask. He appreciated the herbalist's willingness to teach him, and they exchanged lots of stories as she cared for the wound on his head no less than twice a day. Eliza had long since figured out that part of Caleb's interest was that the girl was pretty. She caught Caleb looking at her more than once, but she didn't bring it up.

Caleb went outside as much as he could to walk and stretch; however, he feared going into town for fear of being identified by Roman authorities. Dor and Benji told him that the most likely description the soldier had for him was that of a tall and muscular man. For safety reasons, the rabbis had Caleb shave his beard to be more anonymous. In addition, he wore the sackcloth clothing of a common man. He walked around and worked in the gardens until late in the afternoon and Eliza would leave the company of Dor and Benji and come and join him every day after the mid-day meal. Their routine was to spend time in the garden, then walk outside the city gates, look at the sunset, and talk. They would wait for the last call of the city crier before returning inside the gates before they closed for the evening.

Either Dor or Benji would come and find them and tell them to come to dinner. The rabbis would ask them questions and hold them while they cried. It wasn't until the last evening that the tears began to stop and the insight that comes from passing through grief began to appear.

"I was told by some of the boys in Correae that the setting sun over the sea was beautiful," Eliza said on their last evening. "They say it creates a feeling of peace." Caleb let out a little chuckle before he spoke.

"Most of the boys in Tamar are too scared to travel to the coast, or if they do, they are within the walls of a city behind the doors of an inn by sunset," Caleb shared. Eliza knew that the spirit of adventure was not something that most rabbis knew how to teach.

"In Correae, it is different. Everyone has to travel with their family. We all get taught how to manage Roman coins, and you can't teach the art of negotiation in a schoolroom," she said. She showed Caleb the extra gold coin that she got from her parents, holding the purse of gold and silver at eye level. "Caleb, I want you to see that you and I have a lot of money for this trip. In fact, we have enough to buy our own wagon, a few camels, and perhaps a slave if we need to. This is pure gold from our village, not the unrefined junk that the Romans used to make coins. But we cannot use our money that way. Our village elders have taught us that big transactions draw big attention, and our village's survival depends on protecting secrecy. We need to be as frugal as we can if we want to travel to Rome without any unnecessary attention. A low profile is the best profile, they say." Caleb paused for a moment and gave his opinion. Eliza knew he wasn't motivated by money; in fact, that was one of his more endearing traits.

"I would prefer to get on a horse and ride directly to the coast. You don't want to waste money. I don't want to waste time. Let's find your parents."

"And what do you think would happen if a couple of teenagers rode across the plains, leaving a cloud of dust behind them? We would draw the attention of everyone in that part of Benjamin and Judah before we made it halfway. You cannot be that stupid, can you?" Eliza's sarcasm was well-developed for a seventeen-year-old.

"Shut up, cousin." He knew she was right. He had forgotten that he might now be a marked man. They needed to keep a low profile for the time being.

Meanwhile, Rabbi Dor listened to them formulate their plan to travel to Rome and gave them some feedback. He knew that seeking an audience with the emperor was most likely a once-in-a-lifetime event, and he asked them many questions that they had not yet asked themselves. Once he saw Rufus' ring, signifying his office of the legate, he took their plans to Benji. The two of them decided that it was too risky to send details of their plan to Correae using a courier, so the two of them agreed to personally carry the message to the elders in Correae. They also agreed that no part of the message would be written down. If the Romans ambushed them, they wanted there to be no evidence on them that they were harboring a fugitive. The commitment to let everyone back home know gave Eliza a sense of safety that her other aunts and uncles would know what happened and where Eliza and Caleb were.

The rabbis added what assistance they could to their plan as it formed. There were specific docks at the port that were more friendly to Ebreets than others, and they gave them names to ask for at one of the synagogues outside of town that they could use as their base while they awaited a passage over the sea. Normally, trips to Rome took months to plan, finance, and secure accommodations on a passenger ferry, as precautions had to be taken to guard resources while away. Care of livestock and fields of grain had to be addressed, as well as protection of the home and other personal property, such as carts and raw iron reserves. The two rabbis decided that they would return to Tamar, letting the leadership know that Caleb had survived and was going to Rome to seek a decree from the emperor to free his aunt and uncle. From there, the rabbis would continue their journey on horseback to Correae to let the elders know what had happened to Katya, Matthew, and their daughter Eliza. Once there, they would return toKdron and await their return.

"After you return, we ask one thing of you. We ask that you return here, as we have more to teach you." Dor had a stern look on his face as he asked, and they agreed to return after their current troubles were behind them.

Rabbi Benji gave them final guidance on the evening of the fourth day. "Groups are leaving the city gates every morning, and at least one of them is heading to the coast. Tomorrow, there is a couple with four wagons who are also going directly to Joppa. They will let you go with them at no cost, as a favor to our mission so that you can save your village's money, Eliza. You must appear to be workers if any Romans enter their encampments at the end of the days. You must discard your Ebreet clothing and buy new clothes after you reach Rome."

"I take my clothing off every time after I hunt. It is usually covered in blood from the kill," said Caleb. The rabbi chuckled.

"I should have known," he said, putting his hand on the boy's shoulder.

"That sounds pretty easy," Eliza added. "How long will it take to get to Joppa?"

"You will sleep one night on the coastal plains and arrive near midday on the second day." They nodded in agreement.

"Benji, do you know the people who are in this caravan?" asked Eliza. The rabbi had long ago permitted them to call him by his first name.

"I know of them, but I had not spoken to them before yesterday. I think you can trust them with some of your story, but do not tell them all of it. They are friendly but have not proven yet to be friends. I am assuming you know the difference." Eliza closed her eyes and nodded in affirmation.

On the fifth morning, it was time to pack and get ready to leave. For Eliza, it was common sense to know what sort of preparations were required for them to go on an extended trip such as this one. She remembered how her mother had stood next to her as she made ready all the provisions that she and her father would need the first time that they traveled to the coast three years ago. Eliza asked the cooks to have three loaves of fresh bread ready for her in the morning, asking them to wrap them in a clean, wet cloth to keep them fresh. She purchased dried fruits and meats in case it was not possible to start a cooking fire tomorrow night. She carried extra rope, cloth, metal nails, and a sharp knife. She purchased two bedrolls made from a blend of camel hair and Egyptian cotton. The camel hair kept them fireproof and the Egyptian cotton was comfortable and warm. She had a piece of leather and three skins for water, knowing from experience that they needed two water storage systems and a backup. She had a change of clothes that she wrapped in sheepskin treated with a light amount of mustard oil, keeping the contents waterproof. In the waterproof sheepskins, she also kept a small but thicker wool cloak, a flint, a small piece of steel, and some kindling to start a fire. She added a warm wool cap, as she had heard that Rome was colder than Judah, and she wanted to be comfortable during the winter days as they sailed north into the Roman harbor. She had some wool socks and wool mittens, as well. If their ferry caught a good wind and it was raining, the cold would seem through to their bones, and they needed the wool to keep them comfortable in the bad weather.

Eliza also knew from experience that carrying items to trade with the merchants in distant lands helps establish credibility and would give them a chance to interact with the culture. She grew up thinking that everything in the world was available for purchase on the streets of Rome. That also meant anything could be sold in Rome, too. She asked around in the market and found that purple dyes and Ebreet cinnamon fetched high prices on the streets of Rome this time of year. Eliza filled their backpacks with cinnamon sticks, hoping to sell them once they arrived. She purchased as much as was reasonable in the marketplace, so any interested merchant might see that they were covering their costs and making some profit, but not enough profit to justify additional scrutiny. Most of Eliza's wealth remained in gold and silver coins, unseen to the outside world. Once she had packed all the cinnamon sticks in the dry part of her pack, she put her hands on her hips and faced Caleb.

"OK, cousin. This was your idea, and I am ready to follow you!" she said, leaping into his open arms. She was excited for a real adventure and prayed this time that she saw more than a fox carrying a rabbit. She kissed him and looked him in the eye. She decided to take a page from her mother's toolkit on how to care for your man.

"Caleb, you are a good man. Thank you for doing this for my parents. I will stay beside you and not leave you. I promise," she said. Caleb took a shallow breath and smiled at Eliza.

"I am glad you are coming with me," he said. She accepted his affirmation with another kiss, and he put her down.

"Ok, and we have divided our coins into four different pouches. You and I shall each carry the equivalent of a month's wage within our cloaks. We will keep another month at the bottom of the sheepskins. I know coins don't need to be waterproof, but no one will go looking into a waterproof place for a Roman coin." Caleb nodded at her, acknowledging that this was a good idea.

No one judging them or their clothing would conclude that two teenagers were carrying such immense wealth.

Caleb was preparing and restocking his weapon supply for his part of the preparation. He took his knives to a local blacksmith and had them sharpened, and he took some of Eliza's money to buy a smaller gladius made of Damascus steel that he could hide in his backpack. He did not tell Eliza how much he spent, as he found her stinginess with money annoying. He also replaced his arrows with ones of the highest quality that he could shoot at greater distances and got two replacement bowstrings.

At sunrise the following morning, they met Peter and Elisha, the caravan leader and his wife. Eliza offered to pay them to take them to the coast, but they refused, telling them to climb in one of four carts of olive oil they were taking to Joppa. They were friendly and offered each of them an orange before leaving. Oranges were readily available in Judah this time of year, and they tasted wonderful. Eliza asked to buy two dozen of them, and the woman just told her to take what she liked as part of their tithe to the House of Healing.

The trip to Joppa was uneventful by every measure. Along the journey, the couple stopped for the night in a small town, and Eliza and Caleb adopted a policy of speak-only-when-spoken-to. No one asked their names or where they were from. Peter introduced them as cousins from inland Judah who had a personal matter to attend to in Joppa. No one seemed to care. Caleb and Eliza slept well, ate plenty of food, and seldom talked during the day about their plan. The rest at the House of Healing and the lack of heavy exertion on the cart ride helped Caleb's wounds heal nearly completely, and Eliza was grateful for that.

Once they reached the outskirts of Joppa in the middle of the morning, they finally asked Peter and Elisha a question.

"We need to find a passage to Rome," Eliza said. "What do you recommend?"

The couple looked at each other and smiled. "This time of year, that is easy. Once we reach the port and unload our olive oil, I can ask our buyer if he needs anyone on the ship going to Rome with these olives. If that boat isn't available, people travel between this part of the Empire and Rome every day. It should not be hard to find a passage."

Caleb jumped in. "We do not want to work on the boat or get a free passage. Neither of us has sailed the sea, and we are a little scared. We want a safe passage with a room below deck, and we will gladly pay for it."

Eliza agreed with him for what seemed like the first time in a while.

"Again, it's not a problem," Peter said. His confidence comforted them as he assured them that things would be OK.

Shortly after that, they entered town, and their wagons stopped in front of the docks. There were no less than ten other merchants in line to either load or unload seagoing cargo, and there was lots of conversation up and down the length of the harbor. Caleb and Eliza surveyed their new environment for a moment before they climbed out of the wagon, and Caleb gazed at one of the most magical things he had laid their eyes upon. The Mediterranean was unlike the Sea of Galilee; there was no other side to see. It was as if sailing west would mean falling off the end of the world. He just stared at it as the cart was unloaded.

Eliza was watching the docks and the harbor. They bustled with activity and many people were quickly moving cargo up and down the wooden docks that led from the land into the sea. Caleb watched as some of them loaded and unloaded seagoing vessels. Caleb and Eliza noted that no fewer than twenty boats spread across six docks were in some stage of loading or unloading. The older couple told them to follow them as they walked down one of the docks, asking some questions to find a boat for Caleb and Eliza to board that was going to Rome. Once Peter began a conversation, Caleb took a seat on a small bench halfway down the dock.

"I just want to sit here and watch this. You know, be grateful, like Dor said." Eliza knew what Caleb was talking about.

"Good idea," she said, taking a seat next to Caleb and holding his hand. Part of the training that the rabbis had taught them was to find gratitude in all things throughout the hard work of making peace with the loss of their parents. Dor called it "being present", and he said it would help them stay away from reliving the past. They had been practicing it on the ride here, as they would look at old buildings, studying every detail as they passed. Caleb counted the cattle as they would pass them on the road, and Eliza counted clouds and thought about their shapes. Loss for them was not an event in time, meant to be handled like changing out of sandals once a season. Loss was a process and they were grateful to learn these new skills.

After gazing at all the activity for a while, Caleb grabbed Eliza's hand, and they got down on their knees. Caleb prayed first. "Messiah, thank You for bringing us here uneventfully. Thank You for giving us Your servants in the city to help us begin our healing. We ask that the mercy You showed us to bring us safely here is something we can extend to others as we continue on our journey. Thank you for my cousin and her help getting us here. Let us find her parents."

Eliza kept her eyes closed. "Yeshua, what he said goes for me as well. Give us a safe passage to Rome, and let our pathway to Titus bring You all the glory!"

"Amen," they said.

"I see you are going to try to see the emperor," said Peter, as he had heard their prayers. He had approached them while they were praying, but they were not aware of his presence until he spoke.

They looked at each other before Caleb spoke up. "We are. Have you been to his palace on Palatine Hill? I hear it is beautiful."

The olive oil trader laughed. "I do not think any Ebreet has visited the palace unless they were a slave!"

"We ask, kind sir, that you not tell anyone what you heard us pray," Eliza said.

"Well, if you are going to pray out loud, you must know there shall always be consequences to displaying our faith in public." With that remark, Caleb and Eliza realized that Peter and his wife were also Yeshuians.

"That sounds like something that my parents would say," Caleb said.

"We must not be afraid of displaying our faith publicly. Thank you for reminding us!" Eliza said.

Peter smiled at her appreciation. Too many young people didn't treat their elders with respect, and it was nice seeing that Eliza wasn't like them.

"Try the third dock from the end," he said.

Caleb and Eliza thanked him. They grabbed their backpacks and walked towards what they hoped would be their ride to Rome.

Chapter 14:
Setting Sail

Due to the direction of the wind this time of year, the vessel that Caleb and Eliza booked their passage on was scheduled to depart at noon tomorrow. The greatest risk of wreck occurred near shores, and the direction of the wind traveling away from the coast of Judah was westerly this time of year but predictable only after midday. That meant they needed to maintain their low profile most of the morning.

Once the deckhand who issued them their tickets told them that they would be on the boat for up to two weeks, they immediately made a trip back to the markets of Joppa. Eliza felt a bit stupid for not thinking to ask how long they would be on the boat and she underestimated what they needed.

"We have got to get more provisions before we leave in case something happens. We need to buy an extra barrel of drinking water as well as some more fruit. Remember how they taught us about that sea disease where you do not get enough fruit?" Eliza talked quickly, meaning she was either excited or scared. Caleb wondered who she was talking to. It definitely wasn't him. She gave him no time to answer her questions.

Caleb smiled, knowing better than to react to all of her concerns. She was a detail-oriented, passionate person, and shopping was one of the few places those two skills came together.

"Eliza, relax, please! There will be twenty other people on the boat besides us, including crew, and there will be food." His dismissive tone didn't work with her.

"I am more concerned about the unexpected than I am about delays caused by weather. Let's buy two of the larger sheep bladders

that have been treated in olive oil, so if we capsize, we can float."
Caleb didn't care. It was her money. He needed to save his bow in
case something happened, and everything else was replaceable.

It was too risky to separate, so they decided they would do
the shopping together. That meant Eliza would be in charge. They
walked around the shops near the harbor, smiling and making small
talk with merchants. One of the local shopkeepers seemed safe and
he gave them advice about how to travel by sea. He had come from
Rome several years earlier and he assured them that boats made the
journey up to twice a month. His advice sounded credible.

"Just because you have no experience and are scared doesn't
mean that everyone else is. There will be many people working on
the boat who know what they are doing." Those warm words assured
them.

The next day, they boarded the ship, staring up at the massive twin-sailed vessel in wonder. Neither had been on a boat with a
below-deck section, so they quickly walked through it, looking at all
the rooms and storage features.

"This is more like a small tavern than a boat," Caleb said.

"This vessel looks nice. There is a bathroom, bedding, and
blankets. We won't have to use ours," said Eliza. She had imagined
that they would be sleeping on hardwood every night, but she had
not considered that they would have freshly washed amenities. She
loved it.

As they departed from the docks, the winds took them away
from land at a pace much faster than they had experienced. Caleb
and Eliza stood at the front of the boat, closed their eyes, and felt the
mix of salty water and cold air strike their faces as they proceeded
west. The combination of cooler air temperatures and the motion of
the sea created none of the ill side effects that either of them had been
warned about. They stared at the horizon in the distance and did not
focus on the motion of the boat, and neither of them experienced
seasickness. Soon, Joppa was nothing but a spec in the distance, and
everything in all directions was the great unknown.

The two sails that propelled the boat were made of great rolls
of white cloth. The ropes that held them up were thin and made of

unique materials from the Far East. These ropes were smooth and light, stronger than the thickest of ropes used in Judah to carry timber and stone. As Caleb and Eliza admired them, the captain called down to the front of the boat in Greek. "Never seen silk before, have you?" he asked.

"No, we haven't," Eliza replied. "It is amazing. Where did you get it?"

"I bought all of it at a market in Rome with the wage I got from carrying a group of soldiers."

Caleb looked up at him, holding the end of this new kind of rope. "Does it burn like hemp rope does?"

"It does. It smells like burned feathers. It shrinks first, though. After it burns, add some vinegar, and it cleans up nicely. You two citizens heading home?"

This was the first time either of them had been told that they looked like Roman citizens. "We are not," responded Eliza. The tone of the conversation went limp as the question begged for more than a yes or no answer.

"What are you going to Rome for?" the captain asked. He had no fear of their answer. He was their captain, and he was going to talk to them over the next two weeks. They might as well get used to answering his questions.

Caleb decided a partial answer would work. "We need to get a document and bring it back to handle a transaction we are working on. It involves some other people, too. We are hoping for an uneventful ride, as neither of us has been on the sea before." Caleb was counting on his father's teachings on how to guide a conversation. Mishi had demonstrated that to make the shift; he needed to end the first conversation with a new one that the listener would think he was an expert in.

"What do you recommend for us newcomers to the sea?" Caleb asked.

And it worked. Caleb's question practically begged the captain to tell stories of their adventures. For the rest of the afternoon, Caleb and Eliza listened to the captain and his two crew members tell tales of their travels all over the Mediterranean. They laughed as often as the conversation allowed and gave compliments to the men at each chance, just as they had been taught. There was nothing more valuable for them to establish on this first day at sea than a relationship with the crew who would keep them well-fed and safe.

As the sun neared late afternoon, the captain told the two other crew members to go down and prepare the evening meal. He planned to retire to his quarters for an afternoon nap like most crew and passengers.

"I'm going down, too," Caleb said quietly. He got close to Eliza's ear and whispered to her. "Those guys talked my ear off," Eliza looked at him and smiled.

"Caleb, you did great." Her affirmation filled him and he smiled back at her. He needed her kindness as he navigated the path in front of him. Finally, she spoke again.

"Caleb, I am going to stay up here for a while."

"Suit yourself," said Caleb as he kissed her and went below deck. After a few minutes, she found herself deep in prayer, asking Yahweh to help them secure an audience with everyone they needed to along the way. She spoke in Ebreet under her breath and she kept her eyes closed.

She was startled by a voice in her ear. "Hey, little girl, what are you doing all alone on this here boat?"

She knew enough from her travels to and from Tamar that some of the passengers had been drinking alcohol, like the ones in the taverns she saw the first time she visited Hebron with her father. She turned, feeling a fear not unlike the fear she had felt seeing Tamar in flames.

Before she could act, the man closest to her took another step forward. "I think you shall be our entertainment on this boat," he said, smiling at her, displaying a mouth partially full of teeth. And he smelled like fish. Eliza was disgusted.

One of the men moved to her right and one stood in front of her. The men on each side grabbed her upper arms and held her against the ropes on the edge of the front of the boat while the man in front of her began to untie the string that held up his pants. He stared into her eyes and smiled, and Eliza could sense evil in his heart. Her heart raced and her breathing became short and shallow. The man reached out with one hand and held her cheek gently. She could feel the thick callous on his hands and he ran his thumb over her lips.

"You might be the best part of this two-week boat ride, little girl! What do you say, boys?" he said with a smile that further displayed his bad dental work. Eliza's anxiety was now at all-time highs as the man chuckled and made eye contact with each of his two friends. The men slowly but forcefully pulled Eliza down to the deck until she was sitting with her legs spread.

In her paralysis, Eliza remembered some of what her aunt shared the one time she spoke of her rape. Eliza screamed, remembering that her aunt didn't and wished that she had. Her aunt regretted doing nothing as the Roman soldier raped her, but Eliza was not going to be raped without a fight. Her village elders had told her to fight.

"Let go of me! Let go of me, you animals!" she screamed, nearly in hysterical rage. However, due to the roar of the seas and the wind, her words quickly died out in the air before anyone could hear them.

"Oh, this is how I like them! Nice and feisty. It is better this way," said the man in front of her as he finished untying the last of his pant strings.

"Help!" she yelled again, this time with more desperation in her tone.

The man in front had had enough of her screaming and he stuffed a piece of cloth down her throat. He covered her mouth with a neckerchief that muted her efforts to make noise. She tried to scream, but now it was muffled.

"Hold her down, boys. You will each get your turn." The man in front bent down to untie the strings holding up her lower garments. Eliza had barely tied them after going to the bathroom, as she expected to take them off when she retired for her afternoon nap.

The man in front of Eliza suddenly grunted and his speech stopped. His chest tightened and he lurched forward slightly. A wink of an eye later, he made another lurching motion, but not towards her. Instead, he twisted himself halfway around and attempted to stand up. Eliza looked and saw a pair of arrows sticking out of his backside, one in the upper leg, the other in his buttocks. The man blocked Eliza's view, but soon, he was yanked to the side, and she saw a familiar sight. It was her cousin's massive forearm wrapping around the man's neck.

Her prayers of desperation had been answered, as Caleb must have heard her scream. Caleb dragged the man to the deck with him without releasing his hold on the man's throat. Everyone could see that the man was fighting but was also no longer breathing. His arrows had broken off at the skin, with the metal tip and wooden shafts now in the man's flesh. The more he fought, the deeper the tips of the arrows traveled into his meat. As the man slowed and stopped his struggle, Caleb stood up and addressed the two remaining men.

"This man will die in the next few seconds. I bet you already know that. Swear on your family's honor that you will leave my cousin alone or you will meet the same fate as this scoundrel."

Before the men could respond, Caleb pushed the injured man over the edge of the boat and everyone heard the splash as his body went into the ocean. One of the thugs was no longer a threat. Caleb moved to the place where Eliza was now on the ground. He looked them in the eyes as they knelt next to Eliza, no longer holding her down. Eliza sat up and tied her leggings.

"I did not say that I would kill him. I will let the sea do that. He will bleed out from his backside in the sea, and he will receive the death he deserves." Caleb's tone was flat and matter-of-factual. There was no emotion to focus on. That was the point he desired them to hear. He wanted them to hear his words and not experience merely a loud but powerful body language.

"Who dies next?" he asked, switching eye contact between the two men.

The two men attempted to move away from the edge of the boat. They were not prepared for such cunning resistance and were scared for their lives. They stepped away from Eliza and she jumped to place Caleb between the men and herself, holding him from behind with all of her strength.

Caleb spoke calmly to her in Aramaic, saying what he hoped only she would understand. "Retrieve the new sword and bring it to me."

She got up and walked as quickly as she could to the sleeping holds below deck while Caleb pushed one of the men into the other. He was preparing to bully them.

"So, this is what a good time looks like for you?" Both men stood with their mouths open, looking at the power figure who was dominating them.

"Guess what? Today is your lucky day. I am the offspring of a rape and I swore an oath to kill any man I saw raping a woman. Who will be fed to the sharks next?" He looked back and forth at them, knowing that neither of them would speak, and they would soon begin to panic.

"While I wait for one of you to answer, let me show you something."

Before the men could speak, he reached into his pocket and pulled out Rufus' ring. He put it on and showed it to them. "Unless, of course, you are greater than the nephew of a Roman legate who just witnessed a crime committed by three cowards," he said. In the moment, he was tempted to cower over them, smiling and increasing his threatening words. However, Uncle Rufus' words came back to his mind.

"Use power to the extent that you must, not the extent that you want to. An abuse of power will haunt your soul as you cross that invisible line," he would tell his young nephew.

These men could now see this encounter was not going to have a good ending. Any sense of intoxication from raping Eliza was passed and they were scared for their lives.

"Or would you prefer crucifixion?" were the words he wanted to speak. Instead, he chose to listen to his uncle and not speak, awaiting Eliza's imminent return. He looked back and forth at the two men, praying that Eliza hurry up.

Caleb had the element of surprise moments earlier, but now it was one man against two, and despite his size, any orchestrated attack by the two of them could mean his downfall. Caleb had been speaking loudly enough to hopefully awake the captain, counting on him coming to investigate what all the calamities were.

Caleb glanced down and saw that both men were wearing leather leggings and foot coverings, and he created a plan to assert himself and take away their advantage.

During the next large wave, he yelled out, "Look at that!" as he lowered his knife. As they turned, he pushed both of the men, sending one over the railing and into the sea. The other one fell over the side of the boat but grabbed the rope railing. He hung over the edge of the boat, holding on with one hand.

Eliza came back, running towards Caleb. "Your sword!" she said, handing it to him.

Caleb took the sword and pointed it at the man. "You have two choices now. Let go and swim, or give me your hand and let Damascus Steel cut off your balls."

The man looked at the sword and spoke out of desperation. "I am sorry. Please! I am sorry."

Eliza was appalled by what Caleb had just said and she spoke to him rapidly in Aramaic as she held Caleb's arm. "Caleb, I know this man may deserve death, but remember the lessons on forgiveness. We all deserve to die for our actions. We are not the judge, even though we live in a world where all men want to judge. Let him live, Caleb."

She leaned over the railing and extended her hand to the man without looking at her cousin. Right and wrong were also hers to decide. She spoke Greek in a common way that everyone would understand.

"Sailor, give me your hand. My cousin will not kill you."

Caleb knew Eliza was right. He put the sword in his belt and reached down to help the man up.

"Come on," he said, also extending a free hand to help the man back onto the deck. Once he was back on board, the sailor lay down on the deck in a state of shock. Caleb stood over his with a hand on the hilt of his sword and Eliza held his other hand with both of hers, hoping he wouldn't unsheathe his blade.

The captain finally arrived and was now next to them. He needed no explanation as to what had happened. Without hesitation, he kicked the man in the ribs. The man winced at the force of the impact. Eliza dared not reprimand the captain, but she wanted him to stop as well.

"Get up, you camel! You owe your life to the young girl you tried to rape, for I can tell you, the boy would have done exactly what he said if it wasn't for her stepping in. Go down into the galley and stay there! I will let Rome decide what to do with you once we reach land." He spit on the deck to show his disgust. The man stood up and fled to the galley below. It wasn't until he was gone that anyone said anything.

The captain had both hands on his hips in disbelief. Despite his approval of how he handled the deranged sailors, he viewed Caleb with disgust, as he now knew he was withholding something. In the captain's eyes, Caleb was a liar.

"So, speaking both Aramaic and Ebreet and carrying a legate's ring. Boy, there is a story there! Will you now tell me why you are on this boat?" The captain would not break eye contact with Caleb and he needed to understand that he wanted Caleb to tell him everything, as it was affecting the passengers on his boat. Caleb looked at Eliza; she continued to be in shock and could offer him nothing. She was still clinging to his arm as if it were a lifeboat.

"Fair enough," said Caleb. The captain grumbled.

"Seems like something like this happens all the time nowadays. The world is going to hell no matter what I travel. You two owe me the whole damn story!" he said, pointing at both of them. Eliza agreed with a head nod but was still too scared to speak.

Caleb finally turned to Eliza and she hugged him and wept. All the while, the captain stood next to both of them, realizing that he might have some liability for letting what appeared to be a Roman citizen get assaulted. The captain could see that Caleb was thinking about where to start with his story and he consoled Eliza until she was ready to release her hold on him. Once she let go, the captain spoke to Caleb but looked at Eliza first.

"If that thug comes above deck, you can kill him," the captain offered. "At sea, there is no law other than what the captain says. I say that he is a coward, and you can do whatever you want to him. Based on who that ring says you are, he is dead, anyway."

Caleb thanked the captain and the captain graciously escorted Eliza and Caleb down into the hold where his quarters were. He offered them his room for the afternoon, as it was at the furthest end of the vessel and knew it would make Eliza feel safe. He sat down with them and offered Eliza some strong alcohol. Once she finished the cup, he let her tell her story. Neither man interrupted her between her fits of crying and anger and both men remained in disbelief that all of that happened in broad daylight. The captain thanked Eliza for her bravery. Caleb took her to their room and held her next to him on the bed for the rest of the afternoon.

Caleb reacted as a man would and should react; that is what he told himself. He was protecting his family, just as his father had told him to protect Eliza. However, he now found that he had killed men in consecutive weeks, and his soul was feeling weary from the effects of ending two men's lives. For the rest of the day, as he let Eliza hold him, he continually recalled the look on their faces as he pushed two of them over the edge of the boat and into the sea. The horror on their faces had burned a scar on his soul and it haunted him. Just as Dor and Benji had told him, killing will always be an option to fix a problem; each time he selects that route, it creates new wounds.

As Eliza slept in his arms, he looked at her, quietly speaking to her so as not to wake her.

"Eliza, you are a better person than me," he said, lovingly caressing her, and her hand rested on his chest. Her mouth was open and he could tell she was getting the deep sleep she needed. She had just experienced a life-altering trauma and had nearly been raped. She needed the safety he provided her and the rest. He spoke to her again as she jerked her head; she was having a nightmare and she spoke gibberish.

"Father said you need me. He was right." He closed his eyes and allowed the sting of his tears to roll down his cheeks, somehow wishing he could get the sleep that his cousin was now receiving. His role for the remainder of this trip would be that of Eliza's protector as much as that of the leader. And, right now, there was no more important person in his life than Eliza. Before leaving Joppa, he had not considered that he might be killing more people and he hated thinking that he might have to do it again.

Yet, he replayed the events and believed he did the right thing. She was the victim of an attempted rape. The two who died deserved it. After what seemed to be a hundred instances of reliving the attack, he allowed his weariness to settle in. Finally, he fell asleep holding Eliza.

That evening, Caleb got up to relieve himself over the edge of the boat. The captain was doing the same thing and the two men talked for the first time since Eliza told them how she was assaulted and nearly raped.

"That is a strong cousin you got there. How in the hell did she get the courage to tell you to leave that man alone? I tell you, I would have done exactly what you said you were going to do and not thought twice about it."

Caleb did not answer as he stared at the moonlight reflecting off the sea waves. Caleb found a lot in common with those waves. He would go up and down with his passion, whereas Eliza was more like the horizon, thinking about the sacrifices and what is best for the future. He couldn't say anything like that to the captain, but he did nod in agreement.

"She has that kind of heart, huh?" said the captain.

"Like her aunt and uncle," said Caleb. Caleb flashed back to the scene in Tamar just over a week ago. His mind had already recalled this scene a hundred times as he took the lives of several men trying to avenge the death of his parents and protect Eliza. He continued to relive it, just like the rabbis said he would. He felt the knife go back into the centurion's lower leg as he pulled down and carved the man like he was a dear. He felt the impact on his temple and felt the rapid flow of warm blood down the side of his face. It was as if the battle in Tamar was still raging.

"Captain, you wanted the whole story. I am ready to share it with you." Caleb took a deep breath and turned to face the captain.

"One week ago, I killed several soldiers, including a centurion, trying to protect Eliza's mother and father and my mother and father. Right now, I feel just like I did the day after I killed them." Caleb finished going to the bathroom and faced the captain. Neither of them spoke.

"Why is it the thing that I do not wish to do is the very thing that I do?" he finally asked. The captain chuckled, took a deep breath, and let it out with force.

"That is a great question that has been asked through the ages. As a young man, I would drink too much wine, swearing not to do that again. You know what would happen? I would do it again a few days later, wondering what happened. Seems to me that your wine takes the form of a bow and a sword."

Caleb heard his analogy of comparing drunkenness to murder. It resonated to Caleb's core. His grandfather was a drunk and the analogy meant something. The captain was right and it hurt to hear his words.

"So, what am I supposed to do?" he asked. His question was not rhetorical.

"Do what your cousin there did. Figure out how to forgive. Spend time with people who know how to withhold their desire for vengeance. Learn how to keep your blade in its sheath. Avoid the Roman military. I am telling you this with certainty. They will try to recruit you and get you to join their ranks if they haven't already done so. Shooting a bow accurately on the deck of a boat is no easy task. Just make sure you politely say, 'no', or this haunting you have right now will become a permanent part of your life," he said.

Caleb nodded and laughed inside. He secretly wondered where this captain was last week during his nightmares. As the sun finished setting and became richer, the reds of sunset disappeared, and Caleb spoke again.

"Captain, who do you pray to?" Caleb asked.

"I do not know. I am still working on that," said the captain, slightly laughing.

"Do you know about the Messiah?" Caleb asked.

"Messiah?" the captain said. Caleb had heard that tone before. It brought back fond memories of his mother, and it felt as if his mother was with him, telling him what to do. She told him that nothing filled her soul like sharing the story of the Messiah with a gentile who had not yet heard it. Caleb put his massive hand on the captain's shoulder and they walked back towards the captain's chair at the front of the boat. It was time to take his mother's advice.

"Let me tell you a true story," he said. Caleb stood next to the man as he unwound the mystery of Yeshua on the cross, answering the man's many questions. Caleb's matter-of-fact nature made the conversation relatively fast, with a lot of head-nodding as each processed what the other said. All the while, Eliza stood at the top of the stairs leading down into the galley, with her hands lifted high into the sky, praying for her cousin and the captain. She knew what he was doing, and it filled her soul, too. She thanked God that she and Caleb had great role models as parents. She allowed tears to flow openly as that is what her aunt would do. And now that her aunt was gone, it was her turn to carry that torch of her family's legacy. Eliza was now the woman of the family, and prayer was rich and passionate, which is what women from Naphtali did.

Caleb needed no helper. And just like she needed Caleb, the captain now needed Caleb to share with him the greatest story ever told. And she knew her job was to pray that the most powerful event that could happen in a person's life would occur, just as Yeshua desired.

At that moment, there was no rape. There was no villain. There was no evil other than what exists in the spiritual world. Her aunt had preached that the real enemy is the one in the spiritual world, and the best weapon a young Ebreet girl can unleash is prayer.

As she opened her eyes, she saw Caleb walking towards her. He appeared to be done. He smiled and nodded his head. She knew what that meant. The Captain had accepted Yeshua as the Messiah.

And none of them saw that the lone surviving attacker was watching all of them with curiosity and wonder. He didn't know what had just happened, but he wanted to.

Chapter 15:
The Trust of the Captain

For the next few days, Eliza remained cautious and shaken. Her fear of the unknown remained, and she went nowhere without Caleb or the captain within sight, including the bathroom. Caleb insisted that she be near him all the time and she submitted to his request without resentment. It was the least he could do for not being there during moments he should have been.

The captain asked Caleb questions nearly every day regarding the history of this Messiah, which he wanted to know more about. Caleb remembered much of it but not all, and he would often ask Eliza to come and complete the holes in his knowledge. She had a better memory for that sort of thing. And she was a wonderful storyteller. For all that she lacked in physical strength, she made up for in verbal strength. The captain told both of them he could listen to Eliza talk about Yeshua's miracles and his teachings all day long.

They spotted land on the fourth day. They were too far away to make out any features, but it gave Eliza a feeling of safety that she hadn't had since the incident. Word spread quickly that land was in sight and everyone came to the bow of the boat to see the outcropping of rocks and land in the distance. Eliza went to the top deck with the captain and deckhands, as she had an open invitation to visit the "crew only" section of the boat. She was accustomed to being there and all the men had grown fond of her and her stories. She thought it to be the safest place in the boat. For her part, Eliza was glad to tell all the men about the mystery of the Holy Trinity and the forgiveness of sins. And now, with land in sight, she felt safer.

With land on the horizon, Eliza had many more questions than the captain for the first time.

"Is that Rome?" she asked.

"No, dear, that isn't the city of Rome, but the Roman Empire owns the land on both sides of it. The land to the left is an island called Sicily. It is the biggest in the Mediterranean. The land to the right is Calabria. We will stop at the port of Messene on Calabria. Once we get there, you get your feet dirty. But it is much softer than Judah." That made her laugh.

"Eliza, you won't believe how much you missed the feel of dirt on your feet until you were done. We will get some provisions and be on our way the following day. After that, we will sail to Ostia for about three days."

"Ostia?" Eliza asked.

"Yes, that is the port in Rome that all ships use. Don't worry. It is a short walk from there to downtown."

Eliza looked worried.

"How much colder will it get as we head north?" she asked.

"Not much more than now. Rome feels about the same as the coast of Judah, you know?" he told her rhetorically.

"I am scared, captain. This is my first time sailing the Mediterranean, and this constant motion is something foreign to me. I don't know what to expect," she said.

"We will take care of you, young woman," he said reassuringly. "You will be safe with us. Just do as we tell you, and we will keep you out of harm's way." Eliza smiled and took the captain's arm as she had made a habit of doing since the attempted rape. He put his free arm around her shoulder and drew her in for a sideways hug. As an Ebreet, this would have been an inappropriate act, but Eliza knew that these men were not Ebreet and she had no reason to hold them to standards that they hadn't agreed to. Caleb had seen this and talked with her about the differences in boundaries between Ebreet and Gentiles. They agreed that there was no need to reprimand them or try to teach them the Ebreet way of interacting with others of the opposite sex who were not family. Eliza hungered for the affection of a father figure now.

"It's Eliza," she said. "My name is Eliza, remember? You don't have to call me young girl all the time." Despite his rough exterior, the captain was a sensitive man.

"Yeah, I remember. We are here for you, Eliza," he said, repositioning his arm around her as a father might do. His touch made Eliza feel safe, as she knew he was not like the rapists who had held the same arm that he was holding. It was the same way her father would hold her while he would tell her stories in the evenings. Eliza knew the captain was a good guy in a bad situation; he was not part of the bad situation and shouldn't be equated with it.

"Thank you, captain," she said. His nod acknowledged her the best way he could. He was not a man of words, but she felt his sincere concern for her well-being. He was addressing something deeper; he chose to be her rock as he knew she needed one.

"It is going to be okay, dear," he said. "Whatever happens, it is going to be ok."

Chapter 16:
A Storm That Defines You

The next morning, at sunrise, the captain brought everyone to the top deck. He was not an orator like Mishi, but he knew how to get his point across.

"Do you see those red skies? That means we are in for some bad weather. I am going to try to get us to land before that happens. We will be going as fast as this boat can go. Our goal is to reach Messene before the bad weather hits. Be alert because it will get bumpy as we go full sail and tack this boat as hard as we can!" Before everyone started grumbling, he added, "Do not panic. We will be in sight of land all day long. We will ride along the north shore because it is safer. We will be turning hard all morning to get the most out of this wind until we are near Messene. Hold onto something, and don't be scared. I promise you we have done this before," he said. Everyone could sense that he was not trying to scare them but be a part of the answer. "May whoever you pray to protect us as we travel." That was the last he said.

Eliza smiled as he said that. The captain had gaps in his understanding of what Yeshua could and could not do. So did she, not that long ago.

Caleb looked around at the other passengers on the ship, all conversing with enthusiasm at the news. He had not noticed their identities before, so he took a moment to assess everyone else on the ship. There was a group of six Roman women who were heading back home after visiting their husbands, and they each had one slave with them. They were by far the loudest group and accounted for half of the boat's allotment of passengers. They all had questions, and they each offered their slave to help the captain and the deck-hands with anything they needed. Two older soldiers were traveling home, and no one could tell where they were from as they spoke a language no one understood. The deckhands thought it was Gaelic; others thought it was Saxon. Either way, no one was courageous enough to ask. They added to the conversation in broken Greek, "Good idea…now to drink more!" They raised their fists to the sky and shook them as if this announcement was more about a reason to drink than potential danger. Eliza had already told Caleb that they scared her. Caleb was now standing next to her, and it appeared as if he was about to say something, but she spoke first. He knew she was anxious.

"Caleb, what are we going to do?" she said, speaking loudly in Ebreet, convinced now that no one could understand her.

Caleb knew what to do with Eliza. Normally, he would sug-gest that she toughen up. However, she had reason to be emotionally unstable right now, and he empathized with her. She needed some-thing to do to get her singleness of focus on something else.

"Let's make sure that the sheep bladders are sealed and the stuff we need to keep dry is inside. Would you go below deck and do that?" he asked as politely as he could. She pointed at him and smiled.

"Good idea!" That task kept her busy for a while. His expecta-tions changed and he guessed that giving her something to do would make her feel more secure.

As the skies darkened and the wind and chop picked up, they distracted themselves by staring at Mount Etna on the south side of the Strait of Messene. It was a huge mountain on the island of Sicily in the northwest corner. The size of the snow-covered side and the height of the summits had no parallel in the Golan Heights or Egypt, and they were in awe at its immenseness. Each time a wave would come over the sides of the boat, the mountain's greatness got lost, and they were brought back to the reality of their peril in the rough ride that the captain needed to create. Caleb kept Eliza grounded by reminding her to keep looking at the mountain during moments as the waves hit and the boat violently rocked.

One of the deckhands saw them staring at Etna. "You like Etna? That is a volcano. It spews hot lava, although that hasn't happened in a long time."

"How long ago is a long time?" asked Eliza, feeling more dread than ever.

"Not since I was born. They say the deadly sea monster Typhon was trapped under that mountain by Zeus himself. The hot rock comes from the forges of Hephaestus underneath all that snow."

Neither of the children had been educated in either Greek or Roman theology and they had no idea how to respond. They knew of Yeshua and His power but not of any multi-theistic cults with gods named Typhon and Zeus. But they couldn't deny that smoke was coming from the top of the volcano at the same time that snow was falling on its flanks. They did not understand. Why had they not heard of this place? Had not traveling outside the confines of Naphtali and Benjamin limited their education this much?

Then, with no warning, they rounded a small point on the northern shore and the angle of the waves began to explode on the sides of the boat. With every swell, water would come over the top deck and onto the boat. With the sun already heading towards the horizon, the mates yelled out to the captain.

"Captain, do we make the turn and head to Messene or keep going through this mess?"

The captain made one last look at the horizon before turning towards the mates and barking his orders.

"If we do not go now, we might have to wait till morning. Switch the sails. Let's tack south! Do it!"

With that, the two men decreased the pull on one of the sails and increased the pull on the other. The boat turned south and began to speed up rapidly. The force of the wind took them away from shore and directly towards Messene. The bow raised and fell with the swell, but the water no longer came over the edges. The crew and passengers held on to anything they could find that was stationary. The pattern appeared to be stable, and everyone appeared to have a posture to handle the violence.

Then a large boom came from the front of the boat. The boat abruptly stopped moving forward and two of the women and one of their slaves flew over the edge of the boat and into the sea. The boat had hit something big. The captain quickly stood up and called to the crew, demanding the crew look over the edge and see what had happened. His calm demeanor showed that he had obviously experienced something like this before. The oldest crewman could see over the edge at what had happened. A huge section of the front of the bow had a hole in it big enough to walk through. And half of it was below the water line.

"We hit some rocks and we are taking on water!" The captain didn't need long to process how to handle it.

"Move everyone to the back of the boat and see if we can break free!" The mate, still looking out over the edge, his head in disagreement.

"Captain, what's the point of breaking free of the rocks? We are taking on water." He also experienced damage while on a ship at sea. The captain disagreed immediately as everyone was now watching the two of them discuss what they should do.

"Maybe so, but the boat will at least drift away, and perhaps we can save it later. We aren't far from the land. No one lives if we stay here. Move the people!"

Eliza had just reached the top of the stairs and was in a position to do something. She had just inflated the sheep bladders and packed up all their gear into them. Although she had not seen any water yet, she heard the wood planks at the front of the boat crack like firewood during the impact. Caleb saw the hull break apart. He stood at the top of the stairs, looking down at her.

"Eliza, give me your hand," he yelled and she complied. He pulled her to the top deck and pulled the two bladders up as quickly as he could. He handed one of the inflated bladders to Eliza, slipped the small remaining backpack on her, and loosely attached its belt around her waist.

"Caleb!" she said. He looked at her and saw that she was hyperventilating. As he suspected, she stood in front of him, paralyzed. She had not yet recovered from the attempted rape and was now on a ship that was sinking. He knew she needed him to be calm and lead her through this. He grabbed her forearms and looked her in the eyes.

"Cousin, look at me. We are getting off this boat and swimming to shore! Hold this bladder in front of you and swim toward the closest land you can see. Do not stop until you can stand up and walk. Just follow me and I will lead you there. I promise."

"Ok?" he asked. She nodded furiously in the midst of her hyperventilation, knowing she had no choice.

"Good. Now, follow me." He nodded to her, then jumped off the deck of the boat feet first and disappeared under the waves. He came up from under the water's surface, yelling out her name one more time before he started paddling towards the shore. He held the bladder in front of him and she could see that his bow was over his left shoulder. He kicked his legs and that action was propelling him forward. One of the Roman slaves who was already in the water started to pursue him, but the first swell sent him under the surface and Eliza failed to see him again.

Eliza could see how quickly the boat was taking on water. The Roman women were screaming at their slaves, demanding that they do something. The two soldiers were long since drunk and all but unaware of what was happening. Their situation was dire by every measure and Eliza's world seemed to move in slow motion. She looked as all the different people on the boat began to panic, each asking the other what to do. The Roman women were trying to hold on to all the items that they had purchased, as they didn't want to lose them. The slaves were following the dumbest of orders to get thick jackets out of the hold to keep warm while they waited for a rescue.

"This boat is sinking fast. We won't be here for long," Eliza said out loud. Yet, her feet would not move. She was paralyzed.

She felt more alone than at any time in her life. Watching her parents be captured and feeling powerless to do anything had made her feel feeble. Being nearly raped by three men made her feel frail and vulnerable. However, she was now on a sinking boat and her cousin was already on his way to the shore. Her chest felt hollow, feeling as if it contained some power to prevent her from moving.

But she could not die like this. Her aunt would be disappointed. The elders in her village told her to fight and try to escape. Caleb told her exactly how to follow him and he demonstrated it to her.

Eliza no longer wanted adventure. Are these life-threatening events, like sailing across the ocean in winter, part of an adventure? If that is true, she did not want it anymore. She thought she liked the unknown; now, the unknown was preventing her from moving.

"I love you, Little One," was all she heard. It was a man's voice - not Caleb's or her father's. She had not heard it before. Yet, He was near her, but Eliza couldn't tell which direction he was from her. She took one deep breath and moved to follow Caleb.

"You can do this," was the last thing she said to herself before she felt her feet strike the water's surface, and she submerged. Before Caleb jumped, he told her to keep her eyes closed as she hit the water. Once she surfaced, she reopened them, and she began to feel the shock from the cold water. She felt the winter sea trying to hold her down and move into her bones, but she held the bladder and knew what to do. It was time to stretch her legs out behind her and kick to shore as if it were the last thing she might do.

As her kicking rhythm became stable, she looked around. She saw that she wasn't alone in the water. The two drunks were already attempting to swim in the sea, flailing their arms like chickens might as they tried to fly away from a fox that was chasing them. One of them was already coughing and he would probably go under soon. His fate inspired her to maintain her rhythm of kicking and swimming towards shore.

The situation behind her was too chaotic to understand. She heard more sounds of wood splintering off the bow as the boat tried to separate from the rocks, and she heard screaming and another splash not far from where she landed. This time, though, she did not look back. She could not help them, and she continued kicking. Slowly, she got closer to the shore.

Caleb told her that panicking people might try to take her bladder from her, but Eliza knew what the elders told her. No one was going to take her bladder or her life without a fight. She put it in front of her and began kicking harder to get to the north shore as quickly as she could. She could see the land and it was not far away. She needed to separate from anyone else now in the water who might be coming at her to take her flotation device. She dared not stop and look back again. She needed to separate herself from people trying to come after her, just like Caleb did. And she thanked God that she had gone running in the mornings with Uncle Rufus and Caleb enough to have developed excellent endurance.

What she did not know was that nearly everyone else in the water was clinging to the sides of the boat, scared for their lives. Once she concluded she was halfway to shore, she reached into her soul and extracted enough courage to pause her swim and look back. No one was left on the deck and more than half of the hull was underwater. Most people were clinging to the sinking ship and she could hear women screaming. She also noticed that two other people were swimming in the same direction she was going. She couldn't identify them, but they were closer to the boat than they were to her. She turned back towards Caleb and the land and resumed her kick.

"Be at peace. I need you to go through this, as I have something else in mind for you," said the voice. The man's voice was still nearby.

"Okay," she answered as she paused to capture a few deep breaths and gather herself. "Thank you," was all she could say before the urgency of reaching the land overtook her, and she returned to kicking. Caleb told her that hypothermia would kill her if she stopped and she was not about to allow that to happen. The village elders told her to fight and now was the time to fight. She had a singular focus and she kicked and moved with the waves toward the shore.

She had no idea how much time had elapsed since she hit the cold water. She kept moving steadily, but she could sense that the cold water was draining her energy and she knew she couldn't stay in the water much longer. The sun was overhead and warming her backside, but she began to tire. She saw that the person in front of her had reached land and was standing up, waving, and yelling at her. She tried to speak, but her jaw was shaking uncontrollably, and she couldn't form any words, no matter which language she tried. Moments later, she could understand Caleb's voice.

"Eliza! Keep kicking! You are almost here! I am coming out to help you. Just key on my voice, Eliza!" Caleb's voice gave her hope. Yet, everything in front of her was black and white, and her restricted vision scared her. She knew the loss of color vision meant her body was shutting down non-essential systems, and color vision was one of them. She had to keep moving. If she did not, she would die.

Suddenly, she felt a force on her forearm and then Caleb was in front of her. He lifted her from the water and carried her to shore in his massive arms. As he walked, he looked down at her and smiled. Once they stepped onto dry land, he laid her down on some soft grass and knelt beside her, holding her hand. He removed the bladder and backpack from her and took off all of her exterior clothing that was wet. She wore her undergarments and he handed her a single dry towel that he had ready for her. He rubbed down her head and arms, drying them off.

"Good job!" he said, rubbing her face with his hands to try and warm her up. She smiled, and that made Caleb feel successful.

"This is some cold water, isn't it?" Caleb said to her as he laughed.

"Oh, Caleb! Thank you," she said, and she felt her breathing stabilize.

Quickly, her color vision returned. Concurrently, all fear departed, and she felt Caleb's encouragement.

"Let's get you some dry clothes so you can start to warm up. Here, I think I took your bladder because I have all of your clothes." She smiled at the irony. Caleb had already taken out her thickest cloak and her spare pair of sandals. She covered herself in the cloak and put the dry sandals on her feet.

"Take these clothes and go into the woods to change." He helped her stand up and walked her to the edge of the woods and behind a large tree growing in the dunes. She shivered as she changed her clothes, and she felt the loam under her feet. The soil was rich in nutrients, with plants growing everywhere. She wrapped herself in her warm cloak and stood motionless before she heard Caleb yelling at her. "The faster you change and come back, the faster you will get warm by the fire!"

She stepped out from behind the tree and walked towards the fire that Caleb had built. The sun overhead felt good on her skin, but the ground under her feet felt nothing like it did in Judah. It was soft and void of rocks. It was covered in moss and lichens, and the surrounding woods smelled rich with evergreens like pine and spearmint, a lot like Correae did in the fall. Caleb kept talking to her to keep her focused on preservation.

"Eliza, sit next to the fire," he said. Caleb remained in wet clothes but he seemed less affected by the cold water than she was.

"I feel numb," she said.

"Sit next to the fire and let it do the work of warming you," he said. Once she did, he took off her dry cloak, telling her she would heat up faster with it in her lap.

Everything Caleb said was right. Her torso and hands quickly warmed and her legs felt the comfort of the outer cloak. She sat idle, allowing everything to warm up. Caleb handed Eliza some dried meat and a peeled orange. He also placed a full skin of water next to her, knowing that she would feel her dehydration as soon as she started warming up.

Eliza warmed up quickly and she watched as two surviving swimmers changed directions and navigated themselves toward them. The first one made it to shallow water and stood up.

"Over here," said Eliza, standing up and jumping enthusiastically that someone else had survived. She identified him as one of the deckhands. He waved back at Eliza, came directly towards the campfire, and began warming himself. She spoke to him, knowing he would be too cold to speak back, and Caleb stoked the fire with more driftwood. The first was now roaring with great flames. The deckhand took off his wet outer garments and Caleb took them to hang over a small shrub, next to Eliza's wet clothes. He shook uncontrollably, but the fire warmed him quickly. He was anything but idle, though, and he constantly looked back towards the ship, waving his hands for others to see him.

As the last swimmer neared the shore, the deckhand spoke to Eliza. These were his first words since arriving.

"That is the man who tried to rape you," he said, pointing at the last survivor.

Startled, Caleb grabbed his bow.

"Oh no, he won't!" He notched an arrow and walked towards the water's edge. "That dirty dog! Who does he think he is, trying to come this way?" He readied himself to shoot an arrow into the man as he neared the offshore rocks.

Eliza jumped up and pursued Caleb. She ran up behind him and removed the arrow from its notch on his bow.

"Caleb, don't do that," she said with authority.

"Eliza, what are you doing?" Caleb exclaimed.

"This man made a mistake and is now fighting for his life. Extend him the same courtesy as you did before." Caleb looked angry and puckered his lips. He took a deep breath and exhaled.

"Cousin, you are just…" he stopped short of insulting her and shook his head in disgust. He couldn't finish his thought. It made no sense to him that she treated this man so well despite the evidence that he tried to harm her.

"Caleb, please help him," Eliza said calmly. He gave her his bow, picked up a long stick from the firewood pile, and extended it toward the swimmer. The man began to walk slowly toward the stick, and Eliza noted that he wore an expression of hope.

"Caleb, you know it was your mother who taught me to forgive my enemies. Do you remember her stories of when Yeshua was approached by the Pharisees, who were ready to stone a man who had sinned?"

"Yeah," he said, only partly remembering that story.

"Yeshua said, 'Let the man who has no sin cast the first stone.' The Pharisees realized that none of them were sinless, and none threw any stones."

Her story choice pierced him. Caleb struggled with his identity as a murderer and a defender, and he knew he was a sinner. He took a deep breath and looked at her.

"I guess you're right." Caleb walked out into the sea and helped the man finish stepping out of the water and onto dry land. He acknowledged Caleb's help with a nod and walked towards the fire. Eliza gave him her place out of the smoke but near the warmth.

"Bless you," he said, pausing only for a second to look Eliza in the eye. He sat down, shivering in his wet clothes, hoping to warm up and survive.

Eliza returned to her pack as she was warm enough to move around comfortably. Although much of her pack remained soaked with salt water, everything inside the bladder was dry, and most of the food remained edible. She offered everyone some dried meat and soggy bread. While the three men ate, she quickly accounted for all the coin purses in the middle of the pack. They weighed more than anything else and she was grateful the money was there.

Caleb approached the man who tried to rape Eliza. Although the man was nearing a state of hypothermia, Caleb's anger was not about to be restrained. At least not verbally.

"My cousin spared your life, and I do not know why. You deserve to die. You know that, right?" Caleb towered over the man, and Eliza could see that he was experiencing the same shame he had earlier.

"I am so sorry," the man said, but the shame he felt prevented him from looking Caleb in the eye. He began to cry, first slowly and finally without abandon.

"What are you doing that for? Stop crying!" the deckhand chided. "These folks let you live. Did you see the ring he wears? That is the ring of a ruthless sort of man. No legate would let a crime like yours go unpunished. You are…well, I do not know what you are other than lucky to be alive." The man stopped his crying and stared straight ahead into the fire.

Caleb got up and left to go into the woods, feeling nothing but anger that Eliza was so quick to forgive this villain. Eliza watched the event transpire and she considered following after him, but she let him go. He came back a few moments later, having composed himself. He brought a large bundle of wood and dropped it next to the fire before speaking.

"There is a stream for fresh water and there is lots of wood to burn in the forest. We will need to stay here tonight and come up with a plan in the morning. We will need to get some wood for the fire and keep it stoked during the night." He intentionally walked toward Eliza and stood near her. His intent to protect her was obvious.

For most of the afternoon, the deckhand told stories of his two other shipwrecks. He talked about the Egyptians, the Galls, the Saxons, and just about everyone else other than his own family and friends. And he had fond memories and stories about the captain. Eliza, too, already missed him. She cried for him as the sun set, knowing far too much time had elapsed in that cold water for him to survive. As the sun began to set, the fatigue of the day's stress began to set in, and all of them were ready to sleep.

"My cousin is sleeping all night and the three of us will take a watch," Caleb announced. "I will take my watch first while she sleeps. The rest of you can sleep once you gather more wood. You have my word: I will not slit your throats while you sleep unless you fail to get up and get some wood right now."

"Enough of acting like the tough guy," Eliza said to him in guttural Aramaic. "We need to act like we were raised, you Donkey!" The men were fearful of Caleb, not knowing what Eliza had just said, and they immediately stood up to retrieve their share of the needed firewood from the forest.

"Please wait a moment. What are your names?" she asked the two men.

"I am called Balbinus," said the man who had tried to rape her. "People call me Balbi."

"And I am Priscus," said the deckhand.

"Well, good. Balbi and Priscus. I am Eliza Antiochus and this is my cousin Caleb. We are all lucky to be alive, aren't we?"

"Yes," they said simultaneously.

"I am the daughter of Matthew and Katya from the Ebreet village of Correae in the province of Naphtali. By Roman law, each of you is required to serve us until we release you, as we have saved your lives from an act of the gods."

The two men paused and looked at each other with stoic expressions on their faces. By Roman law, she was right. They lost their freedom when she and Caleb saved them and they were her slaves now. They knew it. Then, they looked at Caleb, and they knew that it would be unwise to rebuke her or seek a way out of servitude. Caleb would kill them without breaking a sweat, and their death would be considered lawful.

"Yes, that is the rule. I know it well," said Balbi. "We understand."

"For now, I have not told you of our plans, but tomorrow, you will help us get back on the way to Rome."

"How do you propose we do that?" Priscus asked.

"Just wait until tomorrow," she said.

Once Caleb saw that Eliza was done talking to the two, he spoke to her in Aramaic.

"And you think I take risks? You just added a known criminal to our lot and a man we knew nearly nothing about."

She replied in Greek so all could hear. "Yeshua added disciples before they were old enough to be worth half their weight in salt. And those young men changed the world. We are going to need help, as we do not know where we are going, and we won't know our way around Rome after we do get there. They will help us."

At that moment, Caleb saw his mother in Eliza. That is how she would have handled the situation. She would have been transparent and quick to shine the light onto stories from the old and new Torah. He looked at her and smiled.

"You are like my mother," he said in Aramaic. Eliza could see the breakthrough in Caleb's heart. If she spoke now, she would cry.

Caleb took a deep breath and spoke instead. "Good night, cousin," was all he could say, and he helped cover her with the single blanket that they had with them. The two of them looked at each other for a few moments, and Caleb put his hand in her beautiful dark brown hair.

"I am glad you put everything in those bladders," Caleb said jokingly.

"I am glad you and your bow made it to shore!" she said, making him laugh.

"As I jumped into the sea, I had to put that bow over my shoulder before swimming to shore. I am not going to lose this." His commitment to his weapons was candid and matter-of-fact, making Eliza feel safe. He truly was a good man to her.

The men soon returned with a large bundle of firewood each and they all watched in silence at the last sunset in the west. Eliza lay under her sleeping blanket not far from the fire while all the men stood around it, as they could not yet fall asleep. Eliza, too, couldn't sleep, but Caleb could see that she felt safe again.

Priscus spoke next. The depth of what had just happened was now beginning to seep into his soul; now, they no longer feared for their lives.

"My boat and my captain are gone," looking into the fire. Everyone nodded. They were all starting to feel loss and trauma from surviving a shipwreck. There were signs of other swimmers in the water and the boat had now disappeared.

Balbi turned towards Eliza as she was sitting up in her bedroll.

"Eliza, thank you for saving my life," he said, using a most contrite tone. "You are a more forgiving woman than any I have known," he added, still staring at the fire. Those words prompted a small but inaudible snort from Caleb, which he hoped no one heard. But they all did.

"I will do what you ask. My life is yours," he continued, bowing his head and turning back to the fire.

"That is the way of our faith, Balbi," she said. Eliza leaned back and quickly fell asleep. The two others joined her and Caleb told Balbi he would wake him in a few hours. Caleb sat near the fire and watched Eliza sleep as he had done several times back in the house of healing. He witnessed her dreaming and her occasional talking, but he couldn't tell who she was talking to. Was she battling some demons? He wondered if she was reliving the attempted rape or if it was something about her parents. She was obviously tormented by something.

It reminded him of what she referenced earlier in one of his school lessons. There was nothing in the real world she was battling as she slept - all her battles were now in her mind. He knew his job as protector was far from over.

Eliza abruptly sat up, nearly panting. Caleb saw her face in the light from the fireplace, and she was tormented.

"You were having a bad dream. Go back to sleep," he said.

"Okay, but Caleb, I am scared," she said, pulling the bedroll up to her chin. Caleb moved next to her and he put one hand on her head. She let her eyes close, and she fell back asleep. All she needed was to feel his touch.

Caleb woke Balbi and finally got his chance to go to sleep, lying where Balbi had been. He placed his sword inside his bedroll and nodded at Balbi. Balbi closed his eyes as he acknowledged the expectation his new masters had on him to keep the watch in the middle of the night to keep them all safe. Caleb stared at Balbi before saying his final prayers, asking God to remove the bitterness he had towards Balbi.

The rest of the night passed without any events.

Chapter 17:
Re-entering Civilization

Priscus had the last watch before sunrise and had already stoked the fire before everyone else woke up. One by one, they woke up and quietly sat next to the fire. Winter meant shorter days, and they all had a full night's sleep. The warm fire and an uneventful night of rest left all of them feeling refreshed. Priscus was obviously gregarious and he started a conversation with Caleb and Eliza as soon as they started moving.

"The Roman fishing village of Reggio up the coast. I bet it is less than a quarter-day walk. We ought to see if we can find it. We won't get any boats to pick us up here. It is too rocky." The coastline where they camped offered no place to land any boat.

"Agreed," Caleb said in a groggy state. "Staying here and waiting is a bad idea. Eliza, what do we have to eat?"

She sat up on her knees and took a deep look inside her backpack before answering him.

"We have more dried meat, but we are out of oranges and nearly out of water." She stood up and walked a few steps towards Caleb's backpack. She reached in and took out what she had packed in his backpack, serving everyone else before taking any for herself. Everyone was grateful to be alive; food in their stomachs was a benefit they weren't expecting.

Since Caleb and Eliza were the only ones in possession of their belongings, everyone watched as the two Ebreet packed up to leave. Caleb was grateful that his clothing had dried out overnight. His bedroll had some moisture in it, but everything else was dry. As he was putting on his pack, Eliza looked at Priscus and spoke up.

"Let's go towards…what did you call it?"

"Reggio!" Eliza took a deep breath and turned to Caleb.

"I promised I would follow you. Lead on, cousin."

They began walking up the coast with Caleb, the tracker, in the front. After a short while, Caleb stopped and surveyed the footprints he was beginning to see. He suggested that they go inland.

"I believe this is a trail that runs parallel to the shore. You can see all the prints on the ground here. If we take it north, we are sure to come up to Reggio. Follow me, but do not talk." He did not wait for an answer before walking. He stopped them after a brief while and knelt on one knee again. "I have been seeing human footprints for a while, but now we have livestock markings. We are close to something."

By mid-morning, they began hearing the sounds of metal striking a rock ahead of them, as well as some cow bells. Soon, some man-made structures appeared and there was a village with about thirty to fifty houses ahead of them. They could see the blacksmith's shack ahead of them, obviously the source of the noises they heard in the forest. Priscus passed Caleb and went to the front of the group.

"Yeah, this is it," said Priscus. "I've sailed by this place too many times to count but haven't stopped here in years. You cannot miss that big red roof over there." He pointed to a two-story inn that had been painted red. "We will find everything we need around there." He stayed in front as everyone walked into the village center via the forested trail. A few of the villagers looked up at them and waved. Eliza immediately waved back, and she asked two of them how they were doing.

"Priscus, I am already glad you are with us," Eliza declared. "Here is the first thing I want you to do. Can you find two rooms for us at a dockside inn and reserve four seats on the next boat to Rome?" For a new slaveowner, Eliza was behaving most cordially.

"Yes, Ms. Eliza. I am on it. You may get some food ordered in the village center. I will come and find you after I talk to the dock-master." Eliza handed him the gold he needed for four tickets to Rome, and Priscus walked away. She motioned for Balbi to follow him. Caleb and Eliza were now alone, and she took a moment to hold her cousin.

"Thank you, again, for looking out for me. I don't know what I would have done without you," she said. Caleb put his hand on her head delicately and kissed the top of her head. He knew that a soft touch filled her soul. But he, too, was reflecting on the boat wreck and had not yet had any privacy to talk to her about it.

"Last night, during my watch, I thought that you might have drowned. I should have made you jump off the boat before me. I feel like I left you." Eliza could tell he was feeling guilty. She knew that he and Priscus had been moving dead bodies from the water before sunrise, thinking she was still asleep. She knew that he was willing to go to any means to protect her.

"You led me by example. There is no greater form of leadership. That is what our King David did many times. I am so grateful you were there for me." Eliza kissed Caleb and looked him in the eye. Caleb's soul was now just as filled as hers.

"Come on. Let's enter the tavern and make the world think we are lovers again!" he said. Eliza laughed and interlocked her fingers in his, and they walked into town, smiling and greeting everyone they met.

This hamlet had a unique blend of greenery and rocky seafront, a geography unknown anywhere in ancient Judah. Caleb had not seen these varieties of trees before. Eliza had no interest in a conversation about treescapes, but she also was not going to leave Caleb's side. Caleb's hunger was starting to get the best of him and he wanted to go straight for the tavern at the center of town. On the way, Eliza made a quick stop at the village center market. She stopped Caleb to engage some of the shopkeepers before their two new slaves returned. She knew that they were close to Rome and she had no idea what Roman fashion or Roman cuisine looked like. After all, she was in another part of the Roman Empire for the first time in her life, and everything seemed exciting. She all but forgot that she was shipwrecked yesterday. She surveyed the vendors and shoppers in the market, looking for those engaged in larger buying or selling operations. She engaged them in conversation, casually trying to inquire about the price of cinnamon here. She carried her pack full of cinnamon, though it was a bit wet. After sharing what it was worth it, she responded with absolutely no body language and thanked them for their help. Caleb reminded her of his hunger and they moved quickly towards the inn. Once they were out of hearing range, she turned and whispered.

"Our cinnamon is worth nearly three times as much as when we bought it back home!" she said, unable to hold back her joy. "Good, but I am hungry," Caleb said. He knew that Eliza needed something other than attempted rape and shipwreck to occupy her mind, and she loved nothing more than a fall Shabbat dance and bartering in the marketplace.

Priscus and Balbi met them as they arrived on the porch outside of the two-story inn and tavern. They also seemed happy.

"I talked to the dockmaster, and it turns out we know some of the same people," said Priscus, smiling. We got four seats to Rome on the next boat," he said, proud of his announcement. Eliza clapped for him and thanked him repeatedly.

The act of re-entering civilization had revitalized all of them. Priscus saw a future back on the sea and Balbi's shame from attempting to rape Eliza was fading and he was able to look at the two young Ebreet and speak.

"I know this village. It will have everything any of us need. This was my favorite port of call," Balbi said.

"What did you discover at the docks about our sunken ship?" Eliza asked Priscus.

"Against all odds, my captain was rescued, as were some of the others on the boat, and they will be continuing to travel to Rome as soon as they can. The local synagogue has put them up in their food storage room. Apparently, they have an outreach for people stranded in the middle of their sea passage, offering food and lodging in exchange for labor. Unfortunately, young masters, nothing is going to Rome today, but there is a vessel leaving tomorrow morning going straight to Rome, and you now have first-class seats." Eliza was excited about seeing the captain and continuing their voyage.

"Let's celebrate with a hot meal," Eliza said.

Caleb led them into the inn using the double doors on the front side that faced the market. The restaurant side of the establishment was relatively empty, as most people were still working or trading in the markets at that time of day. The server approached them, telling them to sit anywhere. Without asking, he brought out four clay mugs of ale, but Eliza politely declined on behalf of all of them. Instead, she got them to bring out some of the soup that they had already been cooking since mid-morning. It was hot and tasted wonderful. Everyone had two cups full before the server engaged them in conversation.

After a few moments of friendly chatter, the server asked them a question. "Would you like to join us tonight at the synagogue? We are talking about the scrolls of Isaiah and his prediction of the Messiah. They came true, you know?"

Caleb looked up at the server and Eliza for approval.

"We would love to," Caleb said.

Little did they know what impact their attendance would have.

Chapter 18:
A Sinner Meets a Savior

With food now entering their stomachs, Eliza and Caleb had a lot of questions about sailing around the Mediterranean. Balbi and Priscus graciously answered every one of them. They wanted to know more about crossing it and what the different ports of call were like. She wanted to know about Alexandria, Gaul, Dalmatia, and Crete. In addition, their server reaffirmed where they were. Reggio was a three-day boat ride to Rome if the weather remained like it is now. Eliza also learned that the ship that they reserved space on served soup exclusively to keep their costs down.

"Why is there so much soup in this part of the world?" Eliza wondered. She knew they needed to get something else to eat for the rest of the trip; otherwise, Caleb would get hungry and angry.

"Caleb, we need to go shopping," she said. Caleb rolled his eyes as he and Eliza did not see shopping in the same light. For her, it was a competitive sport. For him, dealing with a merchant was a utility needed to live life on life's terms.

"I am not shocked," he said with a tint of sarcasm.

The server also told them that this was the low season to travel to Rome. The seas by the coast of Rome were a bit unpredictable in the winter, so no one looked forward to traveling on what could be rough and windy seas. That might be why they so readily found first-class tickets less than a day before sailing. The anxiety of rough seas overcame Eliza again, and she responded by purchasing a second cloak for herself, made strictly of Egyptian cotton. She bought it because it was the warmest garment she had worn, and, for once in her life, the price didn't matter. Caleb told her that hypothermia could have killed her, and she planned for it. He liked her response, though, about trying to make sure that what hurt her before couldn't hurt her again. Dor would be proud, too. It meant that she had learned something in the house of healing.

After they finished their meal and the shopping, they spent the afternoon talking to villagers and hearing stories about this part of the world, all while standing on dry ground. They found comfort in the fact that the earth wasn't moving beneath their feet, and they could relax. The sun was bright and the air was dry, so Caleb and Eliza set out their wet cinnamon sticks on some rocks in a clearing off the trail they had used to walk into the village. They told Balbi to keep watch over the drying cinnamon; once he saw that it was dry, they told him to repack it in their bags. They left him and wandered the town for no other reason than to wander. They laughed at how easy it was to walk on the ground compared to the deck of a moving ship.

That evening, as the sun began to set, their server from earlier found all four of them sitting by the docks, just where he told them to be.

"Thank you for honoring your word and meeting me. As you can imagine, not everyone does."

Caleb smiled and knew what the man was talking about.

"My father invited many people to come and visit him in Tamar, and they said yes more than they said no. However, few came and he would take the same tone that you are using now. I understand what you are feeling and respect you." That gave the man confidence.

" Let me introduce myself now that I am no longer at work." He was not a native Greek speaker, and everyone in the group was curious as to what he called home.

"My name is Avi. I am from Laodicea. Now, I live here. The synagogue I spoke of is a short walk north from the port up that hillside." He pointed to the top of a partially blocked hill.

"Come! Follow me." He began walking towards the path.

Caleb knew from his father's teachings that getting people to follow someone required one person to be enthusiastically responsive. Despite not wanting to sit through a revival celebration, Caleb quickly stood up and followed Avi up the hill. He knew this evening was more to win the souls of Balbi and Priscus than for him and his cousin to sing and dance. Caleb followed Avi, and everyone followed Caleb.

Avi ran ahead of them and was waiting for them before they reached the entrance to the synagogue, holding plates of warm bread, hummus, and dried fish. There were others like him, also offering food to those who were arriving, and there were thick wooden tables outside of the entrance where everyone was sitting and eating their meal. They were all talking and laughing, and Eliza sat herself down with a group of younger women and introduced herself. She showed them her new cloak and they, in turn, all shifted their conversation to shopping. Caleb lost interest in watching his cousin and spoke to Balbi and Priscus instead.

"These Gentiles remind me a lot of the people back home at my synagogue," Caleb observed. Neither Balbi nor Priscus knew what he was talking about, so Caleb decided to use this as a teaching moment.

"Did you know that the Messiah and His disciples used free food more than once to bring together a group to teach them? This strategy is nearly 100 years old." Neither of the men knew that, and they began asking Caleb other questions about the Messiah and his followers. Others gathered to listen. Caleb hoped their curiosity would continue after they entered the synagogue and listened to the teacher.

Meanwhile, the women at Eliza's table listened to her tell her story of the shipwreck. They, too, had many questions. She did the best she could to describe swimming in the sea and sleeping by the shore next to a fire, but she couldn't explain her desire to extend grace to Balbi. These women were believers and Eliza asked them if they would pray for Priscus and Balbi.

As the sky turned a deep red and the sunset was nearly complete, the synagogue rabbi came outside to call them to come inside, carrying a lamp to light the way. As they rose to enter the building, he reminded them not to bring any food in with them and to take off their sandals upon entry.

As Caleb and Eliza approached the entryway and got their chance to greet this rabbi, he stopped them. "Wait. Aren't you Mishi's boy?" he asked Caleb.

"I am," Caleb responded. He knew what was coming next. The rabbis in the house of healing had prepared him. An ongoing loss occurs for someone who loses a celebrity parent or sibling and they meet people who don't know yet.

"How are your parents?"

"I am sorry to tell you this, but my father and mother were killed by Roman soldiers about two weeks ago," he said, looking the rabbi in the eyes. The rabbi was visibly upset and Caleb hugged him.

"I am sorry for your loss," the rabbi replied thoughtfully.

"Thank you very much. Please pray for my cousin and me. That will help us." Caleb put a single hand on the man's shoulder and walked into the synagogue.

This man knew Caleb's parents, but he was a stranger to Caleb. This was not the moment to discuss his parents' demise. Yet, the rabbi's sympathetic words brought up feelings of loss, and Eliza could see that Caleb was hurting. Eliza held Caleb's hand as soon as she saw that her hero was wounded.

After they entered, they met the other rabbi. He also greeted them, placing his hand on their foreheads and blessing them in the Ebreet tradition. As a woman, Eliza expected no such blessing since tradition prevented male and female touching in public unless they were immediate family. She attempted to walk past the rabbi unobtrusively, but he touched her forehead anyway, offering her the same blessing as the men. She was stunned by this instance of cultural and boundary-crossing. These people were Gentiles, and she needed to make peace with the differences.

"Caleb, these people aren't like us, but they know the same Yeshua that we do. But this is still weird," she said.

Eliza remembered how her aunt would teach that Yeshua did not come exclusively for the Ebreet but for every man and woman. She taught this message, reading from the Scriptures she had helped to transcribe. This man obviously had read those teachings and was implementing them his way. In Gentile fashion, this man wanted

Eliza to feel good and know she was loved. Once Eliza saw that message, the night became easier for her.

The message tonight came in the form of storytelling, very much like the way Rabbi Luke taught Caleb's parents. The rabbi shared a story of his recent trip to Rome to visit several men in prison who used to be members of a group he knew and loved. His tale was lively and he told everyone that they were being well taken care of by the local ministry, not wanting food or provisions. He also shared that one of the prison guards had become a Yeshuian. The rabbi told them he had traveled one evening with the guard to their underground synagogue and saw great acts of God's grace despite the structure existing within walking distance of Curia Julia, the home of the Roman Senate. He ended the evening by calling anyone who had not yet believed the message of Yeshua's resurrection to come forward and profess their faith.

Before he could finish his alter call, Balbi went forward. The rabbi greeted him and spoke loud enough for all to hear.

"Do you accept that you are a sinner and that you need a Redeemer to be right with Your maker?" the rabbi asked.

Balbi looked up at the rabbi as a boy might look at his father after he was caught stealing a loaf of bread from a neighbor. "Yes," he said timidly.

"Do you accept the forgiveness of sins that our Messiah offers you, promising to give your life to Him and to serve Him?"

"Yes," he said, this a bit more loudly.

"Just as John the Baptist did many years ago, I baptize you with water to symbolize your commitment to Yeshua. He extends His mercy to you that you may have eternal life. Go forth, Balbi." The rabbi took a small container of water and poured it on Balbi's head.

The next moments were powerful and meaningful for everyone in attendance, but none more than Balbi. The congregation all stood up and began to cheer and clap. Balbi was amazed by the applause. He rubbed the water from his eyes before raising his hands to the sky, asking, "Am I saved yet?" The congregation laughed and applauded, affirming his public profession of faith.

Caleb shook his head and exhaled a single shallow breath with force.

"Had I killed that man, this day would have never come," he whispered to Eliza. She looked him in the eyes and nodded; then, she rested her head on his chest for the moment. Then, she said what she had to say.

"Your mother and father would have been so proud of you, Caleb," she said, looking up and awaiting him to make eye contact with her.

"Kiss me, my warrior," she said, and Caleb poured his affection into her, wrapping her in a hug and telling her that he was grateful that she was so quick to forgive Balbi.

That moment was magical for Eliza. She realized that she needed to validate her cousin if they were going to complete this trip to Rome, meet the emperor, and return to Judah without dying. Caleb had restrained himself by not killing Balbi, and he was now starting to see the fruit of that choice to hold back administering justice. She needed to be more like her father than her mother. She needed to be the giver of affirmation and support, not the recipient all the time.

"Caleb, I love you. You are my hero," she said.

Those were the words of affirmation that the teenage boy needed. He closed his eyes and smiled. Caleb bent his chin down, kissing the top of Eliza's head, rubbing it as he knew she liked. They released after a moment as the congregation began to leave. They politely shared Ebreet goodbyes with others in attendance, noting how few knew to say *kol tuv* at the end of a ceremony in the synagogue.

Eliza and Caleb waited outside for Balbi and Priscus to join them, and Eliza told the women about how happy she was that Caleb didn't kill Balbi. All four of them walked back to the inn, listening to Balbi tell stories of his past without interruption. Once they made it to the inn, Priscus and Balbi retired to their rooms, as did Caleb and Eliza. With a single candle to light their room, Eliza and Caleb spoke about what lay ahead of them.

"Tomorrow, we get back on a boat. It seems like a month has passed since we last sailed," Eliza mused.

"You have matured a lot since we left Rome," said Caleb. She stared at the wall, realizing that he was right. The urgency of what lay ahead became a worry.

"Caleb, how are we going to get to speak with the emperor once we get there?"

"I do not know, but we will find help. I know you want a better answer, but I don't have one. Knowing we will find help is part of my faith, Eliza. I do not need to know in advance. I need courage in the present. Why else do you think I like to hunt?"

She had no response that included words, but she felt incomplete and small in a way that she hadn't felt since she ran away from her parents while they were in shackles. Caleb had something that she did not. He had peace about the future in a way that made her jealous.

Caleb blew out the candle and told her to go to sleep. He said a final prayer himself before closing his eyes. "Lord, thank you for not letting me kill that man. I know he deserved it, but what happened tonight was powerful. Please forgive me for my crimes in the same way you forgave Balbi for his crimes. Amen."

Eliza had her own prayer.

"Great God. Please give me places to be courageous like my cousin. When they come, please give me the awareness that they are upon me and teach me to be like Caleb. Amen."

Chapter 19:
Visions of Bravery

The bedding at the inn was much nicer to sleep on than the shoreline from the night before, and Caleb woke up refreshed. He went for a morning run while Eliza slept, and he took a bath using hot water for the first time in over a week. Finally, Eliza woke up, and Caleb told her to take a bath and start packing. Caleb was very excited and Eliza asked him what happened this morning to energize him.

"I spent time at the docks looking at our new ride. I saw the old captain and he is safe and wishes us well."

"Wow, that is wonderful news. I must see him!" she said. Caleb continued with some smaller conversations, but one sentence stood out above the others.

"You know, half that boat was full of women, and you were the only one to survive the wreck," he said without looking up as he stowed his bedroll on the bottom of his pack. He had no idea that his words had made an impact on her. He was too focused on packing the sheep bladders that saved their lives just two days ago.

"The only woman?" she asked rhetorically. Caleb didn't look up, as he already knew that to be true. He responded with a single grunt.

"Yup."

Eliza had her gear in her hands and just stared at Caleb as he innocuously worked. She was caught in deep thought as she remembered one of her aunt's teachings. The words made sense for the first time.

"Remember how your mom used to teach that prayer is timeless?"

"Yeah. What about it?" Caleb said as he began to seal his bag.

"God hears all of our prayers. It is when we say them that we know they are prayers. Remember how many people prayed for us before we left?"

"Yeah," he said, finally looking up at her.

"All those prayers helped. I think that is why I am alive." He looked up at her.

"That makes sense," he said.

"You know what else? There are times in life when we pray for something and it isn't until we pray that we realize we already have it. It was the act of praying that brought it to your attention." He nodded at her.

"I think about that as I am shooting my bow," Caleb said.

She decided she needed to hear his opinion on something before drawing any conclusions. She had been thinking about it since they went to bed.

"Caleb, this is a serious question, so no dumb answers," she said, trying to be authoritative. Caleb did not stop to look at her but inspected her bladder for leaks or small holes.

"Do you think it was courageous to jump off the boat and swim to shore?" she asked timidly.

Caleb paused and looked at her. He could sense that she was feeling shaky. He decided to answer this the way he thought his father might.

"Somewhat. But it was common sense, too. The boat was not going to float much longer, and we needed to get off of it to survive. But, yeah, it was brave, especially for you or someone like you," he said. That wasn't exactly a perfect answer, but it did make her feel brave.

She nodded, causing Caleb to ask her why.

"When I prayed last night, I asked for God to give me bravery under duress like you have," she said. Caleb set down the bladder and crossed the room to where her wooden framed bed sat in the corner. He put his arms around her waist and pulled her into him, almost as if she was his lover. She rested her head on his chest for a moment; then, he pushed her away so he could look at her while he answered.

"Eliza, it is my job to be brave for both of us. That is how God designed us. I go into battle, and I fight for you. Sure, you are brave, but not in the same way that I am. God has made us man and woman, and we do not have the same calling. My mom and dad were ridiculously brave people to the minute that they died. But it wasn't the same kind of bravery. You know, of all things in this world, you need not worry about having too much gold, and I won't worry about stockpiling too much bravery," he said. He kissed her on the forehead, grabbed his bag, and walked out the door. He yelled out as he walked down the hall towards the exit.

"Hurry up. Let's go," he yelled out.

That is what the affirmation she needed. She grabbed her bag and ran to catch him.

Chapter 20:
Prophecy

It took three minutes to walk from the tavern to the docks despite stopping to buy fresh bread in the market. As they reached the docks, Caleb noted how deep the waters next to the shore and the docks were. The docks were smaller than any of the ones in Judah and barely extended into the Mediterranean, but they could handle any vessel of any size. The shortened walk from dry land to the boat decks reduced loading and unloading time.

They were surprised to find the rabbi waiting for them at the docks.

"I was hoping to meet you. I want to bless you one last time before you leave," he cheerfully said.

As they gave their tickets to the deckhand responsible for boarding everyone and their gear, the rabbi blessed Balbi with the sign of the cross on his forehead and he graciously received it. Eliza had never seen that before, but she loved it.

"I am going to do that," she said, obviously excited.

"Balbi, I wish you well on your travels. You always have a place to stay when you come here," the rabbi said. The rabbi wished the new brother good travels and waved at him as he stepped onto the boat.

"Young Ebreet, stay with me," he said. Once Balbi was gone, the rabbi began speaking to them quietly in their native Ebreet.

"On our journey through life, I have found that all of us have a moment when a small part of our story seems bigger than our whole life. I say that because the Holy Spirit came upon me and gave me a prophecy for you two that I must share with you. I see your next steps will define the pathway you take for generations to come."

They had heard Caleb's father have similar prophecies. They could see the passion in the man's eyes, as tears were flowing like a small river. They knew to listen to the rabbi's next words as if they came directly from the Torah.

He adjusted his robe, closed his eyes, as rabbis often did, and began rocking back and forth. Displaying his mild obesity without shame, he raised his hands and began to speak. His voice cracked, as it often did during these visions. He hummed for a moment before he started prophesizing.

"I saw a scroll being written and the scroll was the story of your family's lives. The first pages included the story of your parents and the middle pages included your story." He paused to take a deep breath.

"Then, the story is of a generation of disciples and students who follow you. Caleb will worship and work for the Lord by the water, and he will lead thousands. Eliza shall worship the Lord as she calls disciples from all walks of life, her direct followers more so than the numbers of the Messiah. Their number shall be nearly a century and will reflect a name and position bestowed by the emperor. Then, of these students, another one shall come. She will come from the most humble of society. She will become beautiful and strong and fearless, and she will be the Lord's possession. She will share the same necklace as you and she will be the most powerful woman in the world, yet her job shall be to serve and feed people across the empire. She shall mentor those who would otherwise not be mentored, and her power shall be hidden while she is in public and beyond imagination during the moments she is in private. And each of you shall mentor her and her parents in profound ways. So says our Lord."

Eliza and Caleb looked at each other in disbelief. They didn't know what to say, and the rabbi continued.

Eliza opened her mouth, about to speak, but no words came out. She looked at Caleb.

The rabbi lowered his hands and opened his eyes. He put his hand on their shoulders. "Little Ones, I have no knowledge of what you are doing in Rome. Your parents' death has grieved us all. Yet I can see that your life is soon to become royal like that of Joseph, although I do not know how."

Finally, words came to Eliza. "Was there anything in your dream about what we do after we arrive in Ostia?"

"I see the two of you before a great throne, opening your hands and extending a gift to a man who sits on that throne. I do not know who he is, nor do I know what the gift might be. I have asked Elohim to show me what the man on the throne gives you, but I have not understood the image. It appears that he extends back to you what you gave him, but it now contains both confidence and power."

"What do you mean you do not understand the image?" asked Caleb, a bit perplexed.

"It appears that he dismisses you, but you do not leave."

The two Ebreet looked at each other, checking if the other understood the message. They were equally perplexed.

"Thank you, teacher," Eliza said earnestly. "That gives me some courage, but I don't know what you are talking about."

"How is it that you feel courage?" asked the rabbi in a curious tone.

"I will tell you our story so far," said Caleb. Caleb put his arm around Eliza and pulled her in close to himself and they walked towards a more secluded spot off the pier. Caleb had finally decided that this man was trustworthy. He paused for a moment before telling the rabbi what had happened since Eliza had arrived in Tamar a few weeks ago.

"I can see that this prophecy has already started. The man on the throne is Titus. I am beginning to see what the writer in my dreams was recording."

Caleb and Eliza saw their new captain standing at the top of the plank, yelling for them to hurry up and get on the boat. The two of them turned, raising their hands in acknowledgment.

"We have to go now, rabbi," said Eliza. Before leaving, Caleb reached into the stash of Eliza's village's coins and he went to give one small bag of them to the rabbi. He looked Eliza in the eye, checking for her approval before handing the man the coins. She nodded.

"May the Messiah remain alive and well in your community. May these coins help you do that." He used words that he had heard his father use.

"Young man, you sound like your father, even if you do not look like him," said the rabbi. Caleb wanted to laugh out loud. He did not tell the rabbi any part of that story. This would not be a good moment to tell the rabbi that he was not biologically his father's son.

"You might want to try to stop killing Romans, especially if you need their help," said the rabbi with a chuckle.

They turned and quickly walked back onto the deck of the heavy wooden sailing ship, pausing briefly to turn around and wave the chubby rabbi farewell. As they went below decks to visit their home for the next three days, they saw Balbi.

"I will guard your stuff, Masters. I will protect it with my life, as you have spared mine twice."

"Thank you, Balbi," said Eliza. She chose to believe that Balbi would be loyal to them. They climbed the steps from the lower deck to the top deck and walked to the front of the boat to watch the ship's departure.

Eliza had a moment of anxiety once the land was too far away to swim to. Today's seas were not completely calm; however, there was also no fear of capsizing. The sky was clear, with no clouds in sight, and the low humidity of the winter breeze felt relaxing. She clung to Caleb much of the morning, but soon, she was walking around and talking to the other passengers. Since they were near the bottom corner of Italy and preparing to turn North towards Rome, the crew asked everyone to gather around the captain for a brief message.

"Ahead of us are the straits of Messene," said the captain, "with a long history of humbling watercraft and crew. We are going to take this vessel right through the middle because that is where it is safest." He said more, but his tone was not anxious.

"He'll get no argument from me!" said the passenger standing behind Eliza. They turned around and greeted a young trader. After a few more moments, the captain finished his briefing, and everyone returned to the task of being a passenger and enjoying their trip to Rome.

"So, are you on your way to Rome to make a small fortune for yourself?" As usual, Caleb was making assumptions as he spoke to the man who spoke up earlier.

"No. Not a chance. I am looking to make a big fortune!" That made Eliza smile.

Caleb recognized the color on the man's robes and identified him as one of the surviving members of the Sadducees. This group had wielded great power in old Jerusalem before the Temple was destroyed. The Sadducees were responsible for maintaining the Temple and several families were living next to his grandparents while he was a boy attending the Temple Mount school. Although the current generation no longer identified the color as that of a Sadducee, Caleb took the risk of his assumption. He had seen his father take such non-verbal risks in the past and felt no fear of failure.

Seeing this man's clothing reminded Caleb of a story that Caleb's father used to tell. Before the Temple fell, the Sadducees were a part of his father's life every day. However, once it fell, the remaining remnant of Ebreet blamed them for failing to protect it and their leaders were publicly stoned by the very stones that made up the Temple. The surviving members of their sect fled and scattered around Judah, and some of them ended up in Tamar. Many mainstream Ebreet considered them to be traitors and failures before God, having not protected the Temple as they had vowed to. A few individual families remained; many of them had become merchants, bartering with Romans and Ebreet and initiating commerce.

"Did you enjoy the stop in that town back there?" the trader asked. "I do not remember seeing you on the boat out of Joppa. Were you on a different boat?"

"We were on a different one," said Eliza. She grabbed Caleb's arm, knowing that her cousin was prone to saying too much if she did not jump into the conversation. "We came here yesterday on a different boat. We visited the synagogue last night and spoke with the rabbi before boarding. Did you get to attend any of the services there?"

"I did not. We were in this port town for less than a day, and I did not want to. People can be mean, you know?"

Hearing those words validated Caleb's assumption. He knew what to say. All that remained was to imitate his father.

"The synagogue experience is unique now, especially for those of us who have had an experience with the Messiah. Isn't it wonderful to be rid of the burdens placed on us by the sins of our past?" Caleb asked. The man remained a bit defensive with his body language and didn't say anything. Caleb let the conversation pause do its work before continuing.

"When the Messiah appeared, everyone thought that He was coming to save us from the oppression of Roman occupation, in the same way that Yahweh saved our ancestors from Pharaoh and Nebuchadnezzar. But He was not here to repeat what His Father had done. He came to fulfill Yahweh's promises that we learned in the scrolls of Isaiah."

"You are not the first person to tell me this," the trader said, staring into the distance.

"What did you hear before?" asked Eliza.

"What you said. But there were more words used."

"Did you consider what you heard by comparing it to the ancient scrolls? A man of your stature must surely be able to read and write in our sacred language."

"No, I did not. I am proud of my family, but I do not want to shame them." Caleb put a hand on the man's shoulder and turned so they were looking in the same direction.

"You know, my parents were teachers of the ancient scrolls and of the message of the Messiah. I will wager that you are a descendant of a Sadducee family," Caleb said, pausing long enough for the words to germinate an honest answer. The man looked briefly at Caleb before looking away. He had been discovered.

As a sign of surrender and respect, Caleb unsheathed his blade and let it fall onto the wooden deck. He put his hand on the man's shoulder and took a single deep breath.

"Why did you just surrender to me?" the man asked.

"So you see that I do not judge you. The message of surrender is central to the sacred scrolls, now that they are complete,"

Eliza could sense that the man wanted more. She began teaching, speaking boldly. Certainly, no Sadducee had experience listening to a woman teach, but the stage had been set, and she was the most qualified person to tell the story.

"The Temple had to fall for the prophecies of Isaiah to come to pass. It was not your family's fault that the Temple fell, no matter how many people have been mean to you. Yahweh required the Temple to fall to show the world that His Son was here," she said, standing close to Caleb.

The man lifted his chin and stared straight ahead. He was formulating words to attach to his thoughts, and they came out slowly. He did not know how to process that he was standing with others who knew of his family history yet were not condemning or scorning him. This was rare, indeed. He spoke slowly.

"My parents were good people. My grandparents and parents had to leave Jerusalem immediately after the Temple fell. We had to take up a disguise to avoid people from stoning us to death for dereliction of duty," he shared. Caleb held his chin and nodded, prompting the man to continue. He and Eliza knew to be patient and let the man share how he created his new world order.

"What could my parents have done to stop any of that? My father was an accountant for the Temple and the Temple school. Those two behemoths that walked up the hill and into the city walls could not have been stopped by any Sadducees," he said with a rhetorical question that he obviously had lingering in his heart for far too long.

Caleb knew that a bit of humility and humor would help all of them through this moment—at least, that was what he was taught.

"My father watched the two behemoths come and he said they smelled bad and were very noisy," he said. That made the man laugh, and he began to speak more openly. And he felt comfortable expressing himself and telling stories from that dark window in his family's past.

For the rest of the day, Eliza explained to the Sadducee the full tale of Yeshua and His message, using the writings from the sacred scrolls that her aunt had taught her. The young man reciprocated with equal openness and shared many tales of his youth during the time his family had fled Jerusalem nearly seventeen years ago while he was nine years old. He asked her some questions, most of which she could either not answer or partially answer. Soon, the sun was ready to set, and all of them were hungry as they had spent the day outside on the deck. Eliza was grateful that she had purchased the thicker cloak and wool scarf. Despite the cold, Caleb and the Sadducee looked a bit sunburned.

"So, now that we have shared this with you, what do you feel in your heart?" asked Eliza. "Do you believe it possible that Yeshua fulfilled the Scripture of our ancestors and was the Messiah?" This was the question that she had been taught to ask once she had finished telling her stories. Her aunt had told her one day at dinner that during the time she would tell the story of Yeshua, she would hear a unique song in her soul. Eliza had not understood what her aunt meant until that moment. A resonance in her soul started as she shared with this man and asked him if he believed.

One of her aunt's teachings came to life and Eliza could hear her aunt talking to her as she spoke.

"Eliza, it is your job to ask; it is the listener's job to accept or refuse. The difference between these jobs must not be confused. It is not upon you nor your story to convince any man or woman to believe in the Messiah. You must open your mouth and tell your story," she would teach.

"I think so. Yes, my family were sinners, and I am a sinner, as well. I can see your point that we all are sinners and in need of a Savior. I did not think that He came to save us from our sins; I thought he was here to save us from the Romans." He began to laugh, and a single tear flowed from his eye.

"Followers of The Way need to eat," said Caleb, breaking the tension. "Let's go get some food since it looks like you are one of us now." Caleb put his entire left arm around the man and his right arm around Eliza, and they walked towards the passenger kitchen, where an unending bowl of soup was awaiting them every day for the next three days.

"Yes, I am one of you, I believe," he shared as they started walking.

This was Eliza's first opportunity to lead another Ebreet to Yeshua. She had seen her aunt and uncle do it, but she had not seen her parents do it, as nearly everyone in Correae already believed. The resonance her aunt spoke of was now loud, and she felt it. It was more than her aunt described. It was poetry. It was a song. It was fulfilling.

The man reached into his royal robes, pulled out a purse of coin, and handed it to them. "Please take this for what you shared with me today."

Eliza raised her hand and refused his offering. Instead, she quoted a portion of the Torah to him. "During the Exodus, the Lord said to Moses, 'Tell the people to bring Me an offering. You are to receive the offering for me from everyone whose heart prompts them to give.' You have been prompted to give. However, please save this to give to one of our underground synagogues in Rome. We have been taught that these synagogues are growing and they need all the help that they can get." He bowed, a sign that he agreed to their conditions.

"I will do that," he said. The man bent over, picked up Caleb's sword, and gave it back to him.

"I don't think I would have listened to you if you hadn't done that. You are a bit scary," said the man, which made Eliza laugh.

They all ate dinner together, talking with other passengers during the meal. They asked everyone why they were traveling to Rome. Many had brought cargo with them to trade. Some had come for education. Some were returning from visits abroad. Some were going to work in the city's public works projects, and some were there to relieve family who had finished a four-month shift on service in Thessalonica and were getting a break. Rome was a melting pot of all the world's cultures and trades, unlike any place in the Promised Land, including Jerusalem, and this boat's passengers reflected that diversity.

The next day, they finished traversing the straits of Messene and the captain yelled down to everyone from the deck. "We have seen the worst of the dangerous currents. We will ride the shore to your right and the east all the way to Rome. This shall be an easy journey, now."

The trader gave Caleb a warm embrace. "Thank you for restoring my family's honor. My elders could not accept their loss of dignity after the Temple was destroyed. I will tell them of Yeshua and show them the same words of the Torah that you showed me, and I pray that they will rest better."

Caleb smiled at the man and put his arm on his shoulder. For a moment, he felt like his mother and father with him, smiling down upon him and were pleased.

"It was my pleasure," he said, bowing his head in respect, as was customary among the Sadducees.

The remaining days passed just as the captain said. They arrived well-rested in Rome early on the fourth day.

Chapter 21:
After the Fire

As the boat entered the mouth of the Tiber River, there were multiple slips from which to dock the watercraft. There were some for fishermen as well as a large one for the military. The most important port was Ostia, which was meant for commerce. It was closest to the city. As they arrived, many of the slips at Ostia were filled with slaving vessels, nearly all coming in from Africa to the south and uncivilized lands to the west. It was clear that the city had been recently damaged by a fire, as some of the docks were burned and unusable. The captain sailed past many ships waiting to dock at Ostia, and the scenes on the decks of those ships were unlike anything that either Caleb or Eliza had heard of.

The decks of the slavers were filled with dark-skinned Egyptian men and women. The slaves were all chained together and they were talking out loud in an unknown language. At first, Eliza thought it was Egyptian, but it didn't sound like it, and she couldn't tell where these people were from. Most were barely clothed and appeared to be freezing and angry. The voices were loud and anytime any of them made a move, they would get whipped. Eliza turned her head away from the violence. Once they passed the last of the slave ships, they entered the section of the port meant for citizen passenger services. Their boat slowed to a near crawl and they were within a rope's throw from their dock as Eliza started asking Balbi some questions. She knew he could understand them.

"What were they saying?"

"They want to know what they are going to do in the city. The man on the shore said they are going to help rebuild the city since the fire."

"Fire?" Eliza said with curiosity.

"It's been a bad year. When I first arrived, the city was burning. Yet, it remained open for business. You know the Romans." Rome was notorious for allowing commerce to continue unfettered, no matter the needs of the poor.

"But what caused it?" she asked.

"Some people said that the old emperor caused it. Some say that Yeshuians started the fire. You know, there are a lot of them here now and some people believe that they did it. I do not believe that, though. I do not know many of you, but none of the ones that I know do things like that." Eliza pressed him for more hypotheses about the cause of the fire.

"Most of the people I know think it was just an accident. You go walking through the different regions of the city and you can see that the Romans do not care about most of the people in this city who aren't Roman royalty. Slave quarters and housing for simple folks are close together and it gets cold and windy in the winter. I think the wind caused a cooking fire to jump from house to house and quarter to quarter. One thing is for sure, though. This new emperor has spent a lot of time trying to rebuild things quickly. No matter who caused it, he is cleaning it up and rebuilding it with purpose. Gotta like that."

Caleb and Eliza were so intent on listening to Balbi's story that they did not notice that their boat was next to unload. Balbi and Caleb gathered all their stuff while Balbi continued.

"The most important thing the new emperor did after the last of the fires were put out was to finish building the Coliseum for all the fighting that people around here love to see. That place is unique on the whole earth! You have to see it one day. That is where everyone goes to have a good time and to do people-watching."

The boat finally came to rest at their slip at the dock. Men from the port immediately jumped onto the boat's main deck, going directly to the captain. They were looking forward to collecting docking fees and getting a copy of the written manifest showing who was on the boat and how much weight in goods they were carrying. They charged a tax per head on board and a tax per human weight of gear and it was the captain's job to pay that sum before anyone or any goods could leave the vessel. To make sure, four Roman soldiers dressed in the most exquisite of armor stood next to the plank, holding javelins in their hands, awaiting the word to allow passengers and cargo exit. Or to kill them. During that moment, everyone's fate was in the hands of the captain, and emotions ran high.

The captain gave them the required coins and the Roman in charge said, "Welcome home, my friends," in open Greek, the kind that everyone spoke.

Caleb picked up his stuff and told Balbi to get the rest. He exhaled once and turned to Eliza.

"The time for talk about how to get to Rome and see the emperor is now complete. Now that we are here, we need to go to him. Let's go."

Eliza took Caleb's hand and followed him into the unknown.

Chapter 22:
Finding What Was Right
in Front of You

The Sadducee whom they had met on the boat left quickly, leaving the harbor area in a great hurry. "I know I will see you again," he said with confidence as he shuffled away. Eliza realized that she had failed to learn the man's name and she felt ashamed.

"What is your name?" she called out.

He put his bags down and told his slaves to stop. "My name is Barkhi. 'Barkhi Hyrcanus of the Manasseh tribe on the coast.' That's what we call ourselves as we speak to others in our sect."

"You are just Barkhi to us," said Caleb from afar. Caleb and Eliza waved at the man as he and his slave left.

"Caleb, you made a difference in his life," Eliza said. Caleb smiled at her and said the obvious. Caleb smiled.

"It is time to go and face this unknown." She knew him to know that he was feeling good and would be at his best. She trusted his leadership and was proud to stand with him.

In front of them stood the most architecturally glorious and culturally sinister place in the history of the human race. It was the capital of the greatest man-made empire, home to statues and architecture known around the world. It was the melting pot of nearly all of the world's ethnicities, and it was the greatest port of commerce in the world. Just the sounds and sights from the docks made the outskirts of Rome a mesmerizing sight.

"Balbi, get those bags, and let's go," said Caleb. Balbi grabbed everyone's bags and they began to walk from the waterfront toward the Palatine Hills of downtown Rome.

"You two do not know what you are in for!" he said as he carried their bags off the boat.

Before they left the harbor district, they were aghast at a scene at the end of the docks where the Roman roads were connected. There was a series of twelve wagons, each with a covered top with open sides. There were between two and six women in each one, each wearing an untied outer cloak and a beautiful headdress. Almost by design, each woman's breasts were exposed, as were their upper legs. Eliza looked pale and spoke under her breath.

"Oh my Lord, the God of Abraham, Issac, and Jacob!" she said. Caleb laughed, as he had not heard Eliza take the Lord's name in vain before. His mother would use similar words as he would come inside the house with the best part of a deer, ready to cook it in a hot pan on the stove, dripping blood all over the floor and doorway. His mother, though, wouldn't stop there with her verbal excesses. She would also get sarcastic and ask if he was reenacting the "Damn Passover" as blood would drip everywhere and yell at him to get "that damn deer flesh out of my house!" The first time she did that, it was scary. Every time after that, it was funny.

It wasn't just the bare chests and legs of the women that caught Eliza's attention. Outside of each wagon was a queue of men waiting to pursue their services. The men were almost exclusively passengers and ship crew who had been sailing the Mediterranean for several weeks and looking to start their time in Rome with a sexual release.

"What are they doing in line?" asked Eliza. Before she finished her next breath, she ascertained what was occurring. Caleb looked at her and knew she was in shock and disbelief that these were not just fairy tales about the sensual nature of Rome. Rome was a heathen culture that had no equal in its depravity, and now, Eliza knew why. Neither Caleb nor Eliza could not stop staring at what they saw.

"You have not heard about this?" asked Balbi.

"I had heard the stories, but it took seeing to believe it," said Caleb. Caleb grabbed Eliza by her shoulder and turned her away from the wagons.

"Eliza, let's get you out of here. This is the evil that lies in the hearts of men that Solomon himself spoke about," he said to Eliza in the purest of Ebreet. She looked up at Caleb as he turned her away and she knew he had what was best for her in mind. His smile melted her heart.

"Ok?" he asked, trying to get her to keep walking. She moved slowly and knew he needed her to go faster so she didn't hear some of the awful words exchanged by the men standing in line.

"I am going to take care of you, but we need to move faster." She smiled and nodded as he instructed her where to walk and to keep her head down.

As they passed between the wagons, every sound from these portable brothels was now audible. Eliza knew the source of those sounds as she slept next to her parents and her mother explained what was happening with great embarrassment as she asked about those sounds. But she could not imagine two people doing and making all those noises for all to see and hear.

"Caleb?" Eliza said, with a sense of desperation. Caleb could feel Eliza's heart beating rapidly as she passed what she thought might have become of her had she been raped and decided she was no longer worthy of marriage.

"Eliza, just keep walking," Caleb said, guiding her through the maze of evil. Eliza thought of what her aunt was able to endure and survive, and she did exactly what her aunt taught her to do: she prayed.

"Yeshua, please let there be a day when women do not mate in the streets like this, talking filth and self-deprecating themselves. Restore our people to Your moral code and redeem us," she said.

For his part, Caleb looked around for the best way to walk but he, too, saw and heard everything. To cope, he focused on the workmanship of the paths and roads that they were now walking on. The roads were exquisitely crafted with stone and hewn brick in alternating color patterns. Some of the pathways that lead into Jerusalem and Hebron looked like this, but this was the first time that either of them had seen the "original" city that the roads and public works in ancient Judah were modeled after. Many of their families and friends were taught that God blessed the people of ancient Judah above all others. It took the teachings of Yael and Mishi to help them understand that the architectural achievements of Rome had long since dwarfed the greatest achievements of God's chosen people.

As they passed by the last of the wagons and set a distance between themselves and the open-air brothel, Caleb released his grip on Eliza and allowed her to look up. They stood at the intersection of a road that ran parallel to the river port and another one that went uphill into the heart of the city of Rome. There was a large stone arch in front of them and fountains were on each side, with water flowing from the mouths of a young boy and a young girl.

"Caleb, that was awful," she said. Caleb knew she was telling the truth, but he also remembered the exposed chest of one of the women they passed. She made eye contact with Caleb and winked at him. It was exhilarating. It left a mark inside of him as if a tattoo had been placed in a secret place in his heart, and he was embarrassed to tell Eliza about it.

Yet, what lay in front of them was the real part of Rome that all of the Empire knew to be its ultimate source of power. This was the entrance to the world's largest commerce center - the place where all people and all goods collide and become markets. Everything, without exception, was for sale here, including small armies, slaves, land, and freedom itself. The money changers were as large as their synagogue back home, and the smelters who tested and melted the precious metals and converted them into Roman coins were as numerous as the flies back home in the summer. Eliza was mesmerized by all of it.

At the center of each intersection and gateway to the markets was a piece of lapis lazuli. The blue rock was larger than a human head. Eliza had seen small pieces of the precious stone, and her mother had a necklace that her father bought her that had it as its centerpiece.

"That one piece of stone in the middle of this road is worth as much as all the land in Correae and all the houses that sit on top of it," Eliza exclaimed. The lavishness seemed unfathomable to her community's sense of financial stewardship. For her, the use of such a great amount of wealth for such a wasteful purpose was sinful. Yet, it was also compelling to stare at. It was the greatest single display of wealth she had seen.

"And to think that the horses just relieve their bowels on this beautiful stone," said Caleb as they stood close together and walked up the hill. He saw a cylindrical container half as tall as a man at the next intersection of the two paths. It was made of a pounded and thin silvery metal. "What is that?" he asked Balbi, walking towards it. He reached it and stared at it. It had a cover made of the same material that looked light and easy to remove and reattach.

"That, young master, is a garbage can," said Balbi with a laugh.

"What is it for?" Caleb was fascinated.

"The Romans have decided that refuse should not be discarded directly on the ground. Garbage of all sorts must be placed in these cans and each night, they are emptied by slaves who carry the contents either to the river or to the city burn pits." Eliza and Caleb looked at each other, first in amazement and then with a sense of respect.

"That is a good idea!" said Caleb, taking note of it.

"Caleb, it works, too. Look at how clean the streets here are!" Eliza said.

"Huh," said Caleb, noticing for the first time that there was no refuse on the ground. "Is that why the rivers are so brown and dirty?" he asked Balbi.

"Hard to say, but that river appears that disgusting brown color all year." Caleb chuckled at the irony of keeping the streets clean but the drinking water was filthy.

"My dad put something like this garbage can outside our synagogue, but he did not use metal. His was made of clay and the slaves emptied them twice a week. He and I would take turns going with the slaves to empty the pots," said Caleb.

"But the idea of doing that for everyone every day sounds ridiculous, but it's also wonderful! It means fewer rotting smells," Eliza added.

"Well, as you can tell, that didn't work too well," said Balbi, sarcastically pointing at the sky, reminding them that the air smelled of sickness.

The three of them finally left the garbage can and walked uphill for a few hundred steps. They reached the crest of the hill and stopped to look around. Ahead and downhill of them were more unknown structures and people but first, they turned around and looked back from whence they came. The colors at the dockside seemed more vibrant now that they were distant from them, with brownish water and brown boats giving way to dark slaves, light-skinned Gauls, and colorful clothing on nearly everyone buying and selling. Combined with the noises of all the languages being spoken on the top of the hill, it felt like they were watching one of the plays that they would see in an amphitheater at the end of each school year.

Caleb was fascinated at the lines of slaves of all skin colors steadily carrying items on their heads up the hill. He could not identify if the men in charge of the slaves were the buyers or the sellers of the merchandise, as they often spoke a language other than any of the four that he knew. Many turned off the main route and took parallel side streets, and they would appear moments later, carrying nothing at all on their heads. Moments later, they would reappear and climb up the hill with another load. It seemed like the lines of slaves were like lines of ants, coming and going all the time. They failed to stop moving, almost as if they were waves in the ocean.

There were baskets made of reeds that grew on the shores of the Nile, full of dolls for the rich children of the Roman nobility. There were small, human-drawn carts of bronze pots of all sizes and shapes. There were men wearing gloves carrying huge wheels of cheese with a smell unlike any they were familiar with. There was a large cart of pre-made torches being pulled by a huge horse. Caleb approached the cart and saw that the torches were soaked in a fluid that Caleb did not recognize. He learned from the vendor that they could burn all night and well into the next day before running out of the flammable liquid pre-soaked into them. It seemed like the parade of commerce might not end but soon, their hunger overtook their curiosity and they all agreed to find some food. They saw a cart two streets away with a vendor selling fresh bread and some thick soup, and they walked that way. They sat on their luggage bags and continued to stare at the sights and listen to the sounds of Rome.

"I want to see the Coliseum," said Caleb. He had heard more about the fabled battle hall than any other place. It had been under construction since before his birth and had recently been finished, and he wanted to see what it looked like compared to the drawings he had seen growing up. He was told it was the largest structure in the city and the highest levels of soldiers and mercenaries would go there to test their skills against each other. That was the place of greatest interest.

"Is that it?" Caleb asked Balbi.

"Yes, it sure is! Emperor Titus finished it in his first year as emperor," Balbi said, with a sense of pride. But then, he also extended some caution.

"I have no experience there, but I hear that it changes a man's soul to watch a fight to the death." Caleb knew that Eliza hated seeing animals die, so he knew she wouldn't like it. But he looked forward to seeing it more than he led on.

"From here, its walls seemed to be like that of a large egg, both oval in shape but with straight walls going upward into the sky." Caleb had read that in one of his father's letters and he could now see what the author meant as they wrote that note.

"And it has no roof," said Balbi.

"Come on, let's go there," Caleb said. Eliza had seen pictures, but she didn't know much more than that. She turned to Balbi and asked him some questions.

"Tell us what happens in there," Eliza asked.

"Men fight inside. Roman citizens call what happens in there 'gladiator battles'," said Balbi. Eliza and Balbi had slowed down to talk and Caleb was anxious to get there and was ahead of them.

"Keep walking! Walk and talk!" Caleb said. Balbi returned to tell Eliza stories.

"Roman soldiers compete to see who is the best fighter, but they do not always fight each other. Sometimes, they fight off great beasts and non-Romans, mostly slaves. When the battle commences, everyone watches them from above and people cheer for who they want to win. The emperor is usually there, as he loves bloodshed. And he decides if the battle must end in death or not. He usually gives a thumbs-up down, meaning fight to the death. Citizens like that the best." He lowered his voice and continued so no one could hear his next words.

"Emperor Titus loves a good gladiator battle, but he does some disturbing things. Sometimes, he tells his soldiers to tie up or wound the opponents to make sure the Roman soldiers win. Without meaning to, he makes commoners cheer for the underdog. It is pretty sick if you ask me," said Balbi.

"I would be interested to see this!" said Caleb.

"And I would not!" added Eliza. Her breathing quickened. It was not a good morning to be a naive girl from Correae walking the streets of downtown Rome for the first time and learning that people pay to watch people kill each other. She had just seen how people pay to have sex in the streets in the middle of the day, and that was bad enough.

Their conversation ended abruptly as they heard a street crier talking about an item of interest to them. He walked around a corner of the Coliseum, speaking loudly.

"Come! Learn that the Messiah has been on earth and He offers forgiveness of sins! Come and meet Him!" He repeated his message twice before moving to another spot, repeatedly looking around for people who might be listening to him.

Caleb and Eliza instinctively approached the crier. After all, he was one of them. As they began to walk that way, Balbi could see they were making a mistake and he stood between them and the crier.

"Do not engage this man. This is folly. The Romans will kill Yeshuians on sight if they conclude you are declaring someone as the Messiah ahead of the emperor. It would be a waste to come all this way to see you talking to a man out in public who can have you killed. I tell you, what you are about to do is folly!"

Caleb ignored him, pushed him aside, and walked towards the crier. His father told him that part of being a believer was standing strong in the presence of evil. Caleb approached the man and he spoke in his native language.

"My name is Caleb, and I am from the tribe of Benjamin. This is my cousin Eliza, from the tribe of Naphtali," he said in Ebreet. "I wish to speak to your rabbi as soon as we can. Will you take us to him?" The man looked at Caleb curiously but he did not reply.

"Speak Greek, you idiot!" said Eliza in her not-so-joking manner. He looked at Eliza with some disgust before addressing the man again using Greek. The man responded.

"Of course," he said. The man understood him this time.

"We meet each evening at sundown at the bottom of the Palatine Hill in the building with the yellow door. Go to the door and knock. One of the assistants will let you in. If you wish to speak to the rabbi alone, come early. Our rabbi works on the docks during the day as he is a fisherman." With that, the man left them and began to walk uphill and away from the Coliseum and towards the docks. He repeated his cry as he moved to the next street corner.

"See there?" said Caleb, feeling successful in getting some information that might lead to an audience with the emperor. Eliza rolled her eyes and shook her head, almost like a disgusted wife. Caleb decided to ignore her attempt to downplay his success.

"We have made our first step!" Caleb looked at Eliza, throwing his arm around her and pulling her in for a kiss on her temple. She resisted at first, but she adorned Caleb's affection. And he needed to hear it from her.

"I am glad you are courageous and approached that crier," she said.

Either way, Caleb was proud to get this information and he wanted to let Eliza celebrate. He needed her smarts and her support as they figured out how to arrange a meeting with the emperor.

"Balbi, you have the rest of the day to do as you like. Meet us at the yellow door at sunset," Caleb said. Caleb could sense what Eliza wanted and he decided to give it to her.

"You, my dear, can now go shopping. And I will take you."

Chapter 23:
A Carrot or a Donkey?

Before speaking a single word to anyone in the main Roman spice market, Eliza walked it from end to end, stopping to eavesdrop on conversations in progress. She smiled a lot and answered questions as casually as she could. Although much of the conversation was unrelated to her stash of cinnamon sticks, she knew that the information she obtained casually about what goods were coming into and leaving the market might come in handy - at least it did in Naphtali, Manessah, and Benjamin.

She heard from a vegetable seller that the Gauls had a bumper wheat harvest and would be bringing in lots of it soon. She also learned there had been a flood during the late autumn in Egypt and some of their crop was lost so that the Gauls would be getting a good price for their grain. She wished she had time to play that as she knew she could have made a lot of money brokering the sale to the Egyptians. She didn't hear anyone speaking Ebreet here and she daydreamed about using her language skills in Greek and Egyptian to broker a profitable deal for her family and village. She loved everything about this environment.

Caleb watched and smiled as Eliza followed her passion to buy and sell. He knew that Eliza was in her element during the moments she navigated a foreign market and negotiated the best value. With no fear of her goods connecting back to the gold ore of Correae, she spoke more openly than she otherwise would have. After her first pass of listening in on all the conversations going on, she decided to engage on her second trip through the line. She introduced herself to several shopkeepers and negotiated fiercely for the best price for her sticks. One shopkeeper attempted to offer her a below-market rate and she responded by pouring several gold coins from her purse and counting them in front of him for no other reason than to show that she knew how to value things. The man changed his tone, offering her a much better price, but Eliza knew others were watching her prowess on display, and she dismissed the man and his efforts to low-ball her. She knew that discarding the man's newer offer would prevent others from attempting to offer her a below-market price. And she was right. By the end of her next passthrough, she had already earned a slang title she would not repeat to Caleb, but she was proud of it. Certainly, it was profane, but it also meant she knew what she was doing.

The largest shop in the market seemed to be staffed by entry-level workers, so she chose not to visit it. Experience taught her that they had a limit as to how high they could go in their offers. She suspected that she would not be able to negotiate above the number the owner had already authorized to offer, making the large shops nearly worthless in larger transactions. The shop next door was not as large, but the owner was present and approachable. Within a few minutes, she had emptied her and her cousin's backpack of their cinnamon sticks and had taken possession of a large weight of newly minted Roman coins that had Titus' face on them. She thanked the man for the transaction and he quickly called over some of his men to pack them up and take them somewhere that she didn't know about. He was most likely going to mark them up and sell them again. She was glad as that is how business works. And she now had his name and she knew she could do business with him again in the future. She handed the empty backpacks to Caleb as well as the very large bag of coins with a smile on her face.

"And that, my dear cousin, is how we make a deal if you are from Correae," she said smugly, adjusting her coin purse and belt now that she had twice as many coins in it. She had learned of a shop that sold tea made the Judean way and she offered to take Caleb to buy him a whole pot for being patient with her while she shopped.

"That was enough profit to justify making this trip three times over," she told Caleb as they walked back towards the edge of the

Coliseum. She gave a few coins to beggars she had seen there earlier. The tea was pricy, but it was the real thing and they loved it.

"Are you ready to go with me to find the rabbi and figure out our purpose?" he asked her once she had finished her last cup.

"Yes," she replied. "It's moments like these that remind me of my purpose in the world and how I am supposed to use it to glorify God. We could have kept all those coins, but the beggars need them more than we do right now. And since we are here to help get my parents out, I needed to do something that they would be proud of."

Her justification gave Caleb a moment to pause. He took a few of her coins and gave them to the beggars as well, blessing them and praying for them just as he had seen his father do many times.

"I am glad you said that, cousin. That would make my parents proud," said Caleb. They had no idea where the yellow door was, so they asked a local food cart owner. He pointed and they were amazed that it was so close. As they approached it, they saw that there was already someone there, also knocking to see the rabbi.

"Barkhi!" said Eliza.

"Hello, friends!" he said, bowing before them,

"Barkhi! You do not need to do that," said Eliza, feeling a bit bashful at his public display of honor. Barkhi was opening his mouth to speak as the door opened.

"What is your business here?" a man asked. Eliza felt empowered by her success in the market, so she did all the talking.

"We are members of The Way and just arrived from Judah. We seek prayer and counsel from the rabbi at the local synagogue." She referred to their faith with the old vocabulary.

"Please wait," he said, closing the door. Within a few seconds, it was opened again by a different person who had a skeptical look about him. He wore a full beard and a rich head of long black hair, but his eyes were bloodshot as if he hadn't slept in days.

"What is it that you want?" He was obviously tired.

Eliza had practiced her words for this moment. "We need to get an audience with the emperor. We are not asking for help with that, but we do need prayer. Does it not say, 'Where two or more are gathered in my name, there I am with them?'" She knew that a Yeshua follower would know this phrase.

"How do you know that?" Eliza took a gamble on her aunt's celebrity status.

"Because my aunt and uncle taught it to me. Do you know Rabbi Mishi and Rabbi Yael?"

The man stood motionless for a few seconds before speaking. "Is this some sort of trick? Have you been sent here by the palace guards?"

"Do you know my parents?" Caleb asked. "Have you been to Tamar?"

"Wow." The man stared back and forth for a moment, trying to sort out what to say next.

"I do know your parents and I have been to Tamar! I cannot believe this!" He gestured for them to enter. "Come in! Come in! Bless you!" he said, taking them through the foyer and into the heart of the synagogue. It had a small and humble altar and within the walls, there was seating for perhaps 200 people.

"I worked all of last night and again much of today, but I will not work these next few days. We have a gathering tonight and I must rest before it. However, I have to show you in and welcome you. You must be Mishi's boy. This is truly unprecedented."

They dropped their bags in a storage niche and they turned around to face him.

"When I was not much older than you, my family traveled to Judah and we met your parents in a house outside of Jerusalem. It was there that they told us their story of meeting Luke."

"That is near the place where my parents met," said Caleb.

"We heard how they met in one of King David's tunnels under the city." The rabbi was now coming back to life and was not about to leave them to go back to sleep.

Eliza jumped on the opportunity to add to the story. "Yael was my aunt! She left our village in the middle of my mother and father's wedding ceremony to travel to Jerusalem to atone for her sins. That is when she found that tunnel!" she added with a near squeal. Caleb shook his head and smiled as he watched his cousin act like a twelve-year-old girl.

"You look like your aunt," said the rabbi. He decided it was time to introduce himself formally.

"My name is John and I am a student of Rabbi Paul. He was our teacher here in the city until he was killed. He spent many of his days in the city's prisons before he died."

"My aunt knew Paul! She told me all about working in the prisons!" said Eliza. Her enthusiasm to be the center of attention was growing. Caleb reached out, took her hand, and pulled her back, hoping she would get the message.

"I see you have many great stories for me. However, I must rest and leave you. Otherwise, I will not be effective this evening. You have access to my assistants while I rest, and you can eat anything you like and use any of our resources. I must go to bed before this place is filled with what everyone thinks are crazy and drunk people." That made Eliza laugh as she recalled the story of Cornelius the Centurion.

"Darkness comes early this time of year, and everyone will want to be inside our closed doors before the sun sets." With that, he excused himself, telling his assistants to do anything that was asked of them.

Eliza and Caleb began a lengthy conversation with the two assistants about the workings of the faith in downtown Rome. Barkhi watched the back-and-forth banter but said nothing as he was learning what had changed since his family left the sect of the Sadducees. Eliza asked them to tell her stories of their life serving the growing population of Yeshuians in Rome. She asked many questions about what it was like to serve those under the city streets.

"My aunt would tell me stories about how much it meant to her to talk to and teach the men who were on death row and living under the city streets. They were hungry for the message of salvation, and she loved writing letters for the men to send to their families. Aunt Yael said she felt the power of the Lord more than at any time in her life. During those stories, time passed effortlessly. I will always miss that time." Once they heard Eliza's story, the men retrieved her some letters written by Paul. Eliza sat down and read them, commenting on them being much like what her aunt used to teach her.

"Can we have a copy of these? Eliza asked. The men agreed and promised to ask one of the interns to record one of the smaller ones starting tomorrow.

"And I know that I must visit these prisons one day and see what all the stories are about."

Caleb sat and patiently listened as he heard a theme that was common throughout the Yeshuian world. There were not enough trained leaders to match the number of people coming into the faith in a risen Messiah. This synagogue was no different. Every seat was taken nearly every night, but the Rabbi who worked there was part-time, as the congregation used nearly all of their tithes to reach out to those who were suffering and in greater need. Volunteers did most of the work to keep the synagogue operating, but all of them had other lives and families to concern themselves with. However, nearly all synagogues lacked trained leaders who were prepared to be pilgrims like the apostle Paul and travel to all parts of the Roman Empire, ready to spread His word, organize people, and tell His story. Caleb wasn't shocked to hear Eliza's response to hearing their stories.

"Someone needs to step up and disciple all these people! We need more people to call to follow. We need to teach everyone about our Lord. Perhaps I should do it?" she rhetorically said. Caleb had seen her organize the students to keep the school beautiful. He had no concerns with her organizational skills, but he couldn't see her calling people disciples. But he encouraged her nonetheless.

"You would be great at it, Eliza. You need to get trained first, though," said Caleb with a bit of loving caution. The assistants smiled as they saw how Caleb was trying to nurture the young woman's desires and they continued to speak back and forth.

"We all need missionaries," said one of the assistants. "We need people who know the scrolls and can teach in different languages to others all around the world. Paul spoke that we need to make saints. If you have the heart to do this, Eliza of Naphtali, please follow your calling. Can we pray for you?" the two men asked.

Eliza looked at them then at Caleb.

"I have not changed my opinion. It still is a great idea," said Caleb. Eliza took a deep breath and agreed to receive their prayer. As soon as they were finished, Caleb decided to bring up the reason they were there.

He said, "We need an audience with the emperor so we can get help freeing her parents."

"Just an audience?" the assistant laughed. "How old are you? Do you realize that approaching the emperor is grounds for death?" Caleb didn't see the sarcasm the way they did. He merely answered them with confidence. He shared a summary of what happened in Tamar and why they wanted the audience. They didn't act supportive, but Caleb could not let that deter him.

"Speaking to the emperor is what we intend to do. I need some help getting an audience. And I think I have something that will help." He pulled out his uncle's ring and put it on his middle finger. He turned it upward so Rufus' rank and the carvings on its face were visible to all. "This belonged to my uncle," he said.

The assistants froze, looking at each other. "Well, that will be your key to getting an audience. Since you want to talk to him, here is what we recommend. His entourage walks by our synagogue all the time."

For the next few minutes, the two assistants helped create a plan to get Caleb and Eliza inside the Coliseum for tomorrow's gladiator battles, where they were sure the emperor would also be. They went back and forth with possible strategies to address what they might encounter once they got near him.

Soon, others began arriving at the synagogue. The first to arrive was a group of women carrying fresh food. There were many loaves of fresh bread, warm meats, vegetables, spices, and aromatic sauces. The women approached the assistants and handed them their purses. "Here is the change," said the eldest one. Without awaiting a response, she continued past everyone and walked directly to the kitchen, her other arm full of greens.

"I am going to the kitchen. I am going to get their opinion," Eliza said, pointing at the women. As she went, she turned back to Caleb and spoke in Aramaic, using a dialect from Correae that she knew he would understand. "Do not be a donkey, but do not be a carrot either."

That meant not opening your mouth and saying things that you may regret, but not closing your eyes and ears and not observing all that is going on around you. Eliza wanted him to exercise discretion to protect their secrets a bit better than he had been doing. His mother hated secrets, and her disdain for them caused her to sin and nearly die on more than one occasion. She knew that the rabbi's defensiveness at their first meeting a few hours ago came from experience that not everyone who call themselves Yeshuian could be trusted.

After Eliza left, the assistants went to prepare other things and Caleb watched the main room of the synagogue fill to capacity. Unlike the sanctuaries of the synagogues back in Judah, this one was filled with tables and chairs. Caleb quickly figured out that these Gentiles ate food in the same room where they worshiped and preached. There were also many homeless men and women, as well as several afflicted attendees who perhaps had leprosy. One group caught his attention more than the others. There was a group of three men, all of whom were blind, and they walked directly to a spot familiar to them, away from all the regular traffic. Then to Caleb's great surprise, Rabbi John reappeared after his nap and hugged these blind men. Caleb was scared of the faces of the blind.

"Caleb, come here!" John yelled out. Instinctively, Caleb walked cautiously towards them and the rabbi. He had no experience interacting with a blind man.

"Yes, Rabbi John," Caleb said with a tone of reverence.

"I want you to meet these men. I call them the three brothers, but they are not related by blood. They all come from Gaelic parts of the empire. I told them that the son of one of the great teachers of the Messiah has come to join us this evening, and they wanted to touch you."

"Touch me?" Caleb was not used to being touched by any man at the first meeting, let alone by a blind man, but it made sense as these men couldn't meet him in the traditional sense.

"Come here, boy," one of the older men said.

Caleb did as they instructed and the men began asking him a series of questions as they ran their hands over him. As they explored his physique, they spoke frequently and often complimented his size and apparent strength. They marveled at the thickness of his arms. They asked him questions about his family, his home, and his wife, though he did not have the latter. One of them told him that a man his size ought to start planning to get a wife.

"Do not you want one yet?" they asked.

Caleb felt ashamed as he had not shared his new awareness of girls with Eliza or anyone else.

"Of course, I want one," he said with confidence. Several others who were watching laughed as Caleb spoke the way he did.

"You are big, strong, and obviously smart. You traveled by sea to Rome with your cousin helping you. You need to tell your parents you want a wife soon," one of them said.

Caleb felt hollow, even though they had intended to compliment and affirm him. At that moment, he knew that his parents would not play a role in his selection of a spouse. He would do it the same way that some sects of Gentiles do, in that the men pick the women themselves.

"Do you not have parents?" they asked. Caleb could see that their blindness was limited to their vision.

"No, sir, I don't." The man began to mumble to himself.

"I will pray that you see her during your meeting tomorrow," the man said. Caleb looked at the rabbi, wondering if this was nonsense or if he meant it. The rabbi looked at Caleb and nodded.

"Caleb, I am sure he told you the truth," he said. Caleb instantly understood why John called him over here. These men were prophets and John was using this moment to teach Caleb that authority is not limited to those who are in power or abundantly blessed.

Caleb looked down and smiled. He grew up with prophets in his home all the time. He had seen their words come to pass too many times to count, and he could not wrap his head around the idea that he might meet his wife soon. For the first time, he wondered if he wanted a wife. Eliza could belittle him on occasion and he hated it. If that is what a wife does, he didn't want one of them. But, he found that he liked the blind men's company a lot.

"Are you a gladiator?" one of them asked.

He chuckled before answering. "No. I came here to see the emperor and get his help finding my cousin's parents. That is why we are here."

"You want to see the emperor? Certainly, you will be a gladiator by this time tomorrow." Caleb looked perplexed at that prophecy. He neither wanted a wife nor a fight. He wanted to help free his aunt and uncle; nothing else mattered.

"We all have a path that we set out on. You, young Caleb, are on your own path, not familiar to any of us. Most of us come looking for relief from Roman oppression. You come looking to challenge and engage Roman authority. We do not see your outcome, only the conflict."

Caleb interrupted him, "I don't seek conflict. Your assistants have helped me with an idea that may get us an audience with the emperor. I need some help and asking the emperor for help is the best idea we have come up with so far." The rabbi smiled at Caleb's feistiness.

"I am not here to offer ideas. I imagine you have heard many ideas from others who are smarter and wiser than us. I do not see your encounter with the emperor resulting in an outcome that does not include death," the rabbi ended. Caleb did not want to hear that.

Caleb was respectful. He did not argue with the rabbi. However, he chose the carrot route as his cousin had specifically advised against it. He excused himself and decided to walk outside for some air.

It took a while to walk against the flow of traffic and step into the evening air. Caleb knew these blind men were not going to help them, but he could not deny that his assistants had some great ideas.

He was not expecting to see the two assistants standing outside with him near a group of four exquisitely dressed Roman soldiers. He watched as one of the assistants handed the change purse to the men, who put their hands on his shoulder and bowed their heads as they departed. Caleb walked to the other side of the street to ask them what they were doing.

"Those men protect us from Roman aristocrats who see us as a threat and seek to harm us," explained one of the assistants. "Those soldiers are also our members and they need that money to bribe others to turn the other cheek. Did you know that there are literally a hundred gatherings across the city just like ours every evening? And there are lots of soldiers just like those men."

Caleb realized that he had misjudged them. He set aside his tendency to be either a donkey or a carrot. "I cannot believe it! You are using member tithes to pay bribes to protect your existence. I have never seen that. Is that okay to do?"

"We are unable to find any words of the Messiah that call self-preservation bad. In fact, our rabbi says that Yeshua Himself said, 'Give to Caesar what is Caesar's and give to God what is God's.' That coin doesn't have God's picture on it," he said, and they all laughed.

"Let's go inside. First, there was food, then a message, and then off to sleep. Do all of them together, and that is good living, yes?" Caleb rhetorically asked. Everyone smiled, nodded, and agreed. They headed to the doors to join everyone else inside.

Chapter 24:
Vengeance Is the Lord's

Caleb sat at a table with the two assistants and they enjoyed the meal. All through the meal, the two assistants reiterated their plan to get Caleb and Eliza an audience with the emperor. They couldn't make any promises but everyone who sat with them and listened agreed that there was an opportunity tomorrow that might not happen again for a few weeks. Since their proposal required spending a lot of money, Caleb knew he needed to talk to Eliza first. Caleb asked the assistants to sit with him to help answer Eliza's inevitable list of questions. They agreed to meet in their guest bedroom after the worship ceremony and talk through their plan as a group.

Once the meal was over, everyone moved the tables to the sides of the room and the chairs were rearranged, facing the makeshift altar. Eliza and Caleb were guests of honor and they sat together near the front, with space on the right side of them for people to walk in and out. The seats were all occupied and Eliza could sense that everyone was watching them.

John got everyone's attention for a moment and told them that the worship service would start in a moment as the women in the kitchen first needed to finish cleaning up and package the extras for the men in the prison.

"I am going to help them," said Eliza, getting up and returning to the kitchen. Caleb pulled on her cloak for a moment to get her attention.

"I have a plan to share with you after this. The two assistants and I want to talk to you in the upstairs room as soon as this is over."

"The women in the kitchen came up with a plan, as well. Let's bring everyone together and combine our ideas," she said.

"Fair enough," said Caleb. Eliza quickly went into the kitchen but quickly returned.

"The workers didn't need my help. They will be out with us shortly and will join us upstairs after this is over," she said.

Caleb took this moment of informality to tell her about his encounter with the blind men and their prophecy. He made a point to mention that he liked how they sincerely complimented him, saying that he did not get that from anyone else.

"Caleb, I am sorry I don't lift you up more often. You are becoming a wonderful man," she said. It made her feel a bit sad that she was not providing her cousin the affirmation and love he needed. She kept reminding herself that his parents were dead and she was his family now. She needed to find a better way to be there for him.

For her part, Eliza shared that the women in the kitchen cooked all the food not just for those who were there but also to serve the men in the city prisons. They made a lot of extra food, and they would take the leftovers the following morning to the prisons, sharing them first with the guards and with the inmates, relaying messages between synagogue leadership and those in jail.

"I have no idea how your mother spoke to all these people during her time with Paul working in prison ministry." She wished she had time to talk to the women in the kitchen, asking if they knew her aunt. It would certainly add to her stories. And it made her wonder what it might be like to serve there, herself. She could sense that she wasn't done thinking about it and wondered if she might have the time to join the women on their visit after the service.

Finally, the last of the women left the kitchen, signaling to John that he could start the service. John got everyone's attention again and took his place behind the makeshift altar near the kitchen's entrance so that everyone could see him. Everyone sang a familiar worship song; afterward, John shared the day's message.

"Here is a letter we received just today from our friend Timothy, who remains in prison," he said as he took out a folded piece of parchment from his tunic. He opened it and read it out loud.

"I thank the Lord every day for your gifts of food. The guards treat me and my cellmates well because of your love. Although we do not often get to send you messages, we look forward to the day we are released and can worship with you. If that day does not come, we are looking forward to the day we will see you at the hands of our Messiah in heaven, who has saved a seat for all who have written His name on their hearts and souls. That is the name of Yeshua."

Many in the crowd spoke up, saying, "It is so!" and "Praise the Messiah!" Neither Eliza nor Caleb had seen this sort of audience participation in a synagogue before, but they liked the new culture. It was obvious that Gentiles could love the Lord as much as God's chosen people could, and Eliza felt happy to see this truth.

Once the congregation had stopped their praise and celebration, the rabbi read the rest of the note.

"Several days ago, we found a knife secretly included in our food. We do not know who gave it to us. One in our group, who has since sought repentance, suggested that we use it to kill the guards and escape from prison. However, we were reminded of the teachings of Luke who says, 'Vengeance is mine, says the Lord.' We knew that this knife was a trap from the enemy to lure us into taking vengeance against our captors. Instead, we called over the guards and gave the knife to them, praying for our group's safety during the exchange. None of us were beaten that day and two of the guards stayed with us, praising the Lord until late evening. Praise God that we were able to use this temptation as a path to true freedom. It is with great joy that I tell you these guards accepted Yeshua as their savior."

Everyone applauded again, but this part of the story made Caleb feel alone. The discussion of passing on vengeful opportunities reminded him of the choices to kill the Roman soldiers in Tamar and to shoot first and speak second while on the boat. This letter cut to the core of Caleb's identity and his biggest struggle from his haunted past. No matter how many times Eliza told him that he had done the right thing to protect her parents and protect her, these thoughts would continue to emerge. In fact, they haunted him.

He already admitted to himself that sparing Balbi's life was against his better judgment, yet history proved it was the right thing to do. Now, the man who he should have struck dead before he left the water has a relationship with Yeshua and a place in eternity. How could both be true?

Caleb tuned out John and his mind entered an altered state. He was caught up in a repetitive thought for which he could not escape. He revisited seeing the men stab the poor villager in the gut and watched the man undo Eliza's pants strings. How is it possible that Yeshua could save a wretch like Balbi and offer him a place in eternity? Was there no unforgivable sin?

As the service came to an end, Caleb found himself in prayer, feeling a deep humility that he was alive, yet so many of those who were around him were dead. And he could not solve the riddle of Balbi's salvation that didn't include a conclusion that he was a sinner without a solution, while Balbi was a sinner with a solution.

"God, what am I? How could you have allowed me to nurture all these weapon skills and not use them to protect your people? How do I restrain myself during those moments Eliza is not here?" he prayed under his breath. His prayers were immediately answered.

"Master, I wanted to say that I am grateful, um, I guess eternally grateful, for you sparing my life last week. What I did was shameful, and I do not know how you exercised restraint and kept me from feeling the bite of your blade or your bow. I should be dead now; instead, I have a place in heaven," said Balbi.

Caleb had no idea that the man was next to him. Indeed, he told Balbi to meet them at the yellow door, but he did not t recall him entering. Yet, there he was.

Caleb smiled and spoke without thinking.

"Balbi, I do not know either. But I am glad that I did not kill you," he said, putting one of his massive hands on Balbi's shoulder as a sign of brotherhood. "I am glad you are here, actually."

Caleb laughed under his breath. He had heard his parents talk about how God's methods can be funny. This must be one of those moments that they talked about. Balbi could now add another part of his identity to Caleb's list: Balbi now also served as Caleb's healer.

Eliza greeted Balbi, speaking kindly to him once he made eye contact with her. After Balbi walked away, she spoke to Caleb.

Caleb had tears rolling down his cheeks. Eliza could see that he was trying to cover his tears.

"You are a good man, Caleb. God has His hand on your heart. He is working great things with you. You are the proof that anything is possible with God. You are the most dear person in the world to me. You know that, right?" Caleb looked at her and nodded in acknowledgment, but he was too distraught to speak.

Eliza's conviction suddenly grew. She needed to take care of this man and she needed to do it with truth and love. They were far from home and taking a risk that might kill them. Caleb was doing everything in his power to protect her, including giving up his life, and he had no one to guide him as he made choices without any advanced notice. They felt a bit inadequate as they had not completed schooling or their Mitzvahs, as they promised their parents they would. Caleb remained unsettled and Eliza was scared for him. Finally, Caleb spoke.

"My parents are dead, Eliza. Even after hearing that message, I would kill the men who killed my parents all over again. I want to kill the men who killed Uncle Rufus, too. What am I supposed to do?"

"I do not know," she said and they stopped talking.

They returned their focus to the rabbi as he gave the congregation some final guidance.

"Tomorrow, there will be a parade before the events in the Coliseum. As the emperor and his entourage walk past us, please do not openly show your disdain. Instead, pray for the man and his salvation. He does not need to be stabbed with a knife for things to be made right. We need to pray for our leaders. Yes, this man has ordered the death of many of our people. But we must not give up on him, in the same way that Yeshua did not give up on us while our ancestors crucified Him during His last days in Jerusalem." Eliza looked at Caleb and they nodded at this man's wisdom. They liked his approach to life.

The crowd began to pray out loud and many of the members held hands. "Jehovah Jireh, come into the heart and soul of this man who has become the emperor and free him of the bondage that comes with his role. Bring him to You!"

"And Yeshua, let me play my part with this emperor," Eliza said. "All I want is my parents back."

As the night activities came to an end, the assistants took Eliza and Caleb to the upper room and they settled in for the evening. The rabbi's assistants and two of the women from the kitchen joined them. The assistants began outlining their plan. To the assistants' amazement, the women began nodding their heads.

"That is exactly what we thought these two should do, as well," they said.

For the next few minutes, the four who called Rome home began suggesting names of people that they would need help from, as well as which shops they needed to visit first thing in the morning. They explained it all to Eliza and Caleb and they politely agreed with each action of the plan. The conversation did not take much time and the four left, leaving Caleb and Eliza alone in the upper room.

"Good night, you two. Get some sleep. Tomorrow will be a very busy day for you!" said the oldest woman, and they departed from the view.

Caleb and Eliza took the pile of blankets and laid all of them out on the floor. They gathered on top of them and just looked at each other.

"That is simply amazing: they all came up with the same plan, independent of each other. I am feeling good about it. Do you think you can act like they told you to?" Eliza asked.

"I sure can. I need to remember how Uncle Rufus acted as he escorted my parents through the empire. The task shouldn't be too hard," he said.

"I do not know if I can do this great act of deception," Eliza said, lacking any sense of confidence.

"I wager 100 gold coins that you can if you practice. Do you want to practice?" asked Caleb.

For the next few moments, the two of them sat on top of the blankets, practicing their personas. Once Eliza felt a bit more comfortable, they crawled under the blankets and blew out the last lit candle. Caleb spooned against her and wrapped his massive arm around her. Eliza held it with her hand and she took only a final deep breath before falling asleep.

Caleb whispered one last thing to Eliza. "Tomorrow will be a very interesting day, cousin. I cannot wait."

"Me, too," Eliza agreed. There was a moment of stillness, but the conviction returned to Eliza. Her words earlier could not be a one-time event meant to last until eternity. She needed to tell him this more often.

"Caleb, I love you," she said.

"I know," said Caleb as he fell asleep.

Chapter 25:
Entrance to the Coliseum

Long before the parade started and passed by the synagogue, Caleb and Eliza awakened to begin what they knew would be a busy and expensive day. They ate a hearty breakfast at the restaurant across the street from the synagogue, where they slept, compared notes and destinations, and agreed to meet back at the synagogue before the parade started.

Eliza's first stop was at the hairdresser's shop. The Roman hairdresser was of the highest social class, and Eliza had to pay twice the normal price for a same-day appointment. Since it was Coliseum Day, many other women of the aristocracy were also seeking grooming. That demand for services kept the woman and her slaves busy, but it gave Eliza a chance to talk to the other women who planned on attending this afternoon's gladiator fights. She mentally dismissed the extra cost as part of the cost of selling the cinnamon. She also got some guidance on how to handle all the men and women whom she would meet during the afternoon. She didn't like what she heard, but she was glad she knew about how people would act in advance. Certainly, she was not going to be a part of an orgy afterward, no matter what the hairdresser told her.

Once her hair was perfect, the women introduced her to a seamstress, promising to clothe her in luxury so she looked like a Roman citizen of great nobility. The royal outfitter had served as the seamstress for house Caesar when she was younger and still a slave. Now she has an established boutique with lots of customers willing to pay top prices to look perfect. She was talkative and loved working on someone new and with darker features and stronger curves than most of the paler Roman women. One of the Gentile women brought her a few pairs of new sandals to try before she selected the ones made of black leather. With all the apparel complete, she went to the local baths for cleansing and an application of oils and perfumes. Once all the beauty agents had done their jobs, she looked into the mirror.

"Wow, ladies," she said, shaking her head in disbelief and spinning around in the mirror, looking at how beautiful she appeared.

"Not quite as tall as Cleopatra but just as stunning and certainly more voluptuous," said the woman who held up the mirror. The women giggled and Eliza covered her mouth as she laughed. Not since her sister's wedding had she gotten this dressed up or felt this beautiful. However, she hated how the dress exposed her legs and chest, and she knew she would not wear this clothing once she went home.

In the meantime, the two assistants took Caleb to a different part of the city filled with unique goods used exclusively by Roman soldiers and gladiators. Had Caleb known of this place yesterday, he would already have visited every one of the shops. There were also butchers in the area, as well as several blacksmiths. He speculated that these men specialized in creating weapons for the gladiators as well as providing red meat to heighten their senses during battle. There were many stalls filled with fabrics from all over the world and many women walked openly in the city, mostly with other women and their slaves, visiting these locations and engaging shopkeepers as if they were long-lost friends. Shopkeepers routinely offered wine to the women, promising them great deals if they purchased an entire bolt of cloth before the end of the day. However, Caleb noticed that most of them were there to stare at men. Caleb was the largest man in the market, and he gathered everyone's attention.

"This market exists for people like you," the assistant said.

"What I mean is this place attracts elite fighting men or people who want to look like they are," he said. Caleb looked around and noticed that there were several displays of exquisite hand-made armor and weapons beyond what anyone might need on an actual battlefield. There were helms, bracers, gauntlets, greaves, and plate armor fit to fight off an elephant. However, after Balbi described what the day's activities might look like, Caleb selected a compromise of showy and comfortable protective wear for their trek into the famous structure that was more social than practical. Caleb purchased the lightest weight mail he could find that would fit under a robe. He purchased a processional robe that included gold threads and double-strength edges to prevent it from tearing. He bought matching lightweight greaves and bracers to protect his arms and legs. Caleb was about to spend nearly half of his money on a gold-trimmed helmet before he found a much smaller one. He liked that it wasn't red as red was affiliated with the Roman military. And it didn't block his field of view like many helmets did.

The last and most important step for Caleb was to get a haircut and beard trimming. He also got his skin oiled and his nails cut. Once he was done, he looked as large and strong as the most powerful of Roman gladiators.

"How do I look?" he asked the last shopkeeper after all the adornments were in place.

"It would scare me to see you in combat," said the shopkeeper. Caleb could tell that the man had said that many times before, and it did not mean much.

"It should suffice to get you into the Coliseum," said one of the assistants. "But that bow you have is junk. It makes the rest of what you are wearing seem like a lie." Caleb laughed out loud. This man had no idea what it meant to be an archer from the tribe of Benjamin.

"I trust this bow more than I trust this haircut," Caleb said tactfully.

"We are done. Let's go find Eliza and do this!" Caleb replied.

The hard work of preparing was now done. Eliza and Caleb had finished with their "costumes" that made them look like royalty. Their plan was simple: look like the Romans, jump in the parade and walk with the Romans, and act like the Romans as they waited their turn to enter. If any problems come up, offer some coins and pray for the best. If all went well, they would pass through the blue gate and get escorted to the section of the Coliseum reserved for those of great wealth and position in society.

Caleb casually walked back to the synagogue and waited for Eliza and her entourage to return. The women returned not long after Caleb did, laughing like schoolgirls on the afternoon before Sabbath. Caleb had never seen Eliza this decorated before and her beauty made him smile.

"You look like a princess, Eliza! Everyone is going to look at you!" said Caleb. Eliza quickly looked down to see if her gown had exposed too much, but Caleb wasn't looking at her body. He was staring at her eyes. He sensed her self-consciousness and he knew it was his turn to affirm her. He put a single hand on her cheek and smiled.

"It will be nearly impossible to find a husband good enough for you. I have never seen you look this good," Caleb said.

"You like it?" she said. Caleb didn't respond. He didn't know how to. They were still children at heart and fancy appearances were not normal for them at this stage of life. Neither of them was familiar with the sexualization of the Roman elite, but they both knew that if they held each other, there would be no place for an aggressor to separate them.

"While you wear that gown, you don't look like a humble girl from Naphtali," Caleb said.

"And with all that armor and your bow, you don't look like the son of a rabbi from Benjamin," Eliza said.

"Tell me. What do you think?" Eliza said, spinning around one time. She sought a positive response from Caleb.

"Eliza, you are beautiful, inside and out. I don't need a gown to see that," he said.

"Good answer," she said, pointing at him and making all the other girls laugh.

All of her traveling clothing had been replaced and the new attire was made from pure white cotton linens with gold trim. Her outer robe had purple ruffles and fine lines of woven gold thread down the center seams, making it clear that she was wealthy. Her palla was full of intricate patterns that Caleb had not seen anywhere in Judah, and he was amazed at the detail. Her hair had been washed, cut, and combed and had been put up into a bun, held in place by a single silver needle worth as much as a camel.

"Every man in the Coliseum will be looking at your chest," Caleb said.

"I know, and I wish that it wasn't true!" Eliza said. She was both excited about the attention and disgusted that it would come with lustful thoughts.

"So, let's try what we have been practicing." Eliza turned around and took a few steps away from Caleb. She abruptly turned and walked directly at him, holding her flowing dress slightly off the ground so it wouldn't drag.

"Your Grace," she said, bowing her head like a Roman woman might if the emperor himself walked past.

"You are a stupid girl!" said Caleb, making both of them laugh. She restarted their drill, and this time, he greeted her like a queen.

"I see you like my appearance, my Lord," Eliza said in perfect Greek. "Would you escort me into the Coliseum for today's activities, my Lord?"

"Come, my Lady," said Caleb, using what they had practiced last night. This task I can do for none other than you, my Princess." He spoke in perfect Greek, using the most honorific words, just as an emperor might speak to his wife at their public wedding.

The crowd of men and women who had been helping them cheered. "You two are the most beautiful couple in all of Rome!" said one of the women who helped deliver food into the prisons. "And you look like you are most wealthy, too."

"They do not just look wealthy. They are wealthy!" Balbi chimed in. Eliza gave him her "I am mad at you" look, and everyone erupted with more laughter. But she didn't deny it. At that moment, Balbi was correct. Had they not been carrying lots of Correae's gold, they could not have afforded all this clothing, armor, weapons, and styling.

In accordance with the plan devised by the two assistants and the women, the full group of synagogue members stood and cheered as the parade approached. After the emperor and his royal entourage had passed, Caleb and Eliza casually joined at the back of the parade, just as the other nobles had done as the parade passed their residences. They walked next to other couples who looked similar to them. Many others fell in behind them as they made their way to the Coliseum. They reached it with the sun directly overhead, and they marched a single lap around the Coliseum, waving to the crowds before they neared the entrance. The emperor and a small group went to the left, and the rest of them were led to the right. Groups of eight Roman soldiers stopped and examined each person who approached the entrance on the right. Before they reached Caleb and Eliza, Caleb put on his uncle's ring and placed the hand that wore it on his sword's hilt.

The soldier in charge looked first at Caleb, then at his ring, before asking them where they wished to sit. Caleb knew that the protocol included stating your house of membership to gain entry. "I am Caleb, nephew of the legate of the Fifth Legion, Rufus of Caesarea, son of the centurion Cornelius." He held forward his hand, showing them his uncle's ring as the assistants instructed him to do.

"We already saw it, my Liege. You are clear to enter. Have a nice day," he said. The head soldier nodded to two others, and they, in turn, called over two escorts to lead them to their seats. Eliza gave each of them a single coin.

"Take them to sixteen beta," he said, bowing as they left his presence and entered the Coliseum.

"Come this way, my Lord and my Lady," said one of the two escorts. Eliza also handed each one of them a copper coin, bowing her head as they received them. One walked ahead of Caleb and Eliza until they reached an outdoor rampart near the center of the stadium that led to the Azure section. The other walked behind them. They passed through a simple arch and into their protected box. Inside were four ornately carved chairs. Caleb took off his outer robe and helped Eliza take off hers. He placed them on one of the unused chairs.

Their entrance was complete. This protected box would be their home for the next few hours. On the right was a large wall that separated their section from the ones used by regular citizens. They had asked the escorts to place them on the boundary of the royalty section. To their left were as many as a hundred boxes, each filled with people who looked just like they did.

Two boxes away sat the emperor of Rome, Titus, looking for someone or something that had not yet arrived.

Caleb's heart did not race. He spoke a single prayer. "Thank you, Jehovah Jireh, for an opportunity to make things right for my aunt and uncle. Protect me from sin and lead us away from anxiety and needless worry. I trust you will free them. Use this man to make that happen."

Chapter 26:
Another Yael

During their superficial strut into the Coliseum, Caleb bent his non-sword arm at the elbow, allowing Eliza to place her arm through his, just as all the other couples in front of them had done. As they walked, Eliza took the time to survey the other men and women in line. Eliza compared Caleb to the other men and she found nearly all of them lacking. Caleb was larger by all physical measures. His arms, chest, and legs were all larger and more powerful in appearance than anyone else's in the Azure line. She felt the callous on his hands and wondered if any of these men had actually done work. It did not matter. She was walking with royalty, and this was the grand adventure she had dreamed about since she was a little girl. However, it was rich in betrayal of her beliefs and she was grateful that this man was here to keep her safe.

The women from the kitchen had let her know that she might feel exposed for the duration of the event. Her gown was low cut in the front, commanding the attention of men, and she observed a few of them staring further down her body. She asked the seamstress to fix the design error, but she smiled and told her that showing skin was part of her admission ticket. Now that she saw the other women in line, she understood what the seamstress meant. Some of the other Roman women wore their palla so that a single breast was exposed and Eliza felt shame looking at them. She had been taught that it was common for all those who attended an event at the Coliseum to display their body for others to see. Eliza's dress exposed more of her skin than any Ebreet should, and men old enough to be her father were looking at her with what she thought was ill intent. Eliza wore a necklace fashioned of perfectly hewn gems and the most detailed of gold links. Only an Ebreet Jeweler could make such intricate artifacts of this quality. That, too, was the subject of attention.

Caleb's physique grabbed the attention of nearly every woman, especially all the older ones. His darker skin and defined frame caught their eye and the smile on his face confirmed to Eliza that he liked the sexual attention. In addition, the gold that he wore was prominently placed. Caleb wore a thick bangle on his left wrist. It was of Ebreet origin and one of the few items that Eliza had carried from home. Its ornate carvings were perfectly etched into the rich metal and it was of better workmanship than anyone else's.

People did not only look at the two of them; many commented on how beautiful they looked. Eliza and Caleb were unfamiliar with the unfiltered comments regarding the flesh of others, and all they knew to do was smile, bow, and extend gratitude at the perception of the compliments. A few said that they must enjoy creating children together and that they need to get together and share the experience one day.

"I know these people think they are being nice, but I find it disgusting. I want you to strike dead the next man who tells me that I have nice breasts and I should share them. I sincerely want to vomit," she said to Caleb in Aramaic. Caleb had his own response.

"Did you see the two women old enough to be my mother trying to take my hand and place it on their breasts? They tried to rub my chest hair, as well. That is revolting." Eliza looked at him and could tell he was telling her the truth. He, too, was appalled at this hedonism.

After entering their designated boxed seats, Eliza picked up a pillow and put it in the place where she would sit today. She looked out at the Coliseum for the first time and she felt safe. She felt like an Ebreet queen from the stories of the prophets. The act of donning lavish clothing and finishing her appearance with perfume and jewelry should have been enough to make this a perfect day. But it was not complete until she stood with Caleb and could see the emperor to her left. She did not look at him for long before she returned her gaze to her cousin. Caleb looked like a proud and seasoned warrior now. He remained her cousin, but he was now more than that. He looked like a man in every way. She felt proud and grateful to be with him, and she knew she was safe in his presence.

"Thank you," she whispered to him as she took her reserved seat inside the Coliseum. It was exciting to be within earshot of the most powerful person in the world. She imagined going back home and trying to tell her family and friends about this moment, but she shook her head and chuckled. They would not understand. She remembered her aunt's story of trying to tell her cousins, Despy and Nava, about her desire to explore the world outside of Correae to no avail. Aunt Despy was now so fat that she couldn't get to the Jerusalem highway anymore. Her smile was as much full of solitude and melancholy as it was of joy.

"You know, my Lord, no one will believe us when we tell them we did this," she said to Caleb, using formal Greek but in a low tone. She knew it was possible that others could overhear their words, so she left her comment vague enough for there to be room for interpretation.

"Perhaps." Caleb copied tone and ambiguity. He knew what she meant.

The Flavian Amphitheatre, as it was called, was over four hundred cubits long, making it much larger than the Temple. At one hundred cubits high, it was taller than Noah's Ark. The Amphitheatre was referred to as one of the "seven wonders" of the world due to its grandeur. Its exterior was concrete and brick, and the concrete surfaces had been painted to hold vibrant colors. These colored facades gave the gates their names. While waiting in line to enter, they heard much small talk about how rich the painted walls looked this time of year as the sun shined upon them. It was remarkable how identical the color of the wall was to the sea.

But what filled the hearts of the Romans who could afford to enter the Coliseum was that human death was on public display for all to see. The sights and sounds that came from the center of the theatre were gruesome ones. Yet, the Romans thought them to be "grand". Orgies afterward were common, confirming her impression that this place and those who entered it were evil. Although neither

Eliza nor Caleb had any intention of attending one of these orgies, they knew they needed to look the part to pass through the security checks. The Romans safeguarded their entrances for good reasons. The number of emperors assassinated in the last fifty years required more than there are fingers to count.

Although the original construction was started under Vespasian, it was not until Titus took the throne last year that the Coliseum was completed. Titus was said to have used much of the wealth he acquired during the siege on Jerusalem to finance the work. To justify his economic investment, Titus sold off the rights to certain days of the month for individuals to hold their events at the Coliseum. Titus would come if he received assurances that gladiators would be present, but he collected royalties on all events, including the ones he did not attend.

Their seats were in boxes, so-called because there was a wall of brick on all sides of them. The back wall was high enough to prevent anyone from looking into their booth from the hallways that lead them there. The walls on each side kept patrons from seeing each other while they were seated. If they stood up and went to the edge, they could see the others in the adjacent box. All pit fighting was in front of them, and nothing was placed there that might impede their vision or experience.

Screened and vetted food vendors started coming through their booth as they saw it occupied. They had a large variety of freshly prepared food to offer as well as many wines to choose from. Caleb and Eliza politely declined all food and beverages and they used the encounters with the vendors to ask a lot of questions about the day's events. All that remained was the small matter of getting an audience with the emperor, who sat two boxes to the left.

As Eliza and Caleb spoke to each other, they noticed that another teenage girl dressed in all white adorned with gold had entered their box and stood near them without speaking. She looked to be a year or two older than they did. Caleb had seen an identical girl in the emperor's box and wondered if she was the same person. She did not appear to be selling anything. Caleb motioned for her to come to them. She had some script she spoke to them that Caleb could tell she had said many times before. He guessed that she was an indentured slave.

"Good afternoon," she said. "I have been assigned to assist you during the time at Coliseum. Tell me what to need and I will give it to you." She had a slight accent and poor Greek grammar. She was obviously not a native Greek speaker.

"So, what events relocated you to Rome as an indentured servant?" Eliza asked in perfect Ebreet. She made sure to use larger nouns and verbs to confirm that she knew the Ebreet from the Torah, not the street version often spoken by Romans who tried to sell to Ebreet.

"Ma'am, I do not…" the girl started.

"What is your name?" Eliza interrupted. "You are like us and a member of the twelve tribes, are you not?"

Caleb followed up Eliza's demanding question with a softer one of his own. "You understand us, yes? You are from the Promised Land of Abraham, Isaac, and Jacob. I am from Benjamin and she is from Naphtali. So, what is your name?" Caleb spoke in a gentle voice, though. He and Eliza had much practice speaking to strangers in alternating tones to get information from them.

"Yael," the girl said in perfect Ebreet. "My name is Yael."

Caleb had just placed a small piece of fresh bread and hummus in his mouth as the young woman spoke. His jaw dropped and some food fell out as she said her name the second time. He quickly apologized and the girl bent over to pick up the dropped piece of food. "Please, you don't have to do that. This incident was my fault," said Caleb. He felt an onslaught of shame that a beautiful woman felt that she needed to pick up food that had fallen from his mouth. As soon as he picked it up, he looked into her eyes.

"You know, Yael was my mother's name," Caleb said as he put the bread into his pocket for disposal later. The girl asked to take it from him and he could not let himself force an Ebreet woman to carry something that was already in his mouth. It was against the Talmud for such a thing. Instead, he took the broom that was in the corner and swept up the crumbs off of the well-swept stone floor. All the while, Yael and Eliza began speaking. Once Caleb was done cleaning up, he looked up and saw that the girls were talking incessantly. Eliza must have said something that triggered this new girl.

"Caleb, she knows your mother!" Eliza said. Caleb's eyes bulged. He could not believe that in the middle of the most hedonistic place in the empire, a remnant of his mother's teaching stood in their presence. Yael spoke to Caleb in their native tongue, no longer trying to hide her heritage.

"When I attended school, one of our rabbis was a woman whose name was also Yael! I was told that she was the only female rabbi in all of the promised land. Eliza says she must be your mother!" Yael covered her mouth to stifle a shriek.

This loud conversation in a foreign tongue brought the attention of the Roman couple in the luxury booth next to theirs, and they peered over the edge to see what the source of the commotion was.

"Please excuse us," Caleb said politely. "We got lost in our storytelling. Please forgive us and enjoy your afternoon," said Caleb, using perfect and polite Greek. The middle-aged couple stepped back from the brick barricade, dismissing the perceived young and irresponsible royals. They leaned back and most likely said something negative about Roman youth these days. Once they were gone, all three of them giggled, holding back their laughter.

Eliza had already figured out that Yael was the concierge and assistant for the day. Eliza and Caleb were new to the Coliseum and their admission included the services of a guide. Yael was assigned to them for the day.

"Yael, can you get people to leave us alone?" Eliza asked. Yael looked up and Caleb and Eliza smiled. Despite being a slave, she had something of value that she knew that they didn't.

"I sure can. Hold on," she said. She stepped outside their suite and hung a "do not disturb" sign above their archway, thereby shutting off vendor visits. She stepped back in and posed for a moment.

"There you go! No one else will come in," she said. Eliza thanked her, but as she looked at Caleb, she could see that Caleb was mesmerized by Yael. In fact, he was almost bashful as he smiled at the woman.

"Caleb!" Eliza said, snapping him from his stupor. There was no doubt that Caleb was beginning to like girls.

"Sorry. I was daydreaming," he said. He quickly returned to eating and looking down at the parade, waiting for it to start. He was embarrassed that Eliza caught him looking at Yael.

Eliza and Yael continued to talk and giggle, and they felt a natural ease with each other that could not have been scripted. Eliza quickly told her how much she hated the clothing that she was wearing, feeling that she was all but exposed for everyone to see her. Yael quickly agreed, wishing for a quality cloak from Judah that she could wear to keep warm as it was windy and not expose her breasts while she leaned forward. Within moments, they were complaining about the taste of some Roman food but also marveling at how much they enjoyed all the selections in the market. Caleb came back after a pause, watching the preparation for the start of the opening ceremonies.

"It is as if you two have known each other for years," he said. He joined them in casual conversation for a moment before the main procession began.

The parade commenced on the Coliseum's main floor. The first to enter were flag bearers and trumpeters. The crowd cheered, and many of the royalty near them called out the names of the gladiators that they had sponsored and had come out to see fight. This distraction gave the newly acquainted friends a chance to interact freely with no concern of eavesdropping.

Perhaps the most special part of the moment was that they all got to be Ebreet children again, leaving behind the burdens that enslavement and foreign occupation created. Caleb picked on the girls as if they were all in school, and the girls found joy in asking him questions that he could not answer. They talked until the parade was nearly over, and all three of them felt safe despite the nearby presence of the enemy of their people.

Caleb was impressed with how much of his mother's teaching this girl knew. He asked her lots of questions, and in return, she provided them with great intelligence about Rome. Eliza and Caleb were amazed that she was a slave and not some employee, as she was intelligent and deliberate in her speech. They learned that Yael worked inside the palace and was "leased" out to the Coliseum management company on a per-event basis. Today, she was sent to this box, but she had tomorrow off from work. She and Eliza already had plans to have tea together first thing, and Eliza told her to meet at the fancy shop outside the synagogue, where she knew that she would get real tea from back home, not the Roman stuff.

Yael was in tune with the community of believers in Rome. She said that there were many synagogues all over the city that proclaimed a risen Messiah. Many of their members were current and former Roman military. A lot of the converts had come to know the Messiah from the remarkable tales related to the prisoner Paul. The city was experiencing a mass awakening of faith, and people were migrating away from their polytheistic roots to Yeshua. Caleb's mother had visited three of them, and all had Roman military and Roman prison guards as members.

"That is amazing. I saw some Roman soldiers outside the synagogue with the yellow door near here. I learned they were helping the brothers and sisters," he said.

"I know that synagogue and Rabbi John," she said.

"Wow," said Caleb, staring into Yael's eyes. Eliza watched the two of them and she sensed more than just curiosity between them.

Yael, though, did not paint a perfect world for Messiah followers in Rome. Most people were not sympathetic to their cause. Most Yeshuian faced physical danger, as Roman citizens, guards, and soldiers considered faith in any god other than the emperor to be unlawful. The followers did not speak out against the emperor in public, as this act often ended in martyrdom. She said that all the local rabbis taught them to follow Yeshua in all things but not to foolishly cast their lives away to make their point. Instead, they were taught to engage in prayer for those who did not know the Messiah as they went about their days in the capital city.

Yael told them that since Titus had become emperor, there had been no edicts that restricted Yeshuians, as there had been under emperor Vespasian or those from the line of Caesar who came before him, but the old edict of no god before Caesar remained. Although outside gatherings in public were not allowed, there were few barriers to having private events or Sabbath gatherings that included traditional Ebreet customs. Members of the Senate disagreed, but Titus would often remind them of their obligation to serve the people, and few defied him.

"This new emperor has been a great blessing to us. This emperor does not see the Messiah as a threat like those who have come before him," Yael said. Caleb had been exclusively listening to them but now needed to say something.

"My uncle Rufus taught me nearly all I know about hunting and combat," Caleb said. "He was best friends with Titus while the two of them served in the army. They traveled the world together, conquering lands and peoples in Britannia, Gaul, and our native Benjamin. Once Rufus saw that a life without belief in the Messiah was meaningless, he quit the military at the rank of the legate and stayed back in the Holy Land. He married Gesher, an Ebreet woman, and he served as a protector for the remaining synagogues that were near Jerusalem. He did not have any children of his own, though." said Caleb, speaking out his new thought.

"Cousin, he loved you like a son," said Eliza. She had told him this before in private but not publicly. Yael watched their exchange and she could see the bond between the two of them. Their intimacy and public display of love seemed genuine, and she wanted to be a part of it.

"You two are a breath of fresh air and a fond memory of my homeland. I am so glad that I got to meet you," Yael said. Caleb abruptly switched the direction of the conversation.

"My uncle was killed a few weeks ago. I have his ring." Caleb held up his left hand, showing her the intricate metal and gemstone artifact on his middle finger. Yael looked at the ring and Caleb, obviously in awe.

"I do not know what to say," she replied. She closed her eyes and was obviously praying. Instantly, Eliza reached out and held her hand. Yael was startled but opened her eyes and saw that it was Eliza.

"I will pray with you," Eliza said.

"Thank you," was all Yael could say. She captured the courage to look Caleb directly in the eye.

"God has a purpose for you being here this very day. He has his hand on you, Caleb of the tribe of Benjamin," Yael said. Caleb looked at her and felt her admiration. None of the girls at school would speak to him as directly as she did, and it further mesmerized him. At that moment, he found himself seeing her beauty and had no interest in breaking eye contact with her. Eliza sensed Caleb's infatuation with Yael and she could see that Yael was enjoying her connection with the large warrior. Their shared affection made Eliza smile.

Yael turned back to Eliza and continued talking about what the emperor had done in the last few weeks. Titus had extended freedom of worship to the polytheistic Greeks and sun god-worshipping Egyptians who had been brought into the city to help with the rebuilding after the fire. She said that Rome was a melting pot of culture and religion these days. Titus saw much value in his vision for a more architectural Rome built for the residents of all Roman lands. He wanted them to have a sense of ownership in the city and its culture. Titus chose to extend a Sabbath grace not just to the Ebreet but to all faiths that had their equivalent of a day of rest.

"The emperor has lots of sexual relations but currently lives with a single concubine, and she is Ebreet! I often serve her."

"Is that the truth?" said Caleb. He wanted some evidence that his uncle's descriptions of the emperor were true. "Does he have excellent aim with a javelin, even at fifty cubits?" he asked. Yael stared at him like he was from the top of Mount Ararat. She had no idea how to respond, but she did the best she could.

"I see His Grace eat, I hear him have sex, I hear him complain, I serve him wine before and after he issues edicts, but I have not seen him throw a javelin." Caleb laughed. He realized he had asked a stupid question.

This did not deter Caleb from trying to beat his chest and tell this beautiful girl about combat and hunting. He repeated tales that his uncle Rufus had told him about his best friend before he had become emperor. He told her how Rufus' father was the famous centurion spoken of in the new writings of their faith. The girls politely listened, but she did not care about hunting or the father of a dead man. However, listening to Caleb was more enjoyable than watching animals and people killed.

"Our parents watched Cornelius the centurion baptize Rufus in my hometown. Titus was invited to that event," said Eliza proudly.

"I have read the letters. Titus has heard of the Messiah from Uncle Rufus," Caleb explained. "Uncle Rufus left Titus after the fall of Jerusalem, but the two of them saw each other many times after that," said Caleb.

Eliza's brain raced as she thought of a way to get to him. She breathed deeply and exhaled slowly. Puzzled, the others looked at her, but they had no idea what was on her mind.

"Do you think you could arrange a meeting with Titus for us?" she asked. Before allowing Yael the chance to answer, Eliza told her the complete story of her parents' capture and their need for help from the emperor.

Yael stared straight ahead in disbelief at what she had just been asked. She nodded and spoke.

"I think so. The emperor is relatively approachable. I have an idea that should work. Stand by my Do Not Disturb sign and look for me to signal you. When you see my signal, come immediately. Once I point you towards the emperor, he will be alone. I can't help you after that."

Eliza said, "Yes!" and jumped up and down. Yael looked at Caleb and pointed at him, saying, "I will pray for you, as your mother taught me how to do that." Caleb smiled at Yael. He liked her persona and it didn't hurt that she was just as beautiful as Eliza.

"And you are part of our answered prayers," he said.

"Let's pray!" Eliza looked to the sky, forgetting where she was, raising her hands to the heavens and speaking out to God, just as she had seen her aunt Yael do countless times. "Living God, Jehovah Jireh, may Your will come to be. Allow me to be a servant and use this man to bring my family back together. I ask these things in Your Son's name. Amen."

Eliza did not know that while she prayed, Caleb and Yael had their eyes locked upon each other. Yael was a part of their solution. Caleb knew it.

Chapter 27:
A Meeting at the Emperor's Throne

Eliza stood by the sign on the wall while Caleb watched the proceedings in the pits below them with great interest. Eliza was on the lookout for a signal from Yael that it was time to meet the emperor. All the while, she kept her part of the agreement and prayed.

Caleb had absorbed everything that Yael had told him about the goings-on inside the Coliseum. Apparently, every event was sponsored either by a specific person or the empire. *Munera* were paid for in advance by wealthy families, and those who purchased the rights to hold these events would sell admission or allow entrance at no cost to earn the adoration of the Roman citizens who attended. Rome, acting as a nation/state, would hold events called *ludi* for citizens as spectacles to display justice and its associated bloodshed. These included great acts of punishment, maiming, and death. The Roman Senate concluded that these events should be public and well-marketed, as they provided the citizens and their slaves something to talk about other than the dullness of their daily lives. The Coliseum provided meaning for what might otherwise be a meaningless life. In addition, during *ludi*, individuals accused of crimes would be fed to wild animals or be forced to fight newer gladiators to give the newer fighters some much-needed experience. This reinforced the consequences of breaking the law, keeping the city fearful of defiance.

During *munera* and *ludi*, the main attraction was the fights that pitted one house's gladiator against another house's gladiator. The outcomes of these battles brought great glory to the winner and death to the loser. Many of the gladiators carried the signa of their sponsoring house on their helmets and armor as advertising for their family and the family's business. Once their gladiator entered combat, a representative from each house would be escorted to the pits below, where they could step out at the conclusion of the battle to celebrate the victory with their gladiator. For the royalty in attendance, the possibility of being present during the celebration made the act of going to the Coliseum worth the cost of investing in a gladiator sponsorship. For the wealthy, supporting a gladiator meant living a life of glory without the risk of dying in battle.

Caleb watched two events from beginning to end while they waited for a signal from Yael. During the first one, a younger man who had been found guilty of stealing from a market vendor on two different occasions had to fight a beast. His penalty was to combat a pack of hungry dogs. He was set free to run on the sand-covered pits while the dogs chased him. Prior to the *ludi*, the dogs were denied any food for three days. The handlers had learned from experience that three days of starvation would make the dogs the most aggressive yet strong enough to overcome him if he fought back. The boy was given a single knife to defend himself.

The boy looked up at the emperor, crying out for mercy, as he climbed on blocks of sandstone and marble placed strategically in the pits for combatants to use as strategic protection. Occasionally, a man on a horse would come out with a whip. He would strike the boy, making him move off the block he was standing on and run for his life to another block while the dogs chased him. It took two whippings before one of the dogs caught the boy by an ankle, and they began tearing into his pinned leg. He kicked in resistance, trying to stab at them, but he failed to stop them. Eventually, a larger male dog sunk its teeth into his other leg, biting through a nerve and leaving the boy immobilized. Caleb thought that the dogs would attempt to sever the arteries in the neck, as they would do with a deer, but they did not. Instead, one of the most disgusting things that any of them had seen came to pass.

The sound of the boy as he was eaten alive caused many of the men in the royalty section to laugh. Despite his love of combat, Caleb could not appreciate what they were seeing; he was disgusted at the justice served in this place. His cousin covered her ears, and

Caleb was aware that it wasn't very pleasant for Eliza to hear these sounds. That boy was nearly his age and was inadequately prepared to defend himself. Caleb found the hearts of the men who orchestrated this event detestable. He thought the fight was unfair, but he did not dare speak up. He had learned from his attempts at retaliation in Tamar that vengeance was not his to administer, so he spoke to himself under his breath. "Vengeance is the Lord's. Lord, you have to solve this one."

As the boy cried out and could no longer resist the starved animals, Caleb recalled one of his father's teachings. "There will come a day when we breathe no more and we will stand in front of the Messiah, the Father, and the Holy Spirit. We will account for our actions. Those who do not have the Messiah will be found guilty of sin, and they will pay a penalty for that sin that makes the worst abomination on earth seem trivial."

And it will be worse than this? Caleb thought.

Once the match was over, three young Egyptian women carrying baskets on their heads came out and picked up the remains of the boy, placing the entrails in their baskets before returning to the caves under the pits. The man on the horse climbed down, calling over the dogs and petting two of them before leading them through a portcullis and down into the dungeons below. The dogs had been fed, and it was time to put them away. Caleb wanted to throw up at the disgusting nature of what he was seeing. Eliza had long since stopped watching.

Caleb could not believe that that boy's life had been given such low value. He imagined that the contents of those baskets would become a meal for another animal living in the dungeons below. He prayed again. "Jehovah Jireh, may that boy's soul be with You now, just as my parents are. This boy did not deserve this grisly end. Let him find peace with You."

Without an intermission, the second event started. This match began with lengthy introductions that were interrupted by cheers from the crowd. A single gladiator from one of the houses of Caesar was introduced and he wore great armor and a gold-covered helmet. On the other side, a tall and powerful-looking Egyptian who was called the "modern Goliath" was introduced to the crowd by the crier. The Egyptian towered over everyone else and wore a helmet and chest covering of leather hide. He carried out three javelins and three spears, which were like ones the Roman military carried but much longer and tipped with what appeared to be a polished form of wrought iron. He set out, placing them in strategic places around the pit as he raised his fists, bringing down floods of applause. The other gladiator carried a single gladius and a small shield of the sort that made gladiators famous.

The emperor and everyone else stood up and stopped talking. He raised his hand and spoke. "You shall fight to the death or until I tell you to stop. Do you understand the penalty of disobedience?" The men looked up and nodded.

"Begin," he said coolly. The crowd erupted with noise, and men yelled down to the pits their recommendations for combat. Caleb could tell that there was a split in loyalties between the Egyptian and the Roman. Everyone in his section rooted for one of the two men, but Caleb could not see any patterns or any favorites on the combat floor.

The Roman charged first, holding his weapon in one hand and his small shield in the other. Caleb loved the size and shape of his weapon. He speculated on how easy it must be to use it compared to the javelin and spear combination that the Egyptians used. But success could occur in close proximity to the swordsman and nowhere else.

As he charged, the soldier raised his fist to the crowd. Nearing the Egyptian, he rolled on the ground as the towering Egyptian launched a javelin at him. The Roman intentionally went to the ground and rolled twice, bringing him close enough to strike. His blade was sharp, and it connected with his opponent. Blood rapidly began to flow from the Egyptian's right leg as the blade sliced deeply. Using a spear, the Egyptian responded by attempting to pierce the fighter but failed to plunge the point into an unarmored location. The fighter rolled again to separate himself from the Egyptian. He stood back up and attempted to run behind a nearby marble block. Although the Egyptian was wounded in his leg, he was able to hurl the javelin at his combatant before he reached cover. It struck with a force hard enough to knock the man down. The Roman's back was not as well armored as his front, and Caleb speculated that the Egyptian hit his kidney. The Egyptian moved to pick up one of his spears and hobbled toward the stunned man, placing minimal weight on his injured ankle. The fighter was able to rotate to expose his more protected front side, and the spear glanced off of his armor. From the ground, the Roman swung at the man's already injured leg, hoping to destroy it. However, he had let himself get too close. The Egyptian knew his spear would not be effective against this man's armor, so he picked up the gladiator and threw him into the air, hoping that the impact and the inward folding of his armor would stun him. On his way up, the armored combatant struck the Egyptian on the shoulder, and the blade bit into his flesh. He dropped the gladiator before he could get him over his head, but the force of the armor on the man's smaller frame made him scream. The Roman clung to his gladius as his life depended on it.

The crowd was cheering so loudly that it was deafening, but Caleb was surprised to see that the Emperor was not cheering. The Egyptian picked the man up a second time and this time, the gladiator struck the Egyptian's forearm. The blow was not solid but his blade was sharp and the Egyptian was unarmored. Blood immediately poured from this new wound. Again, the Egyptian dropped the man and covered the wound with his hand to stop the bleeding, screaming with rage. The fighter used that moment to roll away from this Goliath and attempt to stand up. He could not, as Caleb thought he had broken several ribs and lacked the strength.

Both combatants were now seriously wounded, and the Roman tried to hold his broken ribs in his chest through his armor, his lungs obviously damaged. Men wearing armor were not meant to be thrown. The Egyptian figured this out.

"I think the Egyptian will win," Caleb spoke out loud, but no one was listening. He turned around, and Eliza and Yael were nowhere to be seen. He returned to the battle, fixated on the action.

Although the Egyptian had wounds to his leg, shoulder, and forearm, he was mobile and able to wield all of his weapons. He had two nearby javelins in the arena to use and one was right next to him. In his present state, the injured Roman could not defend indefinitely against assault.

A pattern emerged. The Egyptian would throw javelins at the gladiator as he attempted to close the distance between them. Any time the Roman would attempt to close the gap, the Egyptian would thrust the javelin at the man's exposed legs, and the fighter would be forced to retreat. Eventually, one of the Egyptian's throws struck an exposed part of the gladiator's armor and pierced into his chest. The Roman's cry made the crowd erupt with applause, and Caleb could see that he was now irrecoverably wounded. He reached up and tried to wrench out the javelin, but it was too far into his torso, and his adrenaline had long since faded.

The Egyptian raised his spear to the sky, creating a near-deafening response filled with profane calls to finish the Roman and send him to Hades. The Egyptian thrust his final spear into the exposed thigh of his opponent, permanently sending him to the ground. The Egyptian left the spear in the man's leg and walked to retrieve another as the crowd screamed for him to finish the gladiator. Since the Egyptian's ankle was now beginning to fail him, this took a great deal of time.

The crowd began to chant. Some cheered for the Roman to pull out the spear and get back into the fight. However, his will to fight back was now gone, for he knew that if he pulled out the spear, he could not close the gap on the Egyptian and get close enough to strike at his flesh.

As was the custom, the Roman threw his gladius on the ground in front of the soon-to-be winner and gave up. The Egyptian made no spectacle of the man's choice to submit and he pushed his final spear into his neck and out the other side, spilling the man's blood onto the sand.

Caleb looked into the audience as they rejoiced in the goriness of the ending. He watched and listened as men in the crowd chatted with each other, each suggesting what the combatants could have done differently. Caleb had seen enough. He walked back to where his cousin awaited a signal from Yael. Eliza was glad to see him as she was a bit overwhelmed by blocking out the sounds of the match while watching for Yael.

"Caleb, how you can watch that?" He knew better than to respond. After a brief moment of non-responsiveness, she continued with a different line of conversation.

"I've been thinking. I do not think it was by chance that this Yael knew your mother. I do not think our meeting with her was a chance either. And I know how you are looking at her. Those blind men's prophecy about who you would meet today is making sense." Caleb was too numb to respond to any of that, whether it be true or otherwise.

"Caleb, I think what we are seeing is the presence of Yahweh in this place. God is bigger than circumstance. Our prayers are being answered right now in this place of evil!" Caleb looked at her, and the numbness wore off enough to respond.

"That first boy's prayers weren't answered, nor was that Roman's," Caleb replied. Eliza wasn't watching, so she couldn't respond to that. Yet, she had made more observations that she wanted to share with Caleb before he met the Emperor.

"I've been watching the emperor, too. During the last battle, he seemed distracted. He did not talk to anyone. Caleb, I think he's lonely. He did not drink any wine or eat. After watching how he did not care about that ending, I can tell you that something is missing from his life." He looked at her and down the hallway to see if Yael had emerged yet.

"Uncle Rufus told me many times why he quit the military. He said that no matter how successful he was on the battlefield or in bed, it could not bring him happiness. The emperor hasn't discovered that his heart is the same as Uncle Rufus's in that regard," Caleb said.

"Caleb! Yael is signaling us!" Eliza interrupted. "Let's go!"

They quickly left their box and headed toward Yael, who gestured for them to hurry. She stood near an arch that led to the bathroom.

"The emperor just entered the bathroom during the intermission! If you want an audience with him, go find him in there now."

Caleb nodded at the girls and they wished him well. He took a deep breath and entered the bathroom. He rounded the corner, and there sat Titus, his royal robe hanging on a hook built into the wall next to his toilet. Caleb looked directly at him and addressed him in a confident voice. "I am Rufus' nephew from Judea," he began, pausing long enough for his claim to be processed. He knew that it was the emperor's order that the entire land now be called "Judah," but he also knew that Titus had been there during the years it was known as Judea. He risked offending the emperor in doing this, but challenging him seemed like the quickest way to earn his respect. Titus looked intrigued.

"Your Grace, my family needs your help," he continued. Next came the most difficult part. He needed to be quiet and wait for the emperor to respond.

"And you have some proof that you are his nephew, I assume?" Titus asked.

Caleb had expected this and he had practiced his response with Eliza on the boat ride. He took off his uncle Rufus' ring and casually tossed it to the emperor.

Titus caught it and inspected it. "Incredible," he said. "I remember the day he got this ring."

"My uncle said that when you were boys, you would run outside on the Palatine Hill and the first one to the top of the hill would throw stones at the other while they finished. He said you would catch the stones when he beat you. That is why I threw it to you instead of handing it to you."

"Is that so?" said Titus, cracking a smile. He looked down at the ring and shook his head. Caleb's strategy was working. Fond memories were flooding the emperor's mind.

"Oh, Rufus. I do miss him. He was a great friend. I would die alongside him." It was apparent that emperor Titus, ruler of the Roman Empire and all its lands, was an army boy at heart. Caleb and Eliza's strategy to bring him back to the old memories that he kept of Rufus had succeeded. "So, did Rufus give you this ring, or did you steal it from him? And what is it that you need?"

"I am not here for myself. It is for my family," Caleb said. He turned his head back towards the entrance and called out, "Eliza! Come in here, please."

Although he was done with his ablutions, Titus remained seated as Eliza entered. Yael stayed outside.

"Your Grace," said Eliza as she entered. She acted like a Roman woman might act before approaching the presence of the emperor, bowing down and not making eye contact with him.

"So, you are also Ebreet yet you look and act like a Roman woman of wealth," Titus said, and Eliza caught a glimmer of admiration in his tone. He spoke again, trying to rattle her.

"Well done with your disguise, Little One." He used the Ebreet term of affection. She knew this man to be fond of flesh, and Eliza immediately got scared. Titus saw her fear, and it made him smile.

Titus stood up, washed himself with a water challis, and donned his royal robe again. He walked towards the exit, holding the ring, gesturing for Eliza and Caleb to follow. Yael was at the exit, with her head bowed as the three of them walked out. Once they cleared that area, he turned to them and spoke. "So, how is Rufus these days?" he asked.

"My uncle is dead," Caleb said. "He was killed unarmed in Mishi and Yael's village a few weeks ago. The men who did it were current soldiers of yours."

"Do you remember Mishi?" Eliza interjected. She knew that action was the most valuable method to combat fear. "He was the young rabbi who spent the first days with Rufus after the fall of the Temple!"

"I do. He was the skinny man, but he could talk to anyone and make them feel like he was their friend, and he was quite funny if I remember correctly."

"He was my father," said Caleb, standing up straight. He knew that the Roman military mandated absolute reverence for the bloodline.

Titus stared deep into Caleb's eyes and examined his body as if it were a camel at an auction. The emperor nodded his approval of Caleb's physique, but Caleb remained a bit scared. Caleb appeared strong, but in his heart, he feared that the emperor might ask him why he did not have the physique that his father had at that age. He was not ready for that question. "What happened to those men, the ones who killed old Rufus?" Titus asked instead.

"I killed them, Your Grace," said Caleb.

Titus nodded, wearing an eerie smile that displayed respect. He looked first at Caleb and second at the two girls. Eliza and Yael were holding hands, scared and staring at the two of them interacting. Yael had not seen any man challenge the emperor as Caleb had just done, and she had not seen the Emperor extend respect during a negotiation without any demeaning language.

Caleb no longer had a script of questions for him to follow. All that they had hoped to accomplish was to meet Titus and connect with him. They had already gotten far beyond what they had imagined.

"And how did you do that?" Titus asked. Caleb had just watched how the emperor observed the gladiator battle and he told his story with details that he thought the emperor would appreciate. He included his response to seeing his parents take their last breath as his justification for killing the Romans. He showed him the injury to his forehead that happened right before he slit the throat of the centurion with his counter. He also explained his choice to rip through the calf muscle as deeply as he could before attempting to retreat and proactively strike. He recalled the number of steps he had taken and how he had removed his uncle's ring after Rufus had gestured to him to do so.

"Your recall of the details of such an event is impressive. Rufus trained you well. Yet, I can see that killing a man still shakes you, yes?" he asked.

"Yes, it does shake me. Rufus was my weapons and combat instructor," said Caleb. The emperor paused for a minute before speaking. He was impressed with the young man's courage and honesty.

"So, you killed my soldiers and one of my centurions and you come asking for permission to find this girl's parents to set them free without any consequences for your actions? Is that true?"

"Yes, I do, and yes, it is," said Caleb. "Your Grace," he added quickly. Titus noted how the girls were glued to watching Caleb.

"Well, you are a brave and honest young man. I may give you what you seek, but it will come at a cost. Consider it a consequence for the destruction of my property."

"We're listening," said Eliza. Titus looked back at Eliza for a moment before returning his gaze to Caleb. He pointed a finger back at Eliza and spoke to the young man.

"She also speaks with courage despite not being spoken to."

"Please forgive her," said Caleb. "She is a young woman who wants her parents back. I wish to honor her." That brought a smile to the emperor's face, bigger than anything Caleb had seen during the gladiator fights.

"I will ask you for two things. If you can give me one of them, I may give you what you ask for to set your parents free."

Fear entered their hearts. Whatever the emperor was about to offer would require sacrifice, they were sure. They did not know what he was about to ask.

Chapter 28:
The Choice Versus the Outcome

"Let's not talk out here. Follow me," Titus said. The emperor motioned for them to join him in his royal box without making eye contact. Once they were inside, the emperor spoke while adjusting his robes.

"Your first option is to fight in my pits and entertain me," the emperor said. Yael and Eliza continued to hold hands and stare at Caleb. The emperor could see that Caleb was very special to them, and he quickly formulated his second choice.

"Your Grace, I do not want to kill," Caleb replied without hesitation. His uncle Rufus taught him that responding to a question was important in the military. He wanted to say more but knew that his next step was to be courageous and wait for the emperor to offer an alternative. After all, the emperor had said that he would give Caleb two choices.

"Very well. The alternative is that I will bed these two girls who are quite fond of you. The choice is yours."

"Come here," gestured Titus. Titus walked to the edge of his box so the entire population of the Coliseum could see him and the two girls.

Time stood still for all the Ebreet. Yael looked down, but something overcame Eliza, and she smiled and looked into the emperor's eyes. Caleb stared as the two of them locked eyes and it made him recall a talk with his mother a few weeks ago. She had just told him that she was raped.

"My son, you are a beautiful boy, and you are becoming a beautiful man. Many people admire your strength, but we live in a dangerous world."

"Mom, why did you not fight back? Kick him or something?" Caleb thought it to be a complete weakness that his mother lacked the will or the skill to defend herself, and he remembered his promise not to let that happen on his watch. His mother's answer didn't help.

"I was scared and upset at all the things happening around me. I had just seen atrocities that no person should have to see. But there will come a day during which we all must see what we do not wish to see and do what we do not wish to do. It is my prayer that you act and do not feel as paralyzed as I felt."

Caleb saw this as his moment. It was exactly what his mother was talking to him about. His choice was difficult, with either outcome resulting in people getting hurt. Should he fight and kill innocent people to save his cousin and their new friend, or should he let them be defiled in the same manner that his mother let herself be defiled?

Titus spoke to the girls with authority. "Pull down your robe for all to see and admire your bare chest," he said. Without hesitation, the girls undid their two tie strings and the emperor pulled down their robes, exposing their breasts to the 70,000 people watching the emperor's booth throughout the Coliseum. Eliza began to cry and Yael held Eliza's forearm tightly, staring up into the clouds. Yael had been abused like this in the past and she knew how to cope by pretending that she wasn't there.

That display pushed Caleb over the edge of indecision. It was time to honor the promise he made to his mother. He raised his voice and spoke to Titus using a diminutive language.

"I will not give you my sisters. I will fight!" Caleb yelled. The emperor expected as much, and he turned to look at Caleb and smiled.

"A good and entertaining choice."

Caleb knew that he had just committed to the highest levels of sacrifice by addressing Yael and Eliza as his sisters. That now meant that their honor was his honor, and their dishonor was his dishonor.

Yeshua expressed intimacy each time he called his listeners his brothers and sisters. He called all of his disciples' brothers, not students. His parents had told him that to embrace someone as a brother or sister is to regard them as equal to yourself in all ways. Caleb needed these two people to be equal in importance so that he could kill on their behalf. Titus knew enough about Ebreet custom to know that Caleb was now fully committed to combat.

Caleb moved to reach the girls and he pulled up their robes to help them cover back up. He was embarrassed for them and he swore in Aramaic loud enough for both of them to hear him. He kissed each of them on the cheek, promising to take care of them.

While Caleb comforted them, the emperor called for two additional soldiers and gave the senior one orders to change the sequence of events and place Caleb in the fourth and final slot on the day's docket.

As the girls covered themselves, Yael grabbed Caleb's forearm and forced him to look her in the eye.

"Your sister?" said Yael, literally in disbelief at what she had just heard and the honor she had just received. "I cannot accept that level of honor. Caleb, you and I just met each other!" she said.

"Yes, it is true we just met, but you are wrong. You are worth that level of honor," he said. His conviction was obvious and he placed his hands on her shoulders and stared as deeply into her eyes as he could.

"Ok," she said.

Eliza also pleaded with Caleb: "Please, just let this crazy ultimatum pass. My parents' lives are worth more than my body!" Yael still held his forearm and she pulled to get his attention again.

"Caleb, I need to say something shameful. I am not a virgin," said Yael. "I have been bedded against my will many times." Caleb watched and listened as her voice cracked and Caleb's blood boiled with rage. However, he did not speak. He could only grind his teeth and nod his head. This technique to get him to relent was backfiring on them. Caleb was more committed than ever to fight. However, Yael was not done with her plea.

"Caleb, I can survive rape and I can help Eliza survive rape. Do not give your life so foolishly for us." Eliza's heart shattered as she heard Yael use that word and anger inside of her rose as she relived her aunt's trauma.

Although the girls were crying, Caleb felt more hurt and pain than either of them, but he could not express it. He was the head of the household, called by God to be their protector. Caleb could see right through their combined strategy to sway him with guilt. It did not work, and he did not respond to them, either. He looked at Yael and declared the affection for her that he didn't even know he felt.

"You shall not be required to give yourself to these brutes again. Or anyone, for that matter," he said, making extra effort to control his desire to erupt emotionally.

"Follow us, Palestina," said the two soldiers.

Caleb turned around and walked behind the two soldiers as they escorted him to the preparation area below the pits. As he was about to leave, the two girls made one last effort to dissuade him from casting aside his life.

"Caleb, let us do this instead of you!" Eliza said. "We do not want you to die! What you are thinking is folly! Our sacrifice will pass quickly." The emperor did not know their language, but he could tell the girls did not want him to give in to his desire for bloodshed so quickly. The emperor admired his resolve.

"If you want a combat, I will give it to you," Caleb said firmly to Titus. "Promise me that you will leave my sisters alone and I will fight to the death. Will you promise me this?"

"I am the emperor," Titus said. "I make no promises to anyone, let alone an Ebreet. Remember, I destroyed your Temple."

Caleb knew not to let personal assaults break his focus as a soldier. Uncle Rufus had practiced these sorts of verbal assaults with Caleb as they walked back from their hunts. Caleb allowed the words to pass, and he focused his efforts on his cause. That was the tenant of his teachings.

"My uncle said you were an honorable man. If I kill for you, will you leave my sisters undefiled?"

Caleb was not truly speaking for his sisters. He was speaking for his mother. Caleb had decided that he would gladly give his life to prevent such an event as his mother's rape from happening to another generation of young and beautiful girls.

"Take him down to the pits," the emperor said to the guards. Caleb decided that this meant yes.

Uncle Rufus gave his parents the writings he had acquired of Yeshua's brother, John. One of those writings spoke to him in this moment; it gave him peace. He turned to Eliza and spoke out loud in Greek for all to hear.

"There is no greater love than to lay down one's life for one's friends." The difference between John's word and his word was that Yael and Eliza were now his family.

Chapter 29:
Life Expands and Contracts

Caleb was led through a series of passageways under the Coliseum towards a pre-fight staging area. He could hear the crowd screaming intermittently, but he didn't know why or at what. On the way, they passed an entrance gated by a portcullis that led to the fighting pits, and he could see and hear the combat. Caleb paused to look at the two men currently fighting. One of the combatants was seasoned, fully aware that there was no urgency to end the match. The other one had a look of desperation on his face as he circled the older fighter. They appeared to be injured. Caleb had enough experience as a spectator to know that the screaming he heard happened when one of them shed blood.

"Wait, let's watch for a minute. I have never been this close," Caleb said. They observed for a moment before the soldier pressed for them to keep moving. As the noise reached a crescendo, Caleb wondered who had scored the big hit. Did the patience of the seasoned combatant win, or did the desperation of the younger warrior?

"Who won?" Caleb asked the soldier.

"No one yet. The crowd isn't loud enough for there to have been a victor yet."

"I have no experience with fighting to the death," Caleb said, looking to calm his nerves with small talk.

"What have you done then?" asked the soldier.

"I have hunted animals and killed a couple of Roman soldiers and their centurion. That's about it."

"A centurion? How did you kill the centurion?" Despite Caleb's sincere effort to downplay his prowess, there were fewer than one hundred people alive who could claim single-handedly killing a squad and their centurion.

Caleb told him of the attack on his village. He told him how he used controlled cutting, rolling, and luring to get the centurion to overcommit and leave himself vulnerable. He showed the wound on his forehead, just as he had done with the emperor moments earlier.

"A gladiator who thinks!" said the soldier with genuine respect. Caleb didn't like being called a gladiator, but he had no time to protect. They immediately arrived at the staging area next to the entrance to the pits. Two other young boys approached Caleb and the soldier, asking them what sorts of weapons and armor they wished for.

"I will use my bow. I need some weighted arrows. I also need two hunting knives," Caleb said as clearly as he could to make sure he got exactly what he was looking for. I do not want arrows if they do not have a metal tip. I will keep this light armor that I am wearing," he said, taking off his fancy robe and giving it to the boys to hang up.

"I want some lighter and better-strapped sandals, though." The first boy walked to the side room to get what he asked for.

"What about you?" said one of the young boys.

"I'm good, Mark," said the soldier who had been escorting Caleb to the pits. He took off his cloak and handed it to the boy, who hung it on a nail near the gates. He picked up an ornate shield from a nail on the wall and unsheathed his sword, handing it to the other boy to sharpen and polish.

Caleb's heart fell as he realized that he might have been taken to the pits by the same person he would be fighting. He watched the soldier begin a stretching routine to prepare for combat. A sense of fear came over him. It was obvious that this man had many more years of fighting behind him than Caleb did and that he was on a first-name basis with the boys who assisted the gladiators. Once again, Caleb had talked too much, revealing some of his fighting strategies, and he began to feel a sense of panic.

"Am I fighting you?" Caleb asked the man in a sheepish tone. As he awaited an answer, thoughts raced through his mind. Was it too late to go back and offer his cousin's virginity in exchange? How many of Caleb's weaknesses had the soldier uncovered?

Words from his mother passed into his mind. "Do not be afraid, my son. The Messiah is always with you." Caleb felt strengthened by images and words from his mother. He breathed in and exhaled. He had a new peace.

"No, we are fighting together and I needed to know something about my partner," said the soldier, laughing at how silly Caleb's question sounded.

Caleb laughed with the soldier and placed an arm on his shoulder, an act that connected them. It was another tool he had learned from his uncle. He prayed out loud. "Yeshua, You are in control," he said aloud in Ebreet. "Forgive me for not trusting You."

"What was that?" asked the soldier in Greek.

Caleb responded. "I was just talking in my native language."

The other soldier turned to the two boys. "Who do we fight today?" he asked.

"Two men were found to be worshipping a god other than the emperor. You have probably seen them. They have fought here before," said one of them.

"What god?" Caleb asked. Caleb wanted them to be worshippers of the sun god so that he could justify his upcoming actions. But he knew that he must do this deed regardless of who they worshipped.

"I do not know," said Mark as he sifted through the armory, looking for the best arrows he could find. Once he found them and gave them to Caleb, he took several practice shots into a target made from dried grass, and the arrows were true. The boy retrieved them and gave them back to Caleb.

"Not bad!" said the soldier. Mark gave him back his sword; now, a new edge was placed on it.

Despite weapons, armor, and a partner with whom to share the load of combat, Caleb was not prepared to hunt and kill to save Eliza and Yael. Yet he remembered his parents telling him that the act of being a Yeshuian often meant persecution for your beliefs. He also remembered learning that Paul had hunted and killed Yeshuians before giving himself to the Messiah, but he didn't think his life would come to that. Yet, the consequence of his choice to follow the teachings of Yeshua was now taking a form that his parents had not prepared him for. He must now either kill or allow his cousin and a girl with the same name as his mother to be raped. It was a choice that no one should have to make. He had to decide if the commandment "Thou Shalt Not Kill" applied to him at this moment.

"This is literally a choice between two bad endings!" said Caleb.

The other soldier laughed. "You've killed before, kid. It is not every day that I meet a man who killed a centurion, so I know you can win out there. It takes a lot of battle prowess to earn the title of the centurion, and you have already defeated one. I am not concerned. You have the skills needed to win today. Let's get this done. My family is getting a lot of money for this battle, and we need the coin to make it through the rest of this winter before we can return to our farms north of here."

"So, you are from Gaul?" Caleb remembered his geography.

"I am. My grandfather was a druid, as was his father before him. We were all captured and enslaved during a Roman invasion several decades before I was born. My parents paid for our freedom, and they raised me with my two brothers north of here. Our family calls that place home now."

"Perhaps I can come to visit you once these battles are done, and you are free to return home," said Caleb, looking to calm his nerves. Hope for the future made sense in a pre-combat conversation. Hope for the future was wise. It helps carry a man in combat.

The Gaul extended his hand to Caleb. "My name is Ronan, from Gallia Cisalpina. The Roman idiots just call it Gaul."

At that moment, the portcullis was lifted and two men twice Caleb's age came into view from identical gates on the other side of the pits. One man was armed with a bow and the other held a sword and a spear. Neither wore any armor, helmets, or protective boots. They had darker skin than any Roman or Gaul, and Caleb quickly concluded that they were from Syria, Lebanon, or perhaps coastal Manasseh. He heard they were seasoned combatants and they knew their way around the pit. Their lack of armor meant they would be faster than them, as they were unencumbered. Caleb realized that he was the sole combatant without fighting experience. He needed an advantage.

But what would that be? He quickly recalled Ronan's plan. Ronan would step out from the portcullis and begin trotting towards the two men whom they were supposed to kill. Caleb was to wait a moment before sprinting at full speed to the right, circling behind all the marble blocks that were part of the pit floor. He would attempt to flank them while they were distracted by Ronan's close-range threat of attack.

The battle started without any countdown and Caleb wasn't ready. Ronan left without any prompting to do his part and the combatant wielding a bow launched his first arrow. Ronan failed to stop it with his shield, and it struck him between two rings in his chain mail, burying itself into his chest with a loud thump. Ronan grunted and fell, appearing to have been killed instantaneously. Caleb watched Ronan trying to move, but he lost his focus on his partner once an arrow landed in the sand in front of him.

He responded with a defensive move. He climbed atop a marble block that would afford some protection from another arrow shot as the crowds erupted in glee at the flow of fresh blood in front of Ronan.

Caleb knew that his opponent would be feeling a sense of victory after receiving the crowd's applause. He notched an arrow, jumped down from the marble block to the sand, and ran at full speed in the direction that he thought they would be going to flank him.

He guessed correctly. They were not expecting one man to charge two men from the opposing flank. As they rounded a large block on the right side of the pits, Caleb was waiting for them, with one knee on the ground and his bow fully cocked. Caleb knew that the one with ranged weapons was the bigger threat, and he put an arrow in the archer's upper thigh. The man went down immediately and Caleb could see that the arrow had gone through bone and exited the other side of the leg. He would not be placing any load on that leg and would have to try to shoot without its support.

Caleb ducked behind a sandstone block and updated his combat assessment. Melee-range weapons were now an advantage to Caleb. If he could stay away and preserve his arrows, he would have superior weapons. "Thank you, Yeshua," came from his lips, and he steadied himself to take another shot.

Caleb counted his arrows as Rufus taught him to do. This act would keep him focused and mindful of his resources. His first arrow was not retrievable without first killing that man, leaving him with five arrows remaining. He took a deep breath, let it out, and reappeared to take a second shot. Lightning fast, he sent it into the armpit of the injured man, hearing him yell as the arrow ripped into his lung. He was not dead, but he would no longer discharge his bow that day. That gladiator's day in combat was over, and the match was now even. Each team was down one man. His partner turned around and ran in the opposite direction from whence he came.

Caleb thought for a moment. He anticipated that the other combatant would lose his sense of advantage and be temporarily in shock. Caleb's training kicked in, and he decided to waste an arrow and shoot it in his direction to make it seem like he was pursuing him. Caleb hoped it would speed him up in the same way that tapping on a frog from behind makes him jump. It worked, and Caleb saw the man running counterclockwise in the arena, thinking he was avoiding pursuit.

The other man didn't know that as soon as he sent his arrow, Caleb turned and ran at top speed in the opposite direction as he attempted to flank him. Once the man rounded a corner that should have provided him protection from Caleb, he was startled to see Caleb on one knee, directly in front of him at point-blank range. As the crowd erupted with joy, Caleb launched his arrow as soon as the man appeared. It struck his gut with full force, and the tip had come out on the other side of his ribcage. He would not run again this day and without any ranged weapons, Caleb had him. His lung had a hole in it, and shock would soon set in.

Caleb decided to speak to the combatant, desperately trying to be heard over the crowd's loud noises.

"If I do not kill you, I lose my sisters!" Caleb involuntarily shouted at the gutted man. He quickly notched a second arrow and launched it at point-blank range, piercing the man's gut on the opposite side. It made a loud thud as it hit, causing the crowd to erupt, and Caleb looked up and saw that the emperor was standing up and cheering. Each lung had a hole in it and it was a matter of time before he died.

Caleb knew these two wounds would be fatal and he walked up to the wounded man and kicked the sword away from the man nearest to him. He pulled him across the sand and put him next to the first one. The crowds erupted, calling for a retributive strike by the injured man or for Caleb to decapitate him.

As the two men lay next to each other on the sandy floor of the Coliseum, Caleb blocked out all the crowd noise and recommendations to commit atrocities. Instead, he spoke to them calmly in Ebreet.

"I am a member of The Way. The emperor requires that I kill you to protect my family. I do not wish to do this thing." He stood a spear's length away from where they lay in case either of them found the strength for a last lunging attack.

The one with one lung responded with labor. "We were boys when the Temple fell. We were slaves and served in the Roman militia. If you kill us, it will be an act of mercy. Thank you for your gift to go to eternity with Him."

Caleb was shocked. He stood there, pondering his next move. These men were not just Ebreet but also believers in the Messiah. How could he kill them? He was paralyzed, just like his mother was.

The crowd revolted at his inaction, demanding he do something. They began to chant, "Kill the devil worshippers! Kill the Ebreet!" Caleb could sense his shallow breathing. A part of him wanted to scream out at the trap the emperor had set for him, but he knew to say nothing. His anger would give the emperor more power over him.

Thought of his mother returned. Her honor was as much in his decision-making criteria as were the lives of the two women he declared to be his sisters. He needed to be a man of his word, and his word was that they were sisters. Yet, he did not want to kill brothers in Yeshua, either.

Then, the emperor raised his hand, indicating that everyone should be silent. He stretched his hand forward, with his palm facing down. This meant for the battle to end, there must be death. The emperor made his choice for him.

Caleb turned and screamed in the direction of Titus and his box, unaware that this confrontation was forbidden. "Is this what you want? Is this what you and my uncle used to do? Is this what I must do to protect my sisters?" The crowd looked now not towards the pits and the battle there but at the emperor, awaiting his response. Caleb's public questioning of the emperor was worthy of death by crucifixion. Perhaps if Caleb knew that, he would not have done it. It didn't matter. Titus had a much bigger plan for Caleb and had already begun dictating a letter back to Cornelius regarding this young man of interest.

The emperor's box was acoustically engineered so that anything he spoke would be heard down in the pits.

"Your uncle is dead," Titus replied. "You must make your choice. Will you choose to give me their lives, or shall I bed these whom you call sisters?"

With that, the two soldiers in the emperor's presence pulled down Yael and Eliza's robes again. The girls attempted to cover their exposed breasts with their hands as the crowd laughed. The emperor spoke loud enough for all to hear him.

"Leave yourselves uncovered until he has either finished off the wounded or has agreed that your flesh shall be mine," Titus said to them. The girls dropped their hands to their sides, causing laughter in the crowd and sheer rage inside Caleb. The women he promised to protect were now unprotected and he uniquely could do something about this.

He turned again to face Caleb, again extending the thumbs-down signal. It was time to decide whether to kill two Ebreet or allow himself to be killed. Caleb could hear the emperor dispatch a squad of his most elite soldiers to the entrance to the pits to ensure that one of the two events occurred in a timely manner.

Caleb walked to the injured archer and took out his knife. He slit his throat the same way he killed the centurion a few weeks earlier. Caleb turned away as he heard blood pour out onto the sand, striking the floor of the pits with enough force to make a splashing noise.

Killing a man was not the same thing as killing a deer. Caleb was sick to his stomach. He held the man's head up with his hair until it went limp. He let go, and the man slumped over and hit the ground. He was dead.

The crowd burst into applause and many of the royalty began to laugh. Caleb saw and heard nothing but the emperor. He looked up at him and yelled again with the full force of his lungs. "Is this what you want?" This time, there was no way that the emperor could have heard him. Caleb was caught up in tears of rage and tears of sadness, with these opposing feelings struggling to control him.

Unexpectedly, the remaining Ebreet spoke loud enough for Caleb to hear. The man was addressing God. "For Thine is the kingdom, the power, and the glory, forever and ever. Yeshua, take my soul that I may not trouble this world until You return in glory. Amen."

With tears in his eyes, Caleb slit the second man's throat, looking away not to see his last facial expression. His uncle warned him that the eyes of a dying man would invade the killer's dreams for years. Caleb looked up as the man went limp and saw that the emperor had allowed Eliza and Yael to get dressed.

Caleb felt more emotion at that moment than at any time in his life. It was not at all like seeing his parents killed and returning the act with a retributive strike. It was much worse, as Caleb was now alone, covered in the blood of others who worshipped the same Yahweh as he did. And he knew what came next because Balbi told him about it. It meant accolades and a great reward of gold and silver for his efforts. It was unreconcilable. It was sickening. And, it would be how history remembered him. Few, if any, defeat multiple armed opponents during their first battle as a gladiator. Caleb would be a part of Roman history in the worst possible sense. He would be praised for becoming a gladiator.

Caleb's heart ached. This was not what he had been taught would happen. There was no kingdom of God that he had been promised, no peace that the world could not understand, and no glory in defeating the enemy in battle. All the while, Caleb knew that he would remember the last combatant's last words, even though he might not remember the man's name.

Caleb finally stood up, covered in the blood of his combatants. He saw everyone in the Coliseum giving him a standing ovation. The emperor was no longer in his box, meaning that he was probably heading down to the pit to meet Caleb and offer his reward for a job well done.

Caleb saw that the two young servant boys had already run out and onto the pits. One of them handed him a towel while the other one pulled Ronan back into the cavern.

"He's not dead," the boy said calmly. That comment snapped Caleb from his trance and he engaged the boy.

"Mark, get him some help! And get this man's full name, his parent's name, and his hometown. I will come to find you later."

"Of course," said the boy. Caleb turned his face back to the portcullis, where he expected to meet the royal entourage.

Mark returned with Caleb's original gear and returned the combat equipment to the boy. He also gave Mark his blood-soaked towel after he cleaned up his hands and arms. He took the water, washed his face and hands, and put his sandals back on. He took out five gold coins and gave them to the boys.

"Keep one and give the rest to Ronan," he said. Lastly, the boys gave him his untarnished cloak to put on.

"That was excellent work! You look like a warrior, no matter what clothing or armor you adorn, Caleb. You are blessed, indeed. You are about to address the emperor in front of the entire Coliseum," said Mark.

"I already have met that ugly camel. That is why I am here," he responded. He knew he shouldn't have said that, but he did not care what came with insulting the emperor. The boys did not respond; they merely bowed and left.

There was exactly one arrow in his quiver. He had practiced with it and he knew how it flew better than any of the others. He took it out, placed it on the bowstring, and began walking towards the portcullis.

Chapter 30:
A Night in the Palace

Caleb's battle was the last event of the day and some decided to leave ahead of the victory ceremony and avoid the crowds on the streets. However, most stayed to see the emperor heap praise and coin for those gladiators who defeated strong opponents. The two Caleb had killed had battled together nearly a hundred times, and the regular Coliseum-goers spoke both in praise and wonder at Caleb's accomplishment as a first-timer. Caleb could hear them from above, as they were glad that the emperor, in all his wisdom, had set up the best fight for last. Caleb's emotions were trying to overcome him, but he knew that he must maintain control if he was to have any chance of freedom as he left this place.

As he walked toward the raised portcullis, Emperor Titus stood directly in front of him. Titus wore a crown of silver designs showing interlocking leaves and flowers. His cloak was not the one he had worn in the bathroom some hours earlier but was adorned with golden threads and elaborate patterns, including royal purple hues.

Caleb had another choice to make. He must decide whether to kill Titus as well. His last arrow was ready and he could pull his string and launch a direct hit on the man's heart in one second. Emperors rise to power and fall from it all the time. Why should his uncle's best friend be any different?

But that is not who he wanted to be. He was the son of two murdered parents and this was not the choice they would have wanted him to make. He had to kill those two men to protect his family. In his heart, he knew he did not have to kill the emperor. Instead, he cast the bow to the ground, grumbling. Vengeance had not helped him the last time anyway.

"Good choice," said Titus, clapping for Caleb as he approached. "It wouldn't have worked, anyway," he said, opening his robe and showing him intricate chain mail on his chest, specifically designed to stop crossbow bolts and arrows. It was of the highest quality workmanship and there were no flaws or places where Caleb's arrow would have been able to penetrate. Caleb displayed no reaction to the emperor's display of superior insight, but he did acknowledge that he had outwitted him. Caleb closed his eyes and bowed his head as any defeated soldier learns to do at the end of a training session.

Once Eliza heard the emperor speak to Caleb and saw Caleb's bow on the ground, she considered the environment safe again, and she ran from the back of the entourage and threw herself into Caleb's arms. He lifted her and held her in the air, spinning her around two times, just like he always did. He kissed her and told her he loved her. She was grateful to have her family back. And she kissed Caleb on the lips and told him that she loved him. Yael stood nearby, clapping as well, for this gave her all the validation that she needed that Eliza and Caleb were genuine. They honored their families with love and action. She admired them more than ever.

"I prayed every moment you were gone," Eliza whispered into his ear. Then, she kissed him on the cheek. "You protected me, the two of us, even though you did not have to. You are a good man and your parents would be proud of you."

Caleb set her down and held each side of her face. For the inno-cent fans in the Coliseum, they appeared to be lovers. Yael and Titus both stared at them and their interaction was more interesting than the battle.

"I had to do it for you. I did not have a choice that my mother would be proud of. You will be a good woman one day! Today, I tried to make sure of that," he responded. She fully embraced him and spoke into his ears. "Cousin, thank you for loving me!"

The remaining crowd applauded them, cheering for the two young people. Eliza turned and faced everyone as they stood and cheered. She waved at all of them, taking in her moment of glory.

"I believe they think we are lovers," Eliza said. Caleb laughed and he felt some of the tension subside. They turned around to discover that the emperor was standing next to them.

"Your uncle trained you as I thought he might. The victory and the spoils are yours, Young Ebreet. Tonight, you are my guests at the palace," Titus said.

"So, will you keep your promise?" Caleb asked in a most confronting tone.

"I never made any promise to you." Caleb could feel Titus' arrogance.

Eliza knew that Titus was doing this to impress his entourage and she suspected he was vulnerable to their sway. She spoke up again.

"Your Grace, is it not true that the spoils of battle go to the winner?"

"So, the Ebreet girl speaks again. Young man, you must discipline her for this."

"She speaks for me," said Caleb, honoring his cousin before the emperor. The emperor nodded, but neither of them wanted to know his thoughts.

"Your Highness. I ask you to release the slave girl into my care. Consider her service to you complete," Eliza said with a risky tone of confidence. She gestured for Yael to come to her.

She offered, "In exchange, you may keep all the coin that otherwise goes to the victor."

"You would offer me 500 gold coins for a slave that is not worth 20? What kind of businessperson are you?" he asked. Her aunt also trained Eliza to let insults roll off her. She was an excellent businessperson and didn't need to respond to his nonsense.

"Your Grace, you are mistaken. It is I who am getting the better deal for 500 gold coins," Eliza said, staring him directly in the eye. Titus smiled and nodded his head. He liked Eliza's fight.

The entourage looked at Titus and quietly whispered amongst themselves. She could tell that they loved this girl's aggressive stance upon victory and everyone awaiting the response of the King of the

World. Titus also seemed impressed rather than offended by her presumptuousness.

"Done. The girl is yours for 500 gold coins," he said. "I give you the slave and release her from her service to me and the empire." He motioned to his scribe to record what he had just agreed to, promising to give Yael a copy by the end of the day.

The entourage applauded the emperor as Yael left the back of the entourage and walked towards Eliza and Caleb. Yael dared not express any gratitude in front of any of them. Instead, she stepped behind Eliza and bowed her head. Eliza wanted no part in this public display and servitude; instead, Eliza turned and gave Yael hugs and kisses like the one she gave Caleb. After a moment, Eliza whispered something to Yael, and she began to reciprocate. Caleb stood motionless as the two of them embraced. Many of the women in the crowd were touched, but it meant nothing to the Royal Entourage. They turned and left. Yael was about to thank Caleb, but he was not prepared for an intimate encounter with a girl he was infatuated with. Instead, he focused on what he thought was urgent.

"Come on, let's go. I need to wash up again. I have blood down my shirt and on my legs. This is an awful feeling," said Caleb. He put his bow over his shoulder and began to walk toward the exit.

Eliza turned to follow him but Yael pulled on both of them and spun them back around, forcing them to stop.

"Five hundred gold coins? I am not worth that!" Yael said. Eliza turned her head to the side and made sure that Yael could see that she was crying. Caleb put his arm around Eliza and kissed her on the head again. He looked at Yael and smiled.

"Shalom, Yael. Eliza knows what she is doing. She wouldn't have spent all those coins if you weren't worth it. I have known her my whole life," said Caleb, deferring authority for this decision to his cousin.

"I spoke the truth when I told the emperor that I am the one getting the better deal." Yael stared into Eliza's eyes without speaking. Yael could see that Eliza was sincere and passionate. After a small interlude, Eliza spoke again.

"You are worth every one of those gold coins. You need to believe that," Eliza said. She opened her arms and pulled Yael in for a deep and heartfelt hug.

The Coliseum was emptying and the entourage was out of sight. They had gone towards the palace on this side of the Palatine Hills. Yael spoke again to Eliza.

"I am indebted to you. I do not understand what just happened here. I am your slave now?" she asked.

"You are not indebted to us! Caleb won and I used his winnings to pay for your freedom. Caleb is completely uninjured and all of us are leaving this disgusting place for the last time in our lives. That is what happened! You are not our slave." said Eliza. The countenance on her face was of one filled with peace. She leaned in and kissed Yael on the cheek three times, as her family always did on Shabbat. Yael knew the ritual of Shabbat and she knew that the act of acceptance and welcome was sincere. Caleb repeated Eliza's behavior and wiped a single tear from Yael's eyes, lifting her by the chin.

"Yael, you are family now. Just ask anyone who just watched us," Yael stared into his warm eyes, trying to understand what he had just done to protect her place of honor as a woman in Ebreet society. He treated her as if she were a virgin, worthy of defending with his life.

"I do not know what to say! Thank you! I hate this place, too," Yael said and laughed with a sense of great relief.

"Yael, I bought your freedom, not your servanthood. This isn't a trick. You are free. I am free. Caleb is free."

Yael and Eliza held each other as they walked back to the palace. They entered through the main gate and three slaves approached them that Yael did not know. The slaves were all old enough to be their mothers. "We are here to serve you and prepare you before tonight's events," said the first one.

"What events?" asked Eliza. Then, she remembered what Yael told her to expect and a fear came upon her heart. She was not going to participate in an orgy.

The slaves looked at each other. "We will help you get ready, yes?" the eldest one said. They were guests and certainly not required to participate, but Eliza imagined that many of the others had told Titus that they wished to ravish Eliza this evening. Yael told her there was no such requirement, but Eliza was concerned that Yael might be forced to join. The two of them agreed to stay together, and they followed the slaves into a small building filled with bathing rooms. It was adjacent to the main palace near the top of the Palatine Hill.

"Come with me, young master," said the remaining slave to Caleb. She led him to a room adjacent to the girls. He found himself in a room with a large walk-in pool—larger than his family's kitchen back home.

"Disrobe and enter the pool," said the slave. "You must clean before tonight." Although he was protective of his cousin's public nudity, he had no such limitations on himself and he quickly did as she said. "This is very nice," he said as he settled into the water. He closed his eyes and allowed all the tension from the day's combat to flow from his body and into the water. As he began to fall asleep, he felt someone touching him.

In a startled state, he spun around and saw the slave woman was now naked, covered in perfumes, and rubbing his shoulders. "Please stop!" he said in Ebreet, not thinking if she would understand. Once he realized his mistake, he repeated himself in Greek, this time with a more gracious tone. She stepped back, as she was not in the pool but on its edge. Caleb could see all of her womanhood and he let out a chuckle. He knew this was another attempt by the emperor to control him. The emperor had selected a woman with the same voluptuous curves as Eliza and Yael. Caleb clenched his teeth again, knowing that his only power came from self-control.

"You are new to this place, yes?" asked another man, perhaps twice Caleb's age, who had just entered the pool himself. He engaged Caleb before Caleb could answer him.

"I watched you in battle today, and it was obvious to all of us that you were not fighting for the sake of glory." Caleb was no longer sure who sent this woman to him; either way, he could sense that he was being set up again.

"I do not fight for glory. You watched the fight. You know who and what I fight for," Caleb said. He splashed his face with water, dunked his head underneath the pool, and scrubbed his scalp. When he came back up, he looked at the man and accepted a challis from him. He looked inside and smelled red wine, and Caleb did not trust the wine or the man who gave it to him. He set it on the edge of the pool and spoke to the man with composed thoughts.

"I do not dare to risk my life in the arena for myself. The emperor gave me a choice and I took the one that included fighting for family," said Caleb.

"May I ask what the other choice was?" the man asked. He took a drink from his wine cup and picked up Caleb's. He took a sip to show him that it wasn't poisoned.

"You will need to ask the emperor if you want those details. They are private."

"Perhaps," said the man. Caleb could not read the man nor what he was doing in the water with him. They stared at each other for a moment before the man spoke to the servants.

"Bring more hot water!" Yelled the man. Caleb could now tell that this man had been in the pool before and knew what he was doing. Immediately, two more slaves arrived carrying a large vat of steaming water. They poured it into the pool and the temperature increased dramatically.

"Now that is more like it!" Caleb remarked, looking to change the subject. He dunked under the water's surface again, scrubbing more of his body and coming up to breathe.

"I want you to get used to bathing in luxurious pools such as these. In fact, I have paid the emperor to be here with you right now. I have a business deal for you." The man smiled at Caleb and lifted his challis in a toast.

Caleb was not expecting a business offer. Before he could react, the man began his pitch. "My house would like to sponsor you as our gladiator. You will wear our family's crest and fight for me and my children. We will pay you half a talent of gold for each victory. Couldn't your family use that coin?" Caleb paused, but he couldn't restrain his smile.

Remember my sisters out there? One of them carries half a talent of gold and silver with her right now, and she can negotiate another half a talent when she sells a watermelon to an elephant. Why would I want to kill people for something my family already has?

A sarcastic outburst would mean that the emperor had again taken away his self-control. Instead, he chose not to voice them. He smiled at the man as his question gave him the first moment of clarity he had experienced today.

"I am seventeen years old," he replied. "I wish to live my life to the fullest. I want to marry a beautiful woman from the twelve tribes, have children with her, and have a career that impacts for the good. I do not want to risk my future on a Coliseum floor. I'm sure you understand."

"Very well," said the man as he climbed out of the water and left. "Live your life as you desire. But I will wager my soul that you will fight for the emperor again one day."

Chapter 31:
The Simplicity of the Message

Yael kept quiet while the two of them bathed. They didn't need to talk to enjoy each other, and it felt wonderful to soak in the hot water and relax after watching Caleb nearly kill himself for them. Their bath was a walk-in and the two older women came into the tub with them. The older women scrubbed Eliza and Yael's feet and hands, applying lavender and frankincense to their hair and drying them off using Egyptian cotton towels that were the size of blankets. Marble mosaics covered the inside of their tub walls, and the ceiling had depictions of a great fight in the Coliseum between a young and powerful gladiator and a lion. There was a very young girl playing the lyre in the room with them, and she smiled as she looked at them. Eliza no longer could gauge the people of the palace and she wondered if the lyrist had a tongue. Yael had no such confusion and felt at ease. She spoke to Eliza without any filter on her words.

"When I first came to the palace, I used to serve in a bath like this one," She fell short of retelling her repeated raping in tubs like this one, but Eliza could tell that there was some horrible memory there that had infected her view of herself. She had listened to her aunt talk about rape and she risked a question to her new sister.

"Is this where they took your womanhood from you?" Eliza asked.

"Yes," Yael nodded, forcing herself to smile, but she couldn't say more without crying. Eliza could tell that these memories hurt to recall. She knew Yael was desperate for her to change the topic of conversation.

"Before I return home, I must buy some of these towels to take to my mother," Eliza said. "She will love them. Do you want to get some for your family, too?" she asked Yael.

"Can you afford them?" Yael asked. Eliza nodded yes and told her about the profit she made selling cinnamon.

"I am sharing everything else with you. You can have however many coins you need to buy gifts for your family. I can earn more profit later," Eliza said.

"I will repay you," Yael said.

"No, you won't. This is my gift to share. It is the least I can do since Caleb risked his life for us to be sisters," she said. Yael smiled.

"That is the kindest thing anyone has ever said to me," Yael shared. Eliza smiled and nodded her head in acceptance.

"Egyptian towels and linens for two families of Ebreet!" she announced.

"I know where the Egyptian warehouses are. We can go there as soon as we leave," Yael said.

As they finished drying off and removing the excess frankincense, the two older women had them don pure white robes laced with golden threads. Neither needed anything done to their hair or nails, as they were perfectly made up for the Coliseum. All they needed was to step into new sandals.

"I never thought I would wear Caesar's clothing. Now, I have!" said Yael. She wore a smile and did a quick spin, showing off her flowing robes. Part of being a slave meant exposure to the nicest materials and services that the world has known but without the ability to benefit from them yourself. Yael wore the same sandals she did when she first became a slave a year or so ago. This was a dream come true for her.

"I had never seen one of these Royal Pallas until this morning. Now, I have worn two different ones on the same day!" said Eliza. It took a moment of manipulating the fabric to make sure that it didn't expose her breasts again, but without any men present, it was more of a joke than a matter of shame.

The two of them jokingly exchanged conversations about their friends from school and Yael told Eliza more about the times her aunt would come to teach her at her school. They laughed a lot and neither of them struggled as they looked into each other's eyes. They each needed this level of emotional intimacy after the horrors of the Coliseum.

"Yael, I just met you today, but I feel that I have known you my whole life," Eliza added.

Eliza felt that any sense of filter she had with Yael also needed to drop. If Caleb was a man of God and speaking the truth, the girl was now also her family, like it or not.

"I do not know what to say," said Yael, almost bashfully. "I was a slave earlier today. Now, I am receiving your—" and with that, she broke down and began to cry. Eliza pulled her in, holding her like a young child who had just fallen.

"I do not deserve the love that you and Caleb are showing me right now. I cannot understand this sentiment," she said.

"You know, Caleb started this. I know Caleb, and I know his mom and dad. He was angry when he called us sisters, but I know he will honor that proclamation till the day he dies. You are now a part of our family. You are going to see Correae, Tamar, the House of Healing, and Jerusalem, whether you believe me or not. We are stuck with each other, sister!" said Eliza, trying to break the moment up. Since the older women did not understand Ebreet, they merely smiled and listened to their gibberish.

"And I saw how you and Caleb were looking at each other. Caleb isn't like other men, so you don't have to be scared of him. He had a prophecy about you yesterday. I will let him tell you about it. And I know he finds you attractive." Yael said nothing, but it was obvious that she had been thinking about Caleb since they separated.

"Wait. There are no undergarments to put on," Eliza noted uneasily. "Where are our ones from earlier?" Eliza asked the old woman

"You can have it tomorrow," said the old woman. Instantly, Eliza's countenance changed. She felt a pending sexual assault coming, and she began to relive the attempted rape on the boat. Yael had not yet heard that story, but she was keen about the mental disability and trauma that comes when a woman comes to terms with the reality of her pending rape.

"These pallas are not intended to cover you like clothing. That impedes access to what is inside of them," Yael explained. Eliza paused but didn't speak. She figured out what Yael was alluding to. Her pause turned to shock, and all of her Aunt Yael's teachings came to her. She began to pray.

As soon as she began to pray for courage and strength, the emperor walked in.

"Hello, Little Ones," he said. As he approached the girls, he eyed them like a hungry wolf. He motioned with his hand for the old women and the lyrist to leave, and they left without making a sound.

Eliza looked up at the emperor and smiled.

"Your Grace," she said with the greatest amount of kindness she could. She stared deep into his eyes and she could feel the call to be strong. She felt courage rising up just as she knew what to do. Just like she knew what to do while Caleb went into combat, she prayed.

"Yeshua, You are my Lord and King. This man has no authority not granted by You under heaven. Protect me from the evil one, and I know that the evil one is here. Remind me that this is merely a man and not our real enemy. Satan is the enemy, and I bind him in the name of your Son, Yeshua from Galilee," she prayed.

As she prayed, the emperor sat very close to her and Eliza maintained her smile. Just like Caleb had chosen to overcome his paralysis by challenging the leader of the world, Eliza knew that she must do the same. She turned her head slightly and spoke to the man a hand away from her face.

"Your best friend used to tell me stories of you. Would you like to hear one?"

"Sure," Titus replied indifferently. For her part, Yael remained next to Eliza, but she dared not move, fearing the wrath of a man she knew to be predatory.

"One evening, Rufus was recalling the days leading up to and immediately after the destruction of our Temple. He talked of the great siege engines that the two of you made and the mass crucifixions you performed to mold my people into submission. He spoke of entering the city and tearing down the great Temple that my ancestors treasured above all things except Yahweh Himself." Titus was fascinated to see her ability to separate her feelings for her people's most holy place from his actions from more than seventeen years earlier. He was very impressed at her lack of fear and her apparent indifference to what he was about to do to her.

It was hard for Eliza to gauge whether Titus was listening to her, but she knew that he needed to hear this message. It was her responsibility to say it. It was the Holy Spirit's responsibility for it to germinate.

"And you know what he said he felt afterward?" Eliza stopped to let a dramatic pause do the hard work of making the emperor think. The emperor took a moment but nodded his head no.

"Nothing. He told Caleb and me that he felt nothing at all." She quickly looked at Yael and back at the emperor. Next to her was a flask of red wine. She leaned over, picked up the chalice, took a sip, and set it back down. She needed to let what she had just said do its work inside of this man.

"Rufus spent his career in the Roman military, just as his father before him, and he was now the legate over a legion of soldiers who had done something that no Roman military had succeeded in accomplishing. He said that he was at the top of the world, wouldn't you agree?"

"Almost at the top. I remained above him!" Titus chuckled to himself. With that, Eliza returned briefly to her prayer before she continued.

"He said you were a great leader and great friend. He said that you permitted him to take any spoils that he wanted. He already had enough wealth to build a palace anywhere in the empire. Perhaps two of them. But then, he made the greatest decision of his life. That is what he told Caleb and me. Eliza took another sip of wine and again looked at Yael, winking at her.

"After meeting my uncle Mishi and learning the truth about the Messiah, he agreed to leave his post in the Roman military, retire from his service, and join my aunt and uncle in their pursuit of what truly matters. He stayed behind and protected my family as they ministered to people in the area surrounding ancient Jerusalem."

"I know," Titus said, briefly looking down to where Eliza's golden chalice sat. Something was happening inside of him, and Eliza and Yael could see it like fireworks going off.

"Most of my people did not know that the Messiah had come. They thought there would be a spirit that would come to rid us of the Roman Empire, as there had been other great leaders in the past who had redeemed us." Eliza made great hand gestures to paint motion in the skies above to show the power of these great leaders, but she also finished her hand gestures with a chuckle. She knew that they were not as important as the Messiah. And that motion and grandiosity made Titus laugh, as well.

"But the Messiah who was sent came not to rid us of Roman occupation. No, no, no, indeed! The Messiah who was sent came to rid us of death caused by our sins."

The emperor seemed to be losing interest.

"Uncle Rufus said that the two of you exchanged many letters after you separated," Eliza said, attempting to regain his full attention.

"We did, but I do not remember what he said. That was many years ago."

"I know my uncle's heart. I am sure he asked you if you were happy or not. Did he not invite you to come back to Jerusalem and meet the synagogue that he served in?" She knew that he had, as she had read copies of Rufus' letters.

"Yes, he did." The emperor was now becoming introspective, and the girls could see it. A different nerve in his heart had been touched.

Eliza felt emboldened. It was as if she was made for this moment.

"Uncle Rufus knew that your love of flesh and war could be replaced with a joy fuller than those things. He loved you enough to share that with you. I know he missed you. He cared for me when I was a young girl, and he taught me how to run and remain physically fit. You know, he loved me as if I were his daughter."

The emperor stepped away from them and his form went nearly limp. Some sort of fear had cut to his core and he did not know what to say. He began to see the evil of an act of taking her flesh as it was the daughter of his brother and best friend, and it dawned on him that this act was wrong. He moved away from his position near her to a safer distance on the other side of the pool, signifying respect. Yael looked at Eliza with her mouth wide open. She had not seen anyone, let alone a young girl, have such an effect on him.

"You are not like any of the other Ebreet girls," Titus said, lightly hyperventilating.

"Perhaps. But I am here to serve you right now with the most powerful truth in the history of the world. I can sense that you want to know what it is. Rufus needed it. I need it. Would you like to hear the greatest story ever told?" Titus covered his mouth and nodded his head up and down.

"Yes, I would. Tell me!"

Eliza called the emperor back to her and told him to sit down. She used the diminutive form of the language, just as a teacher might use while talking to a student.

Over the rest of the afternoon, she told him the story and the details of Yeshua's life. As she told the story, she continually remembered how her aunt would speak, mixing in powerful words from the Creator with light humor and personal stories. The shifting patterns and change of methods came naturally to her, and she found a way to connect her stories back to God's message to stories that would mean something to Titus. She used analogies of serving in the military or being a great leader over thousands and tens of thousands. Eliza prayed throughout her storytelling, thanking Jehovah for this chance to tell the story above all stories.

Yet, she was not without fear. She knew that Titus could change his heart in less than a moment, and he could commit atrocities against her like his family had done to Yael. But she also knew that all of history might change if Titus would open his heart to the idea of a need for a Messiah. At every moment she spoke, Eliza saw that she was not only replicating her auntie's words, but she also replicated her tone and her body language. Her aunt had a few phrases that she repeated and built her life upon. This moment was an application of those words.

At this moment, Eliza grew up and her identity was defined. She migrated from a life as a student to a teacher of the law, sharing that Yeshua had come to save us from our sins. All the while, the emperor stared at her like a puppy dog might stare at its new master.

"Confronting those who wish to harm you with truth and love is the most sincere way to approach life," is what her aunt would say.

In her soul, she again felt the resonance that her aunt told her about. It was the same resonance from last week. It made the emperor and the two girls smile.

And it felt good.

Chapter 32:
The Morning After

Yael woke up to the sounds of birds outside the window and a slow winter rain. Eliza was next to her, as the two of them had slept in the same bed. Yael woke up first and she found herself looking into Eliza's eyes. She had butterflies in her stomach. Each inhale caused her to fight back tears as she gently touched Eliza's head and hair, pulling it out of her eyes. Yael had certainly found friends, but more so, she found that these two people were answers to her prayers that she had offered from the bottom of her heart many times over the last half a year.

"Yahweh, thank you for hearing my prayers to get out of this Godforsaken place. Thank you for being so loyal to my cries. And, above all else, thank you for this woman whom you have used to take me from this place. You are such a loving God. Thank you," she said. Before she finished her prayers, tears were streaming down her face and she could hear Caleb stirring. He decided to sleep on the floor next to the girls and the slaves brought him several fluffy quilts to lay down on top of. He was moving, but she heard nothing for a moment. After she sat up, she found herself looking directly at him.

"Caleb!" she said, feeling a bit startled. She wiped the last tears off of her face, ashamed to show Caleb that she was crying.

"Don't tell anybody, but sometimes I wake up and cry when I look at Eliza, too. She is the most generous person I have ever met. And if you knew my mom, you know that my words are not passing in the night." Yael smiled and nodded her head in agreement, but she revered Caleb too much to speak from her heart. She took a deep breath before speaking to him.

"You are an amazing warrior, Mr. Archer from the Tribe of Benjamin," she said, allowing herself to burst out in laughter as a cover for more gratitude that she didn't know how to express.

Eliza woke up, wanting to know why they were making all that noise. Caleb told her to shut up and go back to sleep and that made Yael laugh louder. As they made noise, the servants entered, offering them chamber pots to relieve themselves. No one had any interest in doing such a thing in front of a member of the opposite sex, and Yael sent them away. Eliza was now upright and sitting next to Yael, and she was not going back to sleep.

An older woman came in carrying a concoction of herbs and oils, offering it to the girls.

Eliza took one smell and gave a face of total disgust. Yael raised her hand, saying, "No, thank you," to the older woman.

"This is Caesar soup, designed to prevent pregnancy," the woman said. "The emperor spent much of the night with you two. I am sure you need it," she said.

Yael repeated, "No, thank you," but Eliza was the one to speak up.

"Neither of us was violated," she said.

"Yes, of course," said the old lady as she paused and composed her next thought.

"The emperor will not support the children if you one with him," she said. Eliza looked at Yael and laughed.

"I'm sorry. We weren't joking. We don't need that. We did not have sex. You can leave," she said, and the old woman walked out.

Eliza and Yael continued to giggle about something else, and Caleb spoke as a leader.

"We need to get the hell out of this place," Caleb said. "I almost died yesterday, and you two spent the night alone and wearing clothing that almost exposes your breasts while sitting with the Emperor of the World. What are we still doing here?" he asked. It was a sobering comment, and the girls agreed that they needed to get up, pack, and go back to Judah.

Yael knew the interoperations of the palace better than they did.

"Let me help," she said. She called for a servant to come in. A man entered and she asked him to send a message to the docks to request a boat to take them back to Judah as quickly as possible. She told Eliza to give him a coin; abruptly, the young runner left the palace to secure three seats on the afternoon vessel.

They washed their faces and hands and walked to the top floor of the central building as instructed. On the rooftop sat the emperor and his Ebreet concubine under an awning to keep them dry. He was completing his morning calisthenics. Caleb saw him exercising and smiled as he walked up to him.

"Keeps a man young," Titus said as they came into view. "You know, last night was the first night since I became emperor that I did not bed a woman." The girls looked at the concubine, looking for some sign from her, but they got nothing. Neither girl knew how to respond to such a rash comment.

"I have never bedded a woman and I won't until we complete Erusin and marry," said Caleb with a hint of disdain. Titus had made him kill and he remained enraged that the emperor held such power over him.

"Titus, would you please give me what I need to get my parents back?" Eliza asked. She addressed him using his name and not his office, an act of great intimacy. The first time she did that last night, Yael almost stopped breathing. Now that Eliza had done it a dozen or more times, Yael didn't look up. For his part, the emperor smiled at them and laughed.

"Young Ebreet, you had it the whole time," Titus replied, throwing Caleb back his uncle's ring. "If you carry the confidence that you had down in my Coliseum and wear the ring showing your family's authority, all of my soldiers will comply with your requests. They will help you find them. You did not need to risk your life to come to me."

"Are you serious?" said Caleb, with a blend of shock and disgust. Titus paused, clearly contemplating what he wanted to say next. Then, he spoke to Caleb in an eager voice. "You are a fine young warrior, Caleb. I think you need to come back here to train with my elite soldiers, just like your Uncle and I did. First, go home and find your family. Then, come back."

Caleb just stared at the emperor, withholding words that he wanted to say but knew he would regret. The emperor knew all of that, and he smiled. Caleb had no idea that Titus had already sent a directive home to Cornelius telling him what to do to complete Caleb's training. Titus was doing nothing more than accelerating the young man's growth.

"I can already tell that you are not going to fight in the pits again, but I think you could be a great leader for future generations of soldiers." Titus put his hand on Caleb's shoulder, trying to loosen the young man up.

"That is if you are interested in learning how to be a soldier." Eliza could see Titus's tone with Caleb, and she admired Caleb's restraint of tongue. Caleb knew this to be another assertion of power and control. Caleb smiled but did not speak.

Once he finished speaking to Caleb, he dictated an edict to a scribe and stamped it. Then he handed Eliza the sealed scroll.

"This is what Caleb fought for you to have. It has my seal on it. It instructs anyone in possession of your parents to release them."

"Thank you, Your Grace," she said. Now, the emperor of Rome was addressing her, not her student, so she changed her language to treat him as such. Yael stared in wonder as Eliza navigated a complex social relationship with the most powerful man in the world. Yael knew she was observing an incredible event.

Soon after that, the food arrived, and Titus gestured for all of them to sit and eat with him as his guest. The five of them enjoyed a cheerful breakfast. The runner came back before their meals were complete, saying that their boat was ready now if they wished to leave. Eliza and Yael clapped.

Eliza took out two silver coins from her inner purse and handed them to the runner. "There is a man named Balbi in the marketplace. He sailed over with us. Tell him that we have departed and hope to see him again. Tell him he is released from our service."

Without looking up, Caleb spoke to Eliza.

"I told him he was free two nights ago," Eliza remembered the look on his face while John was talking, and she felt she should have guessed this.

"Caleb, thank you. I love your heart," she said.

"I love your hearts. I am in such awe of you two," said Yael. That public affection in front of the emperor almost embarrassed him, and he stopped eating to look at the group. Both Eliza and Yael were sincere, and it made him smile. Caleb put down his last piece of bread and wiped his face.

"Your Grace, it is time for us to depart," Caleb said respectfully. "Thank you for your help," The two men exchanged a warriors' departures, just as Uncle Rufus had taught Caleb to do. He hated the man yet he wanted to hug him at the same time. He got to experience a part of the Roman empire that few Ebreet lived through, and he had earned the respect of thousands of people. Caleb chuckled to himself as he revealed that this relationship was not that much different than the one he had with Balbi. Yeshua was in control; Caleb was not.

Yael and Eliza bowed, and they prepared to leave.

"Not yet. I have some unfinished business with you, Eliza," he said, thoughtfully looking into her eyes.

"To begin with, what do I call you?" he asked. Everyone could tell that it was a serious question. Eliza smiled and approached the emperor. She reached down and took his hand as if she were his daughter.

"I am Eliza Antiochus. Please call me Eliza. I am pleased that you are open to learning more about the Messiah and his call on your life. My sister Yael has already sent a message to her local synagogue, and the rabbi there will come and speak with you each week. Many men in the prison have a great understanding, perhaps more than I do!" she said, laughing. She placed a single hand on his forearm so he would listen to her.

"Your Grace, the man who taught my aunt, spent many years in your prisons, and many of his followers reside there." Her authority at the moment was undeniable and it was obvious that Titus would do whatever she said. But she didn't answer him. Finally, she released her hold on his forearm and he spoke.

"So, you will not answer me. I have heard your people use the word rabbi. Are you one of them?" Titus asked, almost as if he were a child requesting something from his mother.

Eliza smiled and looked at Caleb. She remembered her aunt talking about the first time someone called her rabbi and how she didn't know how to respond.

"In our culture, the title of rabbi is more than just a name. It is a position in time and society. It is what people remember you for. For our people, there is no higher honor than to become a rabbi. You can train to become a carpenter or a goldsmith, but from those career choices, you become old and lose your skills. Not so with a rabbi. You are always improving, as your mind, your heart, and your soul are the tools you bring when it is time to work." Caleb was sitting with her when she told that story not long before they left. Eliza looked at her cousin and glanced at Yael.

"Rabbi Eliza," Titus said, taking another sip of wine, laughing about something that none of them understood.

"That name, rabbi, seems to work for you and me. For now, I beg your permission to leave and find my parents. As far as teachers are concerned, you must get to know the people in the synagogue near the Coliseum. Rabbi John would love to have you sit with him. He can be the rabbi who teaches you. He has more time than I do, Your Grace. I must go home." The two of them made eye contact, and Titus bowed his head, accepting Eliza's offer. Yael shook her head as she had not seen Titus bow his head to anyone, including a senator or a king from a distant land.

"Very well, I will call for Rabbi John," Titus told them, wishing them safe travels. However, as they turned to leave, he called them back.

"Not yet! I have something else for you, rabbi," he said.

Titus nodded and signaled to a servant standing at the top of the stairs. The servant brought over an ornately carved box made of the finest acacia wood and opened it. Inside was a silver ring that bore the insignia of the house of Flavian, of which Titus and his brother were the leaders. There were perhaps ten such rings in the world.

"Wear this on your dominant ring finger and you will not have any problems anywhere in the empire. You are now a member of my house. I told my brother Domitian just this morning that I am giving you this. I claim you as family, just like you claimed that one," pointing at Yael.

"Thank you. It is beautiful," she said, picking the ring up and putting it on the middle finger of her left hand. They bowed again and left.

Once they cleared the security gates at the entrance to the royal palace, they took to the roads leading to the docks. Yael finally gave in to the little girl inside of herself and all but squealed as she made her announcement.

"I now know two women who are rabbis! And you are also a princess in the Roman Empire!" she said, running her hands on Eliza's shoulders and down her abdomen, as that is where a rabbi's prayer shawl must be hung while out in public.

"Stop teasing me!" said Eliza, pushing her hands away and laughing. Yael returned her hands to rubbing Eliza and they began to laugh. Caleb just smiled and enjoyed the first real feeling of peace he had in days. The reason for their journey had reached fruition and it was time for the long boat ride back to their homeland and the world that awaited them.

As they passed some merchants who had no idea of what had just happened, they looked at the men who were focused on their next transaction and began to laugh. Yael and Eliza were holding hands, as Ebreet women do in public, and they took a moment to ponder what had occurred to them in the palace. Yael spoke first.

"Would you two look down at your hands? Do you see the ring that you each wear?" she asked. Caleb was wearing Rufus' ring and Eliza was wearing the ring of the Flavian dynasty. They did and looked up at the former slave.

"There is a deeper message here. You, Caleb, did not know that you already had what you needed." He looked at her and humbly responded.

"Very true." Yael looked Caleb in the eyes and continued to smile at him. Then, she broke her gaze and turned to her new sister.

"You, Eliza, have what you do not need." Eliza laughed and looked over at Caleb for a second, lifting her ring to show to him.

"Also very true," she said, laughing again.

"And I have the gift of freedom, thanks to you two," she said. With that, she kissed each of them on the cheek as a family member might, and she offered a blessing from the Torah over each of them.

"And I can offer you blessings in the name of our Lord publicly now that a member of the House of Caesar is with me," she said. Eliza smiled and nodded. This was the first real moment of power that came from the ring that exempted her from Roman law.

"Perhaps Eliza will make some good use of that," said Caleb. Eliza was done with all the pomp and she was ready to get down to what she loved to do.

"Let's go to the market and get some of that Egyptian cotton. I want some linen and some towels. Then, we are getting on a boat that is waiting for us and sailing home," she said.

"Can I accept your offer now?" asked Yael. "I want to get some things for my family, especially my little sister. She had probably grown up a lot since I have been gone," she said.

"Anything in my coin purse is yours," she said. She reached into her purse and emptied out half of what she was carrying into a smaller coin pouch. She gave her mostly gold and bronze, but it was enough to buy a hundred towels and sheets and pay to have them shipped all the way to Judah. Caleb was openly upset.

"Eliza, you are unbelievable!" Caleb put his hands on his hips and shook his head from side to side in disgust.

"When I ask for your coin to get something, you give me an evil eye like I am some leper. Yael shows up out of the clouds and you give her a quarter of a talent. This is just not fair."

"She is my sister. You told the emperor yourself, yes?" she said, sounding and acting just like his mother. Caleb stuck his tongue out at her and flared his nostrils. They laughed as they turned and walked towards the markets. The two girls locked their arms together, grabbed their bags, and followed behind Caleb as he served as their protector. Their laughter was interrupted by Caleb's abrupt halt. He turned around and ran back.

"I forgot my belongings at the villa," he said, laughing. "Wait for me!" he said.

"We are going to my favorite café to get some tea," Eliza yelled as he ran off. He extended his right hand, showing a thumbs-up signal, indicating that he got her message.

The girls began laughing again, and they took a seat at the outdoor café next to where they had stopped. Eliza ordered some tea for them and she took Yael's hand.

"If he is going to be your family, you will need to get used to him doing stupid things and forgetting stuff," Eliza said.

She completely missed the look on Yael's face as she called him family.

Chapter 33: The Trip Home, All with New Family

Stepping onto the deck of the watercraft was many things, none of them what the young adults expected. There was no monumental joy or profound satisfaction in knowing they were going home. They remained weary from yesterday's events and the sea waves would be great today. It was winter and bad weather was to be expected. The captain told them to abstain from spicy food or alcohol; otherwise, they would spend the day vomiting off the edge of the boat.

Despite all the bathing, oils, and beautiful clothing, they felt dirty on the inside. None of them were prepared for what Rome had done to them. The flair and lavishness that defined Rome had taken their innocence. Their peers at home were preparing for Bar and Bat Mitzvah, and the families were seeking out spouses for their former classmates. By the time they docked in Joppa, all the twelve tribes would be celebrating the lengthening of days, and there would be dancing and preparations for a new season of planting. Animals in the flocks would birth their offspring this month, and it would be a time of prosperity and growth. Not so for Caleb, Eliza, and Yael.

Each was injured in places where traditional healers could not help them. Memories of atrocities where they were participants assaulted their view of the world and themselves. Last night, after the emperor left them, they talked about how they would celebrate as soon as they left the harbor, but the joy they were yearning for didn't magically arrive as their boat left the port. The waves were horrible and they all were a bit nauseous. The inclement weather didn't last long, and as soon as the horizon wasn't shifting continuously, Yael got up to do something.

"I am going to change into my new clothing," Yael said. She had purchased two new outfits with the coin Eliza had given her, and she went below deck and changed into each one, coming back up and showing them to Eliza and Caleb.

"I like you better in the first one," said Caleb.

"Ok, I will put that one back on," she said, going below deck.

Eliza looked at Caleb and felt her heart beating. She could see what was happening between them. Yael was doing the best she could to be dear to Caleb and her strategy was working. She wanted to try to connect with him with as much effort as he used, but she could not offer her life for him as he had done for her. A beautiful appearance was the best she had to offer besides kind words and prayers.

"You think she is beautiful, don't you?" she said almost rhetorically. Caleb took a deep breath and looked at Eliza.

"Do you think my mother would like her?" he asked. Eliza shouldn't have been shocked by that question, but she was. Instead of answering, she looked down at the deck and paused. However, before she formulated what to say, Caleb spoke from his woundedness.

"I am delusional. There is no way I can marry a girl like her. Her heart is too pure for a murderer like me," he said. Eliza got her first glimpse that Caleb's self-image was deeply wounded by killing the two brothers in front of the emperor. Simultaneously, meeting a beautiful woman whom he could give himself to seemed too good to be true. Eliza and Caleb's mom talked about how Caleb was developing a rescuer personality. Yael was the beautiful maiden he had rescued; he didn't know what to do other than see his own inadequacies.

"Caleb, your heart is beautiful and pure, too. You deserve the sun, the moon, and a girl like Yael. She is good for you," said Eliza, kissing Caleb on the cheek. She knew he needed time alone to absorb that compliment, and she got up. She went to meet the captain and showed him her ring. He did not care. He was not gregarious like their first captain as she had hoped he would be. The two deckhands were equally distant and the best she could gather was that all of them were supposed to have a week off; instead, they found out that the palace gave them a surprise order to sail back to Judah. She quickly figured out that they did not want to be on this ship and anticipated some time away from work.

The logistics of the return voyage were simple. Caleb had arranged for the two girls to share the larger of the two rooms below deck and it came with a pot-belly stove to keep them warm during the upcoming nights. Caleb shared a cabin with an Ebreet man from Joppa. There was another older Ebreet couple, but they were ill and seeking passage home to die and be buried with their ancestors. They seldom spoke to anyone and spent most of their days below deck.

Their trip down the west coast of Italy was uneventful, but as soon as they turned east to go through the Strait of Messene, a storm reached that part of the Mediterranean, forcing their vessel to spend three nights at the port of Messene on the Island of Sicily. Caleb wanted to get a dinghy to take him across the strait so that he could thank the rabbi in Reggio, but neither the captain nor the swells in the sea would allow for it. Instead, the three of them spent nearly all of their time talking to the locals and staying warm by the fire at the inn. The combination of good tea, a warm fire, and excellent food gave Eliza and Yael a greater fondness for each other. They talked about their families as well as the ones that they wanted to have. Yael horribly missed her family and she thought about them every day while she was gone. She showed Eliza the bag of coins she planned to give to her father while she entered the house, and Eliza told her that she should be proud that she was coming home with an offering. It was a noble act to give to your father all of your pay and trust him with the task of using it in the best manner. For the most part, Caleb just listened as he found their banter to be a healing force in his life, and he loved running on the soil of Calabria each morning while the girls were asleep. Finally, he got up the courage to speak what was on his mind on the final morning.

"Eliza, after we get home, are we going to do this together?" Caleb asked.

"What do you mean?" Eliza asked. "Do what together?" She looked perplexed.

Caleb tilted his head to the side, wondering why she was making him say the obvious.

"Shabbat is our heritage. It is part of the commands of the Torah, and Shabbat is the source of many of our shared memories, Eliza. Do I need to say it?" he stared at her, hoping she would get it. She didn't. He looked at Yael, his eyes equally pleading for an answer to the question that was upsetting him.

"Eliza, I don't have a family to go home to! I don't have anyone to live with or celebrate Shabbat with!" Finally, the battle of loneliness was too much for Caleb, and he began to cry. He was experiencing the loss of his mother and his father again. The large and powerful master archer who played the role of a gladiator and the self-controlling man who composed himself like a man twice his age in front of the emperor was now useless. He was overwhelmed by pain and loss and hurt. He began to weep bitterly.

"Caleb, you are my family," said Eliza. He looked at her and nodded. Yael had never seen any man as transparent as Caleb, and she wasn't sure how to behave. He was sincere and she spontaneously decided to be the same way.

"Caleb, you are a beautiful man, and you can have any woman you want. I have faith that you will find a wife and have a family of your own one day," Yael said. Yael's words were sincere, but they were incomplete. She wanted to be his wife. He was everything a woman from the twelve tribes could desire. It was finally her turn to stretch her levels of transparency, and her heart told her it was the right thing to do. She moved to sit next to him, and she pulled on his shirt until he looked at her.

"Caleb, my whole life is in front of me. I would be honored to be your family," she said. Caleb looked at her and paused in a way that Eliza had never seen him pause. Some new thought was forming inside of him, and it was filling the hole left behind by his parent's death. Eliza quickly looked at Yael and saw that she was transfixed on Caleb.

"You two are falling in love, aren't you?" Eliza asked. Yael looked at her and stayed to the course of transparency under stress.

"Yes, we are," she said. Caleb put his hand on his chin and exhaled. He laughed. Eliza knew that meant he had just figured something out that others already knew - his moments of revelation always looked like this. She knew what he would do next. He would agree, then leave to clear his head.

"She is right," he said. Caleb was obviously uncomfortable with discovering his feelings for Yael, yet he also knew that he heard a prophecy that he was to meet his wife.

"I need some air," he said. He stood up and walked out of the inn, leaving his bow, arrows, and knives on the table.

"He's never left those when he goes outside," Eliza said to Yael, pointing at the bow and arrows. It was Eliza's turn to be open and honest.

"Yael, what you just did was beautiful. Caleb is hurting and shocked. Just give him some time. He doesn't know what he is doing," Eliza said. Yael put her head on Eliza's forearm and left it there. Eliza rubbed her head and kissed it as Caleb would do with her.

"I don't know what I am doing, either," Yael said, making both of them laugh.

For the first time since leaving Rome and stepping onto the streets of Rome, Eliza was overwhelmed with joy and gratitude. The emperor called her rabbi. He called Caleb a warrior and invited him back to Rome. Balbi called her generous. The women at the synagogue called her as beautiful as Cleopatra. Yet, none of those accolades meant to her as much as seeing Yael take the risk of telling Caleb that she wished to become his wife. She opened herself up to a man she didn't know without reservation. Eliza was not strong enough to do what Yael just did, and she was humbled by the courage of the former slave girl who had already become a dear friend.

The two girls went to the window and watched Caleb standing next to the local blacksmith. Caleb was speaking with his hands on his hips. He stared at the hot embers, answering questions from the blacksmith. Caleb had thrown himself into the familiar role of befriending an artisan, as his grandfather was one of the engineers and stone masons who worked inside the Temple.

"That is what Caleb does," Eliza said to Yael. Yael had no idea what that comment meant. Yael was reacting to a moment in time, and it felt good to show and receive affection. Caleb was escaping a feeling that he didn't understand, but the two girls knew what it was. But it wasn't limited to Yael and Caleb.

"Eliza, I feel like you and I are welded together already. Maybe you don't think about this, but none of us owe any debt, and we are going home to start a new life. This is so far from slavery that I am processing what it means to be free."

Yael reached out and interlocked her fingers with Eliza's. The intimacy was triangular, with each connection different from the others. Neither Yael nor Eliza needed to speak. They were comfortable holding hands.

Soon, Caleb turned around and walked back toward the inn. The girls watched him approach, and he could see that they were holding hands.

"Girls, I don't know what I am doing. We need to go back and see Benji and Dor," Caleb said. It wasn't a request. He was trying to tell them that he didn't know what to do with the offer of affection that Yael just offered him. He looked at them, wondering what he could say to either of them. Eliza was his family and she was going to be a part of his life forever. Yael was beautiful, intelligent, strong, and infatuated with the idea of a life with him. He had no idea what to do with that. But he loved everything that she was offering him, and she was beautiful.

"I know every man goes through this, but I don't know how to do this. I am a murderer in one breath and infatuated with Yael before I can exhale," he said, laughing with them. He went upstairs to get his running sandals and left to go to the woods for the rest of the afternoon.

With inclement weather keeping the girls indoors, they learned some Roman games to pass the time. They all consumed lots of tea and drank more of the soup. Soon, the soup became the subject of bad jokes. After four days in the port of Messina, they departed and continued to Joppa. They left a letter to the rabbi with the harbormaster to deliver the next time a boat crossed the strait.

This section of the trip was long, and they traveled in a straight line towards Joppa, about a week away. All three of them continued their storytelling as they relived their lives in their tales over the week. The depth of their storytelling seemed unlimited, as their sensitivity to pain was high, thanks to their time in Rome.

For her part, Eliza took on the role of rabbi that the emperor gave her. Eliza would often hold Yael and let her weep bitter tears that had been bottled up with each sexual trauma that she shared. It was as if they were built on top of each other. Rape and disparaging comments were all repeated events in her life during her nine months in Rome, and Eliza wondered how Yael had endured as long as she did.

Caleb and Eliza shared their times in the House of Healing with Yael and they told her that she needed to go there with them after they returned. Caleb recounted what he learned from Rabbi Dor, and Eliza pointed out there were mysteries that she did not understand that the healing rabbis would help her with. They promised to take Yael there. It took several iterations over several days to convince Yael to go there with them; her lone request was that she should go home and see her father.

The days were beginning to lengthen again, but Yael was not able to sleep. She went on the deck to see the stars and let the waves rock her to drowsiness. At the front of the boat stood Caleb, wrapped in the royal cloak that he got for the Coliseum. He looked like the men in the house of Caesar back in Rome, but she knew that he wasn't. She saw a man willing to put himself in harm's way for her. Most other men expected her to be harmed for them. She knew this man was from God. This man was part of her prayers that were being answered.

"You cannot sleep, either?" he asked as she approached.

"No," she said.

Without hesitating, Caleb put his arm around her and pulled her into his chest in the same way that he would do with Eliza. However, instead of kissing her on the head like he did with Eliza, he placed his lips on hers and allowed himself to have his first kiss. Yael's heart fluttered as he did it. She did not dare to tell him that she found him to be powerful and humble, and those were the two most important attributes she wanted in a husband. They stood holding each other for a long time without speaking. Caleb continually rubbed on Yael with his eyes closed. He remained in prayer, occasionally holding her hand. Yael basked in the affection he gave her. His touch was mesmerizing to her soul.

"When I told the emperor that you were my sister, I did that for my mom," he said. Yael pushed him away the slightest amount so she could look up and see into his eyes. She didn't know what he meant.

"You know, my mom got raped by a Roman soldier. She told Eliza and me that story for the first time less than a month ago. I was so mad. Then, I saw that my parents and my uncle killed. You know what I did? I killed the bastards. That was such a stupid choice. The act of killing has haunted me more than seeing my father take his last breath. That is why I cannot sleep," he said.

"Oh, Caleb, I am so sorry," she said, leaning back into his chest. She wrapped her arms around his chest and molded into him. He rocked her until she was ready for sleep. After a few more moments, Caleb motioned towards the stairs, and the two of them headed down to their quarters.

Yael lay in her bed, unable to sleep, as Caleb was on her mind.

Chapter 34:
Back in Judah

When they stepped off the docks in Joppa, they all noticed that it seemed no different than before they had left. But inside each of them, things were very different.

"This place hasn't changed," said Yael, a bit of melancholy in her tone as they walked down the rickety docks. On her left stood Caleb, a towering man with whom she was falling in love. On her right walked Eliza, the most courageous woman she had ever met. She looked at both of them, wondering when one of them might magically become a king or queen or perhaps be surrounded by people who were welcoming them home. Instead, they walked to the end and not one person recognized them or greeted them. Yael's life experience told her that these two were famous; now that all of them were home, Eliza returned to her hidden persona of a village girl from distant Naphtali and Caleb, an archer from the tribe of Dan. Yael knew better than to see them as simple people trying to find their way in the world. However, that was their identity.

"Everything here looks as if nothing has happened," Eliza said. Eliza was feeling melancholic that no one seemed to care about what had just happened to them.

"These docks are falling apart. Someone needs to fix them," said Caleb. The girls looked at each other and smiled.

"Caleb, the prophecy said you will spend your days by the water's edge. Maybe you should fix them," Eliza said. Caleb dismissed her suggestion; he still had not yet come to terms with one of the other parts of the prophecy regarding meeting his future wife in the Coliseum.

They reached the end of the docks and looked out at the crowds of people preparing to sail. It reminded her of the moment she left a little more than a month ago. People were hustling to get last-minute supplies, and people were yelling to get everyone organized and on board so as not to lose any time.

"I am glad I am not sailing for Rome right now," she said.

"I hope they don't get shipwrecked. That thing can't swim into Reggio," said Caleb as he watched one man load his prize donkey. The girls laughed out loud at him, looked up at him, and enjoyed the return of Caleb's sense of humor.

"I hope the world will change now that the emperor has accepted Yeshua as his Messiah; I have been praying about it since we left," said Eliza.

"I could care less about him than I do that ass. I hope he closes the Coliseum for gladiator battles. I want to destroy that place," Caleb said. He was obviously upset at hearing the emperor's name. He changed the topic, hoping to change his attitude. He picked up their massive bundle of Egyptian cotton products and walked onto the sandy ground that defined the shores of the twelve tribes.

"You know, that was a crazy thing you did, sharing the story with the emperor," said Caleb, laughing in his disbelief. "I wonder if mother would have done that. You witnessed to the emperor before he prepared to rape you." Yael spoke more openly now that they were home.

"Caleb, Titus was well-behaved when he sat with Eliza and me. He treated us respectfully," Yael said.

"What about me? Do you think he treated me respectfully?" Caleb said. Yael turned, looked Caleb in the eyes, and smiled. Her stare was one of empathy. Caleb wasn't looking to hear her speak. He wanted to feel her heart and know that she was listening and she delivered her affection for him on a silver platter.

"You are a good man, Caleb," she said. He continued walking, but Eliza and Yael both knew that Caleb needed that.

Caleb found a horse and wagon they used to shuttle their six bags of luggage to the hotel district. It was nearing sunset, and Joppa felt calm after the bustle of Rome. Upon arrival, there were no prostitutes. Best of all, they could understand everything that was being said around them. Caleb told them to wait next outside the archway leading into the hotel district, promising to come right back. He wanted to declare their Egyptian cotton linens and pay the taxes due.

Caleb returned with a look of horror on his face. "Guess what I just heard from the soldiers? The emperor is dead! The soldiers patrolling the docks now said that a note had come in, announcing that he had passed away from a sudden disease. I cannot believe it!"

Yael and Eliza stared at Caleb, wearing an expression that looked like they had each been slapped. They asked Caleb a lot of questions and he couldn't answer them. He called over the soldier who he had been speaking to so that they could get more information. "When did this happen?" Eliza asked the man. "We were in his palace two weeks ago. And how did that message get to Judah so quickly?"

"You were in his palace? How is that possible? You don't belong in the presence of the emperor," the soldier asked. Caleb looked at Eliza and nodded his head. They knew that there would be a moment that required the use of Eliza's ring, and the time was now.

"Your Grace, hold up your hand," Caleb asked Eliza in royal speech. Eliza released part of her grasp on Yael and lifted her left hand, exposing the ring on her middle finger. She turned it around so the soldier could see the rubies and sapphires and read all the inscriptions on it.

"So, do you want to try saying that again?" Eliza asked him, with an attitude like that of a bully. For her part, Yael smiled. The soldier shook his head while he perhaps grunted a few expletives before changing his stance. His tone switched to that of a man speaking to one of his superiors.

"Your Grace, a couple of ships left from Rome the day he died with sealed decrees on each boat from the new emperor declaring Titus' death and Domitian's claim to the throne. They stopped along the way to hand copies of the decrees to dockmasters in all the major ports of the Mediterranean. None of the crew disembarked. They just kept sailing. They sailed in here the day before yesterday. They sailed through a storm in the Strait." That story seemed believable, and they all accepted it as truth.

"We are looking for her parents," Caleb told the soldier. "They were captured, and we have permission from the old emperor to free them from their captors."

"Good luck with that, considering the guy who gave that order is now dead."

"Who did you say was the new emperor?" asked Eliza rhetorically.

"The note said Domitian, Titus' younger brother," said the soldier.

"Great. Same house, same family. Same ring. We did not meet him, but Titus told me that he sent him a message that I am a member of his house, too," said Eliza, making eye contact with Caleb and Yael while wearing her best smile. She, too, had learned the power of action during moments of feeling paralyzed.

The soldier shook his head in disbelief and picked a new tone. The idea of a superior being a woman didn't sit well with him.

"Have you also gone to the top of Mount Olympus and had tea with Zeus?" he asked with great sarcasm.

The girls laughed and Caleb reached forward to grab the man's shoulder. Despite the law mandating that no Ebreet may touch a Roman soldier on duty, Caleb knew this guy would dare not unsheathe his blade to strike a member of the house of the emperor.

"Tell us where to go to get information about her mother's whereabouts," Caleb asked in a soft spoken tone. The soldier wasn't stupid. Caleb was bigger than he was.

"Go to that building over there. Speak with the dockmaster on duty. He will introduce you to the commerce director. He is responsible for all slave traffic in Judah. He can tell you who to talk to in that region."

"Thanks. We need to rent a cart to travel inland for a couple of days. Do you have any recommendations?"

The soldier pointed them to a small shack near the first docks where men were lined up.

"Thank you. I will hire them now and use their services tomorrow." They found a hotel that served Ebreet lamb and hummus and secured two adjacent rooms. They ate dinner and sat by the central fireplace with the other guests. Eliza asked lots of questions but none of them shared any of their stories. They were too unbelievable to be credible. Tomorrow, they would be leaving, and no one would remember them, anyway.

It was obvious to Yael that Caleb did not want to get caught by Eliza casting his eyes on hers. There could be no public display of chemistry in Judah. He was not ready for that social consequence. Yael needed healing as her understanding of sex and men was warped and needed fixing. She also had nightmares on the boat ride, and he had heard her yell out in anger at a man named Jupiter or Juneus; he couldn't tell.

Caleb felt like he needed to say something important at this moment. He did not need to be thinking about a future with Yael.

"We have survived the trauma of the death of my parents and your parents' kidnapping. We have survived a shipwreck and an attempted rape. I have killed multiple men, including our brothers. And here we are, back home, acting as if nothing happened."

He looked around and continued, as his father would often do.

"All the while, God has blessed us with great good. We received blessings and prophecies from a foreign rabbi we were not expecting to meet. We have seen how enthusiastic the underground synagogues in Rome are, and they are growing under the watch and support of the Roman military, of all things. We spent the night in the palace of the emperor and left with his favor. And we have witnessed the greatest conversion to Yeshua since Saul himself became Paul. We are truly blessed." Although Eliza didn't respond, Yael did, and she agreed with Caleb.

"This is the craziest week any Ebreet woman has experienced since Mary herself gave birth to the Messiah! I know you guys have a different plan, but can we go back to the inn, have a meal, and sit by the fire for a little bit? We need to celebrate a safe return."

Chapter 36: The Next Choice, but Not the Last Choice

Caleb chose to sleep in a dormitory-style room with three other men, but he secured a private room for Eliza and Yael to share. They stowed their belongings and walked downstairs to sit by the fire with the other guests. Eliza ordered a large cup of the best wine from Gaza for each of them and they talked into the night.

They began a debate about what to do next. After a few iterations, they all agreed that finding Eliza's parents was the reason they went to Rome, but they had to do two things first. They decided that their next step was to stop at Yael's village and proceed to the house of healing. Eliza and Caleb knew that they were not emotionally prepared to return to Tamar to discover what they might not be ready to handle. The attack had happened a month and a half ago, and the Romans involved were certainly not remaining in the village and waiting for them. The families that Caleb and Eliza knew would be there, and they would have to mourn with them again. They knew that Matthew and Katya could be anywhere, but if they could wait six weeks to be freed, they could wait for one more. Figuring out where to begin their search was the hardest part because they would need to return to Tamar first to pick up the trail. Lastly, Yael's hometown was on the way to the house of healing, so they all agreed to go there tomorrow morning after breakfast. It was only a day away from Joppa, and Yael was excited knowing she would see her family tomorrow.

Yet, even with exciting plans for the future, they still were haunted by their dreams.

"Yael, you repeatedly spoke of a man named Jupiter while you slept. Who is he?" Caleb asked. Yael didn't know that Caleb had watched and listened to her sleep, and she felt ashamed.

"His name is Juneus. He is the man who raped me," she said. Caleb could see that she was hyperventilating and he apologized repeatedly for asking her. Finally, Yael calmed down enough to speak.

"Caleb, I didn't want you to know that. He is gone from my life now and I don't want you to think poorly of me," she said. Eliza held Yael's free hand and leaned forward to look her in the eyes.

"You are wounded and all of us want to see you healed. Caleb and I already guessed that is who Juneus was. We don't think poorly of you. You were repeatedly raped. We want to see you heal, sister," she said. Yael nodded that she understood, but she was too distraught to speak. She kept glancing to see Caleb's response, and he knew he needed to say something to convince her that he still adored her.

"Yael, if we were still on the boat and no one was looking at us, I would hold you and kiss you again," he said. He had already told Eliza that he and Yael had their first, and she, in turn, had talked to Yael about it. It was one of the most wonderful moments that either of them had ever experienced. Yael nodded and smiled at his affirmation. Then, they all leaned back and sat quietly while warming themselves by the fire. Caleb confessed next.

"I have got to make these nightmares come to an end. I cannot sleep without reliving the battle in the Coliseum. I think about Ronan and even the boy Mark. The memories don't stop," he said. Yael and Eliza feared that his sleep deprivation and emotional exhaustion would cause him to unsheathe his sword and kill someone in a moment of rage.

"Do you want to sleep with us tonight? Yael and I can share a bed like we did when we were in the palace," Eliza asked.

"Yes, I would like that," he said. Caleb finished his cup of wine and handed it to Eliza to refill it. His response forced Eliza into some thoughtful introspection. She needed to sort out her sexual assault. She told Caleb that she had already done it with Yael. But it continued to trouble her, and she relived having a rag stuffed down her throat so she couldn't scream.

Yael and Eliza sat at the front of the ship and talked a lot on the ride from Messina to Joppa. The older women in the emperor's kitchen taught Yael that during those moments, a man forces himself on you sexually, a woman is changed in ways that require a healer; girls don't just "get better" in the weeks and years after they have been raped. They need a guide if they wish to heal and become a healthy wife and mother. Yael knew that Eliza relived her assault every day, but she seldom spoke about it because of the shame she felt for not being able to defend herself. Eliza's confession to the two of them wasn't related to sexual assault. It was about her future role in the community.

"When Titus called me rabbi, I felt something. It was like everything came together for me; I can't explain it. Perhaps it is my calling to become a rabbi and raise disciples." Eliza's voice was full of wonder but also trepidation. She knew that there would never be another emperor to befriend and teach, but she loved being a part of people like Balbi and the ship captain's lives. Caleb looked at her and smiled, slightly nodding his head in a joyful agreement.

"You would look good in my mother's robes," he said, lifting his cup of wine in a toast.

For her part, Yael listened as she finished her cup of wine. She was cozy by the fire and felt safe again. The first of the people she loved now knew the name Juneus, and they did not reject her as she feared. Nostalgia and gratitude overcame her for a moment.

"Thank you for getting me out of Rome," she said. She looked at two people who had been complete strangers two weeks ago.

"I can't believe tomorrow you will get to meet my family," she said. She did not fear their judgment. She had firsthand experience of how they treated each other and how they treated her. But she did not know what the circumstances in her home might be these days. She buried her feelings for Caleb for the moment and decided to invest in their joint relationship.

"I am scared to go home. I am glad you two are going with me. The world needs people like you two. Your story is unbelievable. If I weren't standing next to you when you did all those things, I wouldn't believe any of it." They stared at her and smiled. The wine was beginning to loosen Yael's lips a bit.

"Caleb, you were offered the dream of all dreams for a warrior. You could train with the elite guard. And you walked away." Yael took another sip before facing Eliza.

"Eliza, you were offered literally anything you wanted, and you said, 'No, thank you,' and you got on a boat with me for two weeks eating only soup instead!" All of them laughed. The wine certainly provided Yael with some courage to speak out about what she had been feeling.

"I feel guilty that I cannot repay you. Fortunately, you do not want repayment and you do not make me feel guilty. However, now I must return to my family, knowing that they sold me. I must try to forgive them and love them. I think the worst part remains in front of me. I am scared of my father when he sees me," she said. She nervously finished her cup.

"Caleb, I have not connected to anyone like I am with you. You are a beautiful man, and you could have any woman in Judah. et, you are broken, and I wish I could offer you something to help. I can see your eyes. You desire me, but I am so grateful that you don't pursue your desires like the men in the palace did. You are such an honorable man," Yael said.

Eliza knew when her grandfather was drunk, and she sensed Yael was getting that way. Caleb, though, spoke to her as if she had no alcohol in her.

"Yael, this is our story now, not only yours or mine. We will help you with your reunion, even if it only means to be there with you when it happens," said Caleb. She looked up at him and smiled. She dared not say it, but she adored this man.

As they walked to their rooms to go to sleep, Caleb reached over and interlocked his fingers with Yael's. Eliza looked down at Caleb's move and then at the two of them. Eliza knew two weeks ago that this outcome was inevitable. Both of them were vulnerable and completely honest with each other. Yael stared at them and was obviously experiencing something, and she stood motionless. Caleb took her other hand and turned her towards him.

"I will leave you two to say goodnight," Eliza said as she turned to walk away.

"No, stay. You are my family now, and our traditions state that family is supposed to be a part of this process." Eliza smiled. She knew what he meant. Caleb was starting the process of choosing a wife and entering into Erusin. It was uniquely her role to provide warnings and guidance, as she could see things that young couples falling in love cannot. However, Eliza was ill-equipped; the only love relationships she knew were her parents and her dead aunt and uncle.

"Cousin, God has placed us all together. Yael, my cousin needs you, and you need a strong man like Caleb." Eliza wished them goodnight and entered her room. Once the door was closed, Caleb wrapped his arms around Yael, and she put her arms over his shoulders. He bent over and kissed her again.

"When I am with you, I feel full. Fighting for you two gave me a purpose. I have considered what you told me earlier. Perhaps one day we can complete each other and have a family," he said.

Caleb had no idea what he was doing. Ebreet culture mandates that the family be involved in the process of selecting a mate. Eliza was his only family and she did not know what he was doing, either. She had already gone to bed.

"I already told you that I will marry you," she said. He released his hold on her and they went into the bedroom.

"That was quick," said Eliza. They were outside for only a minute.

"Eliza, this is so you don't get jealous," Caleb said. He leaned down and kissed her on the lips. Eliza laughed; she knew that was what they were doing, but Caleb's choice to admit it made her laugh. He was no longer secretive about his feelings for Yael.

"Tomorrow starts a new adventure. Let's get some sleep before we go into the unknown one more time," said Caleb.

The story continued in Book 3, Of Healing and Finding Home.